新時代
商務英語職場應用

跨境電商，新經濟、新模態、大數據、人工智慧

何文賢 編著

財經錢線

▶▶ 前言

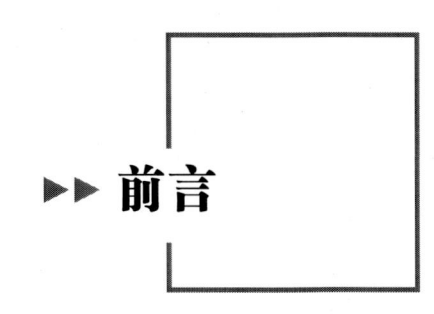

在經濟全球化步伐不斷加快的今天,各國之間的商務交流和貿易往來日益頻繁。對外投資規模、跨境電商產業等的高速發展,新經濟、新模態、大數據、人工智能等商務模式與技術創新不斷湧現,對國際商務英語人才的需求持續增大,要求不斷提高。在這樣的大背景下,各校商務英語專業蓬勃發展,企業的國際化程度迅速提高。而企業對於既具備國際商務英語溝通能力又掌握必備商務技能的高素質商務人才的需求越來越迫切。商務人才在促進貿易關係、交流商業信息、拓展國際業務、贏得海外市場、吸引外國投資等方面起著至關重要的作用。

本教材緊扣新時期商務英語專業的人才培養目標,全面落實複合型、國際化、應用性的專業培養特色,根據商務英語的特點及職場能力要求,在編寫時既遵循傳統教材的編寫模式,又借鑑國內外先進的編寫體例,注重教材內容與新時代職場接軌,針對學生進入職場後的場景,特別是對職場英語的背景知識進行系統介紹,幫助學生累積商務知識,培養商務思維,同時也注重語言技能與商務知識的融合,力求反應真實的商務活動情境,讓學習者不僅能基本掌握商務英語獨特的語言現象和文體風格,而且能從不同側面瞭解國際商務知識,掌握較強的跨文化商務交際能力和實踐技能。

本教材既強調「語言基本功」和「商務英語應用能力」的培養,又重視「商務實踐能力」的培養,內容兼具英語語言知識、商務管理知識、職場文化背景的三重屬性,涉及全球化、區域合作、商業管理、國際商務、金融服務、銀行職能、電子支付、企業責任、IT技術應用以及經濟模式等多方面知識,選材廣泛,體例新穎,應用性強。通過多維度知識體系與商務能力的搭建,幫助財經商貿類專業和英語言文學類專業的學生在鍛煉英語閱讀與寫作能力的同時,成為擁有較高商科專業素養、具備國際化視野、符合現代商務職場需求的高素質人才。

本書由商務英語專業教學團隊負責人何文賢、池玫擔任主編,徐品晶、林山擔任副主編,

其中，何文賢、池玫老師負責教材的統稿和編審工作，陳素慧、薛澤民、林山、陳巧金、林珊、饒衛忠、徐品晶、洪慧玲、林培華、連焰等老師分別參與了 Chapter I 至 Chapter X 的編寫工作，陳文鑠、葉劍老師在資料收集、整理、校對等方面做了大量的工作，在此謹向他們致以衷心的感謝！

書中不足之處在所難免，懇請有關專家學者和廣大讀者不吝賜教，以便我們進一步修改完善。

何文賢、池玫

▶▶ 目錄

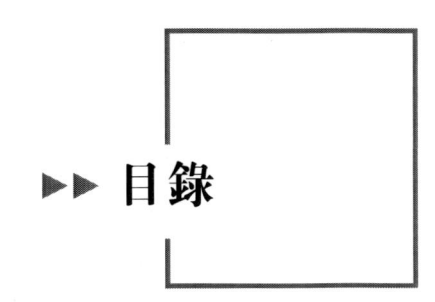

1 / **Chapter I**　**Globalization and International Governance**

32 / **Chapter II**　**Regional Cooperation and Competition**

60 / **Chapter III**　**Business Management**

91 / **Chapter IV**　**Trade and International Agreement**

122/ **Chapter V**　**Central Banking and Global Financial System**

152/ **Chapter VI**　**Financial Instruments and Financial Crises**

183/ **Chapter VII**　**Commercial Law and IPR Protection**

205/ **Chapter VIII**　**IT Industry and Electro-technologies**

246/ **Chapter IX**　**Social Responsibility and Corporate Practice**

269/ **Chapter X**　**Economies and Economic Theories**

Chapter I

Globalization and International Governance

Part I Globalization

Globalization is the process of international integration arising from the interchange of world views, products, ideas and other aspects of culture. Advances in transportation and telecommunications infrastructure, including the rise of the telegraph and its development of Internet, are major factors in globalization, generating further interdependence of economic and cultural activities. The term globalization had been used in its economic sense at least as early as 1981, and in other senses since at least as early as 1944. Theodore Levitt is credited with popularizing the term and bringing it into the mainstream business audience in the later half of the 1980s.

Though scholars place the origins of globalization in modern times, others trace its history long before the European Age of Discovery and voyages to the New World. Large-scale globalization began in the 19th century. In the late 19th century and early 20th century, the connectedness of the world's economies and cultures grew very quickly.

In 2000, the International Monetary Fund (IMF) identified four basic aspects of globalization: trade and transactions, capital and investment movements, migration and movement of people, and the dissemination of knowledge. Further, environmental challenges such as global warming, cross-boundary water and air pollution, and over-fishing of the ocean are linked with globalization. Globalizing processes affect and are affected by business and work organization, economics, socio-cultural resources, and the natural environment.

Humans have interacted over long distances for thousands of years. The overland Silk Road that connected Asia, Africa, and Europe is a good example of the transformative power of trans-local exchange that existed in the 「Old World」. Philosophy, religion, language, the arts, and other aspects of culture spread and mixed as nations exchanged products and ideas. In both the 15th and 16th centuries, Europeans made important discoveries in their exploration of the oceans, including the start of transatlantic travel to the 「New World」 of the Americas. Global movement of people, goods, and ideas expanded significantly in the following centuries. Early on in the 19th century, the development of new forms of transportation (such as the steamship and railroads) and telecommunications that 「compressed」 time and space allowed for increasingly rapid rates of global interchange. In the 20th century, road vehicles, intermodal transport, and airlines made transportation even faster. The advent of electronic communications, most notably mobile phones and the Internet, connected billions of people in new ways by the year 2010.

Trade on the Silk Road was a significant factor in the development of the civilizations of China, the Indian subcontinent, Persia, Europe, and Arabia, opening long-distance, political and economic interactions between the civilizations. Though silk was certainly the major trade item from China, many other goods were traded, and religions, syncretic philosophies, and various technologies, as well as diseases, also travelled along the Silk Routes. In addition to economic trade, the Silk Road served as a means of carrying out cultural trade among the civilizations along its network. The movement of people, such as refugees, artists, craftsmen, missionaries, robbers and envoys, resulted in the exchange of religions, art, languages and new technologies.

The first modern wave of economic globalization began during the period of 1870–1914, marked by transportation expansion, record levels of migration, enhanced communications, trade expansion, and growth in capital transfers. During the mid-nineteenth century, the passport system in Europe dissolved as rail transport expanded rapidly. Most countries issuing passports did not require their carry, thus people could travel freely without them. The standardization of international passports would not arise until 1980 under the guidance of the United Nations International Civil Aviation Organization. From 1870 to 1915, 36 million Europeans migrated away from Europe. Approximately 25 million (or 70%) of these travelers migrated to the United States, while most of the rest reached Canada, Australia, Argentina, and Brazil. Europe itself experienced an influx of foreigners from 1860 to 1910, growing from 0.7% of the population to 1.8%. While the absence of meaningful passport requirements allowed for free travel, migration on such an enormous scale would have been prohibitively difficult if not for technological advances in transportation, particularly the expansion of railway travel and the dominance of steam-powered boats over traditional sailing ships. World railway mileage grew from 205,000 kilometers in 1870 to 925,000 kilometers in 1906, while steamboat cargo tonnage surpassed that of sailboats in the 1890s. Advancements such as the telephone and wireless telegraphy revolutionized telecommunication by providing instantaneous communication. In 1866, the first transatlantic cable was laid beneath the ocean to connect London and New York, while Europe and Asia became connected through new landlines.

Economic globalization grew under free trade, starting in 1860 when the United Kingdom entered into a free trade agreement with France known as the Cobden–Chevalier Treaty. However, the golden age of this wave of globalization endured a return to protectionism between 1880 and 1914. In 1879, German Chancellor Otto von Bismarck introduced protective tariffs on agricultural and manufacturing goods, making Germany the first nation to institute new protective trade policies. In 1892, France introduced the Méline tariff, greatly raising customs duties on both agricultural and manufacturing goods. The United States maintained strong protectionism during most of the nineteenth century, imposing customs duties between 40% and 50% on imported goods. Despite these measures, international trade continued to grow without slowing. Paradoxically, foreign trade grew at a much faster rate during the protectionist phase of the first wave of globalization than during the free trade phase sparked by the United Kingdom.

Unprecedented growth in foreign investment from the 1880s to the 1900s served as the core driver of financial globalization. The worldwide total of capital invested abroad amounted to US $44 billion in 1913 ($1.02 trillion in 2012 dollars), with the greatest share of foreign assets held by the United Kingdom (42%), France (20%), Germany (13%), and the United States (8%). The Netherlands, Belgium, and Switzerland together held foreign investments on par with Germany at around 12%.

The world experienced substantial changes prior to 1914, which created an environment favorable to an increase in and development of international financial centers. Principal among such changes were unprecedented growth in capital flows and the resulting rapid financial center integration, as well as faster communication. Before 1870, London and Paris existed as the world's only prominent financial centers. Berlin and New York soon rose to eminence on par with London and Paris. An array of smaller financial centers became important as they found market niches, such as Amsterdam, Brussels, Zurich, and Geneva. London remained the leading international financial center in the four decades leading up to World War I.

Growth of globalization has never been smooth. One influential event was the late 2000s recession, which was associated with lower growth (such as cross-border phone calls and Skype usage) or even temporarily negative growth (such as trade) of global interconnectedness. The DHL Global Connectedness Index studies four main types of cross-border flow: trade (in both goods and services), information, people (including tourists, students and migrants) and capital. It shows that the depth of global integration fell by about one-tenth after 2008, but by 2013 had recovered well above its pre-crash peak. The report also found a shift of economic activity to emerging economies.

Part II International Governance and Organizations

Globalized society offers a complex web of forces and factors that bring people, cultures, markets, beliefs and practices into increasingly greater proximity to one another. At the same time, it arises various global problems and needs international governance.

An international organization is an organization with an international membership, scope, or presence. There are two main types: International nongovernmental organizations (INGOs), nongovernmental organizations (NGOs) that operate internationally. These include international non-profit organizations and worldwide companies such as the World Organization of the Scout Movement, International Committee of the Red Cross, etc..

Intergovernmental organizations, also known as international governmental organizations (IGOs), are made up primarily of sovereign states (referred to as member states). Examples include the United Nations (UN), Organization for Security and Co-operation in Europe (OSCE), Council of Europe (COE), International Labour Organization (ILO) and International Police Organization (INTERPOL).

The United Nations

Headquarters	New York City (International territory)
Official languages	Arabic Chinese English French Russian Spanish
Membership	193 member states 2 observer states

The United Nations (UN) is an intergovernmental organization established on 24 October 1945 to promote international co-operation. The organization was created following the Second World War to prevent another such conflict. At its founding, the UN had 51 member states; there are now 193. The headquarters of the United Nations is in Manhattan, New York City, and enjoys extraterritoriality. Further main offices are situated in Geneva, Nairobi and Vienna. The organization is financed by assessed and voluntary contributions from its member states. Its objectives include maintaining international peace and security, promoting human rights, fostering social and economic development, protecting the environment, and providing humanitarian aid in cases of famine, natural disaster, and armed conflict.

The UN's mission to preserve world peace was complicated in its early decades by the Cold War between the US and Soviet Union and their respective allies. The organization participated in major actions in Korea and the Congo, as well as approving the creation of the state of Israel in 1947. The organization's membership grew significantly following widespread decolonization in the 1960s, and by the 1970s its budget for economic and social development programmes far outstripped its spending on peacekeeping. After the end of the Cold War, the UN took on major military and peacekeeping missions across the world with varying degrees of success.

The UN has six principal organs: the General Assembly (the main deliberative assembly), the Security Council (for deciding certain resolutions for peace and security), the Economic and Social Council (ECOSOC) (for promoting international economic and social co-operation and development), the Secretariat (for providing studies, information, and facilities needed by the UN), the International Court of Justice (the primary judicial organ), and the United Nations Trusteeship Council (inactive since 1994). UN System agencies include the World Bank Group, the World Health Organization, the World Food Programme, UNESCO, and UNICEF. The UN's most prominent officer is the Secretary-General. Non-governmental organizations may be granted consultative status with ECOSOC and other agencies to participate in the UN's work. The organization won the Nobel Peace Prize in 2001.

Another primary purpose of the UN is 「to achieve international co-operation in solving international problems of an economic, social, cultural, or humanitarian character」. Numerous bodies have been created to work towards this goal, primarily under the authority of the General Assembly and ECOSOC.

The UN Development Programme (UNDP), an organization founded in 1945, is one of the leading bodies in the field of international development. The Food and Agriculture Organization (FAO), also founded in 1945, promotes agricultural development and food security. UNICEF (the United Nations Children's Fund) was created in 1946 to aid European children after the Second World War and expanded its mission to provide aid around the world and to uphold the Convention on the Rights of the Child.

The World Bank Group and International Monetary Fund (IMF) are independent, specialized agencies and observers within the UN framework, according to a 1947 agreement. They were initially formed separately from the UN through the Bretton Woods Agreement in 1944. The World Bank provides loans for international development, while the IMF promotes international economic co-operation and gives emergency loans to indebted countries.

The World Health Organization (WHO), which focuses on international health issues and disease eradication, is another of the UN's largest agencies. In 1980, the agency announced that the eradication of smallpox had been completed. In subsequent decades, WHO largely eradicated polio, river blindness, and leprosy. The Joint United Nations Programme on HIV/AIDS (UNAIDS), begun in 1996, co-ordinates the organization's response to the AIDS epidemic. The UN Population Fund, which also dedicates part of its resources to combating HIV, is the world's largest source of funding for reproductive health and family planning services.

Along with the International Red Cross and Red Crescent Movement, the UN often takes a leading role in coordinating emergency relief. The World Food Programme (WFP), created in 1961, provides food aid in response to famine, natural disasters, and armed conflict. The organization reports that it feeds an average of 90 million people in 80 nations each year. The Office of the United Nations High Commissioner for Refugees (UNHCR), established in 1950, works to protect the rights of refugees, asylum seekers, and stateless people. UNHCR and WFP programmes are funded by voluntary contributions from governments, corporations, and individuals, though the UNHCR's administrative costs are paid for by the UN's primary budget.

Other

Since the UN's creation, over 80 colonies have attained independence. The General Assembly adopted the Declaration on the Granting of Independence to Colonial Countries and Peoples in 1960 with no votes against but abstentions from all major colonial powers. The UN works toward decolonization through groups including the UN Committee on Decolonization, created in 1962. The committee lists seventeen remaining「Non-Self-Governing Territories」, the largest and most populous of which is Western Sahara.

Beginning with the formation of the UN Environmental Programme (UNEP) in 1972, the UN has made environmental issues a prominent part of its agenda. A lack of success in the first two decades of UN work in this area led to the 1992 Earth Summit in Rio de Janeiro, Brazil, which sought to give new impetus to these efforts. In 1988, the UNEP and the World Meteorological Organization (WMO), another UN organization, established the Intergovernmental Panel on Climate Change, which assesses and reports on research on global warming. The UN-sponsored Kyoto Protocol, signed in 1997, set legally binding emissions reduction targets for ratifying states.

The UN also declares and co-ordinates international observances, periods of time to observe issues of international interest or concern. Examples include World Tuberculosis Day, Earth Day, and the International Year of Deserts and Desertification.

G-20

The Group of Twenty (also known as the G-20 or G20) is an international forum for the governments and central bank governors from 20 major economies. The members include 19 individual countries—Argentina, Australia, Brazil, Canada, China, France, Germany, India, Indonesia, Italy, Japan, Mexico, Russia, Saudi Arabia, South Africa, South Korea, Turkey, the United Kingdom and the United States—along with the European Union (EU). The EU is represented by the European Commission and by the European Central Bank. Spain is a permanent invitee of G20 and participates annually of G20 summits.

The G-20 was founded in 1999 with the aim of studying, reviewing, and promoting high-level discussion of policy issues pertaining to the promotion of international financial stability. It seeks to address issues that go beyond the responsibilities of any one organization. Collectively, the G-20 economies account for around 85% of the gross world product (GWP), 80% of world trade and two-thirds of the world population. The G-20 heads of government or heads of state have periodically conferred at summits since their initial meeting in 2008.

On 25 September 2009, the leaders of the group announced that G-20 replaced the G8 as the main economic council of wealthy nations.

The G-20 is the latest in a series of post-World War II initiatives aimed at international coordination of economic policy, which include institutions such as the 「Bretton Woods twins」, the International Monetary Fund and the World Bank, and what is now the World Trade Organization.

Though the G-20's primary focus is global economic governance, the themes of its summits vary from year to year. For example, the theme of the 2006 G-20 meeting was 「Building and Sustaining Prosperity」. The issues discussed included domestic reforms to achieve 「sustained growth」, global energy and resource commodity markets, reform of the World Bank and IMF, and the impact of demographic changes due to an aging world population. In a statement following a meeting of G7 finance ministers on 11 October 2008, US President George W. Bush stated that the next meeting of the G-20 would be important in finding solutions to the burgeoning economic crisis of 2008.

The G-20 Summit was created as a response both to the financial crisis of 2007–2010 and to a growing recognition that key-emerging countries were not adequately included in the core of global economic discussion and governance. After the 2008 debut summit in Washington, D. C., G-20 leaders met twice a year in London and Pittsburgh in 2009, Toronto and Seoul in 2010.

Since 2011, when France chaired and hosted the G-20, the summits have been held only once a year. Russia chaired and hosted the summit in 2013; while the summit was held in Australia in 2014, with Turkey hosting it in 2015.

A number of other ministerial-level G20 meetings have been held since 2010. Agriculture ministerial meetings were conducted in 2011 and 2012; meetings of foreign ministers were held in 2012 and 2013; trade ministers met in 2012 and 2014 and employment ministerial meetings have taken place annually since 2010.

China has taken on the presidency of the G20 at a time when the world economy continues to face significant challenges associated with weakening global trade and investment, anemic economic growth and serious difficulties faced by some emerging markets. In order to address these challenges, the G20 trade ministers gathered in Shanghai in July, 2016 and came up with trade and investment policy recommendations for the G20 Summit, which was held in Hangzhou in September.

President Xi Jinping emphasized that 「building an innovative, invigorated, interconnected and inclusive world economy」 was the theme of the G20 Hangzhou Summit.

He proposed five policy suggestions to counter the global slowdown in economic growth, trade and investment.

The first is to reinforce the G20 trade and investment cooperation mechanism, which includes the institutionalization of the G20 Trade Ministers Meeting and its supporting working groups. The second is to stress the centrality of the multilateral trading system (MTS) in promoting trade liberalization and investment, while standing against trade and investment protectionism. The third is to propel global trade growth by initiating concrete measures for reducing trade costs and promoting e-commerce and the services sector. The fourth is to support policy measures that enable small and medium-sized enterprises (SMEs) and developing countries irrespective of their level of development to participate and derive maximum benefit from this participation in global value chains (GVCs). The fifth is to enhance global investment governance, which is currently fragmented because of numerous investment agreements. For this purpose, China has proposed developing non-binding global investment principles for all G20 members and increasing investment policy coordination.

As the G20 is gradually shifting from a crisis response mechanism to a global economic governance mechanism, the multilateral trading system (MTS) should play the central role in promoting global trade and investment.

Therefore, G-20 Summit should work out a mechanism for ensuring that such bilateral and regional trade agreements conform to the WTO norms and supplement the MTS rather than generating new risks and barriers. The G20 members should clarify the central position of the MTS in the current global trade and economic governance.

The main problem is that G20 members often make decisions but then do not implement them and their declarations have no binding force. China expects that the Hangzhou summit will demonstrate greater political will to address pressing economic challenges. China's economic size, foreign exchange reserves and expertise in infrastructure should stand to translate positive intentions into action.

Part Ⅲ OPEC and the World Economic Forum

In 1949 Venezuela and Iran were the first countries to move towards the establishment of OPEC by approaching Iraq, Kuwait and Saudi Arabia, suggesting that they exchange views and explore avenues for regular and closer communication among petroleum-producing nations.

Organization of the Petroleum Exporting Countries (OPEC), a permanent, international organization headquartered in Vienna, Austria, was established in Baghdad, Iraq on 10-14 September 1960. The formation of OPEC represented a collective act of sovereignty by oil exporting nations, and marked a turning point in state control over natural resources. In the 1960s when the international oil market was largely dominated by a group of multinational companies known as the 「seven sisters」, OPEC ensured that oil companies could not unilaterally cut prices. Its mandate is to 「coordinate and unify the petroleum policies」 of its members and to 「ensure the stabilization of oil markets in order to secure an efficient, economic and regular supply of petroleum to consumers, a steady income to producers, and a fair return on capital for those investing in the petroleum industry.」 In 2014 OPEC comprised twelve members: Algeria, Angola, Ecuador, Iran, Iraq, Kuwait, Libya, Nigeria, Qatar, Saudi Arabia, the United Arab Emirates and Venezuela. Norway and Russia have attended OPEC meetings as observers, indicating that OPEC is not averse to further expansion. Iraq remains a member of OPEC, but Iraqi production has not been a part of any OPEC quota agreements since March 1998.

OPEC was headquartered in Geneva, Switzerland before moving to Vienna, Austria, on September 1, 1965.

The OPEC headquarters in Vienna

The OPEC Conference is the supreme authority of the organization, and consists of delegations normally headed by the Ministers of Oil, Mines and Energy of member countries. The Conference usually meets twice a year (in March and September) and in extraordinary sessions whenever required. It operates on the principle of unanimity, and one member, one vote.

Objectives and Activities
Coordinate International Petroleum Policies

According to the United States Energy Information Administration (EIA), OPEC crude oil production is an important factor affecting global oil prices. OPEC sets production targets for its member nations and generally, when OPEC production targets are reduced, oil prices increase. Projections of changes in Saudi production result in changes in the price of benchmark crude oils. Crude oil benchmark is a crude oil price that serves as a reference price for buyers and sellers of crude oil.

In the 1970s, OPEC began to gain influence and steeply raised oil prices during the 1973 oil crisis in response to US aid to Israel during the Yom Kippur War. It lasted until March 1974. OPEC added to its goals the selling of oil for socio-economic growth of the poorer member nations, and membership grew to 13 by 1975. A few member countries became centrally planned economies.

In a 1979 U.S. District Court decision held that OPEC's pricing decisions have sovereign immunity as 「governmental」 acts of state, as opposed to 「commercial」 acts, and are therefore beyond the legal reach of U.S. courts competition law and are protected by the Foreign Sovereign Immunities Act of 1976.

In the 1980s, the price of oil was allowed to rise before the adverse effects of higher prices caused demand and price to fall. The OPEC nations, which depended on revenue from oil sales, experienced severe economic hardship from the lower demand for oil and consequently cut production in order to boost the price of oil. During this time, environmental issues began to emerge on the international energy agenda. Lower demand for oil saw the price of oil fall back to 1986 levels by 1998–1999.

In the 2000s, a combination of factors pushed up oil prices even as supply remained high. Prices rose to then record-high levels in mid-2008 before falling in response to the 2007 financial crisis. OPEC's summits in Caracas and Riyadh in 2000 and 2007 had guiding themes of stable energy markets, sustainable oil production, and environmental sustainability.

In April 2001, OPEC, in collaboration with other international organizations, such as APEC, Eurostat and IAE, launched the Joint Oil Data Exercise, which became rapidly the Joint Organization Data Initiative (JODI).

In 2003 the International Energy Agency (IEA) and OPEC held their first joint workshop on energy issues and they continued to meet since then to better「understand trends, analysis and viewpoints and advance market transparency and predictability.」

In 2011 Nymex oil future trades reached record highs. By mid-March the Nymex WTI「exceeded 1.5 million futures contracts, 18 times higher than the volume of daily traded physical crude.」OPEC called for more efforts by governments and regulatory bodies to curb excessive speculation in oil futures markets. OPEC claimed this increased volatility in oil prices, disconnected price from market fundamentals.

1973 Oil Embargo

In October 1973, OPEC declared an oil embargo in response to the United States' and Western Europe's support of Israel in the Yom Kippur War of 1973. The result was a rise in oil prices from $ 3 per barrel to $12 starting on 17 October 1973, and ending on 18 March 1974 and the commencement of gas rationing. Other factors in the rise in gasoline prices included a market and consumer panic reaction, the peak of oil production in the United States around 1970 and the devaluation of the U.S. dollar. U.S. gas stations put a limit on the amount of gasoline that could be dispensed, closed on Sundays, and limited the days gasoline could be purchased based on license plates. Even after the embargo concluded, prices continued to rise.

The Oil Embargo of 1973 had a lasting effect on the United States. The Federal government got involved first with President Richard Nixon recommending citizens reduce their speed for the sake of conservation, and later Congress issuing a 55 mph limit at the end of 1973. Daylight saving time was extended year round to reduce electrical use in the American home. Smaller, more fuel efficient cars were manufactured.

On 4 December 1973, Nixon also formed the Federal Energy Office as a cabinet office with control over fuel allocation, rationing, and prices. People were asked to decrease their thermostats to 65 degrees and factories changed their main energy supply to coal.

One of the most lasting effects of the 1973 oil embargo was a global economic recession. Unemployment rose to the highest percentage on record while inflation also spiked. Consumer interest in large gas guzzling vehicles fell and production dropped. Although the embargo only lasted a year, during that time oil prices had quadrupled and OPEC nations discovered that their oil could be used as both a political and economic weapon against other nations.

Responding to War and Low Prices

Leading up to the 1990-1991 Gulf War, the President of Iraq Saddam Hussein recommended that OPEC should push world oil prices up, helping all OPEC members financially. But the division of OPEC countries occasioned by the Iraq-Iran War and the Iraqi invasion of Kuwait marked a low point in the cohesion of OPEC. Once supply disruption fears that accompanied these conflicts dissipated, oil prices began to slide dramatically.

After oil prices slumped at around $ 15 a barrel in the late 1990s, joint diplomacy achieved a slowing down of oil production beginning in 1998.

In 2000, Venezuela President Hugo Chávez hosted the first summit of OPEC in 25 years in Caracas. The next year, however, the September 11, 2001 attacks against the United States, and the following invasion of Afghanistan, and 2003 invasion of Iraq and subsequent occupation prompted a sharp rise in oil prices to levels far higher than those targeted by OPEC themselves during the previous period.

On 19 November 2007, global oil prices reacted violently as OPEC members spoke openly about potentially converting their cash reserves to the euro and away from the US dollar.

In May 2008, Indonesia announced that it would leave OPEC when its membership expired at the end of that year, having become a net importer of oil and being unable to meet its production quota. A statement released by OPEC on 10 September 2008 confirmed Indonesia's withdrawal, noting that it ⌈regretfully accepted the wish of Indonesia to suspend its full Membership in the Organization and recorded its hope that the Country would be in a position to rejoin the Organization in the not too distant future.⌋ Indonesia is still exporting light, sweet crude oil and importing heavier, more sour crude oil to take advantage of price differentials (import is greater than export).

Production Disputes

The economic needs of the OPEC member states often affect the internal politics behind OPEC production quotas. Various members have pushed for reductions in production quotas to increase the price of oil and thus their own revenues. These demands conflict with Saudi Arabia's stated long-term strategy of being a partner with the world's economic powers to ensure a steady flow of oil that would support economic expansion. Part of the basis for this policy is the Saudi concern that expensive oil or supply uncertainty will drive developed nations to conserve and develop alternative fuels. To this point, former Saudi Oil Minister Sheikh Yamani famously said in 1973: ⌈The stone age didn't end because we ran out of stones.⌋

On 10 September 2008, one such production dispute occurred when the Saudis reportedly walked out of OPEC negotiating session where the organization voted to reduce production. Although Saudi Arabian OPEC delegates officially endorsed the new quotas, they stated anonymously that they would not observe them. The New York Times quoted one such anonymous OPEC delegate as saying ⌈Saudi Arabia will meet the market's demand. We will see what the market requires and we will not leave a customer without oil. The policy has not changed.⌋

OPEC Aid

OPEC aid dates from well before the 1973-1974 oil price explosion. Kuwait has operated a program since 1961 (through the Kuwait Fund for Arab Economic Development).

The OPEC Special Fund was conceived in Algiers, Algeria, in March 1975, and formally founded early the following year. A Solemn Declaration reaffirmed the natural solidarity which unites OPEC countries with other developing countries in their struggle to overcome underdevelopment, and called for measures to strengthen cooperation between these countries, operating under a reasoning that the Fund's 「resources are additional to those already made available by OPEC states through a number of bilateral and multilateral channels.」The Fund was later renamed as the OPEC Fund for International Development (OFID).

The Fund became a fully fledged permanent international development agency in May 1980.

The World Economic Forum (WEF)

WORLD
ECONOMIC
FORUM

COMMITTED TO
IMPROVING THE STATE
OF THE WORLD

The World Economic Forum is a Swiss nonprofit foundation, based in Cologny, Geneva. Recognized by the Swiss authorities as the international institution for public-private cooperation, its mission is cited as 「committed to improving the state of the world by engaging business, political, academic, and other leaders of society to shape global, regional, and industry agendas」.

The Forum is best known for its annual winter meeting in Davos, a mountain resort in Switzerland. The meeting brings together some 2,500 top business leaders, international political leaders, selected intellectuals, and journalists to discuss the most pressing issues facing the world. Often this location alone is used to identify meetings, participation, and participants with such phrases as 「a Davos panel」and 「a Davos Man」.

The organization also convenes some six to eight regional meetings each year in locations such as Latin America and East Asia, as well as undertaking two further annual meetings in China and the United Arab Emirates. Beside meetings, the foundation produces a series of research reports and engages its members in sector specific initiatives.

History

The forum, first named the「European Management Forum」, was founded in 1971 by Klaus Schwab, a German-born business professor at the University of Geneva. In the summer of 1971, Schwab invited 444 executives from Western European firms to the first European Management Symposium held in the Davos Congress Centre under the patronage of the European Commission and European industrial associations, where Schwab sought to introduce European firms to American management practices. He then founded the WEF as a nonprofit organization based in Geneva and drew European business leaders to Davos for the annual meetings each January.

Schwab developed the「stakeholder」management approach, which attributed corporate success to managers actively taking account of all interests: not merely shareholders, clients, and customers, but also employees and the communities within which the firm is situated, including governments. Events in 1973, including the collapse of the Bretton Woods fixed-exchange rate mechanism and the Arab-Israeli War, saw the annual meeting expand its focus from management to economic and social issues. It changed its name to the World Economic Forum in 1987 and sought to broaden its vision to include providing a platform for resolving international conflicts, and, for the first time political leaders were invited to the annual meeting in January 1974.

Klaus Schwab, founder and executive chairman, World Economic Forum

Political leaders soon began to use the annual meeting as a neutral platform. The *Davos Declaration* was signed in 1988 by Greece and Turkey, helping them turn back from the brink of war. In 1992, South African President F. W. de Klerk met with Nelson Mandela at the annual meeting, their first joint appearance outside South Africa. At the 1994 annual meeting, Israeli Foreign Minister Shimon Peres and PLO Chairman Yasser Arafat reached a draft agreement on Gaza and Jericho.

Headquartered in Cologny, in 2006 the foundation opened regional offices in Beijing and New York City. It strives to be impartial and is not tied to any political, partisan, or national interests. The foundation is「committed to improving the State of the World」. Until 2012, it had observer status with the United Nations Economic and Social Council; it is under the supervision of the Swiss Federal Council. The foundation's highest governance body is the foundation board.

The foundation is funded by its 1,000 member companies, typically global enterprises with more than five billion dollars in turnover (varying by industry and region). These enterprises rank among the top companies within their industry and/or country and play a leading role in shaping the future of their industry and/or region. Membership is stratified by the level of engagement with forum activities, with the level of membership fees increasing as participation in meetings, projects, and initiatives rises.

Objectives and Activities

The flagship event of the foundation is the invitation-only annual meeting held during the winter at the end of January in Davos, Switzerland, The 2011 annual meeting in Davos was held from 26 to 30 January. The 2012 meeting was held on 25–29 January 2012, with the theme「The Great Transformation: Shaping New Models」. The 2013 meeting was held from 23 to 27 January, with the theme of「Resilient Dynamism,」following founder Klaus Schwab's declaration that「the need for global cooperation has never been greater」. The 2014 meeting was held from 22 to 25 January, with the theme「The Reshaping of the World: Consequences for Society, Politics and Business」.

During the five-day annual meeting in Davos, more than 2,500 participants from slightly fewer than 100 countries gather in Davos. Approximately 1,500 are business leaders drawn from its members, 1,000 of the world's top companies. Besides these, participants included 219 public figures, including 40 heads of state or government, 64 cabinet ministers, 30 heads or senior officials of international organizations, and 10 ambassadors. More than 432 participants were from civil society, including 32 heads or representatives of non-governmental organizations, 225 media leaders, 149 leaders from academic institutions and think tanks, 15 religious leaders of different faiths, and 11 union leaders.

The town is small enough to allow participants to meet anywhere outside the sessions and allows them the greatest opportunities to attend receptions organized by companies and countries. The participants are also taking part in role playing events, such as the Investment Heat Map. Informal winter meetings may have led to as many ideas and solutions as the official sessions. Approximately 2,200 participants gather for the five-day event and attend some of the 220 sessions in the official programme. The winter discussions focus around key issues of global concern (such as international conflicts, poverty, and environmental problems and possible solutions).

As many as 500 journalists from online, print, radio, and television take part, with access to all sessions in the official program, some of which are also webcast. Not all the journalists are given access to all areas, however, all plenary debates from the annual meeting also are available on YouTube.

Participants

In 2011, some 250 public figures (heads of state or government, cabinet ministers, ambassadors, heads or senior officials of international organizations) attended the annual meeting, including: Robert B. Zoellick, Nicolas Sarkozy, Ban Ki-moon, Angela Merkel, Gordon Brown, David Cameron, Min Zhu, Dmitry Medvedev, Kofi Annan, Jacob Zuma, and Chinese former premier Zeng Peiyan.

Al Gore, Bill Clinton, Bill Gates, and Tony Blair are also regular Davos attendees. Past attendees include Henry Kissinger, Nelson Mandela, and Yasser Arafat.

Summer annual Meeting

In 2007, the foundation established the Annual Meeting of the New Champions (also called Summer Davos), held annually in China, alternating between Dalian and Tianjin, bringing together 1,500 participants from what the foundation calls Global Growth Companies, primarily from rapidly growing emerging countries such as China, India, Russia, Mexico, and Brazil, but also including quickly growing companies from developed countries. The meeting also engages with the next generation of global leaders from fast-growing regions and competitive cities, as well as technology pioneers from around the globe. Premier Wen Jiabao has delivered a plenary address at each annual meeting.

Regional Meetings

Every year regional meetings take place, enabling close contact among corporate business leaders, local government leaders, and NGOs. Meetings are held in Africa, East Asia, Latin America, and the Middle East. The mix of hosting countries varies from year to year, but consistently China and India have hosted throughout the decade since 2000.

Young Global Leaders

The group's Forum of Young Global Leaders consists of 800 people chosen by the forum organizers as being representative of contemporary leadership, 「coming from all regions of the world and representing all stakeholders in society」, according to the organization. After five years of participation they are considered alumni.

Social Entrepreneurs

Since 2000, the WEF has been promoting models developed by those in close collaboration with the Schwab Foundation for Social Entrepreneurship, highlighting social entrepreneurship as a key element to advance societies and address social problems. Selected social entrepreneurs are invited to participate in the foundation's regional meetings and the annual meetings where they may meet chief executives and senior government officials.

Global Shapers

In 2011, the World Economic Forum started a global network of people between the ages of 20 and 30 who have shown great potential for future leadership roles in society. The Community of Global Shapers, highlighting Global Shapers is a network of self-organizing local hubs based in each major city around the world. They undertake events and activities intended by the Global Shapers to generate a positive impact within their local community.

As of 21 October 2014 there are 358 Hubs with more than 4,300 Shapers.

The foundation also acts as a think tank, publishing a wide range of reports. In particular, 「Strategic Insight Teams」focus on producing reports of relevance in the fields of competitiveness, global risks, and scenario thinking.

Initiatives

The Global Health Initiative was launched by Kofi Annan at the annual meeting in 2002. The GHI's mission was to engage businesses in public-private partnerships to tackle HIV/

AIDS, tuberculosis, malaria, and health systems.

The Global Education Initiative (GEI), launched during the annual meeting in 2003, brought together international IT companies and governments in Jordan, Egypt, and India that has resulted in new personal computer hardware being available in their classrooms and more local teachers trained in e-learning. This is having a significant effect on the lives of children. The GEI model, which is scalable and sustainable, now is being used as an educational blueprint in other countries including Rwanda.

The Environmental Initiative covers climate change and water issues. Under the Gleneagles Dialogue on Climate Change, the U.K. government asked the World Economic Forum at the G8 Summit in Gleneagles in 2005 to facilitate a dialogue with the business community to develop recommendations for reducing greenhouse gas emissions. This set of recommendations, endorsed by a global group of CEOs, was presented to leaders ahead of the G8 Summit in Toyako and Hokkaido held in July 2008.

The Water Initiative brings together diverse stakeholders such as Alcan Inc., the Swiss Agency for Development and Cooperation, USAID India, UNDP India, Confederation of Indian Industry (CII), Government of Rajasthan, and the NEPAD Business Foundation to develop public-private partnerships on water management in South Africa and India.

In an effort to combat corruption, the Partnering Against Corruption Initiative (PACI) was launched by CEOs from the Engineering and Construction, Energy and Metals, and Mining industries at the annual meeting in Davos during January 2004. PACI is a platform for peer exchange on practical experience and dilemma situations. Approximately 140 companies have joined the initiative.

Awards

The Technology Pioneers Programme recognizes companies that are designing and developing new technologies. The award is given to 30-50 companies each year, comprising, since 2000, more than 400 companies from 5 continents.

The Tech Pioneers are integrated into programme activities with the objective to identify and address future-oriented issues on the global agenda in proactive, innovative, and entrepreneurial ways. By bringing these executives together with scientists, academics, NGOs, and foundation members and partners, the foundation's goal is to shed new light on how technologies may be used to address, for example, finding new vaccines, creating economic growth, and enhancement of global communication.

The Public Eye Awards have been held every year since 2000. It is a counter-event to the annual meeting of the World Economic Forum (WEF) in Davos. Public Eye Awards is a public competition of the worst corporations in the world. In 2011, more than 50,000 people voted for companies that acted irresponsibly. At a ceremony at a Davos hotel, the 「winners」 in 2011 were named as Indonesian palm oil diesel maker, Neste Oil in Finland, and mining company AngloGold Ashanti in South Africa.

「Davos Man」

「Davos Man」 is a neologism referring to the global elite of wealthy (predominantly) men, whose members view themselves as completely「international」. It is similar to the term *Masters of the Universe* attributed to influential financiers on Wall Street.

Davos men supposedly see their identity as a matter of personal choice, not an accident of birth. According to political scientist Samuel P. Huntington, who is credited with inventing the phrase「Davos Man」, they are people who「have little need for national loyalty, view national boundaries as obstacles that thankfully are vanishing, and see national governments as residues from the past whose only useful function is to facilitate the élite's global operations」.

Part Ⅳ IMF, WB and BIS

In the late 1800s, world migration and communication technology facilitated unprecedented growth in international trade and investment. At the onset of World War Ⅰ, trade contracted as foreign exchange markets became paralyzed by money market illiquidity. Countries sought to defend against external shocks with protectionist policies and trade virtually halted by 1933, worsening the effects of the global Great Depression until a series of reciprocal trade agreements slowly reduced tariffs worldwide. Efforts to revamp the international monetary system after World War Ⅱ improved exchange rate stability, fostering record growth in global finance.

The International Monetary Fund (IMF) is an international organization headquartered in Washington, D.C., in the United States, of 188 members working to foster global monetary co-operation, secure financial stability, facilitate international trade, promote high employment and sustainable economic growth, and reduce poverty around the world. Formed in 1944 at the Bretton Woods Conference, it came into formal existence in 1945 with 29 members and the goal of reconstructing the international payment system. Members contribute funds to a pool through a quota system from which countries with payment imbalances can borrow. As of 2010, the fund had SDR476.8 billion, about US $ 755.7 billion at then-current exchange rates. Through this fund, and other activities such as statistics keeping and analysis, surveillance of its members' economies and the demand for self-correcting policies, the IMF works to improve the economies of its members.

The IMF was one of the key organizations of the international economic system; its design allowed the system to balance the rebuilding of international capitalism with the maximization of national economic sovereignty and human welfare. The IMF's influence in the global economy steadily increased as it accumulated more members. The increase reflected in particular the attainment of political independence by many African members and more recently the 1991 dissolution of the Soviet Union because most members in the Soviet sphere of influence did not join the IMF.

IMF「Headquarters」in Washington, D.C.

History

The IMF was originally laid out as a part of the Bretton Woods system exchange agreement in 1944. During the Great Depression, countries sharply raised barriers to trade in an attempt to improve their failing economies. This led to the devaluation of national currencies and a decline in world trade.

This breakdown in international monetary co-operation created a need for oversight. The representatives of 45 governments met at the Bretton Woods Conference in the Mount Washington Hotel in Bretton Woods, New Hampshire, in the United States, to discuss a framework for postwar international economic cooperation and how to rebuild Europe.

There were two views on the role the IMF should assume as a global economic institution. British economist John Maynard Keynes imagined that the IMF would be a co-operative fund upon which the members could draw to maintain economic activity and employment through periodic crises. This view suggested an IMF that helped governments and to act as the U.S. government had during the New Deal in response to World War II. American delegate Harry Dexter White foresaw an IMF that functioned more like a bank, making sure that borrowing states could repay their debts on time. Most of White's plan was incorporated into the final acts adopted at Bretton Woods.

The IMF formally came into existence on 27 December 1945, when the first 29 members ratified its Articles of Agreement. By the end of 1946 the IMF had grown to 39 members. On 1 March 1947, the IMF began its financial operations, and on 8 May France became the first member to borrow from it. As of January 2012, the largest borrowers from the IMF in order were Greece, Portugal, Ireland, Romania, and Ukraine.

Not all members of the IMF are sovereign states, and therefore not all members of the IMF are members of the United Nations. Amidst members of the IMF that are not members of the UN are non-sovereign areas with special jurisdictions that are officially under the sovereignty of full UN members, such as Hong Kong, Macau, and Kosovo. All members of the IMF are also International Bank for Reconstruction and Development (IBRD) members and vice versa.

Apart from Cuba, the other UN states that do not belong to the IMF are Andorra, Liechtenstein, Monaco, Nauru, and North Korea.

Qualifications

Any country or region may apply to be a part of the IMF. Members needed to make periodic membership payments towards their quota, to refrain from currency restrictions unless granted IMF permission, to abide by the Code of Conduct in the IMF Articles of Agreement, and to provide national economic information. However, stricter rules were imposed on governments that applied to the IMF for funding.

Some members have a very difficult relationship with the IMF and even when they are still members they do not allow themselves to be monitored. Argentina, for example, refuses to participate in an Article IV Consultation with the IMF.

Benefits

Members of the IMF have access to information on the economic policies of all members, the opportunity to influence other members' economic policies, technical assistance in banking, fiscal affairs, and exchange matters, financial support in times of payment difficulties, and increased opportunities for trade and investment.

Board of Governors

The Board of Governors consists of one governor and one alternate governor for each member. Each member appoints its two governors. The Board normally meets once a year and is responsible for electing or appointing executive directors to the Executive Board. While the Board of Governors is officially responsible for approving quota increases, Special Drawing Right allocations, the admittance of new members, compulsory withdrawal of members, and amendments to the Articles of Agreement and By-Laws, in practice it has delegated most of its powers to the IMF's Executive Board.

The Board of Governors is advised by the International Monetary and Financial Committee and the Development Committee. The International Monetary and Financial Committee has 24 members and monitors developments in global liquidity and the transfer of resources to developing countries. Countries or regions. The Development Committee has 25 members and advises on critical development issues and on financial resources required to promote economic development in developing countries. They also advise on trade and environmental issues.

Executive Board

24 Executive Directors make up Executive Board. The Executive Directors represent all 188 members in a geographically based roster. Members with large economies have their own Executive Director, but most members are grouped in constituencies representing four or more countries or regions.

Following the 2008 *Amendment on Voice* and *Participation* which came into effect in March 2011, eight members each appoint an Executive Director: the United States, Japan, Germany, France, the UK, China, the Russian Federation, and Saudi Arabia. The remaining 16 Directors represent constituencies consisting of 4 to 22 countries or regions.

Managing Director

The IMF is led by a managing director, who is head of the staff and serves as Chairman of the Executive Board. The managing director is assisted by a First Deputy managing director and three other Deputy Managing Directors. Historically the IMF's managing director has been European and the president of the World Bank has been from the United States. However, this standard is increasingly being questioned and competition for these two posts may soon open up to include other qualified candidates from any part of the world.

In 2011 the world's largest developing countries, the BRICS nations, issued a statement declaring that the tradition of appointing a European as managing director undermined the legitimacy of the IMF and called for the appointment to be merit-based.

Objectives and Activities

The organization's objectives stated in the Articles of Agreement are: to promote international economic co-operation, international trade, employment, and exchange-rate stability, including by making financial resources available to members to meet balance-of-payments needs.

The IMF works to foster global growth and economic stability by providing policy, advice and financing to members, by working with developing members to help them achieve macroeconomic stability, and by reducing poverty. The rationale for this is that private international capital markets function imperfectly and many members have limited access to financial markets. Such market imperfections, together with balance-of-payments financing, provide the justification for official financing, without which many members could only correct large external payment imbalances through measures with adverse economic consequences. The IMF provides alternate sources of financing.

Upon initial IMF formation, its two primary functions were: to oversee the fixed exchange rate arrangements between members, thus helping the governments manage their exchange rates and allowing these governments to prioritize economic growth, and to provide short-term capital to aid balance of payments. This assistance was meant to prevent the spread of international economic crises. The IMF was also intended to help mend the pieces of the international economy after the Great Depression and World War II.

The IMF's role was fundamentally altered after the floating exchange rates after 1971. It shifted to examining the economic policies of members with IMF loan agreements to determine if a shortage of capital was due to economic fluctuations or economic policy. The IMF also researched what types of government policy would ensure economic recovery. The new challenge is to promote and implement policy that reduces the frequency of crises among the emerging market countries or regions, especially the middle-income countries or regions that are vulnerable to massive capital outflows. Rather than maintaining a position of oversight of only exchange rates, their function became one of ⌈surveillance⌋ of the overall macroeconomic performance of members. Their role became a lot more active because the IMF now manages economic policy rather than just exchange rates.

In addition, the IMF negotiates conditions on lending and loans under their policy of conditionality, which was established in the 1950s. Low-income countries or regions can borrow on concessional terms, which mean there is a period of time with no interest rates. The IMF provides emergency assistance via the Rapid Financing Instrument (RFI) to members facing urgent balance-of-payments needs.

Surveillance of the Global Economy

The IMF is mandated to oversee the international monetary and financial system and monitor the economic and financial policies of its members. This activity is known as surveillance and facilitates international cooperation. Since the demise of the Bretton Woods system of fixed exchange rates in the early 1970s, surveillance has evolved largely by way of changes in procedures rather than through the adoption of new obligations. The responsibilities changed from those of guardian to those of overseer of members' policies.

The Fund typically analyses the appropriateness of each member's economic and financial policies for achieving orderly economic growth, and assesses the consequences of these policies for other members and for the global economy.

In 1995 the IMF began work on data dissemination standards with the view of guiding IMF members to disseminate their economic and financial data to the public. The International Monetary and Financial Committee (IMFC) endorsed the guidelines for the dissemination standards and they were split into two tiers: The General Data Dissemination System (GDDS) and the Special Data Dissemination Standard (SDDS).

The primary objective of the GDDS is to encourage members to build a framework to improve data quality and statistical capacity building in order to evaluate statistical needs, set priorities in improving the timeliness, transparency, reliability and accessibility of financial and economic data. Some members initially used the GDDS, but later upgraded to SDDS.

Conditionality of Loans

IMF conditionality is a set of policies or conditions that the IMF requires in exchange for financial resources. The IMF does require collateral from countries or regions for loans but also requires the government seeking assistance to correct its macroeconomic imbalances in the form of policy reform. If the conditions are not met, the funds are withheld. Conditionality is perhaps the most controversial aspect of IMF policies. The concept of conditionality was introduced in a 1952 Executive Board decision and later incorporated into the Articles of Agreement.

These loan conditions ensure that the borrowing country or region will be able to repay the IMF and that the country or region will not attempt to solve their balance-of-payment problems in a way that would negatively impact the international economy.

Conditionality also reassures the IMF that the funds lent to them will be used for the purposes defined by the Articles of Agreement and provides safeguards that the country or region will be able to rectify its macroeconomic and structural imbalances. In the judgment of the

IMF, the adoption by the member of certain corrective measures or policies will allow it to repay the IMF, thereby ensuring that the resources will be available to support other members.

As of 2004, borrowing countries or regions have had a very good track record for repaying credit extended under the IMF's regular lending facilities with full interest over the duration of the loan. This indicates that IMF lending does not impose a burden on creditor members, as lending members receive market-rate interest on most of their quota subscription, plus any of their own-currency subscriptions that are loaned out by the IMF, plus all of the reserve assets that they provide the IMF.

IMF and Globalization

Globalization encompasses three institutions: global financial markets, transnational or transregional companies, and national or regional governments linked to each other in economic and military alliances led by the United States, and rising 「global governments」 such as World Trade Organization (WTO), IMF, and World Bank. These interacting institutions create a new global power system where sovereignty is globalized, taking power and constitutional authority away from nations or regions and giving it to global markets and international bodies. This system institutionalizes global inequality between western countries and the Majority World in a form of global apartheid, in which the IMF is a key pillar.

The establishment of globalised economic institutions has been both a symptom of and a stimulus for globalization. The development of the World Bank, the IMF regional development banks such as the European Bank for Reconstruction and Development (EBRD), and multilateral trade institutions such as the WTO signals a move away from the dominance of the state or region as the exclusive unit of analysis in international affairs.

THE WORLD BANK
IBRD · IDA | WORLD BANK GROUP

The World Bank is an international financial institution that provides loans to developing countries or regions for capital programs. It comprises two institutions: the International Bank for Reconstruction and Development (IBRD) and the International Development Association (IDA). The World Bank is a component of the World Bank Group, and a member of the United Nations Development Group.

The World Bank was created at the 1944 Bretton Woods Conference, along with the International Monetary Fund (IMF). Traditionally, based on a tacit understanding between the United States and Europe, the president of the World Bank has always been selected from candidates nominated by the United States. The World Bank and the IMF are both based in Washington, D.C., and work closely with each other.

Although many countries or regions were represented at the Bretton Woods Conference, the United States and United Kingdom were the most powerful in attendance and dominated the negotiations.

The World Bank Group headquarters bldg. in Washington, D.C.

Objectives and Activities

The World Bank's official goal is the reduction of poverty. According to its Articles of Agreement, all its decisions must be guided by a commitment to the promotion of foreign investment and international trade and to the facilitation of capital investment.

1944–1968

Before 1968, the reconstruction and development loans provided by the World Bank were relatively small. The Bank's staff were aware of the need to instill confidence in the bank. Fiscal conservatism ruled, and loan applications had to meet strict criteria.

The first country to receive a World Bank loan was France. The loan was for US $ 250 million, half the amount requested, and it came with strict conditions. France had to agree to produce a balanced budget and give priority of debt repayment to the World Bank over other governments. World Bank staff closely monitored the use of the funds to ensure that the French government met the conditions. In addition, before the loan was approved, the United States State Department told the French government that its members associated with the Communist Party would first have to be removed. The French government complied with this and removed the Communist coalition government. Within hours, the loan to France was approved.

When the Marshall Plan went into effect in 1947, many European countries began receiving aid from other sources. Faced with this competition, the World Bank shifted its focus to non-European countries. Until 1968, its loans were earmarked for the construction of income-producing infrastructure, such as seaports, highway systems, and power plants, that would generate enough income to enable a borrower country to repay the loan.

1968–1980

From 1968 to 1980, the bank concentrated on meeting the basic needs of people in the developing world. The size and number of loans to borrowers was greatly increased as loan targets expanded from infrastructure into social services and other sectors.

In 1980, the World Bank Administrative Tribunal was established to decide on disputes between the World Bank Group and its staff where allegation of non-observance of contracts of employment or terms of appointment had not been honored.

1980–1989

During the 1980s, the bank emphasized lending to service Third-World debt, and structural adjustment policies designed to streamline the economies of developing countries or regions. UNICEF reported in the late 1980s that the structural adjustment programs of the World Bank had been responsible for「reduced health, nutritional and educational levels for tens of millions of children in Asia, Latin America, and Africa」.

1989–Present

Beginning in 1989, in response to harsh criticism from many groups, the bank began including environmental groups and NGOs in its loans to mitigate the past effects of its development policies that had prompted the criticism. It also formed an implementing agency, in accordance with the Montreal Protocols, to stop ozone-depletion damage to the Earth's atmosphere by phasing out the use of 95% of ozone-depleting chemicals. Since then, in accordance with its so-called「Six Strategic Themes,」the bank has put various additional policies into effect to preserve the environment while promoting development. For example, in 1991, the bank announced that to protect against deforestation, especially in the Amazon, it would not finance any commercial logging or infrastructure projects that harm the environment.

In order to promote global public goods, the World Bank tries to control communicable disease such as malaria, delivering vaccines to several parts of the world and joining combat forces. In 2000, the bank announced a「war on AIDS」, and in 2011, the Bank joined the Stop Tuberculosis Partnership.

Various developments have brought the Millennium Development Goals targets, such as:

1. Eradicate Extreme Poverty and Hunger: From 1990 through 2004, the proportion of people living in extreme poverty fell from almost a third to less than a fifth. Although results vary widely within regions and countries, the trend indicates that the world as a whole can meet the goal of halving the percentage of people living in poverty. Africa's poverty, however, is expected to rise, and most of the 36 countries where 90% of the world's undernourished children live are in Africa. Less than a quarter of countries or regions are on track for achieving the goal of halving under-nutrition.

2. Achieve Universal Primary Education: The percentage of children in school in developing countries or regions increased from 80% in 1991 to 88% in 2005. Still, about 72 million children of primary school age, 57% of them girls, were not being educated as of 2005.

3. Promote Gender Equality: The tide is turning slowly for women in the labor market, yet far more women than men-worldwide more than 60%-are contributing but unpaid family workers. The World Bank Group Gender Action Plan was created to advance women's economic empowerment and promote shared growth.

4. Reduce Child Mortality: There is some improvement in survival rates globally; accelerated improvements are needed most urgently in South Asia and Sub-Saharan Africa. An estimated 10 million-plus children under five died in 2005; most of their deaths were from preventable causes.

5. Improve Maternal Health: Almost all of the half million women who die during pregnancy or childbirth every year live in Sub-Saharan Africa and Asia. There are numerous causes of maternal death that require a variety of health care interventions to be made widely accessible.

6. Combat HIV/AIDS, Malaria, and Other Diseases: Annual numbers of new HIV infections and AIDS deaths have fallen, but the number of people living with HIV continues to grow. In the eight worst-hit southern African countries, prevalence is above 15 percent. Treatment has increased globally, but still meets only 30 percent of needs (with wide variations across countries). AIDS remains the leading cause of death in Sub-Saharan Africa (1.6 million deaths in 2007). There are 300 to 500 million cases of malaria each year, leading to more than 1 million deaths. Nearly all the cases and more than 95 percent of the deaths occur in Sub-Saharan Africa.

7. Ensure Environmental Sustainability: Deforestation remains a critical problem, particularly in regions of biological diversity, which continues to decline. Greenhouse gas emissions are increasing faster than energy technology advancement.

8. Develop a Global Partnership for Development: Donor countries have renewed their commitment. Donors have to fulfill their pledges to match the current rate of core program development. Emphasis is being placed on the Bank Group's collaboration with multilateral and local partners to quicken progress toward the MDGs' realization.

To make sure that World Bank-financed operations do not compromise these goals but instead add to their realization, environmental, social and legal Safeguards were defined. However, these Safeguards have not been implemented entirely yet. At the World Bank's annual meeting in Tokyo 2012 a review of these Safeguards has been initiated which was welcomed by several civil society organizations.

Bank for International Settlements

The Bank for International Settlements (BIS) is an international organization of central banks which fosters international monetary and financial cooperation and serves as a bank for central banks. The BIS carries out its work through subcommittees, the secretariats it hosts and through an annual general meeting of all member banks. It also provides banking services, but only to central banks and other international organizations. It is based in Basel, Switzerland, with representative offices in Hong Kong and Mexico City.

The BIS was established on May 17th, 1930, by an intergovernmental agreement by Germany, Belgium, France, the United Kingdom, Italy, Japan, the United States and Switzerland.

The BIS was originally intended to facilitate reparations imposed on Germany by the Treaty of Versailles after World War I. The need to establish a dedicated institution for this purpose was suggested in 1929 by the Young Committee, and was agreed to in August of that year at a conference at The Hague. A charter for the bank was drafted at the International Bankers Conference in November, and its charter was adopted at a second Hague Conference on January 20, 1930. According to the charter, shares in the bank could be held by individuals and non-governmental entities. The BIS was constituted as having corporate existence in Switzerland on the basis of an agreement with Switzerland acting as headquarters state for the bank. It also enjoyed immunity in all the contracting states.

As a result of allegations that the BIS had helped the Germans loot assets from occupied countries during World War II, the Bretton Woods Conference recommended the liquidation of the Bank for International Settlements at the earliest possible moment. This resulted in the BIS being the subject of a disagreement between the non-governmental U.S. and British delegations. The liquidation of the bank was supported by other European delegates, as well as the United States, but opposed by John Maynard Keynes, head of the British delegation.

Fearing that the BIS would be dissolved by President Franklin Delano Roosevelt, Keynes went to Morgenthau hoping to prevent the dissolution, or have it postponed, but the next day the dissolution of the BIS was approved. However, the liquidation of the bank was never actually undertaken. In April 1945, the new U.S. president Harry S. Truman and the British government suspended the dissolution, and the decision to liquidate the BIS was officially reversed in 1948.

The BIS was originally owned by both governments and private individuals, since the United States and France had decided to sell some of their shares to private investors. BIS shares traded on stock markets, which made the bank an unusual organization: an international organization (in the technical sense of public international law), yet allowed for private shareholders. Many central banks had similarly started as such private institutions; for example, the Bank of England was privately owned until 1946. In more recent years the BIS has bought back its once publicly traded shares. It is now wholly owned by BIS members (central banks) but still operates in the private market as a counterparty, asset manager and lender for central banks and international financial institutions. Profits from its transactions are used, among other things, to fund the bank's other international activities.

Organization of Central Banks

As an organization of central banks, the BIS seeks to make monetary policy more predictable and transparent among its 60-member central banks, except in the case of Eurozone countries which forfeited the right to conduct monetary policy in order to implement the euro. While monetary policy is determined by most sovereign nations, it is subject to central and private banking scrutiny and potentially to speculation that affects foreign exchange rates and especially the fate of export economies. Failures to keep monetary policy in line with reality and make monetary reforms in time, preferably as a simultaneous policy among all 60 member banks and also involving the International Monetary Fund, have historically led to losses in the billions as banks try to maintain a policy using open market methods that have proven to be based on unrealistic assumptions.

Central banks do not unilaterally 「set」 rates, rather they set goals and intervene using their massive financial resources and regulatory powers to achieve monetary targets they set. One reason to coordinate policy closely is to ensure that this does not become too expensive and that opportunities for private arbitrage exploiting shifts in policy or difference in policy, are rare and quickly removed.

Two aspects of monetary policy have proven to be particularly sensitive, and the BIS therefore has two specific goals: to regulate capital adequacy and make reserve requirements transparent.

Regulating Capital Adequacy

Capital adequacy policy applies to equity and capital assets. These can be overvalued in many circumstances because they do not always reflect current market conditions or adequately assess the risk of every trading position. Accordingly, the BIS requires the capital/asset ratio of central banks to be above a prescribed minimum international standard, for the protection of all central banks involved.

The BIS's main role is in setting capital adequacy requirements. From an international point of view, ensuring capital adequacy is the most important problem between central banks, as speculative lending based on inadequate underlying capital and widely varying liability rules causes economic crises as 「bad money drives out good」.

Encouraging Reserve Transparency

Reserve policy is also important, especially to consumers and the domestic economy. To ensure liquidity and limit liability to the larger economy, banks cannot create money in specific industries or regions without limit. To make bank depositing and borrowing safer for customers and reduce risk of bank runs, banks are required to set aside or 「reserve」.

Reserve policy is harder to standardize as it depends on local conditions and is often fine-tuned to make industry-specific or region-specific changes, especially within large developing nations. For instance, the People's Bank of China (PBOC) requires urban banks to hold 7% reserves while letting rural banks continue to hold only 6%, and simultaneously telling all banks that reserve requirements on certain overheated industries would rise sharply or penalties would be laid if investments in them did not stop completely. The PBOC is thus unusual in acting as a national bank, focused on the country not on the currency, but its desire to control asset inflation is increasingly shared among BIS members who fear 「bubbles」, and among exporting countries that find it difficult to manage the diverse requirements of the domestic economy, especially rural agriculture, and an export economy, especially in manufactured goods.

Effectively, the PBOC sets different reserve levels for domestic and export styles of development. Historically, the United States also did this, by dividing federal monetary management into nine regions, in which the less-developed western United States had looser policies.

For various reasons it has become quite difficult to accurately assess reserves on more than simple loan instruments, and this plus the regional differences has tended to discourage standardizing any reserve rules at the global BIS scale. Historically, the BIS did set some standards which favoured lending money to private landowners and for-profit corporations over loans to individuals. These distinctions reflecting classical economics were superseded by policies relying on undifferentiated market values—more in line with neoclassical economics.

Role in Banking Supervision

The BIS provides the Basel Committee on Banking Supervision with its 17-member secretariat, and with it has played a central role in establishing the Basel Capital Accords of 1988 and

2004. There remain significant differences between United States, European Union, and United Nations officials regarding the degree of capital adequacy and reserve controls that global banking now requires. Put extremely simply, the United States, as of 2006, favoured strong strict central controls in the spirit of the original 1988 accords, while the EU was more inclined to a distributed system managed collectively with a committee able to approve some exceptions.

Glossary

Part I

infrastructure   n. 基礎設施；公共建設；下部構造
voyage   n. 航行；航程；旅行記
connectedness   n. 連通性
dissemination   n. 宣傳；散播；傳染（病毒）
philosophy   n. 哲學；哲理；人生觀
exploration   n. 探測；探究；踏勘
interchange   n. 互換；立體交叉道
syncretic   adj. 合一的；融合的；匯合的
refugee   n. 難民，避難者；流亡者，逃亡者
influx   n. 流入；匯集；河流的匯集處
prohibitively   adv. 禁止的；過高的；過分的
dominance   n. 優勢；統治；支配
endure   v. 忍耐；容忍
protectionism   n. 保護主義，貿易保護主義；貿易保護制度
integration   n. 集成；綜合
eminence   n. 顯赫；卓越；高處
negative   adj. 消極的

Part II

conflict   n. 衝突，矛盾；鬥爭；爭執
voluntary   adj. 自願的；志願的；自發的
organ   n. 機構
humanitarian   adj. 人道主義的
uphold   v. 支撐；鼓勵；讚成；舉起
polio   n. 小兒麻痺症（等於 poliomyelitis）；脊髓灰質炎
leprosy   n. 麻瘋病
famine   n. 饑荒；饑餓
abstention   n. 棄權；節制

impetus   n. 動力；促進；衝力
demographic   adj. 人口統計學的；人口學的
reinforce   v. 加強，加固；強化；補充
revitalize   v. 使……復活；使……復興；使……恢復生氣
clarify   v. 澄清；闡明

Part III

sovereignty   n. 主權；主權國家；君主；獨立國
averse   adj. 反對的
crude   adj. 粗糙的；天然的，未加工的
unilateral   adj. 單邊的
revenue   n. 稅收收入；財政收入；收益
speculation   n. 投機；推測；思索
devaluation   n. 貨幣貶值
thermostat   n. 恒溫器；自動調溫器
orchestrate   v. 把……編成管弦樂曲；（美）精心安排；把……協調地結合起來
asylum   n. 庇護；收容所，救濟院
quota   n. 配額；定額
cohesion   n. 凝聚；結合
intellectual   n. 知識分子
academic   adj. 學術的；理論的；學院的
neologism   n. 新詞；新義；新詞的使用

Part IV

revamp   v. 修補；翻新；修改
surveillance   n. 監督；監視
capitalism   n. 資本主義
dissolution   n. 分解，（議會等的）解散；（契約等的）解除
oversight   n. 監督，照管；疏忽
periodic   adj. 週期的；定期的
jurisdictions   n. 司法權，審判權，管轄權
alternate   v. 交替；輪流
compulsory   adj. 義務的；必修的；被強制的
macroeconomic   adj. 宏觀經濟的，總體經濟的
prioritize   v. 給……排出優先級；優先處理；優先考慮
vulnerable   adj. 易受攻擊的，易受……的攻擊；易受傷害的

dissemination　n. 宣傳；散播；
subscription　n. 捐獻；訂閱；訂金；簽署
surveillance　n. 監督；監視
pillar　n. 柱子，柱形物；棟梁
criteria　n. 標準，條件（criterion 的複數）
arbitrage　n. 套匯，套利；仲裁
ideology　n. 意識形態；思想意識；觀念學

Phrases

on par with　與……同等水準
advent of　出現
as well as　也；和……一樣；不但……而且……
focus on　集中於
in cases of　萬一；如果發生；假設
the period of　時期
according to　根據，按照
along with　連同……一起；與……一道；隨同……一起
come up with　提出；想出；趕上
consist of　包含；由……組成
demand for　對……的需求
take place　發生；舉行
lay out　展示；安排；花錢；提議
access to　接近；有權使用；通向……的入口
open up　打開；開發；展示，揭露
the demise of　……的告終；……的消亡
split into　分成，分裂成
attempt to　嘗試，企圖
decide on　決定；選定

Notes

International Monetary Fund（IMF）：國際貨幣基金組織是根據1944年7月在布雷頓森林會議簽訂的《國際貨幣基金協定》，於1945年12月27日在華盛頓成立的。與世界銀行同時成立，並列為世界兩大金融機構之一，其職責是監察貨幣匯率和各國貿易情況，提供技術和資金協助，確保全球金融制度運作正常。其總部設在華盛頓。我們常聽到的「特別提款權」就是該組織於1969年創設的。

Silk Road：絲綢之路，簡稱絲路，一般指陸上絲綢之路，廣義上講又分為陸上絲綢之路和海上絲綢之路。陸上絲綢之路起源於西漢漢武帝派張騫出使西域開闢的以首都長安（今西安）為起點，經甘肅、新疆，到中亞、西亞，並連接地中海各國的陸上通道。它的最初作用是運輸中國古代出產的絲綢。1877年，德國地質地理學家李希霍芬

在其著作《中國》一書中，把「從公元前114年至公元127年間，中國與中亞、中國與印度間以絲綢貿易為媒介的這條西域交通道路」命名為「絲綢之路」，這一名詞很快被學術界和大眾所接受，並正式運用。「海上絲綢之路」是古代中國與外國交通貿易和文化交往的海上通道，該路主要以南海為中心，所以又稱南海絲綢之路。海上絲綢之路形成於秦漢時期，發展於三國至隋朝時期，繁榮於唐宋時期，轉變於明清時期，是已知的最為古老的海上航線。

Bretton Woods Agreement：布雷頓森林協定是第二次世界大戰後以美元為中心的國際貨幣體系協定。布雷頓森林體系是該協定對各國就貨幣的兌換、國際收支的調節、國際儲備資產的構成等問題共同作出的安排所確定的規則、採取的措施及相應的組織機構形式的總和，旨在為二戰之後的各國提供一個堅實的經濟基礎。1973年2月美元進一步貶值，世界各主要貨幣由於受投機商衝擊被迫實行浮動匯率制，至此布雷頓森林體系完全崩潰。布雷頓森林體系崩潰以後，國際貨幣基金組織和世界銀行作為重要的國際組織仍得以繼續存在至今，並發揮重要的國際作用。

World Health Organization（WHO）：世界衛生組織，是聯合國下屬的一個專門機構，總部設置在瑞士日內瓦，只有主權國家才能參加，是國際上最大的政府間衛生組織。世界衛生組織的宗旨是使全世界人民獲得盡可能高水準的健康。世界衛生組織的主要職能包括：促進流行病和地方病的防治；提供和改進公共衛生、疾病醫療和有關事項的教學與訓練；推動確定生物製品的國際標準。

International Red Cross and Red Crescent Movement：紅十字會與紅新月會國際聯合會即為紅十字會，是一個遍布全球的志願救援組織。目的為推動「國際紅十字與紅新月運動」，是全世界組織最龐大，也是最具影響力的類似組織，除了許多國家立法保障其特殊位階外，戰爭時紅十字也常與政府、軍隊緊密合作。

Gulf War：海灣戰爭，包括3個主要軍事行動：沙漠盾牌行動、沙漠風暴行動和海上攔截行動。聯盟軍隊以較小的代價取得決定性勝利，重創伊拉克軍隊。1991年2月27日，美國宣布解放科威特的戰爭結束並於當天午夜停火，伊拉克最終在4月接受了停火協議。海灣戰爭是美軍自越南戰爭後主導參加的第一場大規模局部戰爭。在戰爭中，美軍首次將大量高科技武器投入實戰，展示了壓倒性的制空、制電磁優勢。通過海灣戰爭，美國進一步加強了與波斯灣地區國家的軍事、政治合作，強化了美軍在該地區的軍事存在。

BRICS：金磚國家（BRICS），用巴西（Brazil）、俄羅斯（Russia）、印度（India）、中國（China）和南非（South Africa）的英文首字母組成。由於該詞與英語單詞的磚（Brick）類似，因此被稱為「金磚國家」。2001年，美國高盛公司首席經濟師吉姆·奧尼爾（Jim O'Neill）首次提出「金磚四國」這一概念，特指世界新興市場。

Questions

1. How does the International Monetary Fund identify four basic aspects of globalization?
2. What is UN? How many principal organs does The UN have?
3. Talk about the UN's mission.
4. What role does China play in G-20 members?
5. Please talk about the OPEC objectives and activities.
6. What is「Davos Men」?

Chapter II

Regional Cooperation and Competition

Regional cooperation refers to the political and institutional mechanisms that countries in a general geographical region devise to find and strengthen common interests as well as promoting their national interests, through mutual cooperation and dialogue. It is also an arrangement for enhancing cooperation through regional rules and institutions entered into by states of the same region. Regional integration could have as its objective political or economic goals or in some cases, a business initiative aimed at broader security and commercial purposes.

Regional organizations (ROs) are, in a sense, international organizations (IOs), as they incorporate international membership and encompass geopolitical entities that operationally transcend a single nation state. However, their membership is characterized by boundaries and demarcations characteristic to a defined and unique geography, such as continents, or geopolitics, such as economic blocs. They have been established to foster cooperation and political and economic integration or dialogue among states or entities within a restrictive geographical or geopolitical boundary. They both reflect common patterns of development and history that have been fostered since the end of World War II as well as the fragmentation inherent in globalization. Most ROs tend to work alongside well-established multilateral organizations such as the United Nations. While in many instances a regional organization is simply referred to as an international organization, in many others it makes sense to use the term regional organization to stress the more limited scope of a particular membership.

Part I   G-7 and EU Member States

Group of 7

The Group of Seven (G7) is a governmental forum of leading advanced economies in the world. The forum originated with a 1975 summit hosted by France that brought together representatives of six governments: France, West Germany, Italy, Japan, the United Kingdom, and the United States, thus leading to the name Group of Six or G6. The summit became known as the Group of Seven or G7 in 1976 with the addition of Canada. The G7 is composed of the seven wealthiest developed countries on earth (by national net wealth or by GDP). The G7 countries represent more than 64% of the net global wealth ($ 263 trillion) according to the Credit Suisse Global Wealth Report October 2014.

Since 1975, the group meets annually on summit site to discuss economic policies; since 1987, the G7 finance ministers have met at least semi-annually, up to 4 times a year at stand-alone meetings.

In 1999, the G7 decided to get more directly involved in 「managing the international monetary system」through the Financial Stability Forum, formed earlier in 1999 and the G-20, established following the summit, to 「promote dialogue between major industrial and emerging market countries」.

In 2008 the G7 met twice in Washington D.C. to discuss the global financial crisis of 2007 -2010 and in February 2009 in Rome. The group of finance ministers pledged to take 「all necessary steps」to stem the crisis.

Russia was added to the group from 1998 to 2014, which then became known as the G8. The European Union was represented within the G8 since the 1980s but could not host or chair summits.

The G7 has influenced IMF and World Bank rules of crisis resolution and development, as well as WTO's rules of international trade.

EU Member States

The European Union is a politico-economic union of 28 member states that are located primarily in Europe. It traces its origins from the European Coal and Steel Community (ECSC) and the European Economic Community (EEC), formed by the Inner Six countries in 1951 and 1958, respectively. In the intervening years, the community and its successors have grown in size by the accession of new member states.

The European Union (EU) was formally established when the Maastricht Treaty came into force on 1 November 1993. In 1957, Belgium, France, Italy, Luxembourg, the Netherlands, and West Germany signed the Treaty of Rome, which created the European Economic Community (EEC) and established a customs union. In 1973, the Communities enlarged to include Denmark, Ireland, and the United Kingdom. Greece joined in 1981; Portugal and Spain in 1986. In 1985, the Schengen Agreement led the way toward the creation of open borders without passport controls between most member states and some non-member states. In 1990, after the fall of the Eastern Bloc, the former East Germany became part of the Community as part of a reunited Germany. In 2004, the EU saw its biggest enlargement to date when Cyprus, the Czech Republic, Estonia, Hungary, Latvia, Lithuania, Malta, Poland, Slovakia, and Slovenia joined the Union. On 1 January 2007, Romania and Bulgaria became EU members. On 1 July 2013, Croatia became the 28th EU member. The EU operates through a system of supranational institutions and intergovernmental-negotiated decisions by the member states.

The European Union has seven institutions: the European Parliament, the Council of the European Union, the European Commission, the European Council, the European Central

Bank, the Court of Justice of the European Union and the European Court of Auditors. Competencies in scrutinizing and amending legislation are divided between the European Parliament and the Council of the European Union while executive tasks are carried out by the European Commission and in a limited capacity by the European Council. The monetary policy of the eurozone is governed by the European Central Bank. The interpretation and the application of EU law and the treaties are ensured by the Court of Justice of the European Union. The EU budget is scrutinized by the European Court of Auditors. There are also a number of ancillary bodies which advise the EU or operate in a specific area.

Internal Market

The EU has developed a single market through a standardized system of laws that apply in all member states. The single market involves the free circulation of goods, capital, people, and services within the EU, and the customs union involves the application of a common external tariff on all goods entering the market. Once goods have been admitted into the market they cannot be subjected to customs duties, discriminatory taxes or import quotas, as they travel internally. The non-EU member states of Iceland, Norway, Liechtenstein and Switzerland participate in the single market but not in the customs union. Half the trade in the EU is covered by legislation harmonized by the EU.

Free movement of capital is intended to permit movement of investments such as property purchases and buying of shares between countries.

The free movement of capital is unique insofar as it is granted equally to non-member states.

The free movement of persons means that EU citizens can move freely between member states to live, work, study or retire in another country.

Within the Schengen Area, passport controls have been abolished. EU policies aim to ensure the free movement of people, goods, services, and capital, enact legislation in justice and home affairs, and maintain common policies on trade, agriculture, fisheries, and regional development. In 2012, the EU was awarded the Nobel Peace Prize.

Eurozone

The monetary union was established in 1999 and came into full force in 2002, the year when euro banknotes and coins replaced national currencies in 12 of the member states. Since then, the eurozone has increased to encompass 19 countries.

The euro was introduced in 2002, replacing 12 national currencies. Seven countries have since joined.

Through the Common Foreign and Security Policy, the EU has developed a role in external relations and defense. The union maintains permanent diplomatic missions throughout the world and represents itself at the United Nations, the WTO, the G8, and the G-20.

With a combined population of over 500 million inhabitants, or 7.3% of the world population, the EU in 2014 generated a nominalgross domestic product (GDP) of 18.495 trillion US dollars, constituting approximately 24% of global nominal GDP and 17% when measured in terms of purchasing power parity. As of 2014 the EU has the largest economy in the world, generating a GDP bigger than any other economic union or country. Of the top 500 largest corporations measured by revenue (Fortune Global 500 in 2010), 161 have their headquarters in the EU.

Competition

The EU operates a competition policy intended to ensure undistorted competition within the single market. The Commission as the competition regulator for the single market is responsible for antitrust issues, approving mergers, breaking up cartels, working for economic liberalisation and preventing state aid. For example, in 2001 the Commission for the first time prevented a merger between two companies based in the United States (GE and Honeywell) which had already been approved by their national authority. Another high-profile case against Microsoft, resulted in the Commission fining Microsoft over 777 million following nine years of legal action.

Monetary Union

The seat of the Central Bank in Frankfurt 19 of the 28 member states of the union have adopted the euro as their legal tender.

The creation of aEuropean single currency became an official objective of the European Economic Community in 1969. In 1992, after having negotiated the structure and procedures of a currency union, the member states signed the Maastricht Treaty and were legally bound to fulfill the agreed-on rules including the convergence criteria if they wanted to join the monetary union. The states wanting to participate had first to join the European Exchange Rate Mechanism.

In 1999 the currency union started, first as an accounting currency with eleven member states joining. In 2002, the currency was fully put into place, when euro notes and coins were issued and national currencies began to phase out in the eurozone, which by then consisted of 12 member states. The eurozone (constituted by the EU member states which have adopted the euro) has since grown to 19 countries, the most recent being Lithuania which joined on 1 January 2015. Denmark, the United Kingdom, and Sweden decided not to join the euro.

Since its launch the euro has become the second reserve currency in the world with a quarter of foreign exchanges reserves being in euro. The euro and the monetary policies of those who have adopted it in agreement with the EU, are under the control of the European Central Bank (ECB).

To prevent the joining states from getting into financial trouble or crisis after entering the monetary union, they were obliged in the Maastricht treaty to fulfill important financial obligations and procedures, especially to show budgetary discipline and a high degree of sustainable economic convergence, as well as to avoid excessive government deficits and limit the government debt to a sustainable level.

Some states joined the euro but violated these rules and contracts to an extent that they slid into adebt crisis and had to be financially supported with emergency rescue funds. These states were Greece, Ireland, Portugal, Cyprus and Spain.

Even though the Maastricht treaty forbids eurozone states to assume the debts of other states (「bailout」), various emergency rescue funds had been created by the members to support the debt crisis states to meet their financial obligations and buy time for reforms that those states can gain back their competitiveness.

European Economic Area

The European Economic Area (EEA) is a single market that provides for the free movement of persons, goods, services and capital through three of the four member states of the European Free Trade Association (EFTA) –Iceland, Liechtenstein and Norway–and all 28 member states of the European Union (EU). Pending its ratification by all EEA countries, Croatia, the remaining and most recent EU member state, is applying the EEA Agreement provisionally.

The EEA was established on 1 January 1994 following an agreement between the member states and the EU's predecessor, the European Community. EFTA states which join the EEA are able to participate in the EU's single internal market without being EU members, adopting almost all the relevant EU legislation other than laws regarding agriculture and fisheries. The EEA's decision-shaping processes enable them to influence and contribute to new EEA policy and legislation from an early stage.

One EFTA member, Switzerland, has not joined the EEA but has a series of bilateral agreements with the EU, including a free trade agreement.

Brexit decision sparks EU crisis

**A statue of Winston Churchill is silhouetted by Big Ben
and the Houses of Parliament in central London.**

As the first member to vote to leave the 28-member bloc, the UK's historical referendum has caused a chain reaction, not only in Britain but also in the EU and the international communities. The referendum, which held a 52 percent to 48 percent lead with more than 17 million votes cast for Leave and 16 million for Remain, is not binding but 「advisory」. It does not automatically trigger exit from the EU, which must be confirmed by the British prime minister activating Article 50 of the Lisbon Treaty, beginning a years-long process of exit.

It is clear that this political earthquake will have after-shocks throughout the world.」

European stock markets saw sharply lower opens on Friday, falling by as much as 12 percent, and markets worldwide plunged as the vote counts trickled in Thursday night and Friday morning. The British pound fell to its lowest level since 1985, down more than 10 percent at one point against the US dollar, before staging what may be a temporary recovery. Gold and the Japanese yen went up. Most economists predict that the decision is likely to result in long-term economic damage to the UK, and possible recession.

Part II   ASEAN, APEC and ASEAN

The Association of Southeast Asian Nations is a political and economic organization of ten Southeast Asian countries. It was formed on 8 August 1967 by Indonesia, Malaysia, the Philippines, Singapore, and Thailand. Since then, membership has expanded to include Brunei, Cambodia, Laos, Myanmar (Burma), and Vietnam. Its aims include accelerating economic growth, social progress, and socio-cultural evolution among its members, protection of regional peace and stability, and opportunities for member countries to resolve differences peacefully.

ASEAN covers a land area of 4.4 million km^2, 3% of the total land area of the Earth.

ASEAN territorial waters cover an area about three times larger than its land counterpart. The member countries have a combined population of approximately 625 million people, 8.8% of the world's population. In 2013, the organization's combined nominal GDP had grown to more than US $ 2.4 trillion. If ASEAN were a single entity, it would rank as the seventh largest economy in the world, behind the US, China, Japan, Germany, France, and the United Kingdom.

Flag   Emblem

As set out in the ASEAN Declaration, the aims and purposes of ASEAN are:

· To accelerate economic growth, social progress, and cultural development in the region

· To promote regional peace and stability

· To promote collaboration and mutual assistance on matters of common interest

· To provide assistance to each other in the form of training and research facilities

· To collaborate for the better utilisation of agriculture and industry to raise the living standards of the people

· To promote Southeast Asian studies

· To maintain close, beneficial co-operation with existing international organizations with similar aims and purposes

ASEAN Charter

On 15 December 2008, the members of ASEAN met in the Indonesian capital of Jakarta to launch a charter, signed in November 2007, with the aim of moving closer to 「an EU-style community」. The charter turns ASEAN into a legal entity and aims to create a single free-trade area for the region encompassing 500 million people.

The ASEAN Way

The 「ASEAN Way」 refers to a working process or style that is informal and personal. Policymakers constantly utilize compromise, consensus, and consultation in the informal decision-making process. It above all prioritizes a consensus-based, non-conflictual way of addressing problems. Quiet diplomacy allows ASEAN leaders to communicate without bringing the discussions into the public view. Members avoid embarrassment that may lead to further conflict.

It has been said that the merits of the ASEAN Way might be usefully applied to global conflict management.

ASEAN Plus Three

The leaders of each country felt the need to further integrate the region. Beginning in 1997, the bloc began creating organizations with the intention of achieving this goal. ASEAN Plus Three was the first of these and was created to improve existing ties with the People's Republic of China, Japan, and South Korea. This was followed by the even larger East Asia Summit (EAS), which included ASEAN Plus Three countries as well as India, Australia, New Zealand, United States, and Russia.

In 2006, ASEAN was given observer status at the United Nations General Assembly. In response, the organization awarded the status of 「dialogue partner」 to the UN.

Asia-Pacific Economic Cooperation (APEC)

Asia-Pacific Economic Cooperation

Asia-Pacific Economic Cooperation is a forum for 21 Pacific Rim member economies that promotes free trade throughout the Asia-Pacific region. It was established in 1989 in response to the growing interdependence of Asia-Pacific economies and the advent of regional trade blocs in other parts of the world; to fears that highly industrialised Japan (a member of G8) would come to dominate economic activity in the Asia-Pacific region; and to establish new markets for agricultural products and raw materials beyond Europe.

An annual APEC Economic Leaders' Meeting is attended by the heads of government of all APEC members except Taiwan economic leader (which is represented by a ministerial-level official under the name Chinese Taipei). The location of the meeting rotates annually among the member economies, and a famous tradition, followed for most (but not all) summits, involves the attending leaders dressing in a national costume of the host member.

History

In January 1989, Australian Prime Minister Bob Hawke called for more effective economic cooperation across the Pacific Rim region. This led to the first meeting of APEC in the Australian capital of Canberra in November, chaired by Australian Foreign Affairs Minister and attended by ministers from twelve countries; the meeting concluded with commitments for future annual meetings in Singapore and Korea.

Countries of the Association of Southeast Asian Nations (ASEAN) opposed the initial proposal, instead proposing the East Asia Economic Caucus which would exclude non-Asian countries such as the United States, Canada, Australia, and New Zealand. This plan was opposed and strongly criticized by Japan and the United States.

The first APEC Economic Leaders' Meeting occurred in 1993 when U.S. President Bill Clinton, after discussions with Australian Prime Minister Paul Keating, invited the heads of government from member economies to a summit on Blake Island. He believed it would help bring the stalled Uruguay Round of trade talks back on track. At the meeting, some leaders called for continued reduction of barriers to trade and investment, envisioning a community in the Asia-Pacific region that might promote prosperity through cooperation. The APEC Secretariat, based in Singapore, was established to coordinate the activities of the organization.

Member Economies

APEC currently has 21 members, including most countries or regions with a coastline on the Pacific Ocean. However, the criterion for membership is that the member is a separate economy, rather than a state or region. As a result, APEC uses the term member economies rather than member countries to refer to its members. APEC also includes three official observers: ASEAN, the Pacific Islands Forum and the Pacific Economic Cooperation Council.

India has requested membership in APEC, and received initial support from the United States, Japan and Australia. Officials have decided not to allow India to join for various reasons. India does not border the Pacific Ocean, which all current members do. However, India was invited to be an observer for the first time in November 2011.

Bangladesh, Pakistan, Sri Lanka, Chinese Macau, Mongolia, Laos, Cambodia, Costa Rica, Colombia, Panama, and Ecuador, are among a dozen other economies seeking membership in APEC, in addition to India. Colombia applied for APEC's membership as early as in 1995, but its bid was halted as the organization stopped accepting new members from 1993 to 1996, and the moratorium was further prolonged to 2007 due to the 1997 Asian Financial Crisis. Guam has also been actively seeking a separate membership, citing the example of Chinese Hong Kong, but the request is opposed by the United States, which currently represents Guam.

Objectives and Activities

During the meeting in 1994 in Bogor, Indonesia, APEC leaders adopted the Bogor Goals that aim for free and open trade and investment in the Asia-Pacific by 2010 for industrialized economies and by 2020 for developing economies. In 1995, APEC established a business advisory body named the APEC Business Advisory Council (ABAC), composed of three business executives from each member economy.

APEC has long been at the forefront of reform efforts in the area of business facilitation. Between 2002 and 2006 the costs of business transactions across the region was reduced by 6%, thanks to the APEC Trade Facilitation Action Plan (TFAPI). Between 2007 and 2010, APEC hopes to achieve an additional 5% reduction in business transaction costs. To this end, a new Trade Facilitation Action Plan has been endorsed. According to a 2008 research brief published by the World Bank as part of its Trade Costs and Facilitation Project, increasing transparency in the region's trading system is critical if APEC is to meet its Bogor Goal targets. The APEC Business Travel Card, a travel document for visa-free business travel within the region is one of the concrete measures to facilitate business. In May 2010 Russia joined the scheme, thus completing the circle.

APEC first formally started discussing the concept of a Free Trade Area of the Asia-Pacific (FTAAP) at its summit in 2006 in Hanoi. The proposal for a FTAAP arose due to the lack of progress in the Doha round of World Trade Organization negotiations, and as a way to overcome the「noodle bowl」effect created by overlapping and conflicting elements of the copious free trade agreements—there were approximately 60 free trade agreements in 2007, with an additional 117 in the process of negotiation in Southeast Asia and the Asia-Pacific region. In 2012, ASEAN+6 countries alone had 339 free trade agreements, many of which were bilateral.

The FTAAP is more ambitious in scope than the Doha round, which limits itself to reducing trade restrictions. The FTAAP would create a free trade zone that would considerably expand commerce and economic growth in the region. The economic expansion and growth in trade could exceed the expectations of other regional free trade areas such as the ASEAN Plus Three (ASEAN + China, Japan, and South Korea).

At the 2014 APEC summit in Beijing, APEC leaders agreed to launch 「a collective strategic study」 on the FTAAP, which will be APEC's big goal out into the future.

Part Ⅲ　BRICS and Four Asian Tigers

BRICS is the acronym for an association of five major emerging national economies: Brazil, Russia, India, China and South Africa. The grouping was originally known as 「BRIC」 before the inclusion of South Africa in 2010. The BRICS members are all developing or newly industrialised countries, but they are distinguished by their large, fast-growing economies and significant influence on regional and global affairs; all five are G-20 members. Since 2010, the BRICS nations have met annually at formal summits. Russia currently holds the chair of the BRICS group, and host the group's seventh summit in July 2015.

As of 2014, the five BRICS countries represent almost 3 billion people, or approximately 40% of the world population; as all five members are in the top 25 of the world by population, and four are in the top 10. The five nations have a combined nominal GDP of US $ 16.039 trillion, equivalent to approximately 20% of the gross world product, and an estimated US $ 4 trillion in combined foreign reserves.

Developments

The BRICS Forum, an independent international organization encouraging commercial, political and cultural cooperation between the BRICS nations, was formed in 2011. In June 2012, the BRICS nations pledged $ 75 billion to boost the lending power of the International Monetary Fund (IMF). However, this loan was conditional on IMF voting reforms. In late March 2013, during the fifth BRICS summit in Durban, South Africa, the member countries agreed to create a global financial institution which they intended to rival the western-dominated IMF and World Bank. After the summit, the BRICS stated that they planned to finalize the arrangements for this New Development Bank by 2014. However, disputes relating to burden sharing and location have slowed down the agreements.

At the BRICS leaders meeting in St. Petersburg in September 2013, China committed $ 41 billion towards the pool; Brazil, India and Russia $ 18 billion each; and South Africa $ 5 billion.

On 15 July, 2014, the first day of the BRICS 6th summit in Fortaleza, Brazil, the group of emerging economies signed the long-anticipated document to create the US $ 100 billion New Development Bank (formerly known as the 「BRICS Development Bank」) and a reserve currency pool worth over another US $ 100 billion. Documents on cooperation between BRICS export credit agencies and an agreement of cooperation on innovation were also inked.

Four Asian Tigers

The Four Asian Tigers or Four Asian Dragons is a term used in reference to the highly free and developed economies of Chinese Hong Kong, Singapore, South Korea, and Chinese Taiwan. These nations and regions were notable for maintaining exceptionally high growth rates (in excess of 7 percent a year) and rapid industrialization between the early 1960s (mid-1950s for Chinese Hong Kong) and 1990s. By the end of the 20th century, all four had developed into advanced and high-income economies, specializing in areas of competitive advantage. For example, Singapore Chinese Hong Kong and have become world-leading international financial centers, whereas South Korea and Chinese Taiwan are world leaders in manufacturing information technology. Their economic success stories have served as role models for many developing countries or regions, especially the Tiger Cub Economies.

Overview

Prior to the 1997 Asian financial crisis, the growth of these four Asian tiger economies (commonly referred to as,「The Asian Miracle」) has been attributed to export oriented policies and strong development policies. Unique to these economies were the sustained rapid growth and high levels of equal income distribution. A World Bank report suggests two development policies among others as sources for the Asian miracle: factor accumulation and macroeconomic management.

Chinese Hong Kong's economy was the first out of the four to undergo industrialization with the development of a textile industry in the 1950s. By the 1960s, manufacturing in Chinese Hong Kong had expanded and diversified to include clothing, electronics and plastics for export orientation. Following Singapore's independence from Malaysia, the Economic Development Board formulated and implemented economic strategies to promote the nation's manufacturing sector. Industrial estates were set up and foreign investment was attracted the nation with tax incentives. Meanwhile, Chinese Taiwan and South Korea began to industrialize in the mid-1960s with heavy government involvement including initiatives and policies. Export-orientated industrialization as in Chinese Hong Kong and Singapore was followed by both Chinese Taiwan and South Korea.

By the end of the 1960s, levels in physical and human capital amongst the four countries far exceeded other countries or regions at similar levels of development. This subsequently led to a rapid growth in per capita income levels. While high investments were essential to the economic growth of these countries and regions, the role of human capital was also important. Education in particular is cited as playing a major role in the Asian miracle. The levels of education enrollment in the four Asian tigers were higher than predicted given their level of income. By 1965, all four countries and regions had achieved universal primary education. South Korea in particular had achieved a secondary education enrollment rate of 88% by 1987. There was also a notable decrease in the gap between male and female enrollments during the Asian miracle. Overall these progresses in education allowed for high levels of literacy and cognitive skills.

The creation of stable macroeconomic environments was the foundation upon which the Asian miracle was built. Each of the four Asian tigers managed, to various degrees of success, three variables in: budget deficits, external debt and exchange rates. Each tiger's budget deficits were kept within the limits of their financial limits, as to not destabilize the macro-economy. South Korea in particular had deficits lower than the OECD average in the 1980s. External debt was non-existent for Chinese Hong Kong, Singapore and Chinese Taiwan, as they did not borrow from abroad. Although South Korea was the exception to this, its debt to GNP ratio was quite high during the period 1980-1985, and it was sustained by the nation's high level of exports. Exchange rates in the four Asian tigers had been changed from long-term fixed rate regimes to fixed-but-adjustable rate regimes with the occasional steep devaluation of managed floating rate regimes. This active exchange rate management allowed the 4 tiger economies to avoid exchange rate appreciation and maintain a stable real exchange rate.

Export policies have been the de facto reason for the rise of these four Asian tiger economies. The approach taken has been different among the four countries and regions. Chinese Hong Kong, and Singapore introduced trade regimes that were neoliberal in nature and encouraged free trade, while South Korea and Chinese Taiwan adopted mixed regimes that accommodated their own export industries. In Chinese Hong Kong and Singapore, due to small internal markets, internal prices were linked to external prices. South Korea and Chinese Taiwan introduced export incentives for the traded-goods sector. The governments of Singapore, South Korea and Chinese Taiwan also worked to promote specific exporting industries, which were termed as an export push strategy. All these policies helped these four countries and regions to achieve a economic growth averaging 7.5% each year for three decades and as such they achieved developed economic status.

1997 Asian financial crisis

The 1997 Asian financial crisis had an impact on all of the four Asian tiger economies. South Korea was hit the hardest as its foreign debt burdens swelled resulting in its currency falling between 35% and 50%. By the beginning of 1997, the stock market in Chinese Hong Kong, Singapore, and South Korea also saw losses of at least 60% in dollar terms. However, four Asian tigers recovered from the 1997 crisis faster than other countries due to various economic advantages including their high savings rate (except South Korea) and their openness to trade.

2008 financial crisis

The export-oriented economies of the four Asian tigers which benefited from American consumption, were hit hard by the financial crisis of 2007-2008. By the fourth quarter of 2008, the GDP and GRDP of all four countries and regions fell by an average annualized rate of around 15%. Exports also fell by a 50% annualized rate. Weak internal demand also affected the recovery of these economies. In 2008, retail sales fell 3% in Chinese Hong Kong, 6% in Singapore and 11% in Chinese Taiwan.

As the world recovers from the financial crisis, the four Asian tiger economies have also rebounded strongly. This is due in no small part to each tiger's government fiscal stimulus measures. These fiscal packages accounted for more than 4% of each tiger's GDP and GRDP in

2009. Another reason for the strong bounce back is the modest corporate and household debt in these four countries and regions.

GDP

In 2013, the combined economy of the Four Asian Tigers constituted 3.81% of the world's economy with a total GDP and GRDP of 2,366 billion US dollars. The GDP and GRDP in Hong Kong, Singapore, South Korea and Chinese Taiwan was worth 274.01 billion, 297.94 billion, 1,304.55 billion and 489.21 billion US dollars respectively in 2013, which represented 0.44%, 0.48%, 2.10% and 0.79% of the world economy. Together, their combined economy is close to United Kingdom's GDP of 4.07% of the world's economy.

Part IV ADB and AIIB

ADB Logo

The Asian Development Bank (ADB) is a regional development bank established on 22 August 1966 which is headquartered in Metro Manila, Philippines, to facilitate economic development in Asia. The bank admits the members of the United Nations Economic and Social Commission for Asia and the Pacific (UNESCAP, formerly the Economic Commission for Asia and the Far East or ECAFE) and non-regional developed economies. From 31 members at its establishment, ADB now has 67 members, of which 48 are from within Asia and the Pacific and 19 outside. The ADB was modeled closely on the World Bank, and has a similar weighted voting system where votes are distributed in proportion with members' capital subscriptions. Since 2014, ADB releases annual report of Creative Productivity Index and comparatively includes Finland and United States for the list of Asia-Pacific members.

At the end of 2013, Japan holds the largest proportion of shares at 15.67%. The United States holds 15.56%, China holds 6.47%, India holds 6.36%, and Australia holds 5.81%.

History

1962–1972

The concept of a regional bank was formally mooted at a trade conference organized by the Economic Commission for Asia and the Far East (ECAFE) in 1963 for developing intra-regional trade. Once the ADB was founded in 1966, Japan took a prominent position in the bank; it received the presidency and some other crucial 「reserve positions」 such as the director of the administration department. By the end of 1972, Japan contributed $173.7 million (22.6% of the total) to the ordinary capital resources and $122.6 million (59.6% of the total) to the special funds. In contrast, the United States contributed only $ 1.25 million for the special fund.

The ADB served Japan's economic interests because its loans went largely to Indonesia, Thailand, Malaysia, South Korea and the Philippines, the countries with which Japan had crucial trading ties; these nations accounted for 78.48% of the total ADB loans between 1967 and 1972. Japan tied its special funds contributions to its preferred sectors and regions and procurements of its goods and services, as reflected in its $100 million donation for the Agricultural Special Fund in April 1968.

1972–1986

Japan's share of cumulative contributions increased from 30.4% in 1972 to 35.5% in 1981 and 41.9% in 1986. In addition, Japan was a crucial source of ADB borrowing, 29.4% (out of $ 6,729.1 million) in 1973–1986, compared to 45.1% from Europe and 12.9% from the United States. During this period there was a strong parallel institutional tie between the ADB and the Japanese Ministry of Finance, particularly the International Finance Bureau (IFB).

Since 1986

Japan's share of cumulative contributions increased from 41.9% in 1986 to 50.0% in 1993. In addition, Japan has been a crucial lender to the ADB, 30.4% of the total in 1987–93, compared to 39.8% from Europe and 11.7% from the United States. However, different from the previous period, Japan has become more assertive since the mid-1980s. Japan's plan was to use the ADB as a conduct for recycling its huge surplus capital and a 「catalyst」 for attracting private Japanese capital to the region. After the 1985 Plaza Accord, Japanese manufacturers were pushed by high yen to move to Southeast Asia.

In 2009, ADB obtained member-contributions for its Fifth General Capital Increase of 200%, in response to a call by G20 leaders to increase resources of multilateral development banks so as to support growth in developing countries amid the global financial crisis. With this increase, the bank's capital base tripled from $55 billion to $165 billion.

Objectives and Activities

The ADB played a role in channeling Japanese private capital to Asia by improving local infrastructure. The ADB also committed itself to increasing loans for social issues such as education, health and population, urban development and environment.

The ADB offers 「hard」 loans from ordinary capital resources (OCR) on commercial terms, and the Asian Development Fund (ADF) affiliated with the ADB extends 「soft」 loans from special fund resources with concessional conditions. The ADB borrows from international capital markets with its capital as guarantee.

Effectiveness

All projects funded by ADB are evaluated to find out what results are being achieved, what improvements should be considered, and what is being learned.

There are two types of evaluation: independent and self-evaluation. Self-evaluation is conducted by the units responsible for designing and implementing national or regional strategies, programs, projects, or technical assistance activities. It comprises several instruments, including project/program performance reports, midterm review reports, technical assistance or project/program completion reports, and portfolio reviews. All projects are self-evaluated by the relevant units in a project completion report. ADB's project completion reports are publicly disclosed on ADB's website. Client governments are required to prepare their own project completion reports.

Independent evaluation is a foundation block of organizational learning: It is essential to transfer increased amounts of relevant and high-quality knowledge from experience into the hands of policy makers, designers, and implementers. ADB's Independent Evaluation Department (IED) conducts systematic and impartial assessment of policies, strategies, programs, and projects, including their design, implementation, results, and associated business processes to determine their relevance, effectiveness, efficiency, and sustainability following prescribed methods and guidelines. It also validates self-evaluations. By this process of evaluation, ADB demonstrates three elements of good governance: accountability, by assessing the effectiveness of ADB's operations; transparency, by independently reviewing operations and publicly reporting findings and recommendations; and improved performance, by helping ADB and its clients learn from experience to enhance ongoing and future operations.

Operations evaluation has changed from the beginnings of evaluation in ADB in 1978. Initially, the focus was on assessing after completion the extent to which projects had achieved their expected economic and social benefits. Operations evaluation now shapes decision making throughout the project cycle and in ADB as a whole. Since the establishment of its independence in 2004, IED reports directly to ADB's Board of Directors through the Board's Development Effectiveness Committee. Behavioral autonomy, avoidance of conflicts of interest, insulation from external influence, and organizational independence have made evaluation a dedicated tool—governed by the principles of usefulness, credibility, transparency, and independence—for greater accountability and making development assistance work better. Independent Evaluation at the Asian Development Bank presents a perspective of evaluation in ADB from the beginnings and looks to a future in which knowledge management plays an increasingly important role.

In recent years, there has been a major shift in the nature of IED's work program from a dominance of evaluations of individual projects to one focusing on broader and more strategic studies. Since 2006, acting within the knowledge management framework of ADB, IED has applied knowledge management to lesson learning, using knowledge performance metrics.

Asian Infrastructure Investment Bank (AIIB)

The Asian Infrastructure Investment Bank is an international financial institution proposed by the government of China. The purpose of the multilateral development bank is to provide finance to infrastructure projects in the Asia region; AIIB is regarded by some as a rival for the IMF, the World Bank and the Asian Development Bank (ADB), which are regarded as dominated by developed countries like the United States. The United Nations has addressed the launch of AIIB as 「scaling up financing for sustainable development」 for the concern of Global

Economic Governance.

History

The first news reports about the AIIB appeared in October 2013. The Chinese government has been frustrated with what it regards as the slow pace of reforms and governance, and wants greater input in global established institutions like the IMF, World Bank and Asian Development Bank which it claims are dominated by American, European and Japanese interests.

In April 2014, Chinese Premier Li Keqiang delivered a keynote speech at the opening of the Boao Forum for Asia and said that China was ready to intensify consultations with relevant parties in and outside Asia on the preparations for the Asian Infrastructure Investment Bank.

The Asian Development Bank Institute published a report in 2010 which said that the region requires $ 8 trillion to be invested from 2010 to 2020 in infrastructure for the region to continue economic development. In a 2014 editorial, *The Guardian* newspaper wrote that the new bank could allow Chinese capital to finance these projects and allow it a greater role to play in the economic development of the region commensurate with its growing economic and political clout. But until March 2015, China in the ADB has only 5.47 percent voting right, while Japan and US have a combined 26 percent voting right (13 percent each) with a share in subscribed capital of 15.7 percent and 15.6 percent, respectively. Dominance by both countries and slow reforms underlie China's wish to establish the AIIB, while both countries worry about China's increasing influence.

In June 2014 China proposed doubling the registered capital of the bank from $ 50 billion to $ 100 billion and invited India to participate in the founding of the bank. On October 24, 2014, a signing ceremony held in Beijing formally recognized the establishment of the bank. Twenty-one countries signed the Memorandum of Understanding (MOU), including China, India, Thailand, Malaysia, Singapore, the Philippines, Pakistan, Bangladesh, Brunei, Cambodia, Kazakhstan, Kuwait, Laos, Myanmar, Mongolia, Nepal, Oman, Qatar, Sri Lanka, Uzbekistan, and Vietnam.

U.S. pressure allegedly tried to keep Australia and South Korea from signing up as founding members, despite the fact that they expressed an interest in it. However, both Australia and South Korea have officially applied to join the bank in late March 2015, ignoring objections by the United States. Indonesia's joining was slightly delayed due to their new presidential administration not being able to review the membership in time. Indonesia signed the MOU on 25 November 2014.

In early March 2015, the United Kingdom's Chancellor of the Exchequer, George Osborne, announced that Britain had decided to apply to join the Chinese-led Asian Infrastructure Investment Bank, becoming the first major Western country to do so. The announcement was criticized by the Obama Administration in the United States. A US government official told the *Financial Times*, 「We are wary about a trend toward constant accommodation of China, which is not the best way to engage a rising power.」This official further stated that the British decision was taken after 「no consultation with the US.」In response to the US criticism, the UK claimed that the subject had been discussed between the Chancellor Osborne and the US Treasury Secretary Jack Lew for several months preceding the decision. It was further stated that joining the bank as a founding member will allow Britain to influence the development of the institution. By encouraging Chinese investments in the next generations of nuclear power plants, Osborne announced that「the City of London would become the base for the first clearing house for the yuan outside Asia.」

Following the criticism, the White House National Security Council, in a statement to *The Guardian*, declared,「Our position on the AIIB remains clear and consistent. The United States and many major global economies all agree there is a pressing need to enhance infrastructure investment around the world. We believe any new multilateral institution should incorporate the high standards of the World Bank and the regional development banks. Based on many discussions, we have concerns about whether the AIIB will meet these high standards, particularly related to governance, and environmental and social safeguards. The international community has a stake in seeing the AIIB complement the existing architecture, and to work effectively alongside the World Bank and Asian Development Bank.」

Three other European nations—Germany, France and Italy—soon followed Britain's decision to join the AIIB. German Finance Minister Wolfgang Schäuble stated,「We want to contribute our long-standing experience with international financial institutions to the creation of the new bank by setting high standards and helping the bank to get a high international reputation.」In late March, 2015, the South Korean Ministry of Strategy and Finance announced that it, too, is planning to join the AIIB, citing its potential in benefiting South Korean companies win deals in infrastructural projects as well expanding South Korea's influence in international banking as a founding member.

Membership

As of 15 April 2015, there are 57 Prospective Founding Members (PFM), 37 PFMs in the region, and 20 PFMs outside the region. Almost all Asian countries and most major countries outside Asia had joined the AIIB, except the US, Japan (which dominated the ADB). Belgium, Canada, Czech Republic and Ukraine are considering joining the AIIB. Colombia, Japan, and the United States have no immediate intention to participate. North Korea and Chinese Taiwan were rejected by China to join as a PFM.

Objectives and Activities

The Asian Infrastructure Investment Bank can be construed as a natural inter-national extension of the infrastructure-driven economic development framework that has sustained the rapid economic growth of China since the adoption of the Chinese economic reform under Chairman Deng Xiaoping. It stems from the notion that long-term economic growth can only be achieved through massive, systematic, and broad-based investments in infrastructure assets—in contrast with the more short-term「export-driven」and「domestic consumption」development models favored by mainstream Neoclassical economists and pursued inconsiderately by many developing countries in the 1990s and the first decade of the 21st century with generally disappointing results.

In his March 29, 2015 speech at the Boao Forum for Asia (BFA) annual conference,

President Xi Jinping insisted that「the Chinese economy is deeply integrated with the global economy and forms an important driving force of the economy of Asia and even the world at large. China's investment opportunities are expanding. Investment opportunities in infrastructure connectivity as well as in new technologies, new products, new business patterns, and new business models are constantly springing up. China's foreign cooperation opportunities are expanding. We support the multilateral trading system, devote ourselves to the Doha Round negotiations, advocate the Asia-Pacific free trade zone, promote negotiations on regional comprehensive economic partnership, advocate the construction of the Asian Infrastructure Investment Bank (AIIB), boost economic and financial cooperation in an all-round manner, and work as an active promoter of economic globalization and regional integration」, insisting that the Silk Road Fund and the Asian Infrastructure Investment Bank would foster「economic connectivity and a new-type of industrialization (in the Asia Pacific area), and (thus) promote the common development of all countries as well as the peoples' joint enjoyment of development fruits」.

Part V Arab League, Ecowas and Comesa

Flag   **Emblem**

The Arab League, formally, the League of Arab States is a regional organization of Arab world in and around North Africa, the Horn of Africa, and Southwest Asia. It was formed in Cairo on 22 March 1945 with six members: Kingdom of Egypt, Kingdom of Iraq, Transjordan (renamed Jordan in 1949), Lebanon, Saudi Arabia and Syria. Yemen joined as a member on 5 May 1945. Currently, the League has 22 members, although Syria's participation has been suspended since November 2011, as a consequence of government repression during the ongoing uprising and civil war.

The League's main goal is to「draw closer the relations between members and co-ordinate collaboration between them, to safeguard their independence and sovereignty, and to consider in a general way the affairs and interests of the Arab world」.

Through institutions such as the Arab League Educational, Cultural and Scientific Organization (ALECSO) and the Economic and Social Council of the Arab League's Council of Arab Economic Unity (CAEU), the Arab League facilitates political, economic, cultural, scientific and social programs designed to promote the interests of the Arab world. It has served as a forum for the members to coordinate their policy positions, to deliberate on matters of common concern, to settle some Arab disputes and to limit conflicts such as the 1958 Lebanon crisis. The League has served as a platform for the drafting and conclusion of many landmark documents promoting economic integration. One example is the *Joint Arab Economic Action Charter*, which outlines the principles for economic activities in the region.

Each member state has only one vote in the *League Council*, while decisions are binding only for those members that have voted for them. The aims of the league in 1945 were to strengthen and coordinate the political, cultural, economic, and social programs of its members, and to mediate disputes among them or between them and third parties. Furthermore, the signing of an agreement on Joint Defense and Economic Cooperation on 13 April 1950 committed the signatories to coordination of military defense measures. In the early 1970s, the Economic Council of the League of Arab States put forward a proposal to create the Joint Arab Chambers of Commerce across the European states. This led, under the decree of the League of Arab States no. K1175/D52/G, to the decision by the Arab governments to set up the Arab British Chamber of Commerce which was mandated to: 「promote, encourage and facilitate bilateral trade」between the Arab world and its major trading partner, the United Kingdom.

The Arab League has similarly played a role in shaping school curricula, advancing the role of women in the Arab societies, promoting child welfare, encouraging youth and sports programs, preserving Arab cultural heritage, and fostering cultural exchanges between the member states.

Starting with only six members in 1945, the Arab League today occupies an area spanning around 14 million km^2 and counts 22 members, and 4 observer states. As of 2015, there are a total of 22 members, including 3 of the largest African countries (Sudan, Algeria and Libya), and the largest country in the Middle East (Saudi Arabia).

There has been a continual increase in membership during the second half of the 20th century, with an additional 15 Arab states being admitted.

The area of members of the Arab League covers over 13,000,000 km^2 and straddles two continents: Africa and Asia. The area consists of large arid deserts, namely the Sahara. Nevertheless, it also contains several very fertile lands, such as the Nile Valley, the Jubba and Shebelle valley of Somalia, the High Atlas Mountains, and the Fertile Crescent which stretches over Mesopotamia and the Levant. The area comprises deep forests in southern Arabia, as well as parts of the world's longest river, the Nile.

The Arab League is a political organization which tries to help integrate its members economically, and solve conflicts involving members without asking for foreign assistance. It possesses elements of a member representative parliament while foreign affairs are often dealt with under UN supervision.

The Charter of the Arab League endorsed the principle of an Arab homeland while respecting the sovereignty of the individual member. The internal regulations of the Council of the League and the committees were agreed in October 1951. Those of the Secretariat-General were agreed in May 1953.

At the Cairo Summit of 1964, the Arab League initiated the creation of an organization representing the Palestinian people. The first Palestinian National Council convened in East Jerusalem on 29 May 1964. The Palestinian Liberation Organization was founded during this meeting on 2 June 1964. Palestine was shortly admitted in to the Arab League, represented by the PLO. Today, State of Palestine is a full member of the Arab League.

At the Beirut Summit on 28 March 2002, the league adopted the Arab Peace Initiative, a Saudi-inspired peace plan for the Arab-Israeli conflict. The initiative offered full normalization of the relations with Israel. In exchange, Israel was required to withdraw from all occupied territories, including the Golan Heights, to recognize Palestinian independence in the West Bank and Gaza Strip, with East Jerusalem as its capital, as well as a「just solution」for the Palestinian refugees. The Peace Initiative was again endorsed at 2007 in the Riyadh Summit.

The「Greater Arab Free Trade Area」(GAFTA) is a pan-Arab free trade zone that came into existence in 1997. It was founded by 14 countries: Bahrain, Egypt, Iraq, Kuwait, Lebanon, Libya, Morocco, Oman, Qatar, Saudi Arabia, Sudan, Syria, Tunisia, and the United Arab Emirates. The formation of GAFTA followed the adoption of the「Agreement to Facilitate and Develop Trade Among Arab Countries」(1981) by the Arab League's Economic and Social Council (ESC) and the approval by seventeen Arab League members at a summit in Amman, Jordan of the「Greater Arab Free Trade Area Agreement」(1997). In 2009, Algeria joined GAFTA as the eighteenth member. GAFTA is supervised and run by the ESC.

The members participate in 96% of the total internal Arab trade, and 95% with the rest of the world by applying the following conditions:

1. Instruct the inter-customs fees.

To reduce the Customs on Arab products by 10% annually, the 14 Arab Countries or regions reported their custom tariff programs to the Security Council of the Arab League to coordinate them. Syria was excepted and uses the Brussels tariffs system.

2. Applying the locality of the Arab products.

All members have shared their standards and specifications to help their products move smoothly from one country to another.

The League has also created a project to apply the Arab Agriculture Pact:

Which is to share the standards of the agricultural sector and inject several restrictions and specifications.

The Arab League granted exceptions, which allowed for a customs rate for certain goods to six members for several goods, however requests for additional exceptions were rejected by Morocco, Lebanon and Jordan.

3. Private sectors.

The League created a database and a service to inform and promote the private sector's benefits.

4. Communication.

The Economic and Social Council in its sixty-fifth meeting agreed on pointing a base for communication to ease communication between the members, and to work on easing interaction between the Private and public sectors to further apply the Greater Arab Free Trade Area.

5. Customs Duties.

In the sixty-seventh meeting the Economic and Social Council agreed that a 40% decrease on customs on goods in the past 4 years of the GAFTA would continue and following the decisions at the Amman summit, the members will make efforts to eliminate all customs duties on local goods.

Economic Resources

The Arab League is rich in resources, with enormous oil and natural gas resources in certain members. Another industry that is growing steadily in the Arab League is telecommunications. Within less than a decade, local companies such as Orascom and Etisalat have managed to compete internationally.

Economic achievements initiated by the League amongst members have been less impressive than those achieved by smaller Arab organizations such as the Gulf Cooperation Council (GCC). Among them is the Arab Gas Pipeline, that will transport Egyptian and Iraqi gas to Jordan, Syria, Lebanon, and Turkey. As of 2013, a significant difference in economic conditions exist between the developed oil states of Algeria, Qatar, Kuwait and the UAE, and developing countries like Comoros, Djibouti, Mauritania, Somalia, Sudan and Yemen.

The Arab League also has great fertile lands in South ofthe Sudan, usually referred to as the food basket of the Arab World, the region's instability has not affected its tourism industry, that is considered the fastest growing industry in the region, with Egypt, UAE, Lebanon, Tunisia and Jordan Leading the way. Another industry that is growing steadily in the Arab League is telecommunications.

Economic Community of West African States (ECOWAS)

The Economic Community of West African States is a regional group of fifteen West African countries. Founded on 28 May 1975, with the signing of the Treaty of Lagos, its mission is to promote economic integration across the region.

Considered one of the pillars of the African Economic Community, the organization was founded in order to achieve 「collective self-sufficiency」 for its members by creating a single large trading bloc through an economic and trading union. It also serves as a peacekeeping force in the region. The organization operates officially in three co-equal languages—French, English, and Portuguese.

The ECOWAS consists of two institutions to implement policies—the ECOWAS Commission and the ECOWAS Bank for Investment and Development, formerly known as the Fund for Cooperation until it was renamed in 2001.

The West African Economic and Monetary Union is acustoms union and currency union between the members of ECOWAS. It was established to promote economic integration among countries that share a common currency.

Its objectives include the following:

· Greater economic competitiveness, through open markets, in addition to the rationalization and harmonization of the legal environment

· The convergence of macro-economic policies and indicators

- The creation of a common market
- The coordination of sectoral policies
- The harmonization of fiscal policies

Among its achievements, the Union has successfully implemented macro-economic convergence criteria and an effective surveillance mechanism. It has adopted a customs union and common external tariff and has combined indirect taxation regulations, in addition to initiating regional structural and sectoral policies. A September 2002 IMF survey cited the Union as「the furthest along the path toward integration」of all the regional groupings in Africa.

ECOWAS and the Union have developed a common plan of action on trade liberalization and macroeconomic policy convergence. The organizations have also agreed on common rules of origin to enhance trade, and ECOWAS has agreed to adopt the Union's customs declaration forms and compensation mechanisms.

ECOWAS Bank for Investment and Development Headquarters in Lome.

West African Monetary Zone

Formed in 2000, the West African Monetary Zone (WAMZ) is a group of six countries within ECOWAS that plan to introduce a common currency, the Eco. The six member states of WAMZ are Gambia, Ghana, Guinea, Nigeria and Sierra Leone who founded the organization together in 2000 and Liberia who joined on 16 February 2010. Apart from Guinea, which is Francophone, they are all English speaking countries. Along with Mauritania, Guinea opted out of franc currency shared by all other former French colonies in West and Central Africa.

The WAMZ attempts to establish a strong stable currency to rival franc, whose exchange rate is tied to that of the Euro and is guaranteed by the French Treasury. The eventual goal is for the franc and Eco to merge, giving all of West and Central Africa a single, stable currency. The launch of the new currency is being developed by the West African Monetary Institute based in Accra, Ghana.

Common Market for Eastern and Southern Africa

The Common Market for Eastern and Southern Africa (COMESA) is a free trade area with twenty member states stretching from Libya to Swaziland. COMESA was formed in December 1994, replacing a Preferential Trade Area which had existed since 1981. Nine of the member states formed a free trade area in 2000 (Djibouti, Egypt, Kenya, Madagascar, Malawi, Mauritius, Sudan, Zambia and Zimbabwe), with Rwanda and Burundi joining the FTA in 2004, the Comoros and Libya in 2006, and Seychelles in 2009.

COMESA is one of the pillars of the African Economic Community.

In 2008, COMESA agreed to an expanded free-trade zone including members of two other African trade blocs, the East African Community (EAC) and the Southern Africa Development Community (SADC). COMESA is also considering a common visa scheme to boost tourism.

Glossary

Part I

forum   n. 論壇，討論會
pledge   v. 保證，許諾
primarily   adv. 首先，主要地，根本上
supranational   adj. 超國家的，超民族的
scrutinize   v. 細閱，作詳細檢查
ancillary   adj. 輔助的，副的，從屬的
tariff   n. 關稅表，收費表
legislation   n. 立法，法律
defense   n. 防衛，防護
inhabitant   n. 居民，居住者
antitrust   adj. 反壟斷的
ratification   n. 批准，承認，認可
copious   adj. 豐富的，很多的，多產的
launch   n. 發射，發行，投放市場
sustainable   adj. 可以忍受的，足可支撐的
budgetary   adj. 預算的
rescue   n. 營救，援救，解救
provisionally   adv. 臨時地，暫時地
bilateral   adj. 雙邊的，有兩邊的
referendum   n. 公民投票權，外交官請示書
recession   n. 衰退，不景氣，後退

Part II

accelerate   v. 加速，促進，增加
counterpart   n. 副本，配對物
entity   n. 實體，存在，本質
collaborate   v. 合作
utilization   n. 使用，利用
compromise   v. 妥協，讓步
diplomacy   n. 外交，外交手腕，交際手段

merit   n. 優點，價值，功績
integrate   v. 使……完整，使……成整體
oppose   v. 反對，對抗，抗爭
criterion   n.（批評判斷的）標準，準則，規範，準據
prolong   v. 延長，拖延
forefront   n. 最前線，最前部，最活動的中心
transparency   n. 透明，透明度
scheme   n. 計劃，組合，體制
copious   adj. 豐富的，很多的，多產的
commerce   n. 貿易，商業，商務
ambitious   adj. 野心勃勃的，有雄心的

Part III

inclusion   n. 包含，內含物
nominal   adj. 名義上的
trillion   n.（數）萬億
equivalent   adj. 等價的，相等的，同意義的
reform   n. 改革
rival   v. 與……競爭
notable   adj. 值得注意的，顯著的，著名的
competitive   adj. 競爭的，比賽的，求勝心切的
oriented   adj. 導向的，定向的，以……為方向的
accumulation   n. 積聚，累積，堆積物
estate   n. 房地產
amongst   prep. 在……之中，在……當中（等於 among）
essential   adj. 基本的，必要的，本質的，精華的
literacy   n. 讀寫能力
macroeconomic   adj. 宏觀經濟的，總體經濟的
deficit   n.（財政）赤字，虧損
neoliberal   n. 新自由主義，新自由主義者
regime   n. 政權，政體，社會制度，管理體制
openness   n. 公開，寬闊，率真
consumption   n. 消費，消耗
stimulus   n. 刺激，激勵，刺激物

Part IV

facilitate   v. 促進，幫助，使容易
proportion   n. 比例，占比，部分
moot   v. 提出……供討論
prominent   adj. 突出的，顯著的，傑出的，卓越的
procurement   n. 採購，獲得，取得
index   n. 指標，指數
crucial   adj. 重要的，決定性的
cumulative   adj. 累積的
assertive   adj. 肯定的，獨斷的
infrastructure   n. 基礎設施，公共建設，下部構造
guarantee   n. 保證，擔保，保證人，保證書，
portfolio   n. 公文包，文件夾
impartial   adj. 公平的，公正的
strategic   adj. 戰略上的，戰略的
avoidance   n. 逃避，廢止，職位空缺
frustrate   v. 挫敗，阻撓   v. 失敗，受挫
editorial   adj. 編輯的，社論的
commensurate   adj. 相稱的，同量的，同樣大小的
citing   n. 引用，引證，舉例
mainstream   n. 主流
advocate   v. 提倡，主張，擁護
boost   v. 促進，增加，支援

Part V

suspend   v. 延緩，推遲
safeguard   v. 保護，護衛
deliberate   v. 仔細考慮，商議
dispute   n. 辯論，爭吵
mediate   v. 調停，傳達   v. 調解
signatory   n. 簽約國，簽名人
decree   n. 法令，判決
welfare   n. 福利，幸福
fertile   adj. 富饒的，肥沃的
parliament   n. 議會，國會

territory　n. 領土，領域
tariff　n. 關稅
inject　v. 注入，注射
achieve　v. 取得，獲得
sufficiency　n. 足量，充足，自滿
implement　v. 實施，執行，實現
eliminate　v. 消除，排除
criteria　n. 標準，條件（criterion 的復數）
compensation　n. 補償，報酬，賠償金

Phrases

insofar as 在……的範圍內，到……程度
intend to 打算做……，想要……
break up 打碎，破碎，結束，解散
bound to 一定會，束縛於
acronym for 縮寫
prior to 在……之前，居先
in per capita income 按人均收入計算
impact on 影響，對……衝擊，碰撞
in contrast 與此相反，比較起來
affiliate with 交往；附屬機構
participate in 　參與、分享、參加
in exchange (for sth.) 作為交換
adoption of 採用
agree on 　同意；達成共識
refer to 參考，涉及
opt out of 　決定不參加……，決定（從……）退出

Notes

European Economic Community：歐洲經濟共同體，是歐洲共同體中最重要的組成部分，人們常常把它和歐洲共同體混淆。1957年3月25日，法國、義大利、聯邦德國、荷蘭、比利時、盧森堡六國外長在羅馬簽訂了建立歐洲經濟共同體與歐洲原子能共同體的兩個條約，即《羅馬條約》，於1958年1月1日生效。1965年4月8日，6國簽訂了《布魯塞爾條約》，決定將歐洲煤鋼共同體、歐洲原子能共同體和歐洲經濟共同體統一起來，統稱歐洲共同體。歐洲經濟共同體與歐洲煤鋼共同體、歐洲原子能共同體共同組成歐洲共同體。歐共體是西歐一些主要資本主義國家由政府出面組成的一個經濟和政治集團，本質上是一種國家壟斷資本主義的國際聯盟。總部設在布魯塞爾。

European Exchange Rate Mechanism：歐洲匯率機制，1979年創立，旨在限制歐盟成員國貨幣的匯率波動。ERM 為成員國貨幣的匯率設定固定的中心匯率，允許匯率在中

心匯率上下一定的幅度內波動。據規定，歐盟新成員國在加入歐元區之前，應將其貨幣納入允許匯率在中心匯率上下15%的區間內波動的 ERM-2 體系，為時兩年。

　　Uruguay Round：烏拉圭回合談判，1986年9月在烏拉圭的埃斯特角城舉行了關貿總協定部長級會議，決定進行一場旨在全面改革多邊貿易體制的新一輪談判，故命名為「烏拉圭回合談判」。這是迄今為止最大的一次貿易談判，歷時7年半，於1994年4月在摩洛哥的馬拉喀什結束。談判幾乎涉及所有貿易，從牙刷到遊艇，從銀行到電信，從野生水稻基因到愛滋病治療。參加方從最初的103個，增至談判結束時的125個。

　　Boao Forum：博鰲亞洲論壇（縮寫：BFA），由25個亞洲國家和澳大利亞發起，於2001年2月27日在海南省瓊海市萬泉河入海口的博鰲鎮召開大會，正式宣布成立。論壇為非官方、非營利性、定期、定址的國際組織，為政府、企業及專家學者等提供一個共商經濟、社會、環境及其他相關問題的高層對話平臺，海南博鰲為論壇總部的永久所在地。

　　The Maastricht Treaty：馬斯特里赫特條約，1991年12月9~10日，第46屆歐共體首腦會議在荷蘭的馬斯特里赫特（Maastricht）舉行。經過兩天辯論，代表們通過並草簽了《歐洲經濟與貨幣聯盟條約》和《政治聯盟條約》，統稱《歐洲聯盟條約》（Treaty of Maastricht）即《馬斯特里赫特條約》。1992年2月7日歐共體12國外長和財政部長在荷蘭小鎮馬斯特里赫特正式簽署了該條約，條約也正式生效。這一條約是對《羅馬條約》（Treaty of Rome）的修訂，它為歐共體建立政治聯盟和經濟與貨幣聯盟確立了目標與步驟，是歐洲聯盟成立的基礎。參與簽訂該條約的為原歐共體的12個國家，即：比利時、丹麥、德意志聯邦共和國、希臘、西班牙、法蘭西共和國、愛爾蘭、義大利、盧森堡、荷蘭、葡萄牙和大不列顛及北愛爾蘭聯合王國。芬蘭、奧地利和瑞典於1995年1月1日加入。

　　Pacific Islands Forum：太平洋島國論壇，太平洋島國論壇，原名「南太平洋論壇」，1971年8月5日在新西蘭首都惠靈頓成立，2000年10月，「南太平洋論壇」正式改稱為「太平洋島國論壇」。2012年8月27~31日第43屆太平洋島國論壇領導人系列會議在庫克群島舉行。2018年9月4日，日媒稱中國正在加強對南太平洋島國的影響力。一些國家已經利用中國的融資推進港口、道路建設。各國將在9月4日於瑙魯開幕的太平洋島國論壇峰會上圍繞與中國打交道的方式展開對話。

　　Pacific Economic Cooperation Council：太平洋經濟合作會議，太平洋經濟合作會議（Pacific Economic Cooperation Conference，PECC），旨在研究和促進太平洋地區經濟合作，以增強太平洋沿岸各國之間的經濟聯繫。每18個月舉行一次大會，由不代表政府身分的高級政府官員、企業家和學者三方代表參加。會議設常務委員會，下設若干組。內容涉及漁業合作和發展，農業政策，太平洋經濟展望，礦產及能源，貿易政策，運輸通訊和旅遊，科技與技術，人力資源等等。成員包括澳大利亞、文萊、加拿大、中國、中國臺北、印尼、日本、南朝鮮、馬來西亞、新西蘭、菲律賓、新加坡、太平洋島群國家等。中國1986年加入，在北京設有中國太平洋經濟合作委員會。太平洋經濟合作會議在自由和開放經濟交流的基礎上，本著保持夥伴關係、公平和互相尊重的精神，加強經濟合作，以充分發揮太平洋盆地的潛力。

Questions

1. What are the aims and purposes of ASEAN ?

2. What is APEC? When did the first APEC Economic Leaders' Meeting occur?

3. Why were the costs of business transactions across the region reduced by 6% between 2002 and 2006?

4. What are the five major BRICS members?

5. Talk about the development of BRICS Forum.

6. How does the Asian Development Bank establish? What are its aims?

7. Talk about objectives and activities of the Asian Infrastructure Investment Bank.

Chapter III

Business Management

Business involves in the trade of goods, services, or both to consumers. Business can refer to a particular organization, e.g.「company」,「corporation」, or to an entire market sector, e.g.「the music business」,「agribusiness」.

When business refers to an entire market sector, it is usually classified according to its features, for examples:

· Agriculture and mining businesses produce raw material, such as plants or minerals.

· Financial businesses include banks and other companies that generate profits through investment and management of the capital.

· Information businesses generate profits primarily from the sale of intellectual property and include movie studios, publishers and internet and software companies.

Forms of business ownership vary by jurisdiction, but several common forms exist:

· **Sole proprietorship:** owned by one person and operates for their benefit. The owner may operate the business alone or with other people. A sole proprietor has unlimited liability for all obligations incurred by the business, whether from operating costs or judgement against the business.

· **Partnership:** A partnership is a business owned by two or more people. In most forms of partnerships, each partner has unlimited liability for the debts incurred by the business. The three most prevalent types of for-profit partnerships are general partnerships, limited partnerships, and limited liability partnerships.

· **Corporation:** The owners of a corporation have limited liability and the business has a separate legal personality from its owners. Corporations can be either government-owned or privately owned. They can organize either for profit or as not-for-profit organizations. A privately owned, for-profit corporation is owned by its shareholders, who elect a board of directors to direct the corporation and hire its managerial staff. A privately owned, for-profit corporation can be either privately held by a small group of individuals, or publicly held, with publicly traded shares listed on a stock exchange.

· **Cooperative:** Often referred to as a「co-op」, a cooperative is a limited liability business that can organize for-profit or not-for-profit. A cooperative differs from a corporation in that it has members, not shareholders, and they share decision-making authority. Cooperatives are typically classified as either consumer cooperatives or worker cooperatives. Cooperatives are fundamental to the ideology of economic democracy.

Owners may administer their businesses themselves, or employ managers to do this for them. The efficient and effective operation of a business, and study of this subject, is called management. The major branches of management are organization & HR management, production and service management, financial and marketing management, legal and strategic management.

Part I   Organization & HR management

The character of organization lies in its culture.

Organizational culture represents the collective values, beliefs and principles of organizational members and is a product of such factors as history, product, market, technology, and strategy, type of employees, management style, and national culture. Organizational culture is a set of shared assumptions that guide what happens in organizations by defining appropriate behavior for various situations. It is also the pattern of such collective behaviors and assumptions that are taught to new organizational members as a way of perceiving and, even, thinking and feeling. Thus, organizational culture affects the way people and groups interact with each other, with clients, and with stakeholders. In addition, organizational culture may affect how much employees identify with an organization.

Organizational culture has been shown to have an impact on important organizational outcomes such as performance, attraction, recruitment, retention, employee satisfaction, and employee well-being. Also, organizations with an adaptive culture tend to perform better than organizations with an maladaptive culture.

Leadership

Leadership can be defined as a process of influencing others to agree on a shared purpose, and to work towards shared objectives. A distinction should be made between leadership and management. Managers process administrative tasks and organize work environments. Although leaders may be required to undertake managerial duties as well, leaders typically focus on inspiring followers and creating a shared organizational culture and values. Managers deal with complexity, while leaders deal with initiating and adapting to change. Managers undertake the tasks of planning, budgeting, organizing, staffing, controlling and problem solving. In contrast, leaders undertake the tasks of setting a direction or vision, aligning people to shared goals, communicating, and motivating.

Team effectiveness

Organizations support the use of teams, because teams can accomplish a much greater amount of work in a short period of time than can be accomplished by an individual contributor, and because the collective results of a group of contributors can produce higher quality deliverables. Five elements that are contributors to team effectiveness include:

1. Team composition

The composition of teams is initially decided during the selection of individual contributors that are to be assigned to specific teams and has a direct bearing on the resulting effectiveness of those teams. Aspects of team composition that should be considered during the team selection process include team member: knowledge, skills and abilities (KSAs), personalities, and attitudes.

2. Task design

A fundamental question in team task design is whether or not a task is even appropriate for a team. Those tasks that require predominantly independent work are best left to individuals, and team tasks should include those tasks that consist primarily of interdependent work. When a given task is appropriate for a team, task design can play a key role in team effectiveness.

3. Organizational resources

Organizational support systems impact the effectiveness of teams and provide resources for teams operating in the multi-team environment. In this case, the provided resources include various resource types that teams require to be effective, including facilities, equipment, information, training and leadership. Also identified during team chartering are team-specific resources (e.g., budgetary resources, human resources).

4. Team rewards

Organizational reward systems are a driver for strengthening and enhancing individual team member efforts that contribute towards reaching collective team goals. In other words, rewards that are given to individual team members should be contingent upon the performance of the entire team.

Several design elements of organizational reward systems are needed to meet this objective. The first element for reward systems design is the concept that for a collective assessment to be appropriate for individual team members, the group's tasks must be highly interdependent. If this is not the case, individual assessment is more appropriate than team assessment. A second design element is the compatibility between individual-level reward systems and team-level reward systems. For example, it would be an unfair situation to reward the entire team for a job well done if only one team member did the great majority of the work. That team member would most likely view teams and team work in a negative fashion and not want to participate in a team setting in the future. A final design element is the creation of an organizational culture that supports and rewards employees who believe in the value of teamwork and who maintain a positive mental attitude towards team-based rewards.

5. Team goals

Goals for individual contributors have been shown to be motivating when they contain three elements: (1) difficulty, (2) acceptance, and (3) specificity. In the team setting, goal difficulty is related to group belief that the team can accomplish the tasks required to meet the assigned goal. This belief (collective efficacy) is somewhat counterintuitive, but rests on team member perception that they now view themselves as more competent than others in the organization who were not chosen to complete such difficult goals. This in turn, can lead to higher levels of performance. Goal acceptance and specificity is also applicable to the team setting. When team members individually and collectively commit to team goals, team effectiveness is increased and is a function of increased supportive team behaviors.

As related to the team setting, it is also important to be aware of the interplay between the goals of individual contributors that participate on teams and the goals of the teams themselves. The selection of team goals must be done in coordination with the selection of goals for individuals. Individual goals must be in line with team goals (or not exist at all) to be effective. For example, a professional ball player that does well in his/her sport is rewarded individually for excellent performance. This individual performance generally contributes to improved team performance which can, in turn, lead to team recognition, such as a league championship.

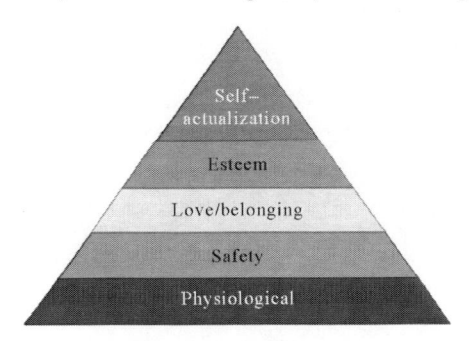

Maslow's hierarchy of needs

Maslow's hierarchy of needs is often portrayed in the shape of a pyramid with the largest, most fundamental levels of needs at the bottom and the need for self-actualization at the top.

Maslow's theory suggests that the most basic level of needs must be met before the individual will strongly desire (or focus motivation upon) the secondary or higher level needs.

Physiological needs

Physiological needs are the physical requirements for human survival. If these requirements are not met, the human body cannot function properly and will ultimately fail. Physiological needs are thought to be the most important; they should be met first.

Air, water, and food are metabolic requirements for survival in all animals, including humans. Clothing and shelter provide necessary protection from the elements. While maintaining an adequate birth rate shapes the intensity of the human sexual instinct.

Safety needs

With their physical needs relatively satisfied, come the individual's safety needs. In the absence of physical safety-due to war, natural disaster, family violence, childhood abuse, etc. -people may (re-) experience stress disorder. In the absence of economic safety-due to economic crisis and lack of work opportunities-these safety needs manifest themselves in ways such as a preference for job security, savings accounts, insurance policies, reasonable disability accommodations, etc.

Love and belonging

After physiological and safety needs are fulfilled, the third level of human needs is interpersonal and involves feelings of belongingness. This need is especially strong in childhood and can override the need for safety as witnessed in children who cling to abusive parents. Deficiencies within this level of Maslow's hierarchy can impact the individual's ability to form and maintain emotionally significant relationships in general, such as:

· Friendship

· Intimacy

· Family

According to Maslow, humans need to feel a sense of belonging and acceptance among their social groups, regardless whether these groups are large or small. For example, some large social groups may include clubs, co-workers, religious groups, professional organizations, sports teams, and gangs. Some examples of small social connections include family members, intimate partners, mentors, colleagues, and confidants. Humans need to love and be loved-both sexually and non-sexually-by others. Many people become susceptible to loneliness, social anxiety, and clinical depression in the absence of this love or belonging element. This need for belonging may overcome the physiological and security needs, depending on the strength of the peer pressure.

Esteem

All humans have a need to feel respected; this includes the need to have self-esteem and self-respect. Esteem presents the typical human desire to be accepted and valued by others. People often engage in a profession or hobby to gain recognition. These activities give the person a sense of contribution or value. Low self-esteem or an inferiority complex may result from imbalances during this level in the hierarchy. People with low self-esteem often need respect from others; they may feel the need to seek fame or glory. However, fame or glory will not help the person to build their self-esteem until they accept who they are internally. Psychological imbalances such as depression can hinder the person from obtaining a higher level of self-esteem or self-respect.

Most people have a need for stable self-respect and self-esteem. Maslow noted two versions of esteem needs: a 「lower」 version and a 「higher」 version. The 「lower」 version of esteem is the need for respect from others. This may include a need for status, recognition, fame, prestige, and attention. The 「higher」 version manifests itself as the need for self-respect. For example, the person may have a need for strength, competence, mastery, self-confidence, independence, and freedom. Deprivation of these needs may lead to an inferiority complex, weakness, and helplessness.

Maslow states that while he originally thought the needs of humans had strict guidelines, the 「hierarchies are interrelated rather than sharply separated」. This means that esteem and the subsequent levels are not strictly separated; instead, the levels are closely related.

Self-actualization

「What a man can be, he must be.」This quotation forms the basis of the perceived need for self-actualization. This level of need refers to what a person's full potential is and the realization of that potential. Maslow describes this level as the desire to accomplish everything that one can, to become the most that one can be. Individuals may perceive or focus on this need very specifically. For example, one individual may have the strong desire to become an ideal parent. In another, the desire may be expressed athletically. For others, it may be expressed in paintings, pictures, or inventions. As previously mentioned, Maslow believed that to understand this level of need, the person must not only achieve the previous needs, but master them.

Personnel recruitment and selection

Personnel recruitment is the process of identifying qualified candidates in the workforce and getting them to apply for jobs within an organization. Personnel recruitment processes include developing job announcements, placing ads, defining key qualifications for applicants, and screening out unqualified applicants.

Personnel selection is the systematic process of hiring and promoting personnel. Personnel selection systems employ evidence-based practices to determine the most qualified candidates. Personnel selection involves both the newly hired and individuals who can be promoted from within the organization. Common selection tools include ability tests, knowledge tests, personality tests, structured interviews, the systematic collection of biographical data, and work samples.

Performance appraisal/management

Performance appraisal or performance evaluation is the process of measuring an individual's or a group's work behaviors and outcomes against the expectations of the job. Performance appraisal is frequently used in promotion and compensation decisions, to help design and validate personnel selection procedures, and for performance management. Performance management is the process of providing performance feedback relative to expectations and improvement information (e.g. coaching, mentoring). Performance management may also include documenting and tracking performance information for organization-level evaluation purposes.

Training and training evaluation

Training is the systematic acquisition of skills, concepts, or attitudes that results in improved performance in another environment. Most people hired for a job are not already versed in all the tasks required to perform the job effectively. Evidence indicates that training is effective and that these training expenditures are paying off in terms of higher net sales and gross profitability per employee. Training can be beneficial for the organization and for employees in terms of increasing their value to their organization as well as their employability in the broader marketplace. Many organizations are using training and development as a way to attract and retain their most successful employees.

Before training design issues are considered, a careful needs analysis is required to develop a systematic understanding of where training is needed, what needs to be taught or trained, and who will be trained. Training needs analysis typically involves a three-step process that includes organizational analysis, task analysis and person analysis. Organizational analysis examines organizational goals, available resources, and the organizational environment to determine where training should be directed. This analysis identifies the training needs of different departments or subunits and systematically assessing manager, peer, and technological support for transfer of training. Organizational analysis also takes into account the climate of the organization and its subunits. For example, if a climate for safety is emphasized throughout the organization or in particular parts of the organization (e.g., production), then training needs will likely reflect this emphasis. Task analysis uses the results from job analysis on determining what is needed for successful job performance and then determines what the content of training should be. Task analysis can consist of developing task statements, determining homogeneous task clusters, and identifying KSAOs (knowledge, skills, abilities, other characteristics) required for the job. With organizations increasingly trying to identify 「core competencies」 that are required for all jobs, task analysis can also include an assessment of competencies. Person analysis identifies which individuals within an organization should receive training and what kind of instruction they need. Employee needs can be assessed using a variety of methods that identify weaknesses that training and development can address. The needs analysis makes it possible to identify the training program's objectives, which in turn, represents the information for both the trainer and trainee about what is to be learned for the benefit of the organization.

Therefore with any training program it is key to establish specific training objectives.

· To identify the abilities required to perform increasingly complex jobs.
· To provide job opportunities for unskilled workers.
· To assist supervisors in the management of an ethnically diverse workforce.
· To retain workers displaced by changing economic, technological, and political forces.
· To help organizations remain competitive in the international marketplace.
· To conduct the necessary research to determine the effectiveness of training programs.

Innovation

Innovation is often considered a form of productive behavior that employees exhibit when they come up with novel ideas that further the goals of the organization. Research indicates if various skills, knowledge, and abilities are present then an individual will be more apt to innovation. These qualities are generally linked to creativity.

In addition to the role and characteristics of the individual, one must consider what it is that may be done on an organizational level to develop and reward innovation. Four specific characteristics that may predict innovation within an organization have been identified as follows.

1. A population with high levels of technical knowledge
2. The organization's level of specialization
3. The level an organization communicates externally
4. Functional Differentiation.

Additionally, organizations could use and institutionalize many participatory system-processes, which could breed innovation in the workplace. Some of these items include providing creativity training, having leaders encourage and model innovation, allowing employees to question current procedures and rules, seeing that the implementation of innovations had real consequences, documenting innovations in a professional manner, allowing employees to have autonomy and freedom in their job roles, reducing the number of obstacles that may be in the way of innovation, and giving employees access to resources (whether these are monetary, informational, or access to key people inside or outside of the organization).

Motivation in the workplace

Work motivation is a set of energetic forces that originate both within as well as beyond an individual's being, to initiate work-related behavior, and to determine its form, direction, intensity, and duration. Motivation can often be used as a tool to help predict behavior, it varies greatly among individuals and must often be combined with ability and environmental factors to actually influence behavior and performance. Because of motivation's role in influencing workplace behavior and performance, it is key for organizations to understand and to structure the work environment to encourage productive behaviors and discourage those that are unproductive.

Motivation serves to direct attention, focusing on particular issues, people, tasks, etc. It also serves to stimulate an employee to put forth effort. Next, motivation results in persistence, preventing one from deviating from the goal-seeking behavior. Finally, motivation results in task strategies, which are patterns of behavior produced to reach a particular goal.

Counterproductive work behavior

Counterproductive work behavior (CWB) can be defined as employee behavior that goes against the goals of an organization. These behaviors can be intentional or unintentional and result from a wide range of underlying causes and motivations. There is evidence that an emotional response (e.g. anger) to job stress (e.g. unfair treatment) can motivate CWBs.

The forms of counterproductive behavior with the most empirical examination are ineffective job performance, absenteeism, job turnover, and accidents. Less common but potentially more detrimental forms of counterproductive behavior have also been investigated including violence and sexual harassment.

Occupational health and wellbeing

Staying vigorous during working hours is important for work-related behavior. Positive relationships are found between job satisfaction and life satisfaction, happiness, positive affect, and the absence of negative affect and feelings of positive wellbeing. The negative health impacts are also looked at on mature-aged unemployment. Results indicated that attempts should be made to reduce physical demands over older employees at work, to help improve their health and well-being.

Part Ⅱ　Production and Service Management

Production is a process of combining various material inputs and immaterial inputs in order to make something for consumption. It is the act of creating output, a good or service which has value and contributes to the utility of individuals.

Factors of Production

In economics, factors of production, resources, or inputs are what is used in the production process in order to produce output—that is, finished goods. The amounts of the various inputs used determine the quantity of output according to a relationship called the production function. There are three basic resources or factors of production: land, labour, and capital. Some modern economists also consider entrepreneurship or time a factor of production. These factors are also frequently labeled 「producer goods」in order to distinguish them from the goods or services purchased by consumers, which are frequently labeled 「consumer goods.」All three of these are required in combination at a time to produce a commodity.

Factors of production may also refer specifically to the primary factors, which are land, labor (the ability to work), and capital goods applied to production. Materials and energy are considered secondary factors in classical economics because they are obtained from land, labour and capital. The primary factors facilitate production but neither become part of the product (as with raw materials) nor become significantly transformed by the production process (as with fuel used to power machinery). Land includes not only the site of production but natural resources above or below the soil. Recent usage has distinguished human capital (the stock of knowledge in the labor force) from labor. Entrepreneurship is also sometimes considered a factor of production. Sometimes the overall state of technology is described as a factor of production. The number and definition of factors varies, depending on school of economics. Many economists today consider 「human capital」(skills and education) as the fourth factor of production, with entrepreneurship as a form of human capital. Yet others refer to intellectual capital. More recently, many have begun to see 「social capital」as a factor, as contributing to production of goods and services.

Means of Production

In economics and sociology, the means of production are physical, non-human inputs used in production, such as machinery, tools and factories, infrastructural capital and natural capital.

The means of production has two broad categories of objects: *instruments of labour* (tools, factories, infrastructure, etc.) and *subjects of labor* (natural resources and raw materials). If creating a good, people operate on the subjects of labor, using the instruments of labor, to create a product; or, stated another way, labour acting on the means of production creates a good.

In an agrarian society the means of production is the soil and the shovel. In an industrial society it is the mines and the factories, and in a knowledge economy the offices and computers. In the broad sense, the 「means of production」 includes the 「means of distribution」 such as stores, the internet and railroads.

Manufacturing

Manufacturing is the production of merchandise for use or sale using labour and machines, tools, chemical and biological processing, or formulation. The term may refer to a range of human activity, from handicraft to high tech, but is most commonly applied to industrial production, in which raw materials are transformed into finished goods on a large scale. Such finished goods may be used for manufacturing other, more complex products, such as aircraft, household appliances or automobiles, or sold to wholesalers, who in turn sell them to retailers, who then sell them to end users—the 「consumers」.

Manufacturing takes turns under all types of economic systems. In a free market economy, manufacturing is usually directed toward the mass production of products for sale to consumers at a profit. In a collectivist economy, manufacturing is more frequently directed by the state to supply a centrally planned economy. In mixed market economies, manufacturing occurs under some degree of government regulation.

The manufacturing sector is closely connected with engineering and industrial design. Examples of major manufacturers in North America include General Motors Corporation, General Electric, Procter & Gamble, General Dynamics, Boeing, Pfizer, and Precision Castparts. Examples in Europe include Volkswagen Group, Siemens, and Michelin. Examples in Asia include Sony, Huawei, Lenovo, Toyota, Samsung, etc.

Economics of manufacturing

Manufacturing is a wealth-producing sector of an economy, whereas a service sector tends to be wealth-consuming. Emerging technologies have provided some new growth in advanced manufacturing employment opportunities in the Manufacturing Belt in the United States. Manufacturing provides important material support for national infrastructure and for national defense.

On the other hand, most manufacturing may involve significant social and environmental costs. The clean-up costs of hazardous waste, for example, may outweigh the benefits of a product that creates it. Hazardous materials may expose workers to health risks. These costs are now well known and there is effort to address them by improving efficiency, reducing waste, and eliminating harmful chemicals. The increased use of technologies such as 3D printing also offer the potential to reduce the environmental impact of producing finished goods through distributed manufacturing.

The negative costs of manufacturing can also be addressed legally. Developed countries regulate manufacturing activity with labor laws and environmental laws. Across the globe, manufacturers can be subject to regulations and pollution taxes to offset the environmental costs of manufacturing activities. Labor unions and craft guilds have played a historic role in the negotiation of worker rights and wages. Environment laws and labor protections that are available in developed nations may not be available in the third world. These are significant dynamics in the ongoing process, occurring over the last few decades, of manufacture-based industries relocating operations to 「developing-world」 economies where the costs of production are significantly lower than in 「developed-world」 economies.

Quality Control

Quality control, or QC for short, is a process by which entities review the quality of all factors involved in production. ISO 9000 defines quality control as 「A part of quality management focused on fulfilling quality requirements」.

This approach places an emphasis on three aspects:

1. Elements such as controls, job management, defined and well managed processes, performance and integrity criteria, and identification of records

2. Competence, such as knowledge, skills, experience, and qualifications

3. Soft elements, such as personnel, integrity, confidence, organizational culture, motivation, team spirit, and quality relationships.

Controls include product inspection, where every product is examined visually, and often using a stereo microscope for fine detail before the product is sold into the external market. Inspectors will be provided with lists and descriptions of unacceptable product defects such as cracks or surface blemishes for example.

The quality of the outputs is at risk if any of these three aspects is deficient in any way.

Quality control emphasizes testing of products to uncover defects and reporting to management who make the decision to allow or deny product release, whereas quality assurance attempts to improve and stabilize production (and associated processes) to avoid, or at least minimize, issues which led to the defect(s) in the first place. For contract work, particularly work awarded by government agencies, quality control issues are among the top reasons for not renewing a contract.

The ISO 9000 family of quality management systems standards is designed to help organizations ensure that they meet the needs of customers and other stakeholders while meeting statutory and regulatory requirements related to a product. ISO 9000 deals with the fundamentals of quality management systems, including the eight management principles upon which the family of standards is based. ISO 9001 deals with the requirements that organizations wishing to meet the standard must fulfill.

Third-party certification bodies provide independent confirmation that organizations meet the requirements of ISO 9001. Over one million organizations worldwide are independently certified, making ISO 9001 one of the most widely used management tools in the world today.

In recent years there has been a rapid growth in China, which now accounts for approximately a quarter of the global certifications.

The ISO 9000 series are based on eight quality management principles.

Principle 1 Customer focus

Organizations depend on their customers and therefore should understand current and future customer needs, should meet customer requirements and strive to exceed customer expectations.

Principle 2 Leadership

Leaders establish unity of purpose and direction of the organization. They should create and maintain the internal environment in which people can become fully involved in achieving the organization's objectives.

Principle 3 Involvement of people

People at all levels are the essence of an organization and their full involvement enables their abilities to be used for the organization's benefit.

Principle 4 Process approach

A desired result is achieved more efficiently when activities and related resources are managed as a process.

Principle 5 System approach to management

It identifies, understands and manages interrelated processes as a system, and contributes to the organization's effectiveness and efficiency in achieving its objectives.

Principle 6 Continual improvement

Continual improvement of the organization's overall performance should be a permanent objective of the organization.

Principle 7 Factual approach to decision making

Effective decisions are based on the analysis of data and information

Principle 8 Mutually beneficial supplier relationships

An organization and its suppliers are interdependent and a mutually beneficial relationship enhances the ability of both to create value

Operations & Project Management

Operations management is an area of management concerned with overseeing, designing, and controlling the process of production and redesigning business operations in the production of goods or services. It involves the responsibility of ensuring that business operations are efficient in terms of using as few resources as needed, and effective in terms of meeting customer requirements. It is concerned with managing the process that converts inputs into outputs.

According to the United States Department of Education, operations management is the field concerned with managing and directing the physical and/or technical functions of a firm or organization, particularly those relating to development, production, and manufacturing. Operations management programs typically include instruction in principles of general management, manufacturing and production systems, factory management, equipment maintenance management, production control, industrial labor relations and skilled trades supervision, strategic manufacturing policy, systems analysis, productivity analysis and cost control, and materials planning. Management, including operations management, is like engineering in that it blends art with applied science. People skills, creativity, rational analysis, and knowledge of technology are all required for success.

Project management is the process and activity of planning, organizing, motivating, and controlling resources, procedures and protocols to achieve specific goals in scientific or daily problems. A project is a temporary endeavor designed to produce a unique product, service or result with a defined beginning and end undertaken to meet unique goals and objectives, typically to bring about beneficial change or added value. The temporary nature of projects stands in contrast with business as usual, which are repetitive, permanent, or semi-permanent functional activities to produce products or services. In practice, the management of these two systems is often quite different, and as such requires the development of distinct technical skills and management strategies.

There have been several attempts to develop project management standards internationally, such as:

· ISO 21500: 2012-Guidance on project management. This is the first project management ISO.

· ISO 31000: 2009-Risk management. Risk management is 1 of the 10 knowledge areas of either ISO 21500 or PMBoK5 concept of project management.

· ISO/IEC/IEEE 16326-2009-Systems and Software Engineering—Life Cycle Processes—Project Management

· GAPPS, Global Alliance for Project Performance Standards-an open source standard describing COMPETENCIES for project and program managers.

· The ISO standards ISO 9000, a family of standards for quality management systems, and the ISO 10006: 2003, for Quality management systems and guidelines for quality management in projects.

· IAPPM, The International Association of Project & Program Management, guide to project auditing and rescuing troubled projects.

An increasing number of organizations are using, what is referred to as, project portfolio management (PPM) as a means of selecting the right projects and then using project management techniques as the means for delivering the outcomes in the form of benefits to the performing private or not-for-profit organization.

Service Management

Service management in the manufacturing context, is integrated into supply chain management as the intersection between the actual sales and the customer. The aim of high performance service management is to optimize the service-intensive supply chains, which are usually more complex than the typical finished-goods supply chain. Most service-intensive supply chains require larger inventories and tighter integration with field service and third parties. They also must accommodate inconsistent and uncertain demand by establishing more advanced information and product flows. Moreover, all processes must be coordinated across numerous service locations with large numbers of parts and multiple levels in the supply chain.

Customer Service

Customer service is the provision of service to customers before, during and after a purchase. Accordingly, it may vary by product, service, industry and individual customer. The perception of success of such interactions is dependent on employees who can adjust themselves to the personality of the guest. Customer service is also often referred to when describing the culture of the organization. It concerns the priority an organization assigns to customer service relative to components such as product innovation and pricing. In this sense, an organization that values good customer service may spend more money in training employees than the average organization, or may proactively interview customers for feedback.

Customer service plays an important role in an organization's ability to generate income and revenue. From that perspective, customer service should be included as part of an overall approach to systematic improvement. One good customer service experience can change the entire perception a customer holds towards the organization.

Customer support is a range of customer services to assist customers in making cost effective and correct use of a product. It includes assistance in planning, installation, training, trouble shooting, maintenance, upgrading, and disposal of a product. These services even may be done at customer's side where he/she uses the product or service. In this case it is called 「at home customer services」or 「at home customer support」.

Regarding technology products such as mobile phones, televisions, computers, software products or other electronic or mechanical goods, it is termed technical support.

Customer service may be provided by a person or by automated means. Examples of automated means are Internet sites. An advantage with automated means is an increased ability to provide service 24-hours a day, which can, at least, be a complement to customer service by persons.

However, in the Internet era, a challenge has been to maintain and/or enhance the personal experience while making use of the efficiencies of online commerce. 「Online customers are literally invisible to you (and you to them), so it's easy to shortchange them emotionally. But this lack of visual and tactile presence makes it even more crucial to create a sense of personal, human-to-human connection in the online arena.」

Recently, many organizations have implemented feedback loops that allow them to capture feedback at the point of experience. For example, National Express has invited passengers to send text messages whilst riding the bus. This has been shown to be useful, as it allows companies to improve their customer service before the customer defects, thus making it far more likely that the customer will return next time. Technology has made it increasingly easier for companies to obtain feedback from their customers. Community blogs and forums give customers the ability to give detailed explanations of both negative as well as positive experiences with a company/organization.

Strategic service management (SSM) is a business strategy that aims to optimize the post-sales service that a company provides, by synchronizing service parts and resources forecasting, service partners, workforce technicians, and service pricing. Benefits of strategic service management can include:

· Increased revenue through the servicing of manufactured products that may be experiencing decreased sales

  · Increased customer loyalty through improved post-sale service performance

  · Heightened asset accountability and tracking

  · Increased worker productivity

  · More knowledgeable workers to prevent common mistakes

Using strategic service management, Avaya reduced service parts inventory from $ 250 million to $ 160 million, Sun Microsystems saved $ 40 million in the first year, and Dell grew service revenues over 20% in one year.

The Customer Service System (CSS) of the BT Group (previously British Telecommunications) is the core operational support system for BT, bringing in 70% of income for the company. BT rolled out CSS nationally in 1989 and provided an integrated system for telephony—order handling, repair handling and billing.

Part III   Financial and Marketing Management

Finance is a field that deals with the allocation of assets and liabilities over time under conditions of certainty and uncertainty. Finance can also be defined as the science of money management. A key point in finance is the time value of money, which states that purchasing power of one unit of currency can vary over time. Finance aims to price assets based on their risk level and their expected rate of return.

Wall Street, the center of American finance

Capital, in the financial sense, is the money that gives the business the power to buy goods to be used in the production of other goods or the offering of a service. (The capital has two types of resources, Equity and Debt).

The deployment of capital is decided by the budget. This may include the objective of business, targets set, and results in financial terms, e.g. the target set for sale, resulting cost, growth, required investment to achieve the planned sales, and financing source for the investment.

A budget may be long term or short term. Long term budgets have a time horizon of 5-10 years giving a vision to the company; short term is an annual budget which is drawn to control and operate in that particular year.

Budgets will include proposed fixed asset requirements and how these expenditures will be financed. Capital budgets are often adjusted annually (done every year) and should be part of a longer-term Capital Improvements Plan.

A cash budget is also required. The working capital requirements of a business are monitored at all times to ensure that there are sufficient funds available to meet short-term expenses.

The cash budget is basically a detailed plan that shows all expected sources and uses of cash when it comes to spending it appropriately.

Corporate finance

Corporate finance deals with the sources of funding and the capital structure of corporations and the actions that managers take to increase the value of the firm to the shareholders, as well as the tools and analysis used to allocate financial resources. Corporate finance generally involves balancing risk and profitability, while attempting to maximize an entity's wealth and the value of its stock, and generically entails three primary areas of capital resource allocation. In the first, 「capital budgeting」, management must choose which 「projects」 (if any) to undertake. The second, 「sources of capital」 relates to how these investments are to be funded: investment capital can be provided through different sources, such as by shareholders, in the form of equity (privately or via an initial public offering), creditors, often in the form of bonds, and the firm's operations (cash flow). Short-term funding or working capital is mostly provided by banks extending a line of credit. The balance between these elements forms the company's capital structure. The third, 「the dividend policy」, requires management to determine whether any unappropriated profit (excess cash) is to be retained for future investment / operational requirements, or instead to be distributed to shareholders. Short term financial management is often termed 「working capital management」.

Corporate finance also includes within its scope business valuation, stock investing, or investment management. An investment is an acquisition of an asset in the hope that it will maintain or increase its value over time that will in hope give back a higher rate of return when it comes to disbursing dividends. In investment management-in choosing a portfolio-one has to use financial analysis to determine what, how much and when to invest. To do this, a company must:

· Identify relevant objectives and constraints: institution or individual goals, time horizon, risk aversion and tax considerations;

· Identify the appropriate strategy: active versus passive hedging strategy

· Measure the portfolio performance

Financial management overlaps with the financial function of the Accounting profession. However, financial accounting is the reporting of historical financial information, while financial management is concerned with the allocation of capital resources to increase a firm's value to the shareholders and increase their rate of return on the investments.

Financial risk management, an element of corporate finance, is the practice of creating and protecting economic value in a firm by using financial instruments to manage exposure to risk, particularly credit risk and market risk. It focuses on when and how to hedge using financial instruments; in this sense it overlaps with financial engineering. Similar to general risk management, financial risk management requires identifying its sources, measuring it, and formulating plans to address these, and can be qualitative and quantitative. In the banking sector worldwide, the Basel Accords are generally adopted by internationally active banks for tracking, reporting and exposing operational, credit and market risks.

Marketing & Advertisement Management

Marketing

Marketing is communicating the value of a product, service or brand to customers, for the purpose of promoting or selling that product, service, or brand.

Marketing techniques include choosing target markets through market analysis and market segmentation, as well as understanding consumer behavior and advertising a product's value to the customer.

From a societal point of view, marketing is the link between a society's material requirements and its economic patterns of response.

Marketing satisfies these needs and wants through exchange processes and building long-term relationships.

Marketing blends art and applied science (such as behavioural sciences) and makes use of information technology.

Marketing is applied in enterprise and organizations through marketing management.

Marketing Management

The Marketing Management is the performance of business activities that directs the flow of goods and services from producer to consumer or user. It is also a strategy which the company turns the sales into the profit and this can be done by either individuals or a group of people that work for demand and supply to direction of goods and services from company to consumer.

Marketing management often finds it necessary to invest in research to collect the data required to perform accurate marketing analysis. As such, they often conduct marketing research to obtain this information.

Marketing research involves conducting research to support marketing activities, and the statistical interpretation of data into information. This information is then used by managers to plan marketing activities, gauge the nature of a firm's marketing environment and attain information from suppliers. Marketing researchers use statistical methods such as quantitative research and qualitative research. Marketers employ a variety of techniques to conduct market research to interpret their findings and convert data into information, some of the more common include:

· Qualitative marketing research, such as focus groups and various types of interviews

· Quantitative marketing research, such as statistical surveys

· Experimental techniques such as test markets

· Observational techniques such as ethnographic (on-site) observation

Marketing managers may also design and oversee various environmental scanning and competitive intelligence processes to help identify trends and inform the company's marketing analysis.

The marketing research process spans a number of stages, including the definition of a problem, development of a research plan, collection and interpretation of data and disseminating information formally in the form of a report. The task of marketing research is to provide management with relevant, accurate, reliable, valid, and current information.

Marketing environment

Staying ahead of the consumer is an important part of a marketer's job. It is important to understand the ⌈marketing environment⌋ in order to comprehend the consumers concerns, motivations and to adjust the product according to the consumers needs. Marketers continually acquires information on events occurring outside the organization to identify trends, opportunities and threats to a business. The six key elements of a marketing scan are the *demographic forces*, *socio-cultural forces*, *economic forces*, *regulatory forces*, *competitive forces*, and *technological forces*. Marketers must look at where the threats and opportunities stem from in the world around the consumer to maintain a productive and profitable business.

The market environment is a marketing term and refers to factors and forces that affect a firm's ability to build and maintain successful relationships with customers. Three levels of the environment are: Micro (internal) environment-forces within the company that affect its ability to serve its customers. Meso environment-the industry in which a company operates and the industry's market(s). Macro (national) environment–larger societal forces that affect the microenvironment.

Market segmentation

Market segmentation pertains to the division of a market of consumers into persons with similar needs and wants. For instance, Kellogg's cereals, Frosties are marketed to children. Crunchy Nut Cornflakes are marketed to adults. Both goods denote two products which are marketed to two distinct groups of persons, both with similar needs, traits, and wants. In another example, Sun Microsystems can use market segmentation to classify its clients according to their promptness to adopt new products.

Market segmentation allows for a better allocation of a firm's finite resources. A firm only possesses a certain amount of resources. Accordingly, it must make choices in servicing specific groups of consumers. In this way, the diversified tastes of contemporary Western consumers can be served better. With growing diversity in the tastes of modern consumers, firms are taking note of the benefit of servicing a multiplicity of new markets.

Marketing Planning

The marketing planning process involves forging a plan for a firm's marketing activities. A marketing plan can also pertain to a specific product, as well as to an organization's overall marketing strategy. Generally speaking, an organization's marketing planning process is derived from its overall business strategy. Thus, when top management are devising the firm's strategic direction or mission, the intended marketing activities are incorporated into this plan. There are several levels of marketing objectives within an organization. The senior management of a firm would formulate a general business strategy for a firm. However, this general business strategy would be interpreted and implemented in different contexts throughout the firm.

Marketing strategy

The field of marketing strategy considers the total marketing environment and its impacts on a company or product or service. The emphasis is on 「an in depth understanding of the market environment, particularly the competitors and customers.」

A given firm may offer numerous products or services to a marketplace, spanning numerous and sometimes wholly unrelated industries. Accordingly, a plan is required in order to effectively manage such products. Evidently, a company needs to weigh up and ascertain how to utilize its finite resources. For example, a start-up car manufacturing firm would face little success should it attempt to rival Toyota, Ford, Nissan, Chevrolet, or any other large global car maker. A marketing strategy differs from a marketing tactic in that a strategy looks at the longer term view of the products, goods, or services being marketed. A tactic refers to a shorter term view. Therefore, the mailing of a postcard or sales letter would be a tactic, but changing marketing channels of distribution, changing the pricing, or promotional elements used would be considered a strategic change.

A marketing strategy considers the resources a firm has, or is required to allocate in effort to achieve an objective. Marketing Strategies include the process and planning in which a firm may be expected to achieve their company goals.

Multi cultural Marketing

Globalization has led firms to market beyond the borders of their home countries, making international marketing highly significant and an integral part of a firm's marketing strategy.

Multicultural marketing (also known as ethnic marketing or cross-cultural marketing) is the practice of marketing to one or more audiences of a specific ethnicity—typically an ethnicity outside of a country's majority culture, which is sometimes called the 「general market.」 Typically, multicultural marketing takes advantage of the ethnic group's different cultural referents—such as language, traditions, celebrations, religion and any other concepts—to communicate to and persuade that audience.

People tend to live within their cultural boundaries; i.e., people have their own cultural values and norms, which influence the way they think, feel and act. People in a particular ethnic group tend to share the language, customs, values, and social views, and these influence people's cognitive (beliefs and motives), affective (emotion and attitude) and behavioral (purchase and consumption) processes. Based on this notion of 「advertising as a mirror,」 cultural values and standards are implanted in ads in such a way that consumers can 「see themselves」 and identify with the characters in the ads and feel affinity with the brands.

It is suggested that the following skills are required in the field of multicultural marketing.

1. To spot patterns that allow subcultures to be grouped together, so that a common marketing strategy may be extended to several subcultures in a group

2. To develop a distinct marketing strategy for each subculture, if there is a significantly distinct cultural dimension that is important to the specific culture

3. To further segment audiences in a subculture, if needed, in terms of cultural affinity, cultural identity or acculturation level.

4. To develop parameters of culturally acceptable marketing stimuli; and

5. To establish a protocol for measuring cultural effectiveness of the stimuli.

Visual marketing

As a key component of modern marketing, visual marketing focuses on the studying and analysing how images can be used to make objects the centre of visual communication. The product and its visual communication become therefore inseparable and their fusion is what reaches out to people, engages them and defines their choices.

Marketing persuades consumer's buying behaviour and Visual Marketing enhances that by factors of recall, memory and identity.

Growing Trends in the usage of Picture Based Websites and social networking platforms like Pinterest, Instagram, Tumblr, Timeline feature of Facebook justifies the fact that people want to believe what they see, and therefore, need for Visual Marketing.

Visual Marketing includes all visual cues like logo, signage, sales tools, vehicles, uniforms, right to your Advertisements, Brochures, Informational DVDs, Websites, everything that meets the Public Eye.

Brand Awareness and Brand Loyalty in Marketing

Brand Awareness

Brand awareness is the extent to which a brand is recognized by potential customers, and is correctly associated with a particular product. Expressed usually as a percentage of the target market, brand awareness is the primary goal of advertising in the early months or years of a product's introduction.

Brand awareness is related to the functions of brand identities in consumers' memory and can be reflected by how well the consumers can identify the brand under various conditions. Brand awareness includes brand recognition and brand recall performance. Brand recognition refers to the ability of the consumers to correctly differentiate the brand they previously have been exposed to. This does not necessarily require that the consumers identify the brand name. Instead, it often means that consumers can respond to a certain brand after viewing its visual packaging images. Brand recall refers to the ability of the consumers to correctly generate and retrieve the brand in their memory.

In marketing, Brand loyalty is where a person buys products from the same manufacturer repeatedly rather than from other suppliers. brand management is the analysis and planning on how that brand is perceived in the market. Developing a good relationship with the target market is essential for brand management. Tangible elements of brand management include the product itself; look, price, the packaging, etc. The intangible elements are the experience that the consumer has had with the brand, and also the relationship that they have with that brand. A brand manager would oversee all of these things.

Brand management is a function of marketing that uses special techniques in order to increase the perceived value of a product. Based on the aims of the established marketing strategy, brand management enables the price of products to grow and builds loyal customers through positive associations and images or a strong awareness of the brand.

Umbrella branding (also called a family brand) is when a firm uses a brand name for two or more products. All products use the same means of identification and have no additional brand names or symbols attached. Umbrella branding does not mean that the whole product portfolio of a firm will fall under one brand name as company can go for different approaches of branding for different product lines.

Umbrella Branding makes different product lines easily identifiable by the consumer by grouping them under one brand name. It provides uniformity reducing marketing cost for firms and helps consumers make a positive association with the products. All products under the same umbrella brand are expected to have a uniform quality and user experience. It is the branding strategy that gives the probability of a brand extension for every possible quality of profile.

Umbrella branding generates savings in brand development and marketing costs over time and can create advertising efficiencies. Consumer's experience in one category may affect their quality perception of another product or service falling under same umbrella brand.

Umbrella branding can be proven effective when customers use information in one advertisement to make an inference about a product with the same brand name. The association can reduce the advertising cost per effective image.

Visual Brand Language

Visual brand language is the unique 「alphabet」 of design elements-such as shape, color, materials, finish, typography and composition-which directly and subliminally communicate a company's values and personality through compelling imagery and design style. This 「alphabet」, properly designed, results in an emotional connection between the brand and the consumer. Visual brand language is a key ingredient necessary to make an authentic and convincing brand strategy that can be applied uniquely and creatively in all forms of brand communications to both employees and customers. Successful Visual Brand Language creates a memorable experience for the consumer, encouraging repeat business and boosting the company's economic health. It is a long-term creative solution that can be leveraged by an executive team to showcase their brand's unique personality.

Brand language is a part of verbal brand identity, includes naming of both corporation and the products they sell as well as taglines, voice, and tone. Another benefit of developing a brand language is the ability for a corporation or product to be recognizable across international borders, while other advertising codes can be misinterpreted, words can be translated to ensure brand unity.

Brand Ambassador

Brand ambassador is a marketing jargon for celebrity endorser or spokesmodel, a person employed by an organization or company to promote its products or services. The brand ambassador is meant to embody the corporate identity in appearance, demeanor, values and ethics. The key element of brand ambassadors lies in their ability to use promotional strategies that will strengthen the customer-product (service) relationship and influence a large audience to buy and consume more. Predominantly, a brand ambassador is known as a positive spokesperson, an opinion leader or a community influencer, appointed as an internal or external agent to boost product/service sales and create brand awareness. Today, brand ambassador as a term has expanded beyond celebrity branding to self branding or personal brand management. Professional figures such as good-will and non-profit ambassadors, promotional models, testimonials and brand advocates have formed as an extension of the same concept, taking into account the requirements of every company.

Advertising

Advertizing is a form of marketing communication used to persuade an audience to take or continue some action, usually with respect to a commercial offering, or political or ideological support.

The purpose of advertising may also be to reassure employees or shareholders that a company is viable or successful. Advertising messages are usually paid for by sponsors and viewed via various old media; including mass media such as newspaper, magazines, television advertisement, radio advertisement, outdoor advertising or direct mail; or new media such as blogs, websites or text messages.

Commercial advertisers often seek to generate increased consumption of their products or services through 「branding」, which involves associating a product name or image with certain qualities in the minds of consumers. Non-commercial advertisers who spend money to advertise items other than a consumer product or service include political parties, interest groups, religious organizations and governmental agencies. Nonprofit organizations may rely on free modes of persuasion, such as a public service announcement (PSA).

Sales promotions are another way to advertise. Sales promotions are double purposed because they are used to gather information about what type of customers one draws in and where they are, and to jumpstart sales. Sales promotions include things like contests and games, sweepstakes, product giveaways, samples coupons, loyalty programs, and discounts. The ultimate goal of sales promotions is to stimulate potential customers to action.

Increasingly, other media are overtaking many of the 「traditional」 media such as television, radio and newspaper because of a shift toward the usage of the Internet for news and music as well as devices like digital video recorders (DVRs) such as TiVo.

Digital signage is poised to become a major mass media because of its ability to reach larger audiences for less money. Digital signage also offers the unique ability to see the target audience where they are reached by the medium. Technological advances have also made it possible to control the message on digital signage with much precision, enabling the messages to be relevant to the target audience at any given time and location which in turn, gets more response from the advertising. Digital signage is being successfully employed in supermarkets. Another successful use of digital signage is in hospitality locations such as restaurants and malls.

Advertising on the World Wide Web is a recent phenomenon. Prices of web-based advertising space are dependent on the 「relevance」 of the surrounding web content and the traffic that the website receives.

In online display advertising, display ads generate awareness quickly. Unlike search, which requires someone to be aware of a need, display advertising can drive awareness of something new and without previous knowledge. Display works well for direct response. Display is not only used for generating awareness, it's used for direct response campaigns that link to a landing page with a clear 「call to action」.

E-mail advertising is another recent phenomenon. Unsolicited bulk E-mail advertising is known as 「e-mail spam」. Spam has been a problem for e-mail users for many years.

A new form of advertising that is growing rapidly is social network advertising. It is online advertising with a focus on social networking sites. This is a relatively immature market, but it has shown a lot of promise as advertisers are able to take advantage of the demographic information the user has provided to the social networking site. Friendertising is a more precise advertising term in which people are able to direct advertisements toward others directly using social network services. As the mobile phone became a new mass medium in 1998 when the first paid downloadable content appeared on mobile phones in Finland, mobile advertising followed, also first launched in Finland in 2000.

Some companies have proposed placing messages or corporate logos on the side of booster rockets and the International Space Station.

Part Ⅳ Legal and Strategic Management

Most legal jurisdictions specify the forms of ownership that a business can take, creating a body of commercial law for each type.

The major factors affecting how a business is organized are usually:

· **The size and scope of the business firm** and its structure, management, and ownership, broadly analyzed in the theory of the firm. Generally a smaller business is more flexible, while larger businesses, or those with wider ownership or more formal structures, will usually tend to be organized as corporations or (less often) partnerships. In addition, a business that wishes to raise money on a stock market or to be owned by a wide range of people will often be required to adopt a specific legal form to do so.

· **The sector and country.** Private profit-making businesses are different from government-owned bodies. In some countries, certain businesses are legally obliged to be organized in certain ways.

· **Limited Liability Companies (LLC)**, limited liability partnerships, and other specific types of business organization protect their owners or shareholders from business failure by doing business under a separate legal entity with certain legal protections. In contrast, unincorporated businesses or persons working on their own are usually not so protected.

· **Tax advantages.** Different structures are treated differently in tax law, and may have advantages for this reason.

· **Disclosure and compliance requirements**. Different business structures may be required to make less or more information public (or report it to relevant authorities), and may be bound to comply with different rules and regulations.

Many businesses are operated through a separate entity such as a corporation or a partnership. Most legal jurisdictions allow people to organize such an entity by filing certain charter documents and complying with certain other ongoing obligations. The relationships and legal rights of shareholders, limited partners, or members are governed partly by the charter documents and partly by the law of the jurisdiction where the entity is organized. Generally speaking, shareholders in a corporation, limited partners in a limited partnership, and members in a limited liability company are shielded from personal liability for the debts and obligations of the entity, which is legally treated as a separate 「person」. This means that unless there is misconduct, the owner's own possessions are strongly protected in law if the business does not succeed.

A few relevant factors to consider in deciding how to operate a business include:

1. General partners in a partnership, plus anyone who personally owns and operates a business without creating a separate legal entity, are personally liable for the debts and obligations of the business.

2. Generally, corporations are required to pay tax just like 「real」 people. In some tax systems, this can give rise to so-called double taxation, because first the corporation pays tax on the profit, and then when the corporation distributes its profits to its owners, individuals have to include dividends in their income when they complete their personal tax returns, at which point a second layer of income tax is imposed.

3. In most countries, there are laws which treat small corporations differently from large ones. They may be exempt from certain legal filing requirements or labor laws, have simplified procedures in specialized areas, and have simplified, advantageous, or slightly different tax treatment.

4. 「Going public」 through a process known as an initial public offering (IPO) means that part of the business will be owned by members of the public. This requires organization as a distinct entity, and compliance with a tighter set of laws and procedures. Most public entities are corporations that have sold shares, but increasingly there are also public LLCs that sell units (sometimes also called shares). A general partnership cannot 「go public.」

Capital may be raised through private means, by aninitial public offering or IPO on a stock exchange, or in other ways.

Businesses that have gone public are subject to regulations concerning their internal governance, such as how executive officers' compensation is determined, and when and how information is disclosed to shareholders and to the public. In the United States, these regulations are primarily implemented and enforced by the United States Securities and Exchange Commission (SEC). Other Western nations have comparable regulatory bodies. The regulations are implemented and enforced by the China Securities Regulation Commission (CSRC) in China. In Singapore, the regulation authority is the Monetary Authority of Singapore (MAS), and in Hong Kong, it is the Securities and Futures Commission (SFC). Major stock exchanges include the Shanghai Stock Exchange, Singapore Exchange, Hong Kong Stock Exchange, New York Stock Exchange and Nasdaq (USA), the London Stock Exchange (UK), the Tokyo

Stock Exchange (Japan), and Bombay Stock Exchange (India). Most countries with capital markets have at least one.

Strategic Management

Strategy is defined as 「the determination of the basic long-term goals of an enterprise, and the adoption of courses of action and the allocation of resources necessary for carrying out these goals.」 Strategies are established to set direction, focus effort, define or clarify the organization, and provide consistency or guidance in response to the environment.

Corporate strategy involves answering a key question from a portfolio perspective: 「What business should we be in?」 Business strategy involves answering the question: 「How shall we compete in this business?」 In management theory and practice, a further distinction is often made between strategic management and operational management. Operational management is concerned primarily with improving efficiency and controlling costs within the boundaries set by the organization's strategy.

Strategic management involves the formulation and implementation of the major goals and initiatives taken by a company's top management on behalf of owners, based on consideration of resources and an assessment of the internal and external environments in which the organization competes.

Strategic management provides overall direction to the enterprise and involves specifying the organization's objectives, developing policies and plans designed to achieve these objectives, and then allocating resources to implement the plans. Strategic management is not static in nature; the models often include a feedback loop to monitor execution and inform the next round of planning.

Strategic management involves the related concepts of strategic planning and strategic thinking. Strategic planning is analytical in nature and refers to formalized procedures to produce the data and analyses used as inputs for strategic thinking, which synthesizes the data resulting in the strategy.

Strategic planning may also refer to control mechanisms used to implement the strategy once it is determined. In other words, strategic planning happens *around* the strategic thinking or strategy making activity.

Strategic thinking involves the generation and application of unique business insights to opportunities intended to create competitive advantage for a firm or organization. It involves challenging the assumptions underlying the organization's strategy and value proposition. It is more about synthesis (i.e. 「connecting the dots」) than analysis (i.e. 「finding the dots」), capturing what the manager learns from all sources (both the soft insights from his or her personal experiences and the experiences of others throughout the organization and the hard data from market research and the like) and then synthesizing that learning into a vision of the direction that the business should pursue. Strategic thinking is the critical part of formulating strategy, more so than strategic planning exercises.

Strategic management is often described as involving two major processes: formulation and implementation of strategy. The two processes are iterative and each provides input for the other.

Formulation of strategy involves analyzing the environment in which the organization operates, then making a series of strategic decisions about how the organization will compete. Formulation ends with a series of goals or objectives and measures for the organization to pursue.

Implementation involves decisions regarding how the organization's resources (i.e. people, process and IT systems) will be aligned and mobilized towards the objectives. Implementation results in how the organization's resources are structured, leadership arrangements, communication, incentives, and monitoring mechanisms to track progress towards objectives, among others.

Running the day-to-day operations of the business is often referred to as 「operations management」 or specific terms for key departments or functions, such as 「logistics management」 or 「marketing management,」 which take over once strategic management decisions are implemented.

SWOT Analysis

By the 1960s, the business policy course at the Harvard Business School included the concept of matching the distinctive competence of a company (its strengths and weaknesses) with its environment (opportunities and threats) in the context of its objectives. This framework came to be known by the acronym SWOT and was 「a major step forward in bringing explicitly competitive thinking to bear on questions of strategy.」

A SWOT analysis is an organized design method used to evaluate the strengths, weaknesses, opportunities and threats complex within the person or the group or the organization where the functional process takes place.

SWOT analysis involves both internal and external factors in an organization. such that the first two elements indicate internal capability and limitations while the last two factors indicate chances in business and limitations. (SW = strength and weakness are internal factors while OT = Opportunities and threats are external issues to a business).

A SWOT analysis, with its four elements in a 2×2 matrix.

Glossary

Part I

agribusiness　n. 農業綜合企業
proprietorship　n. 所有權
jurisdiction　n. 管轄權，權利
prevalent　adj. 普遍的，流行的
maladaptive　adj. 適應不良的，不適應的
deliverables　n. 可交付的成果
conscientiousness　n. 盡責，憑良心辦事
predominantly　adv. 主要地
contingent　adj. 不一定的，偶發的
interdependent　adj. 相互依賴的
counterintuitive　adj. 違法直覺的
interplay　n. 相互作用，相互影響
hierarchy　n. 層級，等級制度
metamotivation　n. 衍生動機
physiological　adj. 生理的
metabolic　adj. 變化的，新陳代謝的
manifest　v. 證明，表明
cling　v. 堅持，附著
confidant　n. 知己，密友
susceptible　adj. 易受影響的，易感動的
inferiority　n. 自卑，下屬，次等
biographical　adj. 傳記的
aptitude　n. 天資，才能
psychometrics　n. 心理測驗學
pertain　v. 屬於，關於
psychomotor　adj. 精神運動的
predispose　v. 預先處置，傾向
homogeneous　adj. 同質的，均勻的
fledged　adj. 成熟的，快會飛的
courtesy　n. 禮貌，恩惠
virtue　n. 美德，優點
institutionalize　v. 使成為慣例
autonomy　n. 自治權
disseminate　v. 宣傳，傳播
absenteeism　n. 曠工

consensus   n. 一致，輿論，合議
vigor   n. 活力，精力
board of directors   董事會
collective value   集體價值
behaviorally anchored   行為錨定

Part Ⅱ

school   n. 流派
accrue   v. 產生，累積
agrarian   adj. 土地的，耕地的
blemish   n. 瑕疵，污點
attributable   adj. 可歸於……的，可歸屬的
approximately   adv. 大約地，近似地
essence   n. 本質，實質，精華
tactical   adj. 戰術的，策略的
endeavor   n. 努力，盡力
constraint   n. 約束，局促
telecommute   v.（利用電腦終端機）遠距離工作
tactile   adj. 觸覺的
automated   adj. 自動化的，機械化的
synchronizing   v. 同步，整步
mainframe   n. 主機，大型機
collectivist economy   集體主義經濟
stereo microscope   立體顯微鏡
military science   兵法
cost effective   有成本效益的，劃算的

Part Ⅲ

disburse   v. 支付，支出
gauge   v. 測量，估計
stem   v. 阻止
denote   v. 表示，指示
promptness   n. 機敏，敏捷
entice   v. 誘使，慫恿
strand   n. 線，串
affinity   n. 密切關係，吸引力

tailor　v. 使合適
moviegoer　n. 常看電影的人
imperative　adj. 必要的，不可避免的
compelling　adj. 引人注目的，激發興趣的
exemplify　v. 例證，例示
tagline　n. 標語，品牌口號
demeanor　n. 風度，舉止，行為
testimonial　n. 證明書，推薦書
parcel　n. 包裹，小包
conglomerate　n. 企業集團，聚合物
jumpstart　v. 安裝，引進
sweepstake　n. 賭金的獨得，彩票
signage　n. 引導標示
initial public offering　首次公開募股
product placement　產品置入，植入式廣告

PartI V

disclosure　n. 披露，揭發
compliance　n. 順從，服從
shielded　adj. 隔離的，屏蔽了的
misconduct　n. 不端行為，處理不當
impose　v. 強加，徵稅
advantageous　adj. 有利的，有益的
initiative　n. 主動權，首創精神，新方案
pre-ordinate　adj. 預定的，預先的
proposition　n. 命題，提議，主題
iterative　adj. 反復的，重複的
competence　n. 能力
collaborative　adj. 合作的，協作的
acronym　n. 首字母縮寫字
elimination　n. 淘汰，消除
strained　adj. 緊張的
flaw　n. 缺點，瑕疵
confidential　adj. 機密的，表示信任的，
unsavory　adj. 難吃的，沒有香味的

Phrases

be in line with　與……一致，和……符合

in the shape of 以……的形式，呈……的形狀
be susceptible to 對……敏感，易患……，易受……影響
screen out 篩選出，淘汰，屏蔽
slack off 偷懶，懈怠
be fueled by 由……刺激引起
put forth 提出，發表
act on 作用於，按照……行事
call for 要求
be concerned with 參與，干預，關心
roll out 鋪開，推出
be drawn to 被---所吸引，考慮，應提請
draw in 引誘，吸引
weigh up 權衡，估量
fall under 受到（影響等），被歸入
be resistant to 對……有抵抗力的
be exempt from 被免除於
be enforced by 被執行，被推動

Notes

Collective Economy：集體經濟，屬於勞動群眾集體所有、實行共同勞動、在分配方式上以按勞分配為主體的社會主義經濟組織。在中國，集體經濟是公有制經濟的重要組成部分，分為農村集體經濟與城鎮集體經濟。農村集體經濟實行鄉鎮、行政村、村民小組的三級所有，土地、林木、水利設施等為集體所有，農民蓋房的宅基地為無償劃撥。城鎮集體經濟又分為「大集體」與「小集體」，其中「大集體」企業受政府行業管理部門領導，參照全民所有制企業的管理與員工待遇；「小集體」為自負盈虧自主經營。勞動者集體所有是指按勞動者的人數平均、共同所有。

Return on Assets：資產回報率，公式為：資產回報率＝稅後淨利潤/總資產。它是用來衡量每單位資產創造多少淨利潤的指標。評估公司相對其總資產值的盈利能力的有用指標。計算的方法為公司的年度盈利除以總資產值，資產回報率一般以百分比表示。有時也稱為投資回報率。

Basel Accords：巴塞爾協議，是巴塞爾委員會制定的在全球範圍內主要的銀行資本和風險監管標準。巴塞爾委員會由來自13個國家的銀行監管當局組成，是國際清算銀行的四個常務委員會之一。由巴塞爾委員會公布的準則規定的資本要求被稱為以風險為基礎的資本要求。1988年7月，頒布第一個準則文件，稱「1988資本一致方針」，又稱「巴塞爾協議」。主要目的是建立防止信用風險的最低資本要求。1996年，巴塞爾協議I作了修正，擴大了範圍，包括了基於市場風險的以風險為基礎的資本要求。1998年，巴塞爾委員會討論了操作風險作為潛在金融風險的重要性，並在2001年公布了許多準則和報告來解決操作風險。2004年6月，頒布新的資本要求準則，稱「巴塞爾協議」。巴塞爾協議的三個支柱包括：最低風險資本要求、資本充足率監管和內部評估過程的市場監管。

EPG：全稱 Electronic Program Guide，即電子節目指南。IPTV 所提供的各種業務的索引及導航都是通過 EPG 系統來完成的。IPTV EPG 實際上就是 IPTV 的一個門戶系統。EPG 系統的界面與 Web 頁面類似，在 EPG 界面上一般都提供各類菜單、按鈕、連結等可供用戶選擇節目時直接點擊的組件；EPG 的界面上也可以包含各類供用戶瀏覽的動態或靜態的多媒體內容。

Questions

1. What is the fundamental factor of training program?

2. What are the basic factors of production? What other factors do people nowadays recommend?

3. Why have many ISO-certified companies achieved better business performance?

4. How does a company analyze its market environment, or what elements are needed to be considered?

5. Give some examples of applications of umbrella branding in the market.

6. What business goals should global advertisers need to consider?

7. What are the advantages of limited liability companies?

8. Form a group of four, choose an organization and use SWOT Analysis to evaluate its competence and weakness.

Chapter IV

Trade and International Agreement

Trade involves the transfer of the ownership of goods or services from one person or entity to another in exchange for other goods or services or for money. Trade includes 「commerce」 and 「financial transaction」.

The original form of trade, barter, saw the direct exchange of goods and services for other goods and services. Later one side of the barter started to involve precious metals, which gained symbolic as well as practical importance. Modern traders generally negotiate through a medium of exchange, such as money. As a result, buying can be separated from selling, or earning. The invention of money greatly simplified and promoted trade. Trade between two traders is called bilateral trade, while trade between more than two traders is called multilateral trade.

Trade exists due to the specialization and division of labor, in which most people concentrate on a small aspect of production, trading for other products. Trade exists between regions because different regions may have a comparative advantage in the production of some tradeable commodity, or because different regions' size may encourage mass production. As such, trade at market prices between locations can benefit both locations.

Retail trade consists of the sale of goods or merchandise from a very fixed location, such as a department store, boutique or kiosk, online or by mail, in small or individual lots for direct consumption or use by the purchaser. Wholesale trade is defined as the sale of goods that are sold as merchandise to retailers, and/or industrial, commercial, institutional, or other professional business users, or to other wholesalers and related subordinated services.

Trading is a value-added function: it is the economic process by which a product finds its end user, in which specific risks are borne by the trader.

Trading can also refer to the action performed by traders and other market agents in the financial markets.

International trade is, in principle, not different from domestic trade as the motivation and the behavior of parties involved in a trade do not change fundamentally regardless of whether trade is across a border or not. The main difference is that international trade is typically more costly than domestic trade. This is due to the fact that a border typically imposes additional costs such as tariffs, time costs due to border delays, and costs associated with country differences such as language, the legal system, or culture.

Another difference between domestic and international trade is that factors of production such as capital and labor are typically more mobile within a country than across countries. Thus, international trade is mostly restricted to trade in goods and services, and only to a lesser extent to trade in capital, labor, or other factors of production. Trade in goods and services can serve as a substitute for trade in factors of production. Instead of importing a factor of production, a country can import goods that make intensive use of that factor of production and thus embody it. An example of this is the import of labor-intensive goods by the United States from China. Instead of importing Chinese labor, the United States imports goods that were produced with Chinese labor.

Part I Products, Goods, Commodities and International Trade

A product can be classified as to be tangible and intangible. A tangible product is a physical object that can be perceived by touch such as a building, vehicle, gadget, or clothing. An intangible product is a product that can only be perceived indirectly such as an insurance policy.

A third type in this is services. Services can be broadly classified under intangible products which can be durable or non durable. Services need high quality control, precision and adaptability. The main factor about services as a type of product is that it will not be uniform and will vary according to who is performing, where it is performed and on whom/what it is being performed.

In retailing, products are called *merchandise*. In manufacturing, products are bought as raw materials and sold as finished goods. In project management, products are the formal definition of the project deliverables that make up or contribute to delivering the objectives of the project. In insurance, the policies are considered products offered for sale by the insurance company that created the contract. In economics and commerce, products belong to a broader category of goods.

Goods, both tangibles and intangibles, may involve the transfer of product ownership to the consumer. Services do not normally involve transfer of ownership of the service itself, but may involve transfer of ownership of goods developed by a service provider in the course of the service. For example, distributing electricity among consumers is a service provided by an electric utility company. This service can only be experienced through the consumption of electrical energy, which is available in a variety of voltages and, in this case, is the *economic goods* produced by the electric utility company. While the service (namely, distribution of electrical energy) is a process that remains in its entirety in the ownership of the electric service provider, the goods (namely, electric energy) is the object of ownership transfer. The consumer becomes electric energy owner by purchase and may use it for any lawful purposes just like any other goods.

The word cargo refers in particular to goods or produce being conveyed-generally for commercial gain-by ship, boat, or aircraft, although the term is now often extended to cover all types of freight, including that carried by train, van, truck, or intermodal container.

Commodities are usually raw materials such as metals and agricultural products, but a commodity can also be anything widely available in the open market. In economics, a commodity is a marketable item produced to satisfy wants or needs. Economic commodities comprise goods and services.

The exact definition of the term commodity is specifically used to describe a class of goods for which there is demand, but which is supplied without qualitative differentiation across a market. That is, the market treats its instances as equivalent or nearly so with no regard to who produced them. As the saying goes, ⌈From the taste of wheat, it is not possible to tell who produced it, a Russian serf, a French peasant or an English capitalist.⌋ Petroleum and copper are other examples of such commodities, their supply and demand being a part of one universal market. Items such as stereo systems, on the other hand, have many aspects of product differentiation, such as the brand, the user interface and the perceived quality. The demand for one type of stereo may be much larger than demand for another.

In contrast, one of the characteristics of a commodity is that its price is determined as a function of its market as a whole. Well-established physical commodities have actively traded spot and derivative markets. Generally, these are basic resources and agricultural products such as iron ore, crude oil, coal, salt, sugar, tea, coffee, beans, soybeans, aluminum, copper, rice, wheat, gold, silver, palladium, and platinum. Soft commodities are goods that are grown, while hard commodities are ones that are extracted through mining.

There is another important class of energy commodities which includes electricity, gas, coal and oil. Electricity has the particular characteristic that it is usually uneconomical to store; hence, electricity must be consumed as soon as it is produced.

International trade is the exchange of goods and services across national borders or territories. In most countries, it represents a significant part of GDP. While international trade has been present throughout much of history, its economic, social, and political importance have increased in recent centuries, mainly because of Industrialization, advanced transportation, globalization, multinational corporations, and outsourcing.

Trading globally gives consumers and countries the opportunity to be exposed to new markets and products. Almost every kind of product can be found in the international market: food, clothes, spare parts, oil, jewelry, wine, stocks, currencies, and water. Services are also traded: tourism, banking, consulting, and transportation.

An absolute trade advantage exists when countries can produce a commodity with less costs per unit produced than could its trading partner. By the same reasoning, it should import commodities in which it has an absolute disadvantage. While there are possible gains from trade with absolute advantage, comparative advantage-that is, the ability to offer goods and services at a lower marginal and opportunity cost-extends the range of possible mutually beneficial exchanges. In a globalized business environment, companies argue that the comparative advantages offered by international trade have become essential to remaining competitive.

Increasing international trade is crucial to the continuance of globalization. Nations would be limited to the goods and services produced within their own borders without international trade.

Empirical evidence for the success of trade can be seen in the contrast between countries such as South Korea, which adopted a policy of export-oriented industrialization, and India, which historically had a more closed policy. South Korea has done much better by economic criteria than India over the past fifty years, though its success also has to do with effective state institutions.

Import and Export

A product that is transferred or sold from a party in one country to a party in another country is an export from the originating country, and an import to the country receiving that product. Imports and exports are accounted for in a country's current account in the balance of payments.

An import is a good brought into a jurisdiction, especially across a national border, from an external source. The party bringing in the good is called an *importer*. The term export means shipping the goods and services out of the port of a country. The seller of such goods and services is referred to as an 「exporter」.

In international trade, the importation and exportation of goods are limited by import quotas and mandates from the customs authority. The importing and exporting jurisdictions may impose a tariff (tax) on the goods. In addition, the importation and exportation of goods are subject to trade agreements between the importing and exporting jurisdictions.

The advent of small trades over the internet such as through Amazon and eBay has largely bypassed the involvement of Customs in many countries because of the low individual values of these trades. Nonetheless, these small exports are still subject to legal restrictions applied by the country of export or import.

Customs

Customs is an authority or agency in a country responsible for collecting tariffs and for controlling the flow of goods, including animals, transports, personal effects, and hazardous items, into and out of a country. The movement of people into and out of a country is normally monitored by immigration authorities, under a variety of names and arrangements. The immigration authorities normally check for appropriate documentation, verify that a person is entitled to enter the country, apprehend people wanted by domestic or international arrest warrants, and impede the entry of people deemed dangerous to the country.

Each country has its own laws and regulations for the import and export of goods into and out of a country, which its customs authority enforces. The import or export of some goods may be restricted or forbidden. In most countries, customs are attained through government agreements and international laws. A customs duty is a tariff or tax on the importation (usually) or exportation (unusually) of goods. Commercial goods not yet cleared through customs are held in a customs area, often called a bonded store, until processed. All authorized ports are recognized customs areas.

Tariff

A tariff is a tax placed on a specific good or set of goods exported from or imported to a country, creating an economic barrier to trade.

Usually the tactic is used when a country's domestic output of the good is falling and imports from foreign competitors are rising, particularly if there exist strategic reasons for retaining a domestic production capability.

Some failing industries receive a protection with an effect similar to a subsidies in that by placing the tariff on the industry, the industry is less enticed to produce goods in a quicker, cheaper, and more productive fashion. The third reason for a tariff involves addressing the issue of dumping. Dumping involves a country producing highly excessive amounts of goods and dumping the goods on another foreign country, producing the effect of prices that are 「too low」. Too low can refer to either pricing the goods from the foreign market at a price lower than charged in the domestic market of the country of origin. The other reference to dumping relates or refers to the producer selling the product at a price in which there is no profit or a loss. The purpose of the tariff is to encourage spending on domestic goods and services. Protective tariffs sometimes protect what are known as infant industries that are in the phase of expansive growth. A tariff is used temporarily to allow the industry to succeed in spite of strong competition. Protective tariffs are considered valid if the resources are more productive in their new use than they would be if the industry had not been started. The infant industry eventually must incorporate itself into a market without the protection of government subsidies. Tariffs can create tension between countries. Such tariffs usually lead to filing a complaint with the World Trade Organization (WTO) and, if that fails, could eventually head toward the country placing a tariff against the other nation in spite, to impress pressure to remove the tariff.

Evasion of customs duties takes place mainly in two ways. In one, the trader under-declares the value so that the assessable value is lower than actual. In a similar vein, a trader can evade customs duty by understatement of quantity or volume of the product of trade. Evasion of customs duty may take place with or without the collaboration of customs officials. Evasion of customs duty does not necessarily constitute smuggling.

Duty-free goods

Many countries allow a traveler to bring goods into the country duty-free. These goods may be bought at ports and airports or sometimes within one country without attracting the usual government taxes and then brought into another country duty-free. Some countries impose allowances which limit the number or value of duty-free items that one person can bring into the country. These restrictions often apply to tobacco, wine, spirits, cosmetics, gifts and souvenirs. Often foreign diplomats and UN officials are entitled to duty-free goods. Duty-free goods are imported and stocked in what is called a bonded warehouse.

Balance of Trade

In International Trade, purchase and sale are replaced by imports and exports. Balance of

Trade is simply the difference between the value of exports and value of imports. Thus, the Balance of Trade denotes the differences of imports and exports of a merchandise of a country during the course of year. It indicates the value of exports and imports of the country in question. If the value of its exports over a period exceeds its value of imports, it is called favourable balance of trade, also known as positive balance or trade surplus, conversely, if the value of total imports exceeds the total value of exports over a period, it is unfavourable balance of trade, also known as negative balance or trade deficit. The favorable balance of trade indicates good economic condition of the country.

Factors that can affect the balance of trade include:

- The cost of production (land, labor, capital, taxes, incentives, etc.) in the exporting economy vise verse those in the importing economy;
- The cost and availability of raw materials, intermediate goods and other inputs;
- Exchange rate movements;
- Multilateral, bilateral and unilateral taxes or restrictions on trade;
- Non-tariff barriers such as environmental, health or safety standards;
- The availability of adequate foreign exchange with which to pay for imports; and
- Prices of goods manufactured at home (influenced by the responsiveness of supply)

In addition, the trade balance is likely to differ across the business cycle. In export-led growth (such as oil and early industrial goods), the balance of trade will improve during an economic expansion. However, with domestic demand led growth (as in the United States and Australia) the trade balance will worsen at the same stage in the business cycle.

Economies such as Japan and Germany, which have savings surpluses, typically run trade surpluses. China, a high-growth economy, has tended to run trade surpluses. A higher savings rate generally corresponds to a trade surplus. Correspondingly, the U.S. with its lower savings rate has tended to run high trade deficits, especially with Asian nations.

Annual trade surpluses are immediate and direct additions to their nations' GDPs while annual trade deficits are the reducers. Small trade deficits are generally not considered to be harmful to either the importing or exporting economy. However, when a national trade imbalance expands beyond prudence (generally thought to be several percent of GDP, for several years), adjustments tend to occur.

A country may rebalance the trade deficit by use of quantitative easing at home. This involves a central bank printing money and making it available to other domestic financial institutions at small interest rates, which increases the money supply in the home economy. Inflation usually results, which devalues in real terms the debt owed to foreign creditors if that debt was instantiated in the home currency.

When an economy is unable to export enough physical goods to pay for its physical imports, it may be able to find funds elsewhere: service exports, for example, are more than sufficient to pay for Hong Kong's domestic goods import. In poor countries, foreign aid may compensate, while in developed economies a capital account surplus caused by sales of assets often offsets a current-account deficit. There are some economies where transfers from nationals working abroad contribute significantly to paying for imports. The Philippines, Bangladesh and Mexico are examples of transfer-rich economies.

While unsustainable imbalances may persist for long periods, the distortions likely to be caused by large flows of wealth out of one economy and into another tend to become intolerable.

Barriers and Protectionism

Trade barriers are generally defined as government laws, regulations, policy, or practices that either protect domestic products from foreign competition or artificially stimulate exports of particular domestic products. While restrictive business practices sometimes have a similar effect, they are not usually regarded as trade barriers. The most common foreign trade barriers are government-imposed measures and policies that restrict, prevent, or impede the international exchange of goods and services.

The barriers can take many forms, including tariffs and non-tariff barriers (NTB) to trade.

Tariff barriers restrict exports while NTBs restrict imports. Non-tariff barriers to trade include import quotas, special licenses, unreasonable standards for the quality of goods, bureaucratic delays at customs, export restrictions, limiting the activities of state trading, export subsidies, countervailing duties, technical barriers to trade, sanitary measures, rules of origin, etc. Sometimes in this list they include macroeconomic measures affecting trade.

Licenses

The most common instruments of direct regulation of imports (and sometimes export) are licenses and quotas. Almost all industrialized countries apply these non-tariff methods. The license system requires that a state (through specially authorized office) issues permits for foreign trade transactions of import and export commodities included in the lists of licensed merchandises. Product licensing can take many forms and procedures. The main types of licenses are general license that permits unrestricted importation or exportation of goods included in the lists for a certain period of time; and one-time license for a certain product importer (exporter) to import (or export). One-time license indicates a quantity of goods, its cost, its country of origin (or destination), and in some cases also customs point through which import (or export) of goods should be carried out. The use of licensing systems as an instrument for foreign trade regulation is based on a number of international level standards agreements. In particular, these agreements include some provisions of the General Agreement on Tariffs and Trade and the Agreement on Import Licensing Procedures, concluded under the WTO.

Quotas

Licensing of foreign trade is closely related to quantitative restrictions-quotas-on imports and exports of certain goods. A quota is a limitation in value or in physical terms, imposed on import and export of certain goods for a certain period of time. This category includes global quotas in respect to specific countries, seasonal quotas, and so-called「voluntary」export restraints. Quantitative controls on foreign trade transactions carried out through one-time license.

Quantitative restriction on imports and exports is a direct administrative form of government regulation of foreign trade. Licenses and quotas limit the independence of enterprises with a regard to entering foreign markets, narrowing the range of countries, which may be entered into transaction for certain commodities, regulate the number and range of goods permitted for import and export. However, the system of licensing and quota imports and exports, establishing firm control over foreign trade in certain goods, in many cases turns out to be more flexible and effective than economic instruments of foreign trade regulation. This can be explained by the fact, that licensing and quota systems are an important instrument of trade regulation of the vast majority of the world.

The consequence of this trade barrier is normally reflected in the consumers' loss because of higher prices and limited selection of goods as well as in the companies that employ the imported materials in the production process, increasing their costs. An import quota can be unilateral, levied by the country without negotiations with exporting country, and bilateral or multilateral, when it is imposed after negotiations and agreement with exporting country. An export quota is a restricted amount of goods that can leave the country. There are different reasons for imposing of export quota by the country, which can be the guarantee of the supply of the products that are in shortage in the domestic market, manipulation of the prices on the international level, and the control of goods strategically important for the country. In some cases, the importing countries request exporting countries to impose voluntary export restraints.

Embargo

Embargo is a specific type of quotas prohibiting the trade. As well as quotas, embargoes may be imposed on imports or exports of particular goods, regardless of destination, in respect of certain goods supplied to specific countries, or in respect of all goods shipped to certain countries. Although the embargo is usually introduced for political purposes, the consequences, in essence, could be economic.

Standards

Standards take a special place among non-tariff barriers. Countries usually impose standards on classification, labeling and testing of products in order to be able to sell domestic products, but also to block sales of products of foreign manufacture. These standards are sometimes entered under the pretext of protecting the safety and health of local populations.

Import deposits

Another example of foreign trade regulations is import deposits. Import deposits is a form of deposit, which the importer must pay the bank for a definite period of time (non-interest bearing deposit) in an amount equal to all or part of the cost of imported goods.

Foreign exchange restrictions

Foreign exchange restrictions and foreign exchange controls occupy a special place among the non-tariff regulatory instruments of foreign economic activity. Foreign exchange restrictions constitute the regulation of transactions of residents and nonresidents with currency and other currency values. Also an important part of the mechanism of control of foreign economic activity is the establishment of the national currency against foreign currencies.

Among the methods of non-tariff regulation should be mentioned administrative and bureaucratic delays at the entrance, which increase uncertainty and the cost of maintaining inventory.

Protectionism

In modern trade arena, trade barriers are identical to protectionism, which is the economic policy of restraining trade between states (countries) through methods such as tariffs on imported goods, restrictive quotas, and a variety of other government regulations designed to allow fair competition between imports and goods and services produced domestically.

This policy contrasts with free trade, where government barriers to trade are kept to a minimum. In recent years, protectionism has become closely aligned with anti-globalization and anti-immigration.

Since the end of World War II, it has been the stated policy of most First World countries to eliminate protectionism through free trade policies enforced by international treaties and organizations such as the World Trade Organization. However, certain policies of First World governments have been criticized as protectionist, such as the Common Agricultural Policy in the European Union, long standing agricultural subsidies and proposed 「Buy American」 provisions in economic recovery packages in the United States.

There is a broad consensus among economists that the impact of protectionism on economic growth (and on economic welfare in general) is largely negative. Heads of the G20 meeting in London on 2 April 2009 pledged 「We will not repeat the historic mistakes of protectionism of previous eras」. Adherence to this pledge is monitored by the Global Trade Alert, providing up-to-date information and informed commentary to help ensure that the G20 pledge is met by maintaining confidence in the world trading system.

Part Ⅱ   Shipment, Insurance and Payment

The term shipment originally referred to transport by sea, but is extended in American English to refer to transport by land or air as well. 「Logistics」, a term borrowed from the military environment, is also fashionably used in the same sense.

Modes of Shipment

Ground

Land or 「ground」 shipping can be by train or by truck (International English: lorry). In air and sea shipments, ground transport is required to take the cargo from its place of origin to the airport or seaport and then to its destination because it is not always possible to establish a production facility near ports due to limited coastlines of countries. Ground transport is typically more affordable than air, but more expensive than sea especially in developing countries like India, where inland infrastructure is not efficient.

Shipment of cargo by trucks, directly from the shipper's place to the destination, is known as a door to door shipment and more formally as multimodal transport. Trucks and trains make deliveries to sea and air ports where cargo is moved in bulk.

Rail Transport

Rail transport is a means of conveyance of passengers and goods, by way of wheeled vehicles running on rails. It is also commonly referred to as train transport. Freight cars (carriages and wagons) can be coupled into longer trains. The operation is carried out by a railway company, providing transport between train stations or freight customer facilities. Railways are a safe land transport system when compared to other forms of transport. Railway transport is capable of high levels of passenger and cargo utilization and energy efficiency, but is often less flexible and more capital-intensive than highway transport is, when lower traffic levels are considered.

Ship

Much shipping is done by actual ships. An individual nation's fleet and the people that crew it are referred to as its merchant navy or merchant marine. Merchant shipping is the lifeblood of the world economy, carrying 90% of international trade with 102, 194 commercial ships worldwide. On rivers and canals, barges are often used to carry bulk cargo.

Air

Cargo was transported by air in specialized cargo aircraft and in the luggage compartments of passenger aircraft. Air freight is typically the fastest mode for long distance freight transport, but also the most expensive.

Intermodal

Intermodal freight transport refers to shipments that involve more than one mode. More specifically it usually refers to the use of intermodal shipping containers that are easily transferred between ship, rail and truck.

Terms of Shipment

Common trading terms used in shipping goods internationally include:

· Free on board (FOB) —the exporter delivers the goods at the specified location (and on board the vessel). Costs paid by the exporter include load, lash, secure and stow the cargo, including securing cargo not to move in the ships hold, protecting the cargo from contact with the double bottom to prevent slipping, and protection against damage from condensation. For example, 「FOB shanghai」 means that the exporter delivers the goods to the Shanghai Port, China, and pays for the cargo to be loaded and secured on the ship. This term also declares that where the responsibility of shipper ends and that of buyer starts. The exporter is bound to deliver the goods at his cost and expense. In this case, the freight and other expenses for outbound traffic are borne by the importer.

· Carriage and freight (now known in the US as 「cost and freight」) (C&F, CFR, CNF): Insurance is payable by the importer, and the exporter pays all expenses incurred in transporting the cargo from its place of origin to the port/airport and ocean freight/air freight to the port/airport of destination. For example, 「C&F Los Angeles」 means that the exporter pays the ocean shipping/air freight costs to Los Angeles. Most of the governments ask their exporters to trade on these terms to promote their exports worldwide such as India and China. Many of the shipping carriers (such as UPS, DHL, FedEx) offer guarantees on their delivery times. These are known as GSR guarantees or 「guaranteed service refunds」; if the parcels are not delivered on time, the customer is entitled to a refund.

· Carriage, insurance and freight (now known in the US as 「cost, insurance and freight」) (CIF): Insurance and freight are all paid by the exporter to the specified location. For example, at CIF Los Angeles, the exporter pays the ocean shipping/air freight costs to Los Angeles including the insurance of cargo. This also states that responsibility of the shipper ends at the Los Angeles port.

Containerization

Containerization is a system of intermodal freight transport using intermodal containers (also called shipping containers and ISO containers) made of weathering steel. The containers have standardized dimensions. They can be loaded and unloaded, stacked, transported efficiently over long distances, and transferred from one mode of transport to another—container ships, rail transport flatcars, and semi-trailer trucks—without being opened. The handling system is completely mechanized so that all handling is done with cranes and special forklift trucks. All containers are numbered and tracked using computerized systems.

The system, developed after World War II, dramatically reduced transport costs, supported the post-war boom in international trade, and was a major element in globalization. Containerization did away with the manual sorting of most shipments and the need for warehousing. It displaced many thousands of dock workers and reduced congestion in ports, significantly shortened shipping time and reduced losses from damage and theft.

Before containerization, goods were usually handled manually as break bulk cargo. Typically, goods would be loaded onto a vehicle from the factory and taken to a port warehouse where they would be offloaded and stored awaiting the next vessel. When the vessel arrived, they would be moved to the side of the ship along with other cargo to be lowered or carried into the hold and packed by dock workers. The ship might call at several other ports before off-loading a given consignment of cargo. Each port visit would delay the delivery of other cargo. Delivered cargo might then have been offloaded into another warehouse before being picked up and delivered to its destination. Multiple handling and delays made transport costly, time consuming and unreliable.

There are five common ISO container standard lengths: 20 ft (6.10 m), 40 ft (12.19 m), 45 ft (13.72 m), 48 ft (14.63 m), and 53 ft (16.15 m). Container capacity is often expressed in twenty-foot equivalent units (TEU). An equivalent unit is a measure of containerized cargo capacity equal to one standard 20 ft (6.10 m) (length) × 8 ft (2.44 m) (width) container. As this is an approximate measure, the height of the box is not considered.

The maximum gross mass for a 20 ft (6.10 m) dry cargo container is 24,000 kg (53,000 lb), and for a 40 ft (12.19 m) container it is 30,480 kg (67,200 lb).

Air freight containers

While major airlines use containers that are custom designed for their aircraft and associated ground handling equipment the IATA (International Air Transport Association) has created a set of standard aluminium container sizes of up to 11.52 m^3 (407 cu ft) in volume.

Container Loading

Full container load

A full container load (FCL) is an ISO standard container that is loaded and unloaded under the risk and account of one shipper and only one consignee. In practice, it means that the whole container is intended for one consignee. FCL container shipment tends to have lower freight rates than an equivalent weight of cargo in bulk. FCL is intended to designate a container loaded to its allowable maximum weight or volume, but FCL in practice on ocean freight does not always mean a full payload or capacity-many companies will prefer to keep a 「mostly」 full container as a single container load to simplify logistics and increase security compared to sharing a container with other goods.

Less-than-container load

Less-than-container load (LCL) is a shipment that is not large enough to fill a standard cargo container. The abbreviation LCL formerly applied to 「less than (railway) car load」 for quantities of material from different shippers or for delivery to different destinations carried in a single railway car for efficiency. LCL freight was often sorted and redistributed into different railway cars at intermediate railway terminals en route to the final destination.

LCL is 「a quantity of cargo less than that required for the application of a carload rate. A quantity of cargo less than that fills the visible or rated capacity of an inter-modal container.」 It can also be defined as 「a consignment of cargo which is inefficient to fill a shipping container. It is grouped with other consignments for the same destination in a container at a container freight station」.

Counter-to-counter Package

In the airline and some other transportation industries, a counter-to-counter package is a quicker (and more expensive) alternative to standard freight for the shipment of small parcels and envelopes. These shipments have size, weight, and content restrictions, and usually may be dropped off and picked up at a ticket counter, luggage service or freight office.

Additional security regulations put into place after September 11, 2001 have eliminated anonymous counter-to-counter shipments. Entities wishing to ship must register to become a known shipper according to the specific directives of the Federal Aviation Administration and the Transportation Security Administration.

Pick and Pack

Pick and pack is a parts of a complete supply chain management process that is commonly used in the retail distribution of goods. It entails processing small to large quantities of product, often truck or train loads and disassembling them, picking the relevant product for each destination and re-packaging with shipping label affixed and invoice included. Usual service includes obtaining a fair rate of shipping from common as well as expediting truck carriers.

Pick and Pack services are offered by many businesses that specialize in supply chain management solutions.

Case picking is the gathering of full cartons or boxes of product. This is often done on a pallet. In the consumer products industry, case picking large quantities of cartons is often an entry level employee's task. There is, however, significant skill required to make a good pallet load of product. Key requirements are that cartons not be damaged, they make good use of the available cube (space) and be quick to assemble.

Warehouse management system products create pick paths to minimize the travel distance of an order selector, but often neglect the need to maximize the use of cube, segregate products that should not touch or minimize damage.

Insurance and Claims

Insurance is the equitable transfer of the risk of a loss, from one entity to another in exchange for payment. It is a form of risk management primarily used to hedge against the risk of a contingent, uncertain loss. An insurer, or insurance carrier, is selling the insurance; the insured, or policyholder, is the person or entity buying the insurance policy. The amount of money to be charged for a certain amount of insurance coverage is called the premium.

The transaction involves the insured assuming a guaranteed and known relatively small loss in the form of payment to the insurer in exchange for the insurer's promise to compensate (indemnify) the insured in the case of a financial (personal) loss. The insured receives a contract, called the insurance policy, which details the conditions and circumstances under which the insured will be financially compensated.

Claims and loss handling is the materialized utility of insurance; it is the actual ⌈product⌋ paid for. Claims may be filed by the insured directly with the insurer or through brokers or agents. The insurer may require that the claim be filed on its own proprietary forms, or may accept claims on a standard industry form.

Insurance company claims departments employ a large number of claims adjusters supported by a staff of records management and data entry clerks. Incoming claims are classified based on severity and are assigned to adjusters whose settlement authority varies with their knowledge and experience. The adjuster undertakes an investigation of each claim, usually in close cooperation with the insured, determines if coverage is available under the terms of the insurance contract, and if so, the reasonable monetary value of the claim, and authorizes payment.

Payment

A payment is the transfer of an item of value from one party (such as a person or company) to another in exchange for the provision of goods, services or both, or to fulfill a legal obligation.

The simplest and oldest form of payment is barter, the exchange of one good or service for another. In the modern world, common means of payment by an individual include money, cheque, debit, credit, or bank transfer, and in trade such payments are frequently preceded by an invoice or result in a receipt. However, there are no arbitrary limits on the form a payment can take and thus in complex transactions between businesses, payments may take the form of stock or other more complicated arrangements.

There are two types of payment methods: exchanging and provisioning. Exchanging is to change coin, money and banknote in terms of the price. Provisioning is to transfer money from one account to another. In this method, a third party must be involved. Credit card, debit card, cheque, money transfers, and recurring cash or ACH (Automated Clearing House) disbursements are all electronic payments methods.

Letter of Credit (L/C)

In international transactions, A letter of credit is often used to ensure that payment will be received where the buyer and seller may not know each other and are operating in different countries. In this case the seller is exposed to a number of risks such as credit risk, and legal risk caused by the distance, differing laws and difficulty in knowing each party personally. A letter of credit provides the seller with a guarantee that they will get paid as long as certain delivery conditions have been met. For this reason the use of letters of credit has become a very important aspect of international trade.

After a contract is concluded between a buyer and a seller, the buyer's bank supplies a letter of credit to the seller (Picture 1).

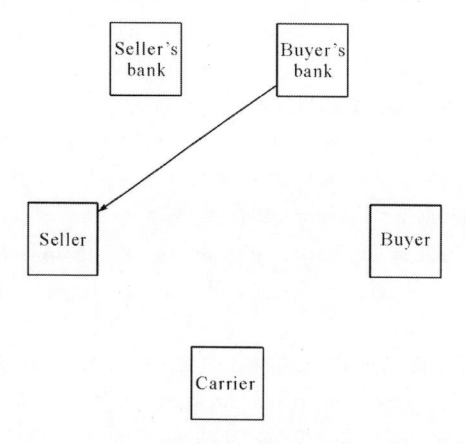

L/C Payment Picture 1

Seller consigns the goods to a carrier in exchange for a bill of lading (Picture 2).

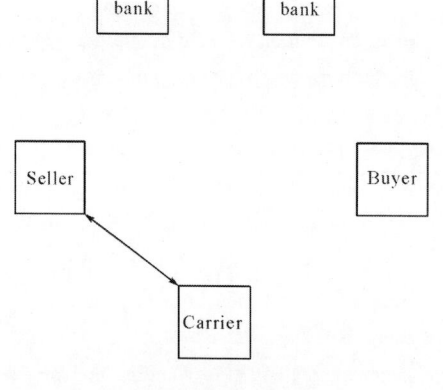

L/C Payment Picture 2

Seller provides the bill of lading to bank in exchange for payment. Seller's bank then provides the bill to buyer's bank, who provides the bill to buyer (Picture 3).

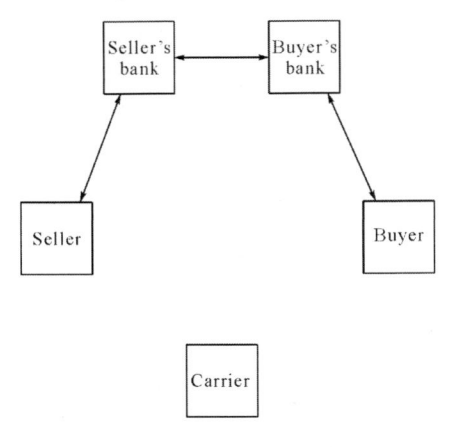

L/C Payment Picture 3

Buyer provides the bill of lading to carrier and takes delivery of the goods (Picture 4).

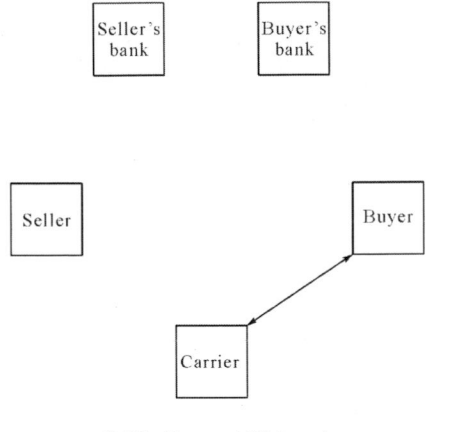

L/C Payment Picture 4

A **letter of credit** is a document from a bank guaranteeing that a seller will receive payment in full as long as certain delivery conditions have been met. In the event that the buyer is unable to make payment on the purchase, the bank will cover the outstanding amount.

The bank that writes the letter of credit will act on behalf of the buyer and make sure that all delivery conditions have been met before making the payment to the seller. Most letters of credit are governed by rules promulgated by the International Chamber of Commerce known as Uniform Customs and Practice for Documentary Credits. Letters of credit are typically used by importing and exporting companies particularly for large purchases and will often negate the need by the buyer to pay a deposit before delivery is made.

Part Ⅲ Special Zones and Free Trade Agreements

Special Economic Zone (SEZ)

The term special economic zone is commonly used as a generic term to refer to any modern economic zone. In these zones business and trades laws differ from the rest of the country. Broadly, SEZs are located within a country's national borders. The aims of the zones include: increased trade, increased investment, job creation and effective administration. To encourage businesses to set up in the zone, financially libertarian policies are introduced. There policies typically regard investing, taxation, trading, quotas, customs and labour regulations. Additionally, companies may be offered tax holidays.

The creation of special economic zones by the host country may be motivated by the desire to attract foreign direct investment (FDI). The benefits a company gains by being in a Special Economic Zone may mean it can produce and trade goods at a globally competitive price. The operating definition of an economic zone is determined individually by each country.

Modern SEZs appeared from late 1950s in industrial countries. The first was in Shannon Airport in Clare, Ireland. From the 1970s onward, zones providing labor-intensive manufacturing have been established, starting in Latin America and East Asia. These zones attracted investment from multinational corporations.

A recent trend has been for African countries to set up SEZs in partnership with China.

Free Economic Zones (FEZ)

Free economic zones or free zones (FZ) are a class of special economic zone (SEZ) designated by the trade and commerce administrations of various countries. The term is used to designate areas in which companies are taxed very lightly or not at all in order to encourage economic activity. The taxation rules are determined by each country. The World Trade Organization (WTO) Agreement on Subsidies and Countervailing Measures (SCM) has content on the conditions and benefits of free zones. A free economic zone may also be called a free port.

Free Port

A free port or free zone, sometimes also called a bonded area is a port or other area with relaxed jurisdiction of customs or related national regulations.

Most commonly a free port is a special customs area or small customs territory with generally less strict customs regulations (or no customs duties and/or controls for transshipment). Earlier in history, some free ports like Hong Kong enjoyed political autonomy. Many international airports have free ports, though they tend to be called customs areas, customs zones, or international zones.

Free Trade Zone (FTZ)

A free trade zone is a specific class of special economic zone. They are a geographic area where goods may be landed, handled, manufactured or reconfigured, and re-exported without the intervention of the customs authorities. Only when the goods are moved to consumers within the country in which the zone is located do they become subject to the prevailing customs duties. Free-trade zones are organized around major seaports, international airports, and national frontiers—areas with many geographic advantages for trade. It is a region where a group of countries has agreed to reduce or eliminate trade barriers. Free trade zones can also be defined as labor-intensive manufacturing centers that involve the import of raw materials or components and the export of factory products.

Export Processing Zone (EPZ)

An export processing zone is a specific type of FTZ, set up generally in developing countries by their governments to promote industrial and commercial exports. Most FTZs located in developing countries: Brazil, Colombia, India, Indonesia, El Salvador, China, the Philippines, Malaysia, Bangladesh, Pakistan, Mexico, Costa Rica, Honduras, Guatemala, Kenya, Sri Lanka, Mauritius and Madagascar have EPZ programs.

China has specific rules differentiating an EPZ from a FTZ. For example, 70% of goods in EPZs must be exported, but there is no such quota for FTZs.

Free Trade Agreements

Free trade is a policy in international markets in which governments do not restrict imports or exports. Free trade is exemplified by the European Union / European Economic Area and the North American Free Trade Agreement, which have established open markets. Most nations are today members of the World Trade Organization (WTO) multilateral trade agreements. However, most governments still impose some protectionist policies that are intended to support local employment, such as applying tariffs to imports or subsidies to exports. Governments may also restrict free trade to limit exports of natural resources. Other barriers that may hinder trade include import quotas, taxes and non-tariff barriers, such as regulatory legislation.

Free trade policies generally promote the following features:

· Trade of goods without taxes (including tariffs) or other trade barriers (e.g., quotas on imports or subsidies for producers)

· Trade in services without taxes or other trade barriers

· The absence of 「trade-distorting」 policies (such as taxes, subsidies, regulations, or laws) that give some firms, households, or factors of production an advantage over others

· Unregulated access to markets

· Unregulated access to market information

· Inability of firms to distort markets through government-imposed monopoly or oligopoly power

· Trade agreements which encourage free trade.

· A common market is usually referred to as the first stage towards the creation of a single market. It usually is built upon a free trade area with relatively free movement of capital and of services, but not so advanced in reduction of the rest of the trade barriers.

· A single market is a type of trade bloc in which most trade barriers have been removed (for goods) with some common policies on product regulation, and freedom of movement of the factors of production (capital and labour) and of enterprise and services. The goal is that the movement of capital, labour, goods, and services between the members is as easy as within them. The physical (borders), technical (standards) and fiscal (taxes) barriers among the member states are removed to the maximum extent possible. These barriers obstruct the freedom of movement of the four factors of production.

· A unified market is the last stage and ultimate goal of a single market. It requires the total free movement of goods, services (including financial services), capital and people without regard to national boundaries.

Free-trade Area

A free-trade area is the region encompassing a trade bloc whose member countries have signed a free trade agreement (FTA). Such agreements involve cooperation between at least two countries to reduce trade barriers—import quotas and tariffs— and to increase trade of goods and services with each other. If people are also free to move between the countries, in addition to FTA, it would also be considered an open border. It can be considered the second stage of economic integration.

Unlike a customs union, members of a free-trade area do not have a common external tariff, which means they have different quotas and customs, as well as other policies with respect to non-members. To avoid tariff evasion (through re-exportation) the countries use the system of certification of origin most commonly called rules of origin, where there is a requirement for the minimum extent of local material inputs and local transformations adding value to the goods. Only goods that meet these minimum requirements are entitled to the special treatment envisioned by the free trade area provisions.

A free-trade area is a result of a free-trade agreement (a form of trade pact) between two or more countries. Free-trade areas and agreements (FTAs) are cascadable to some degree-if some countries sign agreements to form a free-trade area and choose to negotiate together (either as a trade bloc or as a forum of individual members of their FTA) another free-trade agreement with another country (or countries) -then the new FTA will consist of the old FTA plus the new country (or countries).

The aim of a free-trade area is to reduce barriers to exchange so that trade can grow as a result of specialization, division of labour, and most importantly viacomparative advantage. The theory of comparative advantage argues that in an unrestricted marketplace each source of production will tend to specialize in that activity where it has comparative (rather than absolute) advantage. The theory argues that the net result will be an increase in income and ultimately wealth and well-being for everyone in the free-trade area. But the theory refers only to aggregate wealth and says nothing about the distribution of wealth; in fact there may be significant losers, in particular among the recently protected industries with a comparative disadvantage. In principle, the overall gains from trade could be used to compensate for the effects of reduced trade barriers by appropriate inter-party transfers.

North American Free Trade Agreement

The North American Free Trade Agreement (NAFTA) is an agreement signed by Canada, Mexico, and the United States, creating a trilateral rules-based trade bloc in North America.

The agreement came into force on January 1, 1994. It superseded the Canada-United States Free Trade Agreement between the U.S. and Canada.

The goal of NAFTA was to eliminate barriers to trade and investment between the U.S., Canada and Mexico. The implementation of NAFTA on January 1, 1994 brought the immediate elimination of tariffs on more than one-half of Mexico's exports to the U.S. and more than one-third of U.S. exports to Mexico. Within 10 years of the implementation of the agreement, all U.S.-Mexico tariffs would be eliminated except for some U.S. agricultural exports to Mexico that were to be phased out within 15 years. Most U.S.-Canada trade was already duty-free. NAFTA also seeks to eliminate non-tariff trade barriers and to protect the intellectual property right of the products.

Free Warehouse

While a special economic zone is a location which is a geographical area that has been carefully charted and recorded (sometimes these areas are known as bonded logistics parks). Free warehouse (a public bonded warehouse) is a building or premises guarded and locked by Customs. Within this building or these premises, anyone can store goods.

Depending on different countries, it is difficult to choose what kind of warehouse should be chosen for different situations, for example, goods may be entered for temporary warehouse and afterwards for consuming locally or they may be transported out-bound to another country and are placed in warehouse for a while, or they are entered for warehouse waiting for retailers to transfer them.

Under such a complex circumstances, many importers and exporters try to use automation to help manage issues in bonded warehouse which, to some extent, can respond rapidly to customer orders and dispatch products

Bonded Warehouse

A bonded warehouse, or bond, is a building or other secured area in which dutiable goods may be stored, manipulated, or undergo manufacturing operations without payment of duty. It may be managed by the state or by private enterprise. In the latter case a customs bond must be posted with the government. This system exists in all developed countries of the world.

Upon entry of goods into the warehouse, the importer and warehouse proprietor incur liability under a bond. This liability is generally cancelled when the goods are:

- exported; or deemed exported;
- withdrawn for supplies to a vessel or aircraft in international traffic;
- destroyed under Customs supervision; or
- withdrawn for consumption domestically after payment of duty.

While the goods are in the bonded warehouse, they may, under supervision by the customs authority, be manipulated by cleaning, sorting, repacking, or otherwise changing their condition by processes that do not amount to manufacturing. After manipulation, and within the warehousing period, the goods may be exported without the payment of duty, or they may be withdrawn for consumption upon payment of duty at the rate applicable to the goods in their manipulated condition at the time of withdrawal. In the United States, goods may remain in the bonded warehouse up to five years from the date of importation. Bonded warehouses provide specialized storage services such as deep freeze or bulk liquid storage, commodity processing, and coordination with transportation, and are an integral part of the global supply chain.

Duty-free Shops

Duty-free shops (or stores) are retail outlets that are exempt from the payment of certain local or national taxes and duties, on the requirement that the goods sold will be sold to travelers who will take them out of the country. Which products can be sold duty-free vary by jurisdiction, as well as how they can be sold, and the process of calculating the duty or refund the duty component.

However, some countries impose duty on goods brought into the country, though they had been bought duty-free in another country, or when the value or quantity of such goods exceed an allowed limit. Duty-free shops are often found in the international zone of international airports, sea ports, and train stations but goods can be also bought duty-free on board airplanes and passenger ships. They are not as commonly available for road or train travelers, although several border crossings between the United States and both Canada and Mexico have duty-free shops for car travelers. In some countries, any shop can participate in a reimbursement system, such as *Global Blue* and *Premier Tax Free* where a sum equivalent to the tax is paid, but then the goods are presented to the customs and the sum reimbursed on exit.

These outlets were abolished for intra-EU travelers in 1999, but are retained for travelers whose final destination is outside the EU. They also sell to intra-EU travelers but with appropriate taxes. Some special member state territories such as Aland, Livigno and the Canary Islands, are within the EU but outside the EU tax union, and thus still continue duty-free sales for all travelers.

Some duty-free shops operate in central business districts away from airports or other ports. In Japan, for example, any visitor whose passport indicates that they have been in the country for less than six months can buy duty-free items.

In Thailand, the King Power chain has shops where duty-free items are pre-purchased and delivered separately to the airport to be picked up on departure. For certain other purchases, a VAT refund may be claimed at the airport upon departure.

In the Philippines, there is one shopping mall called the Duty Free Philippines Fiestamall, which is located a few miles away from Ninoy Aquino Airport as opposed to being at the airport itself. It is the only shopping mall of its kind in the world. The goods that are sold in this mall are often imported products which come from around the world (mainly from USA, Asia and Australasia) and are not found in any other shopping malls in the country, aside from duty-free malls. Tourists, visitors and returning citizens of Philippines often pay a visit to this mall shortly after their arrival (since only arriving passengers and their companions are allowed access). In order to gain entry, a passport is needed to be presented and registered at the Customer Registration Counter at the entrance of the mall. The customer will then be issued a shopping card; these shopping cards must be presented to the cashier for validation of purchases. Arriving customers are given a certain tax-free allowance on purchases and anything in excess will be subject to local and national taxes. In the past, the mall used to only accept US dollar and Philippine peso but in recent years, it had begun accepting other currencies such as Japanese yen, Brunei dollar, Australian dollar, British pound, Canadian dollar, Swiss franc, Saudi riyal, Bahraini dinar, and Thai baht. Currency exchange booths are also available inside the mall if a customer wishes to exchange currencies into Philippine pesos or US dollars. Credit cards can also be used for purchasing goods.

Part IV   The World Business Organizations and Their Functions

Chamber of Commerce

A chamber of commerce (or board of trade) is a form of business network, for example, a local organization of businesses whose goal is to further the interests of businesses. Business owners in towns and cities form these local societies to advocate on behalf of the business community. Local businesses are members, and they elect a board of directors or executive council to set policy for the chamber. The board or council then hires a President, CEO or Executive Director, plus staffing appropriate to size, to run the organization.

The first chamber of commerce was founded in 1599 in Marseille, France. Another official chamber of commerce would follow 65 years later, probably in Bruges, then part of the Spanish Netherlands.

As a non-governmental institution, a chamber of commerce has no direct role in the writing and passage of laws and regulations that affect businesses. It may however, lobby in an attempt to get laws passed that are favorable to businesses.

International Chamber of Commerce

ICC
International Chamber of Commerce
The world business organization

The International Chamber of Commerce (ICC) is the largest, most representative business organization in the world. Its hundreds of thousands of member companies in over 180 countries have interests spanning every sector of private enterprise.

ICC has three main activities: rule setting, dispute resolution, and policy advocacy. Because its member companies and associations are themselves engaged in international business, ICC has unrivalled authority in making rules that govern the conduct of business across borders. Although these rules are voluntary, they are observed in countless thousands of transactions every day and have become part of international trade.

ICC keeps the United Nations, the World Trade Organization, and many other intergovernmental bodies, both international and regional, in touch with the views of international business. ICC was the first organization granted general consultative status with the United Nations

Economic and Social Council.

The International Chamber of Commerce was founded in 1919 to serve world business by promoting trade and investment, open markets for goods and services, and the free flow of capital. The organization's international secretariat was established in Paris and the ICC's International Court of Arbitration was created in 1923.

ICC's supreme governing body is the World Council, consisting of representatives of national committees. The World Council elects ICC's highest officers, including the Chairman and the Vice-Chairman, each of whom serves a two-year term. The Chairman, Vice-Chairman and the Honorary Chairman (the immediate past Chairman) provide the organization with high-level world leadership. They play an important role in ICC section.

International Secretariat

The ICC International Secretariat, based in Paris, is the operational arm of ICC. It develops and carries out ICC's work programs, feeding business views into intergovernmental organizations on issues that directly affect business operations. The International Secretariat is led by the Secretary General, who is appointed by the World Council.

Dispute Resolution Services

ICC's administered dispute resolution services help solve difficulties in international business. ICC Arbitration is a private procedure that leads to a binding and enforceable decision.

The International Court of Arbitration of the International Chamber of Commerce steers ICC Arbitration and has received 20,000 cases since its inception in 1923. Over the past decade, the Court's workload has considerably expanded.

The Court's membership has also grown and now covers 85 countries and territories. With representatives in North America, Latin and Central America, Africa and the Middle East and Asia, the ICC Court has significantly increased its training activities on all continents and in all major languages used in international trade.

Staged all over the world, ICC events range from large topical conferences to training sessions for small groups. These smaller courses share ICC's expertise on commercial arbitration and dispute resolution mechanisms as well as ICC's trade tools including Incoterms© rules, uniform customs and practice for documentary credits (UCP) and international contracts.

In 1951 ICC established the World Chambers Federation (WCF), formerly the International Bureau of Chambers of Commerce. WCF is the unique global forum uniting the worldwide network of more than 12,000 chambers of commerce and industry. It aims to facilitate the exchange of best practice and the development of new global products and services for chambers, and foster international partnerships between chambers and other stakeholders to help local businesses grow. WCF is a non-political, non-governmental body, with its membership comprising local, regional, national, bilateral and transnational chambers of commerce, as well as public-law and private-law chambers.

With a history spanning over 400 years, chambers today exist in almost every country and business community around the world.

WCF also organizes the World Chambers Congress every two years in a different region of the world. The Congress is the only international forum for chamber leaders and professionals to share best practices, exchange insights, develop networks, address the latest business issues affecting their communities, and learn about new areas of innovation from chambers around the world.

The World Trade Organization (WTO)

The WTO comes from the GATT (General Agreement on Tariffs and Trade). In 1947, 23 countries concluded the GATT at a UN conference in Geneva. Delegates intended the agreement to suffice while members would negotiate creation of a UN body to be known as the International Trade Organization (ITO). As the ITO never became ratified, GATT became the *de facto* framework for later multilateral trade negotiations. Members emphasized trade reciprocity as an approach to lowering barriers in pursuit of mutual gains. The agreement's structure enabled its signatories to codify and enforce regulations for trading of goods and services. GATT was centered on two precepts: trade relations needed to be equitable and nondiscriminatory, and subsidizing non-agricultural exports needed to be prohibited. As such, the agreement's most favored nation clause prohibited members from offering preferential tariff rates to any nation or region that it would not otherwise offer to fellow GATT members. In the event of any discovery of non-agricultural subsidies, members were authorized to offset such policies by enacting countervailing tariffs. The agreement provided governments with a transparent structure for managing trade relations and avoiding protectionist pressures.

The Uruguay Round of GATT multilateral trade negotiations took place from 1986 to 1994, with 123 nations or regions becoming party to agreements achieved throughout the negotiations. Among the achievements were trade liberalization in agricultural goods and textiles, the General Agreement on Trade in Services, and agreements on intellectual property rights issues. The key manifestation of this round was the Marrakech Agreement signed in April 1994, which established the World Trade Organization (WTO). The WTO is a chartered multilateral trade organization, charged with continuing the GATT mandate to promote trade, govern trade relations, and prevent damaging trade practices or policies. It became operational in January 1995. Compared with its GATT secretariat predecessor, the WTO features an improved mechanism for settling trade disputes since the organization is membership-based and not dependent on consensus as in traditional trade negotiations. This function was designed to address prior weaknesses, whereby parties in dispute would invoke delays, obstruct negotiations, or fall back on weak enforcement. In 1997, WTO members reached an agreement which committed to softer restrictions on commercial financial services, including banking services, securities trading, and insurance services. These commitments entered into force in March 1999, consisting of 70 governments accounting for approximately 95% of worldwide financial services.

Organisation for Economic Co-operation and Development (OECD)

The Organisation for Economic Co-operation and Development is an international economic organisation of 34 countries, founded in 1961 to stimulate economic progress and world trade. It is a forum of countries describing themselves as committed to democracy and the market economy, providing a platform to compare policy experiences, seeking answers to common problems, identify good practices and coordinate domestic and international policies of its members.

In 1948, the OECD originated as the Organisation for European Economic Co-operation (OEEC) to help administer the Marshall Plan (which was rejected by the Soviet Union and its satellite states). This would be achieved by allocating American financial aid and implementing economic programs for the reconstruction of Europe after World War II, where there had been similar efforts in the Economic Cooperation Act of 1948 of the United States of America, which stipulated the Marshall Plan that had also taken place elsewhere in the world to war-torn Republic of China and post-war Korea, but the American recovery program in Europe was the most successful one.

In 1961, the OEEC was reformed into the Organisation for Economic Co-operation and Development by the Convention on the Organisation for Economic Co-operation and Development and membership was extended to non-European states. Most OECD members are high-income economies with a very high Human Development Index (HDI) and are regarded as developed countries.

Since 1949, it was headquartered in the Château de la Muette in Paris, France. After the Marshall Plan ended, the OEEC focused on economic issues.

In the 1950s, the OEEC provided the framework for negotiations aimed at determining conditions for setting up a European Free Trade Area, to bring the European Economic Community of the six and the other OEEC members together on a multilateral basis. In 1958, a European Nuclear Energy Agency was set up under the OEEC.

By the end of the 1950s, with the job of rebuilding Europe effectively done, some leading countries felt that the OEEC had outlived its purpose, but could be adapted to fulfill a more global mission. It would be a hard-fought task, and after several sometimes fractious meetings in Paris starting in January 1960, a resolution was reached to create a body that would deal not only with European and Atlantic economic issues, but devise policies to assist less developed countries. This reconstituted organization would bring the US and Canada, who were already OEEC observers, on board as full members. It would also set to work straight away on bringing in Japan.

Following the 1957 Rome Treaties to launch the European Economic Community, the Convention on the Organisation for Economic Co-operation and Development was drawn up to reform the OEEC. The Convention was signed in December 1960 and the OECD officially superseded the OEEC in September 1961. It consisted of the European founder countries of the OEEC plus the United States and Canada, The official founding members are:

· Austria	· Germany	· Luxembourg	· Sweden
· Belgium	· Greece	· The Netherlands	· Switzerland
· Canada	· Iceland	· Norway	· Turkey
· Denmark	· Ireland	· Portugal	· United Kingdom
· France	· Italy	· Spain	· United States

During the next 12 years Japan, Finland, Australia, and New Zealand also joined the organisation. Yugoslavia had observer status in the organization starting with the establishment of the OECD until its dissolution as a nation.

The OECD created agencies such as the OECD Development Centre (1961), International Energy Agency (IEA, 1974), and Financial Action Task Force on Money Laundering.

In 1989, the OECD started to assist countries in Central Europe to prepare market economy reforms. In 1990, the Centre for Co-operation with European Economies in Transition was established, and in 1991, the Programme 「Partners in Transition」 was launched for the benefit of Czechoslovakia, Hungary, and Poland. This programme also included a membership option for these countries. As a result of this, Poland, Hungary, the Czech Republic, and Slovakia, as well as Mexico and South Korea became members of the OECD between 1994 and 2000.

Reform and further enlargement

In the 1990s, a number of European countries, now members of the European Union, expressed their willingness to join the organisation. In 1995, Cyprus applied for membership, but, according to the Cypriot government, it was vetoed by Turkey. In 1996, Estonia, Latvia, and Lithuania signed a Joint Declaration expressing willingness to become full members of the OECD. Slovenia also applied for membership that same year. In 2005, Malta applied to join the organisation. The EU is lobbying for admission of all EU member states. Romania reaffirmed in 2012 its intention to become a member of the organization. In September 2012, the government of Bulgaria confirmed it will apply for full membership before the OECD Secretariat.

In 2003, the OECD established a working group headed by Japan's Ambassador to the OECD to work out a strategy for the enlargement and co-operation with non-members. On 16 May 2007, the OECD Ministerial Council decided to open accession discussions with Chile, Estonia, Israel, Russia and Slovenia and to strengthen co-operation with Brazil, China, India, Indonesia and South Africa through a process of enhanced engagement. Chile, Slovenia, Israel and Estonia all became members in 2010.

In 2011, Colombia expressed the country's willingness to join the organisation during a speech at the OECD headquarters.

In 2013, the OECD decided to open membership talks with Colombia and Latvia. It also announced its intention to open talks with Costa Rica and Lithuania in 2015.

Other countries that have expressed interest in OECD membership are Peru, Malaysia. and Kazakhstan.

The OECD defines itself as a forum of countries committed to democracy and the market economy, providing a setting to compare policy experiences, seek answers to common problems, identify good practices, and co-ordinate domestic and international policies. Its mandate covers economic, environmental, and social issues. It acts by peer pressure to improve policy and implement 「soft law」 —non-binding instruments that can occasionally lead to binding treaties. In this work, the OECD cooperates with businesses, with trade unions and with other representatives of civil society.

In 1976, the OECD adopted the Declaration on International Investment and Multinational Enterprises, which was rewritten and annexed by the OECD Guidelines for Multinational Enterprises in 2000.

Among other areas, the OECD has taken a role in co-ordinating international action on corruption and bribery, creating the OECD Anti-Bribery Convention, which came into effect in February 1999. It has been ratified by thirty-eight countries.

The OECD has also constituted an anti-spam task force, which submitted a detailed report, with several background papers on spam problems in developing countries. It works on the information economy and the future of the Internet economy.

PISA

The OECD publishes the Programme for International Student Assessment (PISA), which is an assessment that allows educational performances to be examined on a common measure across countries.

Glossary

Part I

perceive   v. 感知
precision   n. 精確性
adaptability   n. 適應性
derivative   adj. 派生的，引出的
negotiate   v. 談判
subordinated   adj. 附屬的；居次要地位的
empirical   adj. 經驗主義的，完全根據經驗的
mandate   n. 授權
apprehend   v. 逮捕
evasion   n. 逃避
incentives   n. 激勵；獎勵
availability   n. 可用性
responsiveness   n. 回應能力
surpluses   n. 盈餘
instantiate   v. 實體化；舉例說明
bureaucratic   adj. 官僚的；官僚政治的
sanitary   adj. 衛生的
macroeconomic   adj. 宏觀經濟的
provision   n. 規定；條款
embargo   n. 禁運；禁令
deposit   n. 存款；押金
pledge   v. 保證，許諾；n. 保證，承諾，誓言
reiterate   v. 重申；反復地做

Part II

conveyance   n. 運輸；運輸工具
incur   v. 招致，引發
containerization   n. 集裝箱化
consignment   n. 運送；托付物
unreliable   adj. 不可靠的；靠不住的
consignee   n. 收件人
redistribute   v. 重新分配
segregate   v. 使隔離；使分離
premium   n. 保費；保險費
compensate   v. 補償，賠償
arbitrary   adj. 任意的
disbursement   n. 支付，支出
infrastructure   n. 基礎設施；公共建設
beneficiary   n. 受益人，受惠者
stipulation   n. 條款；規定
promulgate   v. 公布；發布
reimbursement   n. 償付，償還
manipulate   v. 操縱；操作
permissions   n. 許可
authenticate   v. 認證；鑒定
curtail   v. 縮減
ratify   v. 批准；認可
embassy   n. 大使館

Part III

host   n. 主人；主持人
designated   adj. 制定的，特指的
autonomy   n. 自治，自治權
reconfigure   v. 重新配置
intervention   n. 介入，干預
unregulated   adj. 未經調解的
monopoly   n. 壟斷
oligopoly   n. 寡頭壟斷
obstruct   v. 阻礙；妨礙

encompass　v. 包含；包圍
envision　v. 設想；想像；預想
ascadable　adj. 層疊的
supersede　v. 取代；代替
implementation　n. 實施；履行
intellectual　n. 知識分子；adj. 智力的
retailer　n. 零售商
dutiable　adj. 應納稅的；應徵稅的
supervision　n. 監管，監督，管理
withdrawal　n. 退貨；收回
fragrances　n. 香水
peso　n. 比索（貨幣）
reclaimable　adj. 可收回的

Part IV

Marseille　n. 馬賽市
Bruges　n. 布魯日（比利時西北部城市）
representative　n. 代表，典型；adj. 典型的，有代表性的
dispute　n. 爭端
unrivalled　adj. 無與倫比的；無敵的
priority　n. 優先；優先權
secretariat　n. 秘書處
arbitration　n. 公斷，仲裁
affiliation　n. 聯盟
enforceable　adj. 可執行的；可實施的
inception　n. 起初
revised　adj. 修訂的
foster　v. 培養；養育，撫育；抱（希望等）
bureau　n. 局，處
framework　n. 框架，骨架；結構，構架
reciprocity　n. 互惠
signatory　n. 簽署國；簽約國
nondiscriminatory　adj. 不歧視的，一視同仁的
headquarters　n. 總部；指揮部；司令部
Yugoslavia　n. 南斯拉夫
dissolution　n. 解散
Czechoslovakia　n. 捷克斯洛伐克

Phrases

be classified as   列為；歸類稱為……
according to   根據，按照；據……所說；如；比照
regard to   關於，至於
in exchange for   交換
be subject to   使服從，使遭受；容易遭受，受……管制
be responsible for   為……負責，是造成……的原因
check for   檢查
be entitled to   享有；有權要求
bring into   使達到……；把……拿入；使開始生效；使清楚地被人理解［知道］
apply to   適用於；運用；致力於；塗抹
license for   向……頒發……許可證；批准；准許
regardless of   不管，不顧，無，不拘
be identical to   與……相同
be bound to   勢必會；一定
trade on   利用
specialize in   專修；專攻，精通，以……為專業
result in   引起，導致，以……為結局；落得；致使
take the form of   採取……的形狀，表現為……的形式
on behalf of   為了……的利益；代表……
be approved by   經……批准
substitute for   替換；用……代替，代替；抵換
be defined as   規定
with respect to   關於，談到
be exempt from   使免除，使免做
as opposed to   與……相對
be eligible for   適宜於；有……的資格的，合格的
appropriate to   將分配給……
set out   規定
range from   從……到……範圍
in pursuit of   追求
apply for   申請；聲請

Notes

GDP：國內生產總值（Gross Domestic Product，簡稱 GDP），是指在一定時期內（一個季度或一年），一個國家或地區的經濟中所生產出的全部最終產品和勞務的價值，常被公認為衡量國家經濟狀況的最佳指標。它不但可反應一個國家的經濟表現，還可以反應一國的國力與財富。

WTO：世界貿易組織（World Trade Organization，簡稱 WTO），中文簡稱是世貿組

織。1994年4月15日，在摩洛哥的馬拉喀什市舉行的關貿總協定烏拉圭回合部長會議決定成立更具全球性的世界貿易組織，以取代成立於1947年的關貿總協定。世界貿易組織是當代最重要的國際經濟組織之一，有「經濟聯合國」之稱。自2001年12月11日開始，中國正式加入WTO，標誌著中國的產業對外開放進入了一個全新的階段。

ISO：國際標準化組織（International Organization for Standardization，簡稱ISO）。ISO一來源於希臘語「ISOS」，即「EQUAL」，有平等之意。國際標準化組織（ISO）是由各國標準化團體（ISO成員團體）組成的世界性的聯合會，制定國際標準工作通常由ISO的技術委員會完成。中國是ISO的正式成員，代表中國的組織為中國國家標準化管理委員會（Standardization Administration of China，簡稱SAC）。1946年10月14日至26日，中、英、美、法、蘇共25個國家的64名代表集會於倫敦，正式表決通過建立國際標準化組織（ISO），該組織於1947年2月23日宣告正式成立。ISO負責除電工、電子領域和軍工、石油、船舶製造之外的很多重要領域的標準化活動。ISO的最高權力機構是每年一次的「全體大會」，其日常辦事機構是中央秘書處，設在瑞士日內瓦。ISO的宗旨是「在世界上促進標準化及其相關活動的發展，以便於商品和服務的國際交換，在智力、科學、技術和經濟領域開展合作。」

SEZ：經濟特區（Special Economic Zone，簡稱SEZ）。1979年4月鄧小平首次提出要開辦「出口特區」，後於1980年3月，「出口特區」改名為「經濟特區」，並在深圳加以實施。按其實質，經濟特區也是世界自由港區的主要形式之一。以減免關稅等優惠措施為手段，通過創造良好的投資環境，鼓勵外商投資，引進先進技術和科學管理方法，以達促進特區所在國經濟技術發展的目的。經濟特區實行特殊的經濟政策，靈活的經濟措施和特殊的經濟管理體制，並堅持以外向型經濟為發展目標。中國最早的經濟特區為深圳、珠海、汕頭和廈門。

FTZ：自由貿易區（Free Trade Zone，簡稱FTZ）。指簽訂自由貿易協定的成員國和地區相互徹底取消商品貿易中的關稅和數量限制，使商品在各成員國和地區之間可以自由流動。但是，各成員國和地區仍保持自己對來自非成員國進口商品的限制政策。有的自由貿易區只對部分商品實行自由貿易，如「歐洲自由貿易聯盟」內的自由貿易商品只限於工業品，而不包括農產品。這種自由貿易區被稱為「工業自由貿易區」。有的自由貿易區對全部商品實行自由貿易，如「拉丁美洲自由貿易協會」和「北美自由貿易區」，對區內所有的工農業產品的貿易往來都免除關稅和數量限制。

OECD：經濟合作與發展組織（Organization for Economic Co-operation and Development，簡稱OECD），中文簡稱經合組織，是全球市場經濟國家組成的政府間國際經濟合作組織。它的前身是成立於1948年的歐洲經濟聯合體（OEEC），該組織成立的目的是幫助執行致力於第二次世界大戰以後歐洲重建的馬歇爾計劃。1961年創建的經合組織取代了歐洲經濟合作組織，其宗旨為幫助各成員國家的政府實現可持續性經濟增長和就業，成員國生活水準上升，同時保持金融穩定，從而為世界經濟發展作出貢獻。

Questions

1. As China's GDP ranks second in the world, in your opinion, please give a projection of when China will be the first in the world in term of GDP, and illustrate what are the opportunities and threats for China, both internally and externally.

2. What's the economic policy of protectionism? Please deseribe how to eliminate protectionism by the most First World countries since the end of World War II.

3. In which year did China formally join the WTO? What are your views on China's entry into WTO?

4. How many ways can be done as International Trade Payment method and what are they?

5. What's the largest and most representative business organization in the world and what are the main activities of the organization?

Chapter V

Central Banking and Global Financial System

Government control of money is documented in the ancient Egyptian economy (2750-2150 BC). The Egyptians measured the value of goods with a central unit called shat. As many other currencies, the shat was linked to gold. The value of a shat in terms of goods was defined by government administrations. Other cultures in Asia Minor later materialized their currencies in the form of gold and silver coins.

In the Middle Ages and the early modern period, a network of professional banks was established in Southern and Central Europe. The institutes built a new tier in the financial economy. The monetary system was still controlled by government institutions, mainly through the coinage prerogative. Banks, however, could use book money to create deposits for their customers. Thus, they had the possibility to issue, lend and transfer money autonomously without direct governmental control.

In order to consolidate the monetary system, a network of public exchange banks was established at the beginning of the 17th century in main European trade centers. The Amsterdam Wisselbank was founded as a first institute in 1609. Further exchange banks were located in Hamburg, Venice and Nuremberg. The institutes offered a public infrastructure for cashless international payments. They aimed to increase the efficiency of international trade and to safeguard monetary stability. The exchange banks thus fulfilled comparable functions to modern central banks.

The global financial system is the worldwide framework of legal agreements, institutions, and both formal and informal economic actors that together facilitate international flows of financial capital for purposes of investment and trade financing. Since emerging in the late 19th century during the first modern wave of economic globalization, its evolution is marked by the establishment of central banks, multilateral treaties, and intergovernmental organizations aimed at improving the transparency, regulation, and effectiveness of international markets.

Part I Functions of Central Banks

A central bank, or reserve bank is an institution that manages a state's currency, money supply, and interest rates. Central banks usually oversee the commercial banking system of their respective countries. In contrast to a commercial bank, a central bank possesses a monopoly on increasing the monetary base in the state, and prints the national currency, which usually serves as the state's legal tender. Examples include the European Central Bank (ECB), the Bank of Japan, the Bank of England, the Federal Reserve of the United States and the People's Bank of China.

In the past, the term 「national bank」 has been used synonymously with 「central bank」, but it is no longer used in this sense today. Some central banks may have the words 「National Bank」 in their name; conversely if a bank is named in this way, it is not automatically considered a central bank. National banks can either be an ordinary private bank which operates nationally, or a bank owned by the state, especially in developing countries.

A **state bank** is generally a financial institution that is chartered by a state. It differs from a reserve bank in that it does not necessarily control monetary policy, but instead usually offers only retail and commercial services.

The primary function of a central bank is to control the nation's money supply (monetary policy), through active duties such as managing interest rates, setting the reserve requirement, and acting as a lender of last resort to the banking sector during times of bank insolvency or financial crisis. Central banks also have supervisory powers, intended to prevent bank runs and to reduce the risk that commercial banks and other financial institutions engage in reckless or fraudulent behavior. The chief executive of a central bank is normally known as the Governor, President or Chairman.

Functions of a central bank

1. Implementing monetary policies

The term 「monetary policy」 refers to the actions undertaken by a central bank, such as the Federal Reserve, to influence the availability and cost of money and credit to help promote national economic goals. What happens to money and credit affects interest rates (the cost of credit) and the performance of an economy. The Federal Reserve Act of 1913 gave the Federal Reserve authority to set monetary policy in the United States.

Central banks implement a country's chosen monetary policy. At the most basic level, this involves establishing what form of currency the country may have, whether a fiat currency, gold-backed currency, currency board or a currency union. When a country has its own national currency, this involves the issue of some form of standardized currency, which is essentially a form of promissory note: a promise to exchange the note for 「money」 under certain circumstances. Historically, this was often a promise to exchange the money for precious metals in some fixed amount. Now, when many currencies are fiat money, the 「promise to pay」 consists of the promise to accept that currency to pay for taxes.

A central bank may use another country's currency either directly, or indirectly. In the latter case, exemplified by Bulgaria and Latvia, the local currency is backed at a fixed rate by the central bank's holdings of a foreign currency.

The expression 「monetary policy」 may also refer more narrowly to the interest-rate targets and other active measures undertaken by the monetary authority.

The main monetary policy instruments available to central banks are open market operation, bank reserve requirement, interest rate policy, re-lending and re-discount, and credit policy. While capital adequacy is important, it is defined and regulated by the Bank for International Settlements, and central banks in practice generally do not apply stricter rules.

To enable open market operations, a central bank must holdf oreign exchange reserves and official gold reserves. It will often have some influence over any official or mandated exchange rates: Some exchange rates are managed, some are market based and many are somewhere in between.

The goals of monetary policy are mainly to ensure high employment, price stability and economic growth.

2. Determining Interest rates

By far the most visible and obvious power of many modern central banks is to influence market interest rates; contrary to popular belief, they rarely 「set」 rates to a fixed number. Although the mechanism differs from country to country, most use a similar mechanism based on a central bank's ability to create as much fiat money as required.

The mechanism to move the market towards a 「target rate」 (whichever specific rate is used) is generally to lend money or borrow money in theoretically unlimited quantities, until the targeted market rate is sufficiently close to the target. Central banks may do so by lending money to and borrowing money from a limited number of qualified banks, or by purchasing and selling bonds. As an example of how this functions, the Bank of Canada sets a target overnight rate, and a band of plus or minus 0.25%. Qualified banks borrow from each other within this band, but never above or below, because the central bank will always lend to them at the top of the band, and take deposits at the bottom of the band; in principle, the capacity to borrow and lend at the extremes of the band are unlimited. Other central banks use similar mechanisms.

It is also notable that the target rates are generally short-term rates. The actual rate that borrowers and lenders receive on the market will depend on credit risk, maturity and other factors. For example, a central bank might set a target rate for overnight lending of 4.5%, but rates for five-year bonds might be 5%, 4.75%, or, in cases of inverted yield curves, even below the short-term rate. Many central banks have one primary 「headline」 rate that is quoted as the 「central bank rate」. In practice, they will have other tools and rates that are used, but only one that is rigorously targeted and enforced.

The rate at which the central bank lends money can indeed be chosen at will by the central bank; For example, the U.S. central-bank lending rate is known as the Fed funds rate.

The Fed sets a target for the Fed funds rate, which its Open Market Committee tries to match by lending or borrowing in the money market. The Fed is the head of the central-bank because the U.S. dollar is the key reserve currency for international trade. The global money market is a USA dollar market. All other currencies markets revolve around the U.S. dollar market. Accordingly the U.S. situation is not typical of central banks in general.

A typical central bank has several interest rates or monetary policy tools it can set to influence markets.

· Marginal lending rate (currently 0.30% in the Eurozone) -a fixed rate for institutions to borrow money from the central bank. (In the USA this is called the discount rate).

· Main refinancing rate (0.05% in the Eurozone) -the publicly visible interest rate the central bank announces. It is also known as minimum bid rate and serves as a bidding floor for refinancing loans. (In the USA this is called the federal funds rate).

· Deposit rate, generally consisting of interest on reserves and sometimes also interest on excess reserves (−0.20% in the Eurozone) -the rates parties receive for deposits at the central bank.

These rates directly affect the rates in the money market, the market for short term loans. Especially a central bank controls certain types of short-term interest rates. These influence the stock and bond markets as well as mortgage and other interest rates. The European Central Bank for example announces its interest rate at the meeting of its Governing Council; in the case of the U.S. Federal Reserve, the Federal Reserve Board of Governors.

Both the Federal Reserve and the ECB are composed of one or more central bodies that are responsible for the main decisions about interest rates and the size and type of open market operations, and several branches to execute its policies. In the case of the Federal Reserve, they are the local Federal Reserve Banks; for the ECB they are the national central banks.

3. Controlling the nation's entire money supply

Similar to commercial banks, central banks hold assets (government bonds, foreign exchange, gold, and other financial assets) and incur liabilities (currency outstanding). Central banks create money by issuing interest-free currency notes and selling them to the public (government) in exchange for interest-bearing assets such as government bonds. When a central bank wishes to purchase more bonds than their respective national governments make available, they may purchase private bonds or assets denominated in foreign currencies.

The European Central Bank remits its interest income to the central banks of the member countries of the European Union. The US Federal Reserve remits all its profits to the U.S. Treasury. This income, derived from the power to issue currency, usually belongs to the national government. The state-sanctioned power to create currency is called the Right of Issuance. Throughout history there have been disagreements over this power, since whoever controls the creation of currency controls the income.

Through open market operations, a central bank influences the money supply in an economy. Each time it buys securities (such as a government bond or treasury bill), it in effect creates money. The central bank exchanges money for the security, increasing the money supply while lowering the supply of the specific security. Conversely, selling of securities by the central bank reduces the money supply.

Open market operations usually take the form of:

· Buying or selling securities (「direct operations」) to achieve an interest rate target in the interbank market.

· Temporary lending of money for collateral securities (「Reverse Operations」or「repurchase operations」, otherwise known as the「repo」market). These operations are carried out on a regular basis, where fixed maturity loans (of one week and one month for the ECB) are auctioned off.

· Foreign exchange operations such as foreign exchange swaps.

All of these interventions can also influence the foreign exchange market and thus the exchange rate. For example the People's Bank of China and the Bank of Japan have on occasion bought several hundred billions of U.S. Treasuries, presumably in order to stop the decline of the U.S. dollar versus the Renminbi and the Yen.

All banks are required to hold a certain percentage of their assets as capital, a rate which may be established by the central bank or the banking supervisor. For international banks, including the 55 member central banks of the Bank for International Settlements, the threshold is 8% of risk-adjusted assets, whereby certain assets (such as government bonds) are considered to have lower risk and are either partially or fully excluded from total assets for the purposes of calculating capital adequacy. Partly due to concerns about asset inflation and repurchase agreements, capital requirements may be considered more effective than reserve requirements in preventing indefinite lending: when at the threshold, a bank cannot extend another loan without acquiring further capital on its balance sheet.

Historically, bank reserves have formed only a small fraction of deposits, a system called fractional reserve banking. Banks would hold only a small percentage of their assets in the form of cash reserves as insurance against bank runs. Over time this process has been regulated and insured by central banks. Such legal reserve requirements were introduced in the 19th century as an attempt to reduce the risk of banks overextending themselves and suffering from bank runs, as this could lead to knock-on effects on other overextended banks.

As the early 20th century gold standard was undermined by inflation and the late 20th century fiat dollar hegemony evolved, and as banks proliferated and engaged in more complex transactions and were able to profit from dealings globally on a moment's notice, these practices became mandatory, if only to ensure that there was some limit on the ballooning of money supply. Such limits have become harder to enforce. The People's Bank of China retains (and uses) more powers over reserves because the yuan (Reminbi) that it manages is a non-convertible currency.

Loan activity by banks plays a fundamental role in determining the money supply. The central-bank money after aggregate settlement-「final money」-can take only one of two forms:

· physical cash, which is rarely used in wholesale financial markets.

· central-bank money which is rarely used by the people.

The currency component of the money supply is far smaller than the deposit component. Currency, bank reserves and institutional loan agreements together make up the monetary base, called M1, M2 and M3. The Federal Reserve Bank stopped publishing M3 and counting it as part of the money supply in 2006.

To influence the money supply, some central banks may require that some or all foreign exchange receipts (generally from exports) be exchanged for the local currency. The rate that is used to purchase local currency may be market-based or arbitrarily set by the bank. This tool is generally used in countries with non-convertible currencies or partially convertible currencies. The recipient of the local currency may be allowed to freely dispose of the funds, required to hold the funds with the central bank for some period of time, or allowed to use the funds subject to certain restrictions. In other cases, the ability to hold or use the foreign exchange may be otherwise limited.

In this method, money supply is increased by the central bank when it purchases the foreign currency by issuing (selling) the local currency. The central bank may subsequently reduce the money supply by various means, including selling bonds or foreign exchange interventions.

In some countries, central banks may have other tools that work indirectly to limit lending practices and otherwise restrict or regulate capital markets. For example, a central bank may regulate margin lending, whereby individuals or companies may borrow against pledged securities. The margin requirement establishes a minimum ratio of the value of the securities to the amount borrowed.

Central banks often have requirements for the quality of assets that may be held by financial institutions; these requirements may act as a limit on the amount of risk and leverage created by the financial system. These requirements may be direct, such as requiring certain assets to bear certain minimum credit ratings, or indirect, by the central bank lending to counterparties only when security of a certain quality is pledged as collateral.

4. Regulating and supervising the banking industry

In some countries a central bank, through its subsidiaries, controls and monitors the banking sector. In other countries banking supervision is carried out by a government department such as the UK Treasury, or by an independent government agency (for example, UK's Financial Conduct Authority). It examines the banks' balance sheets and behavior and policies toward consumers. Apart from refinancing, it also provides banks with services such as transfer of funds, bank notes and coins or foreign currency. Thus it is often described as the ⌈bank of banks⌋.

Many countries such as the United States will monitor and control the banking sector through different agencies and for different purposes, although there is usually significant cooperation between the agencies. For example, money center banks, deposit-taking institutions, and other types of financial institutions may be subject to different (and occasionally overlapping) regulation. Some types of banking regulation may be delegated to other levels of government, such as state or provincial governments.

Any cartel of banks is particularly closely watched and controlled. Most countries control bank mergers and are wary of concentration in this industry due to the danger of groupthink and runaway lending bubbles based on a single point of failure, the credit culture of the few large banks.

Central banks in most developed nations are institutionally designed to be independent from political interference, though limited control by the executive and legislative bodies usually exists.

In the 2000s there has been a trend towards increasing the independence of central banks as a way of improving long-term economic performance. However, while a large volume of economic research has been done to define the relationship between central bank independence and economic performance, the results are ambiguous.

Advocates of central bank independence argue that a central bank which is too susceptible to political direction or pressure may encourage economic cycles (「boom and bust」), as politicians may be tempted to boost economic activity in advance of an election, to the detriment of the long-term health of the economy and the country. In this context, independence is usually defined as the central bank's operational and management independence from the government.

Part II　The U.S. Federal Reserve System

The United States Congress passed the Federal Reserve Act in 1913, giving rise to the Federal Reserve System.

The Federal Reserve System (also known as the Federal Reserve, and informally as the Fed) is the central banking system of the United States. Over time, the roles and responsibilities of the Federal Reserve System have expanded, and its structure has evolved. Events such as the Great Depression in the 1930s were major factors leading to changes in the system.

The U.S. Congress established three key objectives for monetary policy in the Federal Reserve Act: Maximum employment, stable prices, and moderate long-term interest rates. The first two objectives are sometimes referred to as the Federal Reserve's dual mandate. Its duties have expanded over the years, and as of 2009 also include supervising and regulating banks, maintaining the stability of the financial system and providing financial services to depository institutions, the U.S. government, and foreign official institutions.

The Federal Reserve System's structure is composed of the presidentially appointed Board of Governors or Federal Reserve Board (FRB), partially presidentially appointed Federal Open Market Committee (FOMC), non presidentially appointed twelve regional Federal Reserve Banks located in major cities throughout the nation, numerous privately owned U.S. member banks and various advisory councils. The federal government sets the salaries of the Board's seven governors. Nationally chartered commercial banks are required to hold stock in the Federal Reserve Bank of their region, which entitles them to elect some of their board members. The FOMC sets monetary policy and consists of all seven members of the Board of Governors and the twelve regional bank presidents, though only five bank presidents vote at any given time: the president of the New York Fed and four others who rotate through one-year terms. Thus, the Federal Reserve System has both private and public components to serve the interests of the public and private banks. The structure is considered unique among central banks. It is also unusual in that the United States Department of the Treasury, an entity outside of the central bank, creates the currency used. The Fed considers the Federal Reserve System ⌈ an independent central bank because its monetary policy decisions do not have to be approved by the President or anyone else in the executive or legislative branches of government, it does not receive funding appropriated by the Congress, and the terms of the members of the Board of Governors span multiple presidential and congressional terms. ⌋

The primary motivation for creating the Federal Reserve System was to address banking panics. Before the founding of the Federal Reserve System, the United States underwent several financial crises. Today the Federal Reserve System has responsibilities in addition to ensuring the stability of the financial system. Current functions of the Federal Reserve System include:

1. Addressing the problem of bank panics

Banking institutions in the United States are required to hold reserves-amounts of currency and deposits in other banks-equal to only a fraction of the amount of the banks' deposit liabilities owed to customers. This practice is called fractional-reserve banking. As a result, banks usually invest the majority of the funds received from depositors. On rare occasions, too many of the bank's customers will withdraw their savings and the bank will need help from another institution to continue operating; this is called a bank run. Bank runs can lead to a multitude of social and economic problems. The Federal Reserve System was designed as an attempt to prevent or minimize the occurrence of bank runs, and possibly act as a lender of last resort when a bank run does occur.

2. Check clearing system

Because some banks refused to clear checks from certain others during times of economic uncertainty, a check-clearing system was created in the Federal Reserve system.

By creating the Federal Reserve System, Congress intended to eliminate the severe financial crises that had periodically swept the nation, especially the sort of financial panic that occurred in 1907. During that episode, payments were disrupted throughout the country because many banks and clearing houses refused to clear checks drawn on certain other banks, a practice that contributed to the failure of otherwise solvent banks. To address these problems, Congress gave the Federal Reserve System the authority to establish a nationwide check-clearing system. The System, then, was to provide not only an elastic currency-that is, a currency that would expand or shrink in amount as economic conditions warranted-but also an efficient and equitable check-collection system.

3. Lender of last resort

In the United States, the Federal Reserve serves as the lender of last resort to those institutions that cannot obtain credit elsewhere and the collapse of which would have serious implications for the economy. It took over this role from the private sector 「clearing houses」 which operated during the Free Banking Era; whether public or private, the availability of liquidity was intended to prevent bank runs.

4. Fluctuations

Through its discount window and credit operations, Reserve Banks provide liquidity to banks to meet short-term needs stemming from seasonal fluctuations in deposits or unexpected withdrawals. Longer term liquidity may also be provided in exceptional circumstances. The rate the Fed charges banks for these loans is called the discount rate (officially the primary credit rate).

By making these loans, the Fed serves as a buffer against unexpected day-to-day fluctuations in reserve demand and supply. This contributes to the effective functioning of the banking system, alleviates pressure in the reserves market and reduces the extent of unexpected movements in the interest rates. For example, on September 16, 2008, the Federal Reserve Board authorized an $85 billion loan to stave off the bankruptcy of international insurance giant American International Group (AIG).

5. Central bank

In its role as the central bank of the United States, the Fed serves as a banker's bank and as the government's bank. As the banker's bank, it helps to assure the safety and efficiency of the payments system. As the government's bank, or fiscal agent, the Fed processes a variety of financial transactions involving trillions of dollars. Just as an individual might keep an account at a bank, the U.S. Treasury keeps a checking account with the Federal Reserve, through which incoming federal tax deposits and outgoing government payments are handled. As part of this service relationship, the Fed sells and redeems U.S. government securities such as savings bonds and Treasury bills, notes and bonds. It also issues the nation's coin and paper currency. The U.S. Treasury, through its Bureau of the Mint and Bureau of Engraving and Printing, actually produces the nation's cash supply and, in effect, sells the paper currency to the Federal Reserve Banks at manufacturing cost, and the coins at face value. The Federal Reserve Banks then distribute it to other financial institutions in various ways.

6. Federal funds

Federal funds are the reserve balances (also called Federal Reserve Deposits) that private banks keep at their local Federal Reserve Bank. The purpose of keeping funds at a Federal Reserve Bank is to have a mechanism for private banks to lend funds to one another. This market for funds plays an important role in the Federal Reserve System as it is what inspired the name of the system and it is what is used as the basis for monetary policy. Monetary policy is put into effect partly by influencing how much interest the private banks charge each other for the lending of these funds.

7. Balance between private banks and responsibility of governments

The system was designed out of a compromise between the competing philosophies of privatization and government regulation.

Agrarian and progressive interests, led by William Jennings Bryan, favored a central bank under public, rather than banker, control. But the vast majority of the nation's bankers, concerned about government intervention in the banking business, opposed a central bank structure directed by political appointees.

The legislation that Congress ultimately adopted in 1913 reflected a hard-fought battle to balance these two competing views and created the hybrid public-private, centralized-decentralized structure that we have today.

In the current system, private banks are for-profit businesses but government regulation places restrictions on what they can do. The Federal Reserve System is a part of government that regulates the private banks. The balance between privatization and government involvement is also seen in the structure of the system. Private banks elect members of the board of directors at their regional Federal Reserve Bank while the members of the Board of Governors are selected by the President of the United States and confirmed by the Senate. The private banks give input to the government officials about their economic situation and these government officials use this input in Federal Reserve policy decisions. In the end, private banking businesses are able to run a profitable business while the U.S. government, through the Federal Reserve System, oversees and regulates the activities of the private banks.

8. Government regulation and supervision

Members of the Board frequently testify before congressional committees, such as the House Financial Services Committee hearing. The Senate equivalent of the House Financial Services Committee is the Senate Committee on Banking, Housing, and Urban Affairs.

The Board of Governors also plays a major role in the supervision and regulation of the U. S. banking system. It has supervisory responsibilities for state – chartered banks that are members of the Federal Reserve System, bank holding companies (companies that control banks), the foreign activities of member banks, the U.S. activities of foreign banks, and Edge Act and ⌈agreement corporations⌋ (limited-purpose institutions that engage in a foreign banking business). The Board and, under delegated authority, the Federal Reserve Banks, supervise approximately 900 state member banks and 5,000 bank holding companies.

Some regulations issued by the Board apply to the entire banking industry, whereas others apply only to member banks, that is, state banks that have chosen to join the Federal Reserve System and national banks, which by law must be members of the System. The Board also issues regulations to carry out major federal laws governing consumer credit protection, such as the Truth in Lending, Equal Credit Opportunity, and Home Mortgage Disclosure Acts. Many of these consumer protection regulations apply to various lenders outside the banking industry as well as to banks.

Members of the Board of Governors are in continual contact with other policy makers in government. They frequently testify before congressional committees on the economy, monetary policy, banking supervision and regulation, consumer credit protection, financial markets, and other matters.

The Board has regular contact with members of the President's Council of Economic Advisers and other key economic officials. The Chair also meets from time to time with the President of the United States and has regular meetings with the Secretary of the Treasury. The Chair has formal responsibilities in the international arena as well.

9. National payments system

The Federal Reserve plays an important role in the U.S. payments system. The twelve Federal Reserve Banks provide banking services to depository institutions and to the federal government. For depository institutions, they maintain accounts and provide various payment services, including collecting checks, electronically transferring funds, and distributing and receiving currency and coin. For the federal government, the Reserve Banks act as fiscal agents, paying Treasury checks; processing electronic payments; and issuing, transferring, and redeeming U.S. government securities.

The Federal Reserve plays a vital role in both the nation's retail and wholesale payments systems, providing a variety of financial services to depository institutions. Retail payments are generally for relatively small-dollar amounts and often involve a depository institution's retail clients-individuals and smaller businesses. The Reserve Banks' retail services include distributing currency and coin, collecting checks, and electronically transferring funds through the automated clearinghouse system. By contrast, wholesale payments are generally for large-dollar amounts and often involve a depository institution's large corporate customers or counterparties, including other financial institutions. The Reserve Banks' wholesale services include electronically transferring funds through the Fed wire Funds Service and transferring securities issued by the U.S. government, its agencies, and certain other entities through the Fed wire Securities Service. Because of the large amounts of funds that move through the Reserve Banks every day, the System has policies and procedures to limit the risk to the Reserve Banks from a depository institution's failure to make or settle its payments.

10. Interbank lending

The Federal Reserve sets monetary policy by influencing the Federal funds rate, which is the rate of interbank lending of excess reserves. The rate that banks charge each other for these loans is determined in the interbank market and the Federal Reserve influences this rate through the three「tools」of monetary policy described below.

Tool	Description
Open market operations	Purchases and sales of U.S. Treasury and federal agency securities-the Federal Reserve's principal tool for implementing monetary policy. The Federal Reserve's objective for open market operations has varied over the years. During the 1980s, the focus gradually shifted toward attaining a specified level of the federal funds rate (the rate that banks charge each other for overnight loans of federal funds, which are the reserves held by banks at the Fed), a process that was largely complete by the end of the decade.
Discount rate	The interest rate charged to commercial banks and other depository institutions on loans they receive from their regional Federal Reserve Bank's lending facility-thediscount window.
Reserve requirements	The amount of funds that a depository institution must hold in reserve against specified deposit liabilities.

The Federal Reserve implements U.S. monetary policy by affecting conditions in the market for balances that depository institutions hold at the Federal Reserve Banks. By conducting open market operations, imposing reserve requirements, permitting depository institutions to hold contractual clearing balances, and extending credit through its discount window facility, the Federal Reserve exercises considerable control over the demand for and supply of Federal Reserve balances and the federal funds rate. Through its control of the federal funds rate, the Federal Reserve is able to foster financial and monetary conditions consistent with its monetary policy objectives.

Effects on the quantity of reserves that banks used to make loans influence the economy. Policy actions that add reserves to the banking system encourage lending at lower interest rates thus stimulating growth in money, credit, and the economy. Policy actions that absorb reserves work in the opposite direction. The Fed's task is to supply enough reserves to support an adequate amount of money and credit, avoiding the excesses that result in inflation and the shortages that stifle economic growth.

Part III   Gold Standard

A gold standard is a monetary system in which the standard economic unit of account is based on a fixed quantity of gold. Three types can be distinguished: specie, exchange, and bullion.

· In the *gold specie standard* the monetary unit is associated with the value of circulating gold coins or the monetary unit has the value of a certain circulating gold coin, but other coins may be made of less valuable metal.

· The *gold bullion standard* is a system in which gold coins do not circulate, but the authorities agree to sell gold bullion on demand at a fixed price in exchange for the circulating currency.

· The *gold exchange standard* usually does not involve the circulation of gold coins. The main feature of the gold exchange standard is that the government guarantees a fixed exchange rate to the currency of another country that uses a gold standard, regardless of what type of notes or coins are used as a means of exchange. This creates a *de facto* gold standard, where the value of the means of exchange has a fixed external value in terms of gold that is independent of the inherent value of the means of exchange itself.

In modern times, the British West Indies was one of the first regions to adopt a gold specie standard. In 1717, Sir Isaac Newton, the master of the Royal Mint, established a new mint ratio between silver and gold that had the effect of driving silver out of circulation and putting Britain on a gold standard.

A formal gold specie standard was first established in 1821, when Britain adopted it following the introduction of the gold sovereign by the new Royal Mint at Tower Hill in 1816. The United Province of Canada in 1853, Newfoundland in 1865, and the United States and Germany in 1873 adopted gold. The United States used the eagle as its unit, Germany introduced the new gold mark, while Canada adopted a dual system based on both the American gold eagle and the British gold sovereign.

Australia and New Zealand adopted the British gold standard, as did the British West Indies, while Newfoundland was the only British Empire territory to introduce its own gold coin. Royal Mint branches were established in Sydney, Melbourne and Perth for the purpose of minting gold sovereigns from Australia's rich gold deposits.

The gold specie standard came to an end in the United Kingdom and the rest of the British Empire with the outbreak of World War I.

Impact of World War I

By the end of 1913, the classical gold standard was at its peak but World War I caused many countries to suspend or abandon it. The main cause of the gold standard's failure to resume its previous position after World War 1 was 「the Bank of England's precarious liquidity position and the gold-exchange standard.」A run on sterling caused Britain to impose exchange controls that fatally weakened the standard; convertibility was not legally suspended, but gold prices no longer played the role that they did before. In financing the war and abandoning gold, many of the belligerents suffered drastic inflations. Price levels doubled in the US and Britain, tripled in France and quadrupled in Italy. Exchange rates change less, even though European inflations were more severe than America's. This meant that the costs of American goods decreased relative to those in Europe. Between August 1914 and spring of 1915, the dollar value of US exports tripled and its trade surplus exceeded $ 1 billion for the first time.

Ultimately, the system could not deal quickly enough with the large balance of payments deficits and surpluses; this was previously attributed to downward wage rigidity brought about by the advent of unionized labor, but is now considered as an inherent fault of the system that arose under the pressures of war and rapid technological change. In any case, prices had not reached equilibrium by the time of the Great Depression, which served to kill off the system completely.

For example, Germany had gone off the gold standard in 1914, and could not effectively return to it because War reparations had cost it much of its gold reserves. During the Occupation of the Ruhr the German central bank issued enormous sums of non-convertible marks to support workers who were on strike against the French occupation and to buy foreign currency for reparations; this led to the German hyperinflation of the early 1920s and the decimation of the German middle class.

The US did not suspend the gold standard during the war. The newly created Federal Reserve intervened in currency markets and sold bonds to 「sterilize」some of the gold imports that would have otherwise increased the stock of money. By 1927 many countries had returned to the gold standard. As a result of World War 1 the United States, which had been a net debtor country, had become a net creditor by 1919.

Gold bullion replaces gold specie as standard

The gold specie standard ended in the United Kingdom and the rest of the British Empire at the outbreak of World War I. Treasury notes replaced the circulation of gold sovereigns and gold half sovereigns. Legally, the gold specie standard was not repealed. The end of the gold standard was successfully effected by the Bank of England through appeals to patriotism urging citizens not to redeem paper money for gold specie. It was only in 1925, when Britain returned to the gold standard in conjunction with Australia and South Africa that the gold specie standard was officially ended.

The British Gold Standard Act 1925 both introduced the gold bullion standard and simultaneously repealed the gold specie standard. The new standard ended the circulation of gold specie coins. Instead, the law compelled the authorities to sell gold bullion on demand at a fixed price, but only in the form of bars containing approximately four hundred troy ounces (12 kg) of fine gold.

The interwar partially backed gold standard was inherently unstable, because of the conflict between the expansion of liabilities to foreign central banks and the resulting deterioration in the Bank of England's reserve ratio. France was then attempting to make Paris a world class financial center, and it received large gold flows as well.

The gold standard was blamed in 1920s for prolonging the economic depression which started in 1929 and lasted for about a decade. Adherence to the gold standard prevented the Federal Reserve from expanding the money supply to stimulate the economy. Some economists place the blame for the severity and length of the Great Depression, mostly due to the deliberate tightening of monetary policy even after the gold standard. They blamed the US major economic contraction in 1937 on tightening of monetary policy resulting in higher cost of capital, weaker securities markets, reduced net government contribution to income, the undistributed profits tax and higher labor costs.

The forced contraction of the money supply resulted in deflation. Even as nominal interest rates dropped, inflation-adjusted real interest rates remained high, rewarding those who held onto money instead of spending it, further slowing the economy. Recovery in the United States was slower than in Britain, in part due to Congressional reluctance to abandon the gold standard and float the U.S. currency as Britain had done.

In the early 1930s, the Federal Reserve defended the dollar by raising interest rates, trying to increase the demand for dollars. This helped attract international investors who bought foreign assets with gold.

Gold exchange standard

After the Second World War, a system similar to a gold standard and sometimes described as a 「gold exchange standard」was established by the Bretton Woods Agreements. Under this system, many countries fixed their exchange rates relative to the U.S. dollar and central banks could exchange dollar holdings into gold at the official exchange rate of $ 35 per ounce; this option was not available to firms or individuals. All currencies pegged to the dollar thereby had a fixed value in terms of gold.

Starting in the 1959 – 1969 administration of President Charles de Gaulle and continuing until 1970, France reduced its dollar reserves, exchanging them for gold at the official exchange rate, reducing US economic influence. This, along with the fiscal strain of federal expenditures for the Vietnam War and persistent balance of payments deficits, led U.S. President Richard Nixon to end international convertibility of the U.S. dollar to gold on August 15, 1971 (the 「Nixon Shock」).

Formal abandonment of the Gold Standard

The classical gold standard was established in 1821 by the United Kingdom as the Bank of England enabled redemption of its banknotes for gold bullion. France, Germany, the United States, Russia, and Japan each embraced the standard one by one from 1878 to 1897, marking its international acceptance. The first departure from the standard occurred in August 1914 when these nations erected trade embargoes on gold exports and suspended redemption of gold for banknotes. Following the end of World War I on November 11, 1918, Austria, Hungary, Germany, Russia, and Poland began experiencing hyperinflation. Having informally departed from the standard, most currencies were freed from exchange rate fixing and allowed to float. Most countries throughout this period sought to gain national advantages and bolster exports by depreciating their currency values to predatory levels. A number of countries, including the United States, made unenthusiastic and uncoordinated attempts to restore the former gold standard. The early years of the Great Depression brought about bank runs in the United States, Austria, and Germany, which placed pressures on gold reserves in the United Kingdom to such a degree that the gold standard became unsustainable. Germany became the first nation to formally abandon the post-World War I gold standard when the Dresdner Bank implemented foreign exchange controls and announced bankruptcy on July 15, 1931. In September 1931, the United Kingdom allowed the pound sterling to float freely. By the end of 1931, a host of countries including Austria, Canada, Japan, and Sweden abandoned gold. Following widespread bank failures and a hemorrhaging of gold reserves, the United States broke free of the gold standard in April 1933.

As of 2013, no countries use a gold standard. From 1936 until 2000 the Swiss Franc was based on a 40% gold-reserve. Gold reserves are held in significant quantity by many nations as a means of defending their currency and hedging against the US dollar, which forms the bulk of liquid currency reserves worldwide. Both gold coins and gold bars are traded in liquid markets and serve as a private store of wealth.

Part IV   Bretton Woods System

As the inception of the United Nations as an intergovernmental entity slowly began formalizing in 1944, delegates from 44 of its early member states met at a hotel in Bretton Woods, New Hampshire for the United Nations Monetary and Financial Conference, now commonly referred to as the Bretton Woods conference. Delegates remained cognizant of the effects of the Great Depression, struggles to sustain the international gold standard during the 1930s, and related market instabilities. Whereas previous discourse on the international monetary system focused on fixed versus floating exchange rates, Bretton Woods delegates favored pegged exchange rates for their flexibility. Under this system, nations would peg their exchange rates to the U.S. dollar, which would be convertible to gold at $ 35 USD per ounce. This arrangement is commonly referred to as the Bretton Woods system. Rather than maintaining fixed rates, nations would peg their currencies to the U.S. dollar and allow their exchange rates to fluctuate within a 1% band of the agreed-upon parity. To meet this requirement, central banks would intervene via sales or purchases of their currencies against the dollar. Members could adjust their pegs in response to long-run fundamental disequillibria in the balance of payments, but were responsible for correcting imbalances via fiscal and monetary policy tools before resorting to re-pegging strategies. The adjustable pegging enabled greater exchange rate stability for commercial and financial transactions which fostered unprecedented growth in international trade and foreign investment. This feature grew from delegates' experiences in the 1930s when excessively volatile exchange rates and the reactive protectionist exchange controls that followed proved destructive to trade and prolonged the deflationary effects of the Great Depression. Capital mobility faced de facto limits under the system as governments instituted restrictions on capital flows and aligned their monetary policy to support their pegs.

An important component of the Bretton Woods agreements was the creation of two new international financial institutions, the International Monetary Fund (IMF) and the International Bank for Reconstruction and Development (IBRD). Collectively referred to as the Bretton Woods institutions, they became operational in 1947 and 1946 respectively. The IMF was established to support the monetary system by facilitating cooperation on international monetary issues, providing advisory and technical assistance to members, and offering emergency lending to nations experiencing repeated difficulties restoring the balance of payments equilibrium. Members would contribute funds to a pool according to their share of gross world product, from which emergency loans could be issued. Member states were authorized and encouraged to employ capital controls as necessary to manage payments imbalances and meet pegging targets, but prohibited from relying on IMF financing to cover particularly short-term capital hemorrhages. While the IMF was instituted to guide members and provide a short-term financing window for recurrent balance of payments deficits, the IBRD was established to serve as a type of financial intermediary for channeling global capital toward long-term investment opportunities and postwar reconstruction projects. The creation of these organizations was a crucial milestone in the evolution of the international financial architecture, and some economists consider it the most significant achievement of multilateral cooperation following World War II. Since the establishment of the International Development Association (IDA) in 1960, the IBRD and IDA are together known as the World Bank. While the IBRD lends to middle-income developing countries, the IDA extends the Bank's lending program by offering concessional loans and grants to the world's poorest nations.

Flexible exchange rate regimes: 1973-present

Although the exchange rate stability sustained by the Bretton Woods system facilitated expanding international trade, this early success masked its underlying design flaw, wherein there existed no mechanism for increasing the supply of international reserves to support continued growth in trade. The system began experiencing insurmountable market pressures and deteriorating cohesion among its key participants in the late 1950s and early 1960s. Central banks needed more U.S. dollars to hold as reserves, but were unable to expand their money supplies if doing so meant exceeding their dollar reserves and threatening their exchange rate pegs. To accommodate these needs, the Bretton Woods system depended on the United States to run dollar deficits. As a consequence, the dollar's value began exceeding its gold backing. During the early 1960s, investors could sell gold for a greater dollar exchange rate in London than in the United States, signaling to market participants that the dollar was overvalued.

France voiced concerns over the artificially low price of gold in 1968 and called for returns to the former gold standard. Meanwhile, excess dollars flowed into international markets as the United States expanded its money supply to accommodate the costs of its military campaign in the Vietnam War. Its gold reserves were assaulted by speculative investors following its first current account deficit since the 19th century. In August 1971, President Richard Nixon suspended the exchange of U.S. dollars for gold as part of the Nixon Shock. The closure of the gold window effectively shifted the adjustment burdens of a devalued dollar to other nations. Speculative traders chased other currencies and began selling dollars in anticipation of these currencies being revalued against the dollar. These influxes of capital presented difficulties to foreign central banks, which then faced choosing among inflationary money supplies, largely ineffective capital controls, or floating exchange rates. Following these woes surrounding the U.S. dollar, the dollar price of gold was raised to $ 38 USD per ounce and the Bretton Woods system was modified to allow fluctuations within an augmented band of 2.25% as part of the Smithsonian Agreement signed by the G-10 members in December 1971. The agreement delayed the system's demise for a further two years. The system's erosion was expedited not only by the dollar devaluations that occurred, but also by the oil crises of the 1970s which emphasized the importance of international financial markets in petrodollar recycling and balance of payments financing. Once the world's reserve currency began to float, other nations began adopting floating exchange rate regimes.

The post-Bretton Woods financial order: 1976

As part of the first amendment to its articles of agreement in 1969, the IMF developed a new reserve instrument called special drawing rights (SDRs), which could be held by central banks and exchanged among themselves and the Fund as an alternative to gold. SDRs entered service in 1970 originally as units of a market basket of sixteen major vehicle currencies of countries whose share of total world exports exceeded 1%. The basket's composition changed over time and presently consists of the U.S. dollar, euro, RMB, Japanese yen, and British pound. Beyond holding them as reserves, nations can denominate transactions among themselves and the Fund in SDRs, although the instrument is not a vehicle for trade. In international transactions, the currency basket's portfolio characteristic affords greater stability against the uncertainties inherent with free floating exchange rates. Special drawing rights were originally equivalent to a specified amount of gold, but were not directly redeemable for gold and instead served as a surrogate in obtaining other currencies that could be exchanged for gold. The Fund initially issued 9.5 billion SDR from 1970 to 1972.

IMF members signed the Jamaica Agreement in January 1976, which ratified the end of the Bretton Woods system and reoriented the Fund's role in supporting the international monetary system. The agreement officially embraced the flexible exchange rate regimes that emerged after the failure of the Smithsonian Agreement measures. In tandem with floating exchange rates, the agreement endorsed central bank interventions aimed at clearing excessive volatility. The agreement retroactively formalized the abandonment of gold as a reserve instrument and the Fund subsequently demonetized its gold reserves, returning gold to members or selling it to provide poorer nations with relief funding. Developing countries and countries not endowed with oil export resources enjoyed greater access to IMF lending programs as a result. The Fund continued assisting nations experiencing balance of payments deficits and currency crises, but began imposing conditionality on its funding that required countries to adopt policies aimed at reducing deficits through spending cuts and tax increases, reducing protective trade barriers, and contractionary monetary policy.

The second amendment to the articles of agreement was signed in 1978. It legally formalized the free-floating acceptance and gold demonetization achieved by the Jamaica Agreement, and required members to support stable exchange rates through macroeconomic policy. The post-Bretton Woods system was decentralized in that member states retained autonomy in selecting an exchange rate regime. The amendment also expanded the institution's capacity for oversight and charged members with supporting monetary sustainability by cooperating with the Fund on regime implementation. This role is called IMF surveillance and is recognized as a pivotal point in the evolution of the Fund's mandate, which was extended beyond balance of payments issues to broader concern with internal and external stresses on countries' overall economic policies.

Under the dominance of flexible exchange rate regimes, the foreign exchange markets became significantly more volatile. In 1980, newly elected U.S. President Ronald Reagan's administration brought about increasing balance of payments deficits and budget deficits. To finance these deficits, the United States offered artificially high real interest rates to attract large inflows of foreign capital. As foreign investors' demand for U.S. dollars grew, the dollar's value appreciated substantially until reaching its peak in February 1985. The U.S. trade deficit grew to $ 160 billion in 1985 as a result of the dollar's strong appreciation. The G5 met in September 1985 at the Plaza Hotel in New York City and agreed that the dollar should depreciate against the major currencies to resolve the United States' trade deficit and pledged to support this goal with concerted foreign exchange market interventions, in what became known as the Plaza Accord. The U.S. dollar continued to depreciate, but industrialized nations became increasingly concerned that it would decline too heavily and that exchange rate volatility would increase. To address these concerns, the G7 held a summit in Paris in 1987, where they agreed to pursue improved exchange rate stability and better coordinate their macroeconomic policies, in what became known as the Louvre Accord. This accord became the provenance of the managed float regime by which central banks jointly intervene to resolve under-and overvaluations in the foreign exchange market to stabilize otherwise freely floating currencies. Exchange rates stabilized following the embrace of managed floating during the 1990s, with a strong U.S. economic performance from 1997 to 2000 during the Dot-com bubble. After the 2000 stock market correction of the Dot-com bubble the country's trade deficit grew, the September 11 attacks increased political uncertainties, and the dollar began to depreciate in 2001.

Part V Global financial crises and double-sworded integration

While the global financial system is edging toward greater stability, governments must deal with differing regional or national needs. Some nations are trying to orderly discontinue unconventional monetary policies installed to cultivate recovery, while others are expanding their scope and scale. Emerging market policymakers face a challenge of precision as they must carefully institute sustainable macroeconomic policies during extraordinary market sensitivity without provoking investors to retreat their capital to stronger markets. Nations' inability to align interests and achieve international consensus on matters such as banking regulation has perpetuated the risk of future global financial catastrophes.

Global financial crisis

Following the market turbulence of the 1990s financial crises and September 11 attacks on the U.S. in 2001, financial integration intensified among developed nations and emerging markets, with substantial growth in capital flows among banks and in the trading of financial derivatives and structured finance products. Worldwide international capital flows grew from $ 3 trillion to $ 11 trillion U.S. dollars from 2002 to 2007, primarily in the form of short-term money market instruments. The United States experienced growth in the size and complexity of firms engaged in a broad range of financial services across borders, ending limitations on commercial banks' investment banking activity. Industrialized nations began relying more on foreign capital to finance domestic investment opportunities, resulting in unprecedented capital flows to advanced economies from developing countries, as reflected by global imbalances which grew to 6% of gross world product in 2007 from 3% in 2001.

The global financial crisis precipitated in 2007 and 2008 shared some of the key features exhibited by the wave of international financial crises in the 1990s, including accelerated capital influxes, weak regulatory frameworks, relaxed monetary policies, herd behavior during investment bubbles, collapsing asset prices, and massive deleveraging. The systemic problems originated in the United States and other advanced nations. Similar to the 1997 Asian crisis, the global crisis entailed broad lending by banks undertaking unproductive real estate investments as well as poor standards of corporate governance within financial intermediaries. Particularly in the United States, the crisis was characterized by growing securitization of non-performing assets, large fiscal deficits, and excessive financing in the housing sector. While the real estate bubble in the U.S. triggered the financial crisis, the bubble was financed by foreign capital flowing from many different countries. As its contagious effects began infecting other nations, the crisis became a precursor for the global economic downturn now referred to as the Great Recession. In the wake of the crisis, total volume of world trade in goods and services fell 10% from 2008 to 2009 and did not recover until 2011. The global financial crisis demonstrated the negative effects of worldwide financial integration, sparking discourse on how and whether some countries should decouple themselves from the system altogether.

Eurozone crisis

A series of currency devaluations and oil crises in the 1970s led most countries to float their currencies. The world economy became increasingly financially integrated in the 1980s and 1990s due to capital account liberalization and financial deregulation. A series of financial crises in Europe, Asia, and Latin America followed with contagious effects due to greater exposure to volatile capital flows. The global financial crisis, which originated in the United States in 2007, quickly propagated among other nations and is recognized as the catalyst for the worldwide Great Recession. A market adjustment to Greece's noncompliance with its monetary union in 2009 ignited a sovereign debt crisis among European nations known as the Eurozone crisis.

In 2009, a newly elected government in Greece revealed the falsification of its national budget data, and that its fiscal deficit for the year was 12.7% of GDP as opposed to the 3.7% espoused by the previous administration. This news alerted markets to the fact that Greece's deficit exceeded the eurozone's maximum of 3% outlined in the Economic and Monetary Union's Stability and Growth Pact. Investors concerned about a possible sovereign default rapidly sold Greek bonds. Given Greece's prior decision to embrace the euro as its currency, it no longer held monetary policy autonomy and could not intervene to depreciate a national currency to absorb the shock and boost competitiveness, as was the traditional solution to sudden capital flight. The crisis proved contagious when it spread to Portugal, Italy, and Spain (together with Greece these are collectively referred to as the PIGS). Ratings agencies downgraded these countries' debt instruments in 2010 which further increased the costliness of refinancing or repaying their national debts. The crisis continued to spread and soon grew into a European sovereign debt crisis which threatened economic recovery in the wake of the Great Recession. In tandem with the IMF, the European Union members assembled a €750 billion bailout for Greece and other afflicted nations. Additionally, the ECB pledged to purchase bonds from troubled eurozone nations in an effort to mitigate the risk of a banking system panic. The crisis is recognized by economists as highlighting the depth of financial integration in Europe, contrasted with the lack of fiscal integration and political unification necessary to prevent or decisively respond to crises. During the initial waves of the crisis, the public speculated that the turmoil could result in a disintegration of the eurozone and an abandonment of the euro.

Future of global financial system

The global financial crisis and Great Recession prompted renewed discourse on the architecture of the global financial system. These events called to attention financial integration, inadequacies of global governance, and the emergent systemic risks of financial globalization.

Since the establishment in 1945 of a formal international monetary system with the IMF empowered as its guardian, the world has undergone extensive changes politically and economically. This has fundamentally altered the paradigm in which international financial institutions operate, increasing the complexities of the IMF and World Bank's mandates. The lack of adherence to a formal monetary system has created a void of global constraints on national macroeconomic policies and a deficit of rule-based governance of financial activities.

The Council on Foreign Relations' assessment of global finance notes that excessive institutions with overlapping directives and limited scopes of authority, coupled with difficulty aligning national interests with international reforms, are the two key weaknesses inhibiting global financial reform. Nations do not presently enjoy a comprehensive structure for macroeconomic policy coordination, and global savings imbalances have abounded before and after the global financial crisis to the extent that the United States' status as the steward of the world's reserve currency was called into question. Post-crisis efforts to pursue macroeconomic policies aimed at stabilizing foreign exchange markets have yet to be institutionalized. The lack of international consensus on how best to monitor and govern banking and investment activity threatens the world's ability to prevent future global financial crises. The slow and often delayed implementation of banking regulations that meet Basel III criteria means most of the standards will not take effect until 2019, rendering continued exposure of global finance to unregulated systemic risks. Despite Basel III and other efforts by the G20 to bolster the Financial Stability Board's capacity to facilitate cooperation and stabilizing regulatory changes, regulation exists predominantly at the national and regional levels.

The IMF has reported that the global financial system is on a path to improved financial stability, but faces a host of transitional challenges borne out by regional vulnerabilities and policy regimes. One challenge is managing the United States' disengagement from its accommodative monetary policy. Doing so in an elegant, orderly manner could be difficult as markets adjust to reflect investors' expectations of a new monetary regime with higher interest rates. Interest rates could rise too sharply if exacerbated by a structural decline in market liquidity from higher interest rates and greater volatility, or by structural deleveraging in short-term securities and in the shadow banking system (particularly the mortgage market and real estate investment trusts). Other central banks are contemplating ways to exit unconventional monetary policies employed in recent years. Some nations however, such as Japan, are attempting stimulus programs at larger scales to combat deflationary pressures. The Eurozone's nations implemented myriad national reforms aimed at strengthening the monetary union and alleviating stress on banks and governments. Yet some European nations such as Portugal, Italy, and Spain continue to struggle with heavily leveraged corporate sectors and fragmented financial markets in which investors face pricing inefficiency and difficulty identifying quality assets. Banks operating in such environments may need stronger provisions in place to withstand corresponding market adjustments and absorb potential losses. Emerging market economies face challenges to greater stability as bond markets indicate heightened sensitivity to monetary easing from external investors flooding into domestic markets, rendering exposure to potential capital flights brought on by heavy corporate leveraging in expansionary credit environments. Policymakers in these economies are tasked with transitioning to more sustainable and balanced financial sectors while still fostering market growth so as not to provoke investor withdrawal.

Part Ⅵ   Bank Regulations and the World Famous Banking Corporations

Bank regulations are a form of government regulation which subject banks to certain requirements, restrictions and guidelines. This regulatory structure creates transparency between banking institutions and the individuals and corporations with whom they conduct business, among other things.

Given the interconnectedness of the banking industry and the reliance that the national (and global) economy hold on banks, it is important for regulatory agencies to maintain control over the standardized practices of these institutions. Supporters of such regulation often hinge their arguments on the「too big to fail」notion. This holds that many financial institutions (particularly investment banks with a commercial arm) hold too much control over the economy to fail without enormous consequences. This is the premise for government bailouts, in which government financial assistance is provided to banks or other financial institutions that appear to be on the brink of collapse. The belief is that without this aid, the crippled banks would not only become bankrupt, but would create rippling effects throughout the economy leading to systemic failure.

Objectives of bank regulation

The objectives of bank regulation, and the emphasis, vary between jurisdictions. The most common objectives are:

1. Prudential—to reduce the level of risk to which bank creditors are exposed (i.e. to protect depositors)

2. Systemic risk reduction—to reduce the risk of disruption resulting from adverse trading conditions for banks causing multiple or major bank failures

3. Avoid misuse of banks—to reduce the risk of banks being used for criminal purposes, e.g. laundering the proceeds of crime

4. To protect banking confidentiality

5. Credit allocation—to direct credit to favored sectors

6. It may also include rules about treating customers fairly and having corporate social responsibility (CSR)

The world famous banks
HSBC

HSBC Holdings plc is a British multinational banking and financial services company headquartered in London, United Kingdom. It is the world's third largest bank by assets. It was established in its present form in London in 1991 by the Hongkong and Shanghai Banking Corporation Limited to act as a new group holding company. The origins of the bank mainly lies in Hong Kong, and also to a lesser extent Shanghai, where branches were first opened in 1865. The HSBC name is derived from the initials of the Hongkong and Shanghai Banking Corporation. The company was first formally incorporated in 1866. The company continues to see both the United Kingdom and Hong Kong as its 「home markets」.

HSBC has around 6,600 offices in 80 countries and territories across Africa, Asia, Europe, North America and South America, and around 60 million customers. As of 2012, it was the world's largest bank in terms of assets and sixth-largest public company, according to a composite measure by *Forbes* magazine.

HSBC is organized within four business groups: Commercial Banking; Global Banking and Markets (investment banking); Retail Banking and Wealth Management; and Global Private Banking.

Barclays

Barclays is a British multinational banking and financial services company headquartered in London. It is an universal bank with operations in retail, wholesale and investment banking, as well as wealth management, mortgage lending and credit cards. It has operations in over 50 countries and territories and has around 48 million customers. As of 31 December 2011 Barclays had total assets of US $ 2.42 trillion, the seventh-largest of any bank worldwide.

Barclays is organized within these business clusters: Corporate and Investment Banking, Wealth and Investment Management; and Retail and Business Banking.

Barclays traces its origins to a goldsmith banking business established in the City of London in 1690. James Barclay became a partner in the business in 1736. In 1896 several banks in London and the English provinces, including Backhouse's Bank and Gurney's Bank, united as a joint-stock bank under the name Barclays and Co. Over the following decades Barclays expanded to become a nationwide bank. In 1967, Barclays deployed the world's first cash dispenser. Barclays has made numerous corporate acquisitions, including of London, Provincial and South Western Bank in 1918, British Linen Bank in 1919, Mercantile Credit in 1975, the Woolwich in 2000 and the North American operations of Lehman Brothers in 2008.

Bank of America

Bank of America

Bank of America (abbreviated as **BofA**) is an American multinational banking and financial services corporation headquartered in Charlotte, North Carolina. It is the second largest bank holding company in the United States by assets. As of 2013, Bank of America is the twenty-first largest company in the United States by total revenue. In 2010, *Forbes* listed Bank of America as the third biggest company in the world.

This segment provides its products and services through operating 5,100 banking centers, 16,300 ATMs, call centers, and online and mobile banking platforms. Its Consumer Real Estate Services segment offers consumer real estate products comprising fixed and adjustable-rate first-lien mortgage loans for home purchase and refinancing needs, home equity lines of credit, and home equity loans.

The bank's 2008 acquisition of Merrill Lynch made Bank of America the world's largest wealth management corporation and a major player in the investment banking market. According to the Scorpio Partnership Global Private Banking Benchmark 2014 it had assets under management (AuM) of 1,866.6 (USD Bn) an increase of 12.5% on 2013.

The company held 12.2% of all bank deposits in the United States in August 2009, and is one of the Big Four banks in the United States, along with Citigroup, JPMorgan Chase and Wells Fargo—its main competitors. Bank of America operates—but doesn't necessarily maintain retail branches—in all 50 states of the United States, the District of Columbia and more than 40 other countries. It has a retail banking footprint that serves approximately 50 million consumer and small business relationships at 5,151 banking centers and 16,259 automated teller machines (ATMs).

Citigroup

Citigroup Inc. or Citi is an American multinational banking and financial services corporation headquartered in Manhattan, New York City. Citigroup was formed from one of the world's largest mergers in history by combining the banking giant Citicorp and financial conglomerate Travelers Group in October 1998. As of January 2015, it is the third largest bank holding company in the US by assets. Its largest shareholders include funds from the Middle East and Singapore. At its height until the global financial crisis of 2008 Citigroup was the largest company and bank in the world by total assets with 357,000 employees. In 2007, Citigroup was one of the primary dealers in US Treasury securities. Citigroup had the world's largest financial services network, spanning 140 countries with approximately 16,000 offices worldwide and holds over 200 million customer accounts in more than 140 countries.

Citigroup suffered huge losses during the global financial crisis of 2008 and was rescued in November 2008 in a massive stimulus package by the U.S. government. On February 27, 2009, Citigroup announced that the US government would take a 36% equity stake in the company by converting US $ 25 billion in emergency aid into common stock with a US Treasury credit line of $ 45 billion to prevent the bankruptcy of the largest bank in the world at the time. The government guaranteed losses on more than $ 300 billion troubled assets and injected $20 billion immediately into the company. In exchange, the salary of the CEO was $1 per year and the highest salary of employees was restricted to $500,000 in cash and any amount above $500,000 had to be paid with restricted stock that could not be sold until the emergency government aid was repaid in full. The US government also gained control of half the seats in the Board of Directors, and the senior management was subjected to removal by the US government if there were poor performance. By December 2009, the US government stake was reduced to 27% majority stake from a 36% majority stake after Citigroup sold $21 billion of common shares and equity in the largest single share sale in US history, surpassing Bank of America's $19 billion share sale one month prior. Eventually by December 2010, Citigroup repaid the emergency aid in full and the US government received an additional $12 billion profit in selling its shares. US Government restrictions on pay and oversight of the senior management were removed after the US government sold its remaining 27% stake as of December 2010.

Glossary

Part I

transparency   n. 透明度
monopoly   n. 壟斷
insolvency   n. 破產
reckless   adj. 不計後果的
fraudulent   adj. 不正當的
adequacy   n. 充足性
maturity   n. 成熟度
rigorously   adv. 嚴格地
mortgage   n. 抵押
remit   v. 減免
repo   n. 回購
hegemony   n. 霸權
aggregate   adj. 聚合的
arbitrarily   adv. 隨意處置地
merger   n. 兼併
ubiquitous   adj. 無處不在的
legislature   n. 立法機關
sub-optimal   adj. 不是最理想的
intrinsic   adj. 內在的
multilateral treaties   多邊條約
fiat currency   法定貨幣
knock-on effects   連鎖反應

Part II

inception   n. 出現
alleviate   v. 緩和
presidentially   adv. 以總統的資格
eliminate   v. 消除
warrant   v. 允許
implication   n. 影響
fluctuation   n. 波動
agrarian adj. 土地的
appointee   n. 任命的官員
hybrid   adj. 混合的
congressional   adj. 國會的
deliberation   n. 商議
arena   n. 舞臺
ascertain   v. 確定
speculative   adj. 推測性的
clearinghouse   n. 票據交換所
foster   v. 形成
stifle   v. 扼殺
explicitly   adv. 明確地
mandates   n. 任務

Part III

bullion   n. 金條
de facto   事實上
inherent   adj. 內在的，固有的
sovereign   n. 金鎊
territory   n. 領土，領域
precarious   adj. 不確定的
convertibility   n. 可兌換性
belligerent   n. 交戰人，交戰國
surplus   n. 順差，盈餘
equilibrium   n. 平衡
reparations   n. 賠償
hyperinflation   n. 惡性通貨膨脹

patriotism　n. 愛國主義
interwar　adj. 兩次戰爭之間的
deterioration　n. 惡化
budgetary　adj. 預算的
deflationary　adj. 通貨緊縮的
imminent　adj. 即將到來的
redemption　n. 贖回
bolster　n. 支持
predatory　adj. 掠奪性的
hemorrhaging　n. 流失
amend　v. 修訂

Part IV

intergovernmental　adj. 政府間的
cognizant　adj. 瞭解的
convertible　adj. 可交換的
agreed-upon　adj. 相互認同的
disequilibria　n. 不平衡
unprecedented　adj. 空前的
protectionist n，貿易保護主義者
facilitate　v. 促進
align　v. 調整
intermediary　n. 仲介，中間人
channel　v. 引導
concessional　adj. 優惠的
insurmountable　adj. 難以克服的
cohesion　n. 凝聚力
campaign　n. 戰役，活動
erosion　n. 崩潰
oversight　n. 監督
volatile　adj. 不穩定的
coordinate　v. 調整
provenance　n. 起因

Part V

macroeconomic　adj. 宏觀經濟的
provoke　v. 激怒
perpetuate　v. 保持
precipitate　v. 加速
securitization　n. 資產證券化
trigger　v. 引發，引起
contagious　adj. 感染性的，蔓延性的
precursor　n. 先驅，前導
propagate　v. 傳播
catalyst　n. 催化劑
ignite　v. 激起
falsification　n. 造假
espouse　v. 支持
bailout　n. 救助
turmoil　n. 動亂
disintegration　n. 瓦解
vulnerability　n. 漏洞
plague　v. 困擾，折磨
robust　adj. 健全的
vulnerable　adj. 易受攻擊的
headquarter　v. 總部設在……
codify　v. 編纂
paradigm　n. 模式
exacerbate　v. 惡化
combat　v. 應對
leveraged　adj. 舉債的

Part VI

interconnectedness　n. 關聯性
hinge　v. 取決於
premise　n. 前提
collapse　n. 崩潰，倒閉
prudential　adj. 謹慎的
leeway　n. 餘地，退路

disclose   v. 公開，揭露
multinational   adj. 跨國的，多國的
allege   v. 宣稱，提出
constituent   n. 部分
capitalisation   n. 總值
controversy   n. 爭議
goldsmith   n. 金匠，金器商
outlet   n. 銷售點
shareholder   n. 股東
takeover   n. 收購
segment   n. 部分
lawsuit   n. 訴訟
enormous   adj. 大量的
surpass   v. 超過
predecessor   n. 前身

Phrases

denominate in   用……定名
a small fraction of   一小部分
ratio of   比率
be enshrined in   載入、納入
give rise to   引起
stave off   避開
a quantity of   一些
be blamed (for)   因……而受到指責
in contact with   與……有聯繫
in tandem with   同……合作，與……一起
be recognized as   被認為是，被公認為
adherence to   遵守
take place   發生
on the brink of   瀕臨
be tied to   束縛於，依賴於
be issued with   被配給，被發予
be derived from   起源於，來自
put pressure on   施加壓力
be restricted to   僅限於，局限於
be considered to   被認為

Notes

ECB：歐洲中央銀行，簡稱歐洲央行，總部位於德國法蘭克福，成立於1998年6

月1日，其負責歐盟歐元區的金融及貨幣政策。ECB 是根據 1992 年《馬斯特里赫特條約》的規定於 1998 年 7 月 1 日正式成立的，是為了適應歐元發行流通而設立的金融機構，同時也是歐洲經濟一體化的產物。

Panic of 1907：1907 年恐慌，又稱 1907 年大恐慌、1907 年銀行危機、1907 年金融危機，是指於 1907 年在美國發生的金融危機。

FOMC：聯邦公開市場委員會，隸屬於聯邦儲備系統，主要任務在決定美國貨幣政策，透過貨幣政策的調控，來達到經濟成長及物價穩定兩者間的平衡。聯邦公開市場委員會的最主要工作是利用公開市場操作，從一定程度上影響市場上貨幣的儲量。

Gallup Poll：蓋洛普民意測驗，指由蓋洛普設計的用以調查民眾的看法、意見和心態的一種測試方法，產生於 20 世紀 30 年代。它根據年齡、性別、教育程度、職業、經濟收入、宗教信仰等六個標準，在美國各州進行抽樣問卷調查或電話訪談，然後對所得材料進行統計分析，得出結果。此方法仍在美國經常運用，並有相當高的權威性。

IBRD：國際復興開發銀行，又稱「世界銀行」，是指根據 1944 年 7 月的《國際復興開發銀行協定》建立的國際金融機構。1945 年 12 月 27 日成立，1946 年 6 月營業，1947 年 11 月成為聯合國專門機構之一，總部設在美國華盛頓。

IDA：國際開發協會，世界銀行的兩大附屬機構之一。1960 年 9 月 24 日正式成立，同年 11 月開始營業。該協會宗旨為對低收入的國家提供條件優惠的長期貸款，以促進其經濟的發展。貸款對象僅限於成員國政府，主要用於發展農業、交通運輸、電子、教育等方面。貸款不收利息，只對已支付額每年收取 0.75% 的手續費。

SDR：特別提款權，亦稱「紙黃金」（Paper Gold），最早發行於 1969 年，是國際貨幣基金組織根據會員國認繳的份額分配的，可用於償還國際貨幣基金組織債務、彌補會員國政府之間國際收支逆差的一種帳面資產。其價值目前由美元、歐元、人民幣、日元和英鎊組成的一籃子儲備貨幣決定。會員國在發生國際收支逆差時，可用它向基金組織指定的其他會員國換取外匯，以償付國際收支逆差或償還基金組織的貸款，還可與黃金、自由兌換貨幣一樣充當國際儲備。因為它是國際貨幣基金組織原有的普通提款權以外的一種補充，所以稱為特別提款權。

Questions

1. What are the functions of a central bank? Please list and explain them.

2. What is the central banking system of the United States? What is its structure and its function?

3. What is a gold standard? How many types of a gold standard can be distinguished?

4. How did the Bretton Woods financial order rise? What can be regarded as the important component of Bretton Woods agreements?

5. Why does the author mention「The global financial crisis demonstrated the negative effects of worldwide financial integration, sparking discourse on how and whether some countries should decouple themselves from the system altogether」?

6. Please explain the definition of Bank Regulation and its objective.

7. How many world famous banks do you know and what are they?

Chapter VI

Financial Instruments and Financial Crises

Financial instruments are monetary contracts between parties. They can be created, traded, modified and settled. They can be cash (currency), evidence of an ownership interest in an entity (share), or a contractual right to receive or deliver cash (bond). Financial instruments can be either cash instruments or derivative instruments: Cash instruments-instruments whose value is determined directly by the markets. They can be securities, which are readily transferable, and instruments such as loans and deposits, where both borrower and lender have to agree on a transfer. Derivative instruments-instruments which derive their value from the value and characteristics of one or more underlining entities such as an asset, index, or interest rate. They can be exchange-traded derivatives and over-the-counter (OTC) derivatives.

A financial crisis is any of a broad variety of situations in which some financial assets suddenly lose a large part of their value. In the 19th and early 20th centuries, many financial crises were associated with banking panics, and many recessions coincided with these panics. Other situations that are often called financial crises include stock market crashes and the bursting of other financial bubbles, currency crises, and sovereign defaults. Financial crises directly result in a loss of paper wealth but do not necessarily result in significant changes in the real economy.

Part I Securities and Investment

Bond and Bond Market

In finance, a bond is an instrument of indebtedness of the bond issuer to the holders. It is a debt security, under which the issuer owes the holders a debt and, depending on the terms of the bond, is obliged to pay them interest (the coupon) and/or to repay the principal at a later date, termed the maturity date. Interest is usually payable at fixed intervals (semiannual, annual, sometimes monthly). Very often the bond is negotiable, i.e. the ownership of the instrument can be transferred in the secondary market. This means that once the transfer agents at the bank medallion stamp the bond, it is highly liquid on the second market.

Thus a bond is a form of loan or IOU (sounded 「I owe you」): the *holder* of the bond is the lender (creditor), the *issuer* of the bond is the borrower (debtor), and the *coupon* is the interest. Bonds provide the borrower with external funds to finance long-term investments, or, in the case of government bonds, to finance current expenditure.

Bonds are issued by public authorities, credit institutions, companies and supranational institutions in the primary markets. The most common process for issuing bonds is through underwriting. When a bond issue is underwritten, one or more securities firms or banks, forming a syndicate, buy the entire issue of bonds from the issuer and re-sell them to investors. The security firm takes the risk of being unable to sell on the issue to end investors. Primary issuance is arranged by *bookrunners* who arrange the bond issue, have direct contact with investors and act as advisers to the bond issuer in terms of timing and price of the bond issue. The bookrunner is listed first among all underwriters participating in the issuance in the tombstone ads commonly used to announce bonds to the public. The bookrunners' willingness to underwrite must be discussed prior to any decision on the terms of the bond issue as there may be limited demand for the bonds.

In contrast, government bonds are usually issued in an auction. In some cases both members of the public and banks may bid for bonds. In other cases only market makers may bid for bonds. The overall rate of return on the bond depends on both the terms of the bond and the price paid. The terms of the bond, such as the coupon, are fixed in advance and the price is determined by the market.

In the case of an underwritten bond, the underwriters will charge a fee for underwriting. An alternative process for bond issuance, which is commonly used for smaller issues and avoids this cost, is the private placement bond. Bonds sold directly to buyers and may not be tradeable in the bond market.

Historically an alternative practice of issuance was for the borrowing government authority to issue bonds over a period of time, usually at a fixed price, with volumes sold on a particular day dependent on market conditions.

Some companies, banks, governments, and other sovereign entities may decide to issue bonds in foreign currencies as it may appear to be more stable and predictable than their domestic currency. Issuing bonds denominated in foreign currencies also gives issuers the ability to access investment capital available in foreign markets. The proceeds from the issuance of these bonds can be used by companies to break into foreign markets, or can be converted into the issuing company's local currency to be used on existing operations through the use of foreign exchange swap hedges. Foreign issuer bonds can also be used to hedge foreign exchange rate risk. Some foreign issuer bonds are called by their nicknames, such as the 「samurai bond」. These can be issued by foreign issuers looking to diversify their investor base away from domestic markets. These bond issues are generally governed by the law of the market of issuance, e.g., a samurai bond, issued by an investor based in Europe, will be governed by Japanese law. Not all of the following bonds are restricted for purchase by investors in the market of issuance.

· Eurodollar bond, a U.S. dollar-denominated bond issued by a non-U.S. entity outside the U.S

· Kangaroo bond, an Australian dollar-denominated bond issued by a non-Australian entity in the Australian market

· Maple bond, a Canadian dollar-denominated bond issued by a non-Canadian entity in the Canadian market

· Formosa bond, a non-New Taiwan Dollar-denominated bond issued by a non-Taiwan entity in the Taiwan market

· Panda bond, a Chinese renminbi-denominated bond issued by a non-China entity in the People's Republic of China market

At the time of issue of the bond, the interest rate and other conditions of the bond will have been influenced by a variety of factors, such as current market interest rates, the length of the term and the creditworthiness of the issuer.

These factors are likely to change over time, so the market price of a bond will vary after it is issued. The market price is expressed as a percentage of nominal value. Bonds are not necessarily issued at par (100% of face value, corresponding to a price of 100), but bond prices will move towards par as they approach maturity (if the market expects the maturity payment to be made in full and on time) as this is the price the issuer will pay to redeem the bond. This is referred to as 「Pull to Par」. At other times, prices can be above par (bond is priced at greater than 100), which is called trading at a premium, or below par (bond is priced at less than 100), which is called trading at a discount.

Bond Market

The bond market (also debt market or credit market) is a financial market where participants can issue new debt, known as the primary market, or buy and sell debt securities, known as the secondary market. This is usually in the form of bonds, but it may include notes, bills, and so on.

An important part of the bond market is the government bond market, because of its size and liquidity. Government bonds are often used to compare other bonds to measure credit risk. Because of the inverse relationship between bond valuation and interest rates, the bond market is often used to indicate changes in interest rates or the shape of the yield curve, the measure of 「cost of funding」.

Bond markets, unlike stock or share markets, sometimes do not have a centralized exchange or trading system. Rather, in most developed bond markets such as the U.S., Japan and western Europe, bonds trade in decentralized, dealer-based over-the-counter markets. In such a market, market liquidity is provided by dealers and other market participants committing risk capital to trading activity. In the bond market, when an investor buys or sells a bond, the counterparty to the trade is almost always a bank or securities firm acting as a dealer. In some cases, when a dealer buys a bond from an investor, the dealer carries the bond 「in inventory」, i.e. holds it for his own account. The dealer is then subject to risks of price fluctuation. In other cases, the dealer immediately resells the bond to another investor.

Bond markets can also differ from stock markets in that, in some markets, investors sometimes do not pay brokerage commissions to dealers with whom they buy or sell bonds. Rather, the dealers earn revenue by means of the spread, or difference, between the price at which the dealer buys a bond from one investor—the 「bid」price—and the price at which he or she sells the same bond to another investor—the 「ask」or「offer」price. The bid/offer spread represents the total transaction cost associated with transferring a bond from one investor to another.

Bond market participants are similar to participants in most financial markets and are essentially either buyers (debt issuer) of funds or sellers (institution) of funds and often both.

Participants include:

- Institutional investors
- Governments
- Traders
- Individuals

Because of the specificity of individual bond issues, and the lack of liquidity in many smaller issues, the majority of outstanding bonds are held by institutions like pension funds, banks and mutual funds. In the United States, approximately 10% of the market is held by private individuals.

Bonds are bought and traded mostly by institutions like central banks, sovereign wealth funds, pension funds, insurance companies, hedge funds, and banks. Insurance companies and pension funds have liabilities which essentially include fixed amounts payable on predetermined dates. They buy the bonds to match their liabilities, and may be compelled by law to do this. Most individuals who want to own bonds do so through bond funds. Still, in the U.S., nearly 10% of all bonds outstanding are held directly by households.

Bonds typically pay interest at set intervals. Bonds with fixed coupons divide the stated coupon into parts defined by their payment schedule, for example, semi-annual pay. Bonds with floating rate coupons have set calculation schedules where the floating rate is calculated shortly before the next payment. Zero-coupon bonds do not pay interest. They are issued at a deep discount to account for the implied interest.

Because most bonds have predictable income, they are typically purchased as part of a more conservative investment scheme. Nevertheless, investors have the ability to actively trade bonds, especially corporate bonds and municipal bonds with the market and can make or lose money depending on economic, interest rate, and issuer factors.

The volatility of bonds (especially short and medium dated bonds) is lower than that of equities (stocks). Thus bonds are generally viewed as safer investments than stocks, but this perception is only partially correct. Bonds do suffer from less day-to-day volatility than stocks, and bonds' interest payments are sometimes higher than the general level of dividend payments. Bonds are often liquid-it is often fairly easy for an institution to sell a large quantity of bonds without affecting the price much, which may be more difficult for equities-and the comparative certainty of a fixed interest payment twice a year and a fixed lump sum at maturity is attractive. Bondholders also enjoy a measure of legal protection: under the law of most countries, if a company goes bankrupt, its bondholders will often receive some money back (the recovery amount), whereas the company's equity stock often ends up valueless.

Bond prices can become volatile depending on the credit rating of the issuer-for instance if the credit rating agencies like Standard & Poor's and Moody's upgrade or downgrade the credit rating of the issuer. An unanticipated downgrade will cause the market price of the bond to fall. As with interest rate risk, this risk does not affect the bond's interest payments (provided the issuer does not actually default), but puts at risk the market price, which affects mutual funds holding these bonds, and holders of individual bonds who may have to sell them.

A corporate bond is a bond issued by a corporation in order to raise financing for a variety of reasons such as to ongoing operations, M&A, or to expand business. The term is usually applied to longer-term debt instruments, with maturity of at least one year. Corporate debt instruments with maturity shorter than one year are referred to as commercial paper.

Bond interest is taxed as ordinary income, in contrast to dividend income, which receives favorable taxation rates. However many government and municipal bonds are exempt from one or more types of taxation.

A government bond is a bond issued by a national government, generally with a promise to pay periodic interest payments and to repay the face value on the maturity date. Government bonds are usually denominated in the country's own currency. Another term similar to government bond is 「sovereign bond」. Technically any bond issued by a sovereign entity is a sovereign bond but sometimes the term is used to refer to bonds issued in a currency other than the sovereign's currency. If a government or sovereign is close to default on its debt the media often refer to this as a sovereign debt crisis.

The terms on which a government can sell bonds depend on how creditworthy the market considers it to be. International credit rating agencies will provide ratings for the bonds, but market participants will make up their own minds about this.

Futures and Futures Market

A futures exchange or futures market is a central financial exchange where people can trade standardized futures contracts; that is, a contract to buy specific quantities of a commodity or financial instrument at a specified price with delivery set at a specified time in the future. Such instruments are priced according to the movement of the underlying asset (stock, physical commodity, index, etc.).

The first modern organized futures exchange began in 1710 at the Dojima Rice Exchange in Osaka, Japan.

The United States followed in the early 19th century. Chicago has the largest future exchange in the world, the Chicago Mercantile Exchange. Chicago is located at the base of the Great Lakes, close to the farmlands and cattle country of the Midwest, making it a natural center for transportation, distribution, and trading of agricultural produce. Gluts and shortages of these products caused chaotic fluctuations in price, and this led to the development of a market enabling grain merchants, processors, and agriculture companies to trade in 「to arrive」 or 「cash forward」 contracts to insulate them from the risk of adverse price change and enable them to hedge. In March 2008 the Chicago Mercantile Exchange announced its acquisition of NYMEX Holdings, Inc., the parent company of the New York Mercantile Exchange and Commodity Exchange.

For most exchanges, forward contracts were standard at the time. However, most forward contracts were not honored by both the buyer and the seller. For instance, if the buyer of a corn forward contract made an agreement to buy corn, and at the time of delivery the price of corn differed dramatically from the original contract price, either the buyer or the seller would back out. Additionally, the forward contracts market was very illiquid and an exchange was needed that would bring together a market to find potential buyers and sellers of a commodity instead of making people bear the burden of finding a buyer or seller.

In 1848 the Chicago Board of Trade (CBOT) was formed. Trading was originally in forward contracts; the first contract (on corn) was written on March 13, 1851. In 1865 standardized futures contracts were introduced.

The Chicago Produce Exchange was established in 1874, renamed the Chicago Butter and Egg Board in 1898 and then reorganized into the Chicago Mercantile Exchange (CME) in 1919. Following the end of the postwar international gold standard, in 1972 the CME formed a division called the International Monetary Market (IMM) to offer futures contracts in foreign currencies: British pound, Canadian dollar, German mark, Japanese yen, Mexican peso, and Swiss franc.

In 1881 a regional market was founded in Minneapolis, Minnesota, and in 1883 introduced futures for the first time. Trading continuously since then, today the Minneapolis Grain Exchange (MGEX) is the only exchange for hard red spring wheat futures and options.

The 1970s saw the development of the financial futures contracts, which allowed trading in the future value of interest rates. These (in particular the 90-day Eurodollar contract introduced in 1981) had an enormous impact on the development of the interest rate swap market.

Today, the futures markets have far outgrown their agricultural origins. With the addition of the New York Mercantile Exchange (NYMEX) the trading and hedging of financial products using futures dwarfs the traditional commodity markets, and plays a major role in the global financial system.

In terms of trading volume, the National Stock Exchange of India in Mumbai is the largest stock futures trading exchange in the world, followed by JSE Limited in Sandton, Gauteng, South Africa.

Stock and Stock Market

Stocks can be categorized in various ways. One common way is, by the country where the company is domiciled. For example, Nestlé and Novartis are domiciled in Switzerland, so they may be considered as part of the Swiss stock market, although their stock may also be traded at exchanges in other countries.

A stock market or equity market is the aggregation of buyers and sellers of stocks (also called shares); these may include securities listed on a stock exchange as well as those only traded privately.

Stock participants

One of the many things people always want to know about the stock market is, 「How do I make money investing?」There are many different approaches; two basic methods are classified by either fundamental analysis or technical analysis. Fundamental analysis refers to analyzing companies by their financial statements found in SEC filings, business trends, general economic conditions, etc. Technical analysis studies price actions in markets through the use of charts and quantitative techniques to attempt to forecast price trends regardless of the company's financial prospects.

A few decades ago, worldwide, buyers and sellers were individual investors, such as wealthy businessmen, usually with long family histories to particular corporations. Over time, markets have become more 「institutionalized」; buyers and sellers are largely institutions (e.g., pension funds, insurance companies, mutual funds, index funds, exchange-traded funds, hedge funds, investor groups, banks and various other financial institutions).

The rise of the institutional investor has brought with it some improvements in market operations. There has been a gradual tendency for 「fixed」(and exorbitant) fees being reduced for all investors, partly from falling administration costs but also assisted by large institutions challenging brokers' oligopolistic approach to setting standardized fees.

Importance of Stock Market

The stock market is one of the most important ways for companies to raise money, along with debt markets which are generally more imposing but do not trade publicly. This allows businesses to be publicly traded, and raise additional financial capital for expansion by selling shares of ownership of the company in a public market. The liquidity that an exchange affords the investors enables their holders to quickly and easily sell securities. This is an attractive feature of investing in stocks, compared to other less liquid investments such as property and other immoveable assets. Some companies actively increase liquidity by trading in their own shares.

History has shown that the price of stocks and other assets is an important part of the dynamics of economic activity, and can influence or be an indicator of social mood. An economy where the stock market is on the rise is considered to be an up-and-coming economy. In fact, the stock market is often considered the primary indicator of a country's economic strength and development.

Rising share prices, for instance, tend to be associated with increased business investment and vice versa. Share prices also affect the wealth of households and their consumption. Therefore, central banks tend to keep an eye on the control and behavior of the stock market and, in general, on the smooth operation of financial system functions.

Exchanges also act as the clearing house for each transaction, meaning that they collect and deliver the shares, and guarantee payment to the seller of a security. This eliminates the risk to an individual buyer or seller that the counterparty could default on the transaction.

The smooth functioning of all these activities facilitates economic growth in that lower costs and enterprise risks promote the production of goods and services as well as possibly employment.

The financial system in most western countries has undergone a remarkable transformation. One feature of this development is disintermediation. A portion of the funds involved in saving and financing, flows directly to the financial markets instead of being routed via the traditional bank lending and deposit operations. The general public interest in investing in the stock market, either directly or through mutual funds, has been an important component of this process.

The trend towards forms of saving with a higher risk has been accentuated by new rules for most funds and insurance, permitting a higher proportion of shares to bonds. Similar tendencies are to be found in other developed countries. In all developed economic systems, such as the European Union, the United States, Japan and other developed nations, the trend has been the same: saving has moved away from traditional (government insured) ⌈bank deposits to more risky securities of one sort or another⌋.

A second transformation is the move to electronic trading to replace human trading of listed securities.

Stock Market Bubble

A stock market bubble is a type of economic bubble taking place in stock markets when market participants drive stock prices above their value in relation to some system of stock valuation.

Bubbles occur not only in real-world markets, with their inherent uncertainty and noise, but also in highly predictable experimental markets. Two famous early stock market bubbles were the Mississippi Scheme in France and the South Sea bubble in England. Both bubbles came to an abrupt end in 1720, bankrupting thousands of unfortunate investors.

The two most famous bubbles of the twentieth century, the bubble in American stocks in the 1920s just before the Great Depression and the Dot-com bubble of the late 1990s were based on speculative activity surrounding the development of new technologies. The 1920s saw the widespread introduction of an amazing range of technological innovations including radio, automobiles, aviation and the deployment of electrical power grids. The 1990s was the decade when Internet and e-commerce technologies emerged.

Stock market bubbles frequently produce hot markets in initial public offerings, since investment bankers and their clients see opportunities to float new stock issues at inflated prices. These hot IPO markets misallocate investment funds to areas dictated by speculative trends, rather than to enterprises generating longstanding economic value. Typically when there is an over abundance of IPOs in a bubble market, a large portion of the IPO companies fail completely, never achieve what is promised to the investors, or can even be vehicles for fraud.

Stock Market Crash

A stock market crash is often defined as a sharp dip in share prices of stocks listed on the stock exchanges. In parallel with various economic factors, a reason for stock market crashes is also due to panic and investing public's loss of confidence. Often, stock market crashes end speculative economic bubbles.

There have been famous stock market crashes that have ended in the loss of billions of dollars and wealth destruction on a massive scale. An increasing number of people are involved in the stock market, especially since the social security and retirement plans are being increasingly privatized and linked to stocks and bonds and other elements of the market. There have been a number of famous stock market crashes like the Wall Street Crash of 1929, the stock market crash of 1973-1974, the Black Monday of 1987, the Dot-com bubble of 2000, and the Stock Market Crash of 2008.

Since the early 1990s, many of the largest exchanges have adopted electronic 「matching engines」 to bring together buyers and sellers, replacing the open outcry system. Electronic trading now accounts for the majority of trading in many developed countries. Computer systems were upgraded in the stock exchanges to handle larger trading volumes in a more accurate and controlled manner.

Part Ⅱ Stock Exchanges and Regulayang Commissions

Trade in stock markets means the transfer for money of a stock or security from a seller to a buyer. This requires these two parties to agree on a price. Equities (Stocks or shares) confer an ownership interest in a particular company.

The purpose of a stock exchange is to facilitate the exchange of securities between buyers and sellers. A potential buyer bids a specific price for a stock, and a potential seller asks a specific price for the same stock. Buying or selling at market means you will accept any ask price or bid price for the stock, respectively. When the bid and ask prices match, a sale takes place, on a first-come-first-served basis if there are multiple bidders or askers at a given price. Exchanges may also cover other types of security such as fixed interest securities or indeed derivatives.

Some exchanges are physical locations where transactions are carried out on a trading floor, by a method known as open outcry. This method is used in some stock exchanges and commodity exchanges, and involves traders entering oral bids and offers simultaneously. An example of such an exchange is the New York Stock Exchange. The other type of stock exchange is a virtual kind, composed of a network of computers where trades are made electronically by traders. An example of such an exchange is the NASDAQ.

New York Stock Exchange

The New York Stock Exchange (NYSE), sometimes known as the 「Big Board」, is an American stock exchange located at 11 Wall Street, Lower Manhattan, New York City, New York, United States. It is the world's largest stock exchange by market capitalization of its listed companies at US $ 19.69 trillion as of May 2015. The average daily trading value was approximately US $ 169 billion in 2013.

The NYSE trading floor is located at 11 Wall Street and is composed of 21 rooms used for the facilitation of trading. A fifth trading room, located at 30 Broad Street, was closed in February 2007. The main building, located at 18 Broad Street, between the corners of Wall Street and Exchange Place, was designated a National Historic Landmark in 1978, as was the 11 Wall Street building.

The NYSE is owned by Intercontinental Exchange, an American holding company. Previously, it was part of NYSE Euronext (NYX), which was formed by the NYSE's 2007 merger with the fully electronic stock exchange Euronext. NYSE and Euronext now operate as divisions of Intercontinental Exchange.

The New York Stock Exchange (NYSE) is a physical exchange, with a hybrid market for placing orders both electronically and manually on the trading floor. Orders executed on the trading floor enter by way of exchange members and flow down to a floor broker, who goes to the floor trading post specialist for that stock to trade the order. The specialist's job is to match buy and sell orders using open outcry. If a spread exists, no trade immediately takes place—in this case the specialist should use his/her own resources (money or stock) to close the difference after his/her judged time. Once a trade has been made the details are reported on the 「tape」 and sent back to the brokerage firm, which then notifies the investor who placed the order. Although there is a significant amount of human contact in this process, computers play an important role, especially for so-called 「program trading」.

The NYSE is open for trading Monday through Friday from 9:30 a.m. -4:00 p.m. ET, with the exception of holidays declared by the Exchange in advance.

The NYSE trades in a continuous auction format, where traders can execute stock transactions on behalf of investors. They will gather around the appropriate post where a specialist broker, who is employed by a NYSE member firm, acts as an auctioneer in an open outcry auction market environment to bring buyers and sellers together and to manage the actual auction. They do on occasion (approximately 10% of the time) facilitate the trades by committing their own capital and as a matter of course disseminate information to the crowd that helps to bring buyers and sellers together. The auction process moved toward automation in 1995 through the use of wireless hand held computers (HHC). The system enabled traders to receive and execute orders electronically via wireless transmission.

The movements of the prices in a market or section of a market are captured in price indices called stock market indices, of which there are many, e.g., the S&P, the FTSE and the Euronext indices. Such indices are usually market capitalization weighted, with the weights reflecting the contribution of the stock to the index. The constituents of the index are reviewed frequently to include/exclude stocks in order to reflect the changing business environment.

The Dow Jones Industrial Average, also called the Industrial Average, the Dow Jones, the Dow Jones Industrial, the Dow 30, or simply the Dow, is astock market index, and one of several indices created by *Wall Street Journal* editor and Dow Jones & Company co-founder Charles Dow. The industrial average was first calculated on May 26, 1896. The averages are named after Dow and one of his business associates, statistician Edward Jones. It is an index that shows how 30 large publicly owned companies based in the United States have traded during a standard trading session in the stock market.

The NYSE trading floor in August 2008

Many of the people who ring the bell are business executives whose companies trade on the exchange. However, there have also been many famous people from outside the world of business that have rung the bell. Athletes such as Joe DiMaggio of the New York Yankees and Olympic swimming champion Michael Phelps, entertainers such as rapper Snoop Dogg and members of the band Kiss, and politicians such as Mayor of New York City Rudy Giuliani and President of South Africa Nelson Mandela have all had the honor of ringing the bell. Two United Nations Secretaries General have also rung the bell. On April 27, 2006, Secretary-General Kofi Annan rang the opening bell to launch the United Nations Principles for Responsible Investment. On July 24, 2013, Secretary-General Ban Ki-moon rang the closing bell to celebrate the NYSE joining the United Nations Sustainable Stock Exchanges initiative.

In addition there have been many bell-ringers who are famous for heroic deeds, such as members of the New York police and fire departments following the events of 9/11, members of the United States Armed Forces serving overseas, and participants in various charitable organizations. The reception they receive is often significantly more vocal than that accorded to even the most famous celebrities.

There have also been several fictional characters that have rung the bell, including Mickey Mouse, the Pink Panther, Mr. Potato Head, etc.

NASDAQ

The NASDAQ Stock Market, commonly known as the NASDAQ (currently Nasdaq), is an American stock exchange. It is the second-largest exchange in the world by market capitalization, behind only the New York Stock Exchange. The exchange platform is owned by The NASDAQ OMX Group, which also owns the OMX stock market network and several other US stock and options exchanges.

The NASDAQ is a virtual listed exchange, where all of the trading is done over a computer network. The process is similar to the New York Stock Exchange. However, buyers and sellers are electronically matched. One or more NASDAQ market makers will always provide a bid and ask price at which they will always purchase or sell 「their」 stock.

NASDAQ was founded in 1971 by the National Association of Securities Dealers (NASD). When the NASDAQ began trading on February 8, 1971, it was the world's first electronic stock market. At first, it was merely a *quotation system* and did not provide a way to perform electronic trades. The NASDAQ helped lower the spread (the difference between the bid price and the ask price of the stock) but was unpopular among brokerages which made much of their money on the spread.

NASDAQ eventually assumed the majority of major trades formerly executed by the over-the-counter (OTC) system of trading, although there are still numerous securities traded in this fashion. As late as 1987, the NASDAQ exchange was still commonly referred to as 「OTC」 in media and also in the monthly Stock Guides issued by Standard & Poor's Corporation.

Over the years, NASDAQ became more of a stock market by adding trade and volume reporting and automated trading systems. NASDAQ was also the first stock market in the United States to start trading online, highlighting NASDAQ-traded companies (usually in technology) and closing with the declaration that NASDAQ is 「the stock market for the next hundred years.」 Its main index is the NASDAQ Composite, which has been published since its inception.

In 1992, NASDAQ joined with the London Stock Exchange to form the first intercontinental linkage of securities markets. The National Association of Securities Dealers spun off NASDAQ in 2000 to form a publicly traded company, the NASDAQ Stock Market, Inc.

In 2006, the status of NASDAQ was changed from a stock market to a licensed national securities exchange.

To qualify for listing on the exchange, a company must be registered with the United States Securities and Exchange Commission (SEC), must have at least three market makers (financial firms that act as brokers or dealers for specific securities) and must meet minimum requirements for assets, capital, public shares, and shareholders.

The European Association of Securities Dealers Automatic Quotation System (EASDAQ) was founded originally as a Europeanequivalent to NASDAQ. It was purchased by NASDAQ in 2001 and became NASDAQ Europe. Operations were shut down, however, as a result of the burst of the dot-com bubble. In 2007, NASDAQ Europe was revived as Equiduct, and is currently operating under Börse Berlin.

On June 18, 2012, NASDAQ became a founding member of the United Nations Sustainable Stock Exchanges initiative on the eve of the United Nations Conference on Sustainable Development (Rio+20).

London Stock Exchange (LSE)

The London Stock Exchange is a stock exchange located in the City of London in the United Kingdom. As of December 2014, the Exchange had a market capitalization of US $ 6.06 trillion (short scale), making it the third-largest stock exchange in the world by this measurement (the largest in Europe, ahead of Euronext). The Exchange was founded in 1801 and its current premises are situated in Paternoster Square close to St Paul's Cathedral in the City of London. The Exchange is part of the London Stock Exchange Group.

Issuer services help companies from around the world to join the London equity market in order to gain access to capital. The LSE allows companies to raise money, increase their profile and obtain a market valuation through a variety of routes, thus following the firms throughout the whole IPO process.

The London Stock Exchange runs several markets for listing, giving an opportunity for different sized companies to list. International companies can list a number of products in London including shares, depositary receipts and debt, offering different and cost-effective ways to raise capital. In 2004 the Exchange opened a Hong Kong office and has attracted more than 200 companies from the Asia-Pacific region.

There are also two specialized markets:

Professional Securities Market facilitates the raising of capital through the issue of specialist debt securities or depositary receipts (DRs) to professional investors. Specialist Fund

Market is designed to accept more sophisticated fund vehicles, governance models and security. It is suitable only for institutional, professional and highly knowledgeable investors. The securities available for trading on the London Stock Exchange:
- Bonds, including retail bonds
- Covered warrants
- Exchange-traded products
- Exchange-traded funds
- Global depositary receipts (GDRs)
- Common stock
- Structured products

Tokyo Stock Exchange

The main trading room of the Tokyo Stock Exchange, where trading is currently completed through computers.

The Tokyo Stock Exchange or TSE for short, is a stock exchange located in Tokyo, Japan. It is the third largest stock exchange in the world by aggregate market capitalization of its listed companies. It had 2,292 listed companies with a combined market capitalization of US $ 4.09 trillion as of April 2015.

In July 2012 a planned merger with the Osaka Securities Exchange was approved by the Japan Fair Trade Commission. The resulting entity, the Japan Exchange Group (JPX) was launched on January 1, 2013.

Shanghai Stock Exchange

The Shanghai Stock Exchange (SSE) is a stock exchange that is based in the city of Shanghai, China. It is one of the two stock exchanges operating independently in the People's Republic of China, the other is the Shenzhen Stock Exchange. Shanghai Stock Exchange is the world's 3rd largest stock market by market capitalization at US $ 5.5 trillion as of May 2015. Unlike the Hong Kong Stock Exchange, the Shanghai Stock Exchange is still not entirely open to foreign investors.

The SSE Composite Index is a stock market index of all stocks (A shares and B shares) that are traded at the Shanghai Stock Exchange.

The SZSE Component Index is an index of 40 stocks that are traded at the Shenzhen Stock Exchange.

Hong Kong Stock Exchange

The Hong Kong Stock Exchange (HKSE) is a stock exchange located in Hong Kong. It is Asia's third largest stock exchange in terms of market capitalization behind the Tokyo Stock Exchange and Shanghai Stock Exchange, and the sixth largest in the world behind Euronext. As of 30 November 2013, the Hong Kong Stock Exchange had 1,615 listed companies, 776 of which are from mainland China, 737 from Hong Kong and 102 from abroad (e.g. Cambodia, Italy, Kazakhstan, etc.) Hong Kong Exchanges and Clearing is the holding company for the exchange.

The Hang Seng Index (HSI) is a free float-adjusted market capitalization-weighted stock market index in Hong Kong. It is used to record and monitor daily changes of the largest companies of the Hong Kong stock market and is the main indicator of the overall market performance in Hong Kong. 48 constituent companies represent about 60% of capitalization of the Hong Kong Stock Exchange.

HSI was started on November 24, 1969, and is currently compiled and maintained by Hang Seng Indexes Company Limited, which is a wholly owned subsidiary of Hang Seng Bank, one of the largest banks registered and listed in Hong Kong in terms of market capitalization. It is responsible for compiling, publishing and managing the Hang Seng Index and a range of other stock indexes. Hang Seng, despite being a public company, is held in majority by British financial firm HSBC.

Where there are exchanges, there are exchanges' monitors, for examples, U.S. Securities and Exchange Commission.

U.S. Securities and Exchange Commission

Seal of the U.S. Securities and Exchange Commission

The U.S. Securities and Exchange Commission (SEC) is an agency of the United States federal government. It holds primary responsibility for enforcing the federal securities laws, proposing securities rules, and regulating the securities industry, the nation's stock and options exchanges, and other activities and organizations, including the electronic securities markets in the United States.

The SEC has a three-part mission: to protect investors; maintain fair, orderly, and efficient markets; and facilitate capital formation.

The enforcement authority it received from Congress enables the SEC to bring civil enforcement actions against individuals or companies alleged to have committed accounting fraud, provided false information, or engaged in insider trading or other violations of the securities law. The SEC also works with criminal law enforcement agencies to prosecute individuals and companies alike for offenses that include a criminal violation.

To achieve its mandate, the SEC enforces the statutory requirement that public companies submit quarterly and annual reports, as well as other periodic reports. In addition to annual financial reports, company executives must provide a narrative account, called the ⌈management discussion and analysis⌋ (MD&A), which outlines the previous year of operations and explains how the company fared in that time period. MD&A will usually also touch on the upcoming year, outlining future goals and approaches to new projects. In an attempt to level the playing field for all investors, the SEC maintains an online database called EDGAR (the Electronic Data Gathering, Analysis, and Retrieval system) online from which investors can access this and other information filed with the agency.

Quarterly and semiannual reports from public companies are crucial for investors to make sound decisions when investing in the capital markets. Unlike banking investment in the capital markets is not guaranteed by the federal government. The potential for big gains needs to be weighed against equally likely losses. Mandatory disclosure of financial and other information about the issuer and the security itself gives private individuals as well as large institutions the same basic facts about the public companies they invest in, thereby increasing public scrutiny while reducing insider trading and fraud.

The SEC makes reports available to the public through the EDGAR system. The SEC also offers publications on investment-related topics for public education. The same online system also takes tips and complaints from investors to help the SEC track down violators of the securities laws. The SEC adheres to a strict policy of never commenting on the existence or status of an ongoing investigation.

China Securities Regulatory Commission (CSRC)

The China Securities Regulatory Commission is an institution of the State Council of the People's Republic of China (PRC), with ministry-level rank. It is the main regulator of the securities industry in China.

China's Securities Law (passed December 1998, effective July 1, 1999), the nation's first comprehensive securities legislation, grants CSRC 「authority to implement a centralized and unified regulation of the nationwide securities market in order to ensure their lawful operation.」 The CSRC oversees China's nationwide centralized securities supervisory system, with the power to regulate and supervise securities issuers, as well as to investigate, and impose penalties for, 「illegal activities related to securities and futures.」 The CSRC is empowered to issue Opinions or Guideline Opinions, non-legally binding guidance for publicly traded corporations. Its functions are similar to that of the Securities and Exchange Commission in the United States.

Among its responsibilities include:

· Formulating policies, laws and regulations concerning markets in securities and futures contracts.

· Overseeing issuing, trading, custody and settlement of equity shares, bonds, investment funds.

· Supervising listing, trading and settlement of futures contracts; futures exchanges; securities and futures firms.

Part Ⅲ Wall Street and its Significance

Wall Street

Street sign

Wall Street is a 0.7-mile-long (1.1 km) street running eight blocks, roughly northwest to southeast, from Broadway to South Street on the East River in the Financial District of lower Manhattan, New York City. Over time, the term has become a metonym for the financial markets of the United States as a whole, the American financial sector (even if financial firms are not physically located there), or signifying New York-based financial interests.

Anchored by Wall Street, New York City has been called both the most economically powerful city and the leading financial center of the world, and the city is home to the world's two largest stock exchanges by total market capitalization, the New York Stock Exchange and NASDAQ. Several other major exchanges have or had headquarters in the Wall Street area, including the New York Mercantile Exchange, the New York Board of Trade, and the former American Stock Exchange.

Wall Street itself and the Financial District as a whole are crowded with highrises. Further, the loss of the World Trade Center has spurred development on a scale that had not been seen in decades. In 2006, Goldman Sachs began building a tower near the former Trade Center site. Tax incentives provided by federal state and local governments encouraged development. A new World Trade Center complex, centered on Daniel Libeskind's Memory Foundations plan, is in the early stages of development and one building has already been replaced. The centerpiece to this plan is the 1,776-foot (541 m) tall new World Trade Center (formerly known as the Freedom Tower). New residential buildings are sprouting up, and buildings that were previously office space are being converted to residential units, also benefiting from tax incentives. A new Fulton Center is planned to improve access. In 2007, the Maharishi Global Financial Capital of New York opened headquarters at 70 Broad Street near the NYSE, in an effort to seek investors.

Looking west toward Trinity Church; a crowd on Wall Street is pictured in the foreground

The first months of 2008 was a particularly troublesome period which caused Federal Reserve chairman Ben Bernanke to「work holidays and weekends」and which did an「extraordinary series of moves.」It bolstered U.S. banks and allowed Wall Street firms to borrow「directly from the Fed.」These efforts were highly controversial at the time, but from the perspective of 2010, it appeared the Federal exertions had been the right decisions. By 2010, Wall Street firms were getting back to their old selves as engine rooms of wealth, prosperity and excess, with residential, commercial, retail and hotels booming in the third largest business district in the country. The NYSE closed two of its trading floors in a move towards transforming itself into an electronic exchange. Wall Street investment banking fees in 2012 totaled approximately $ 40 billion, while senior bank officers managing risk and compliance functions earned as much as $ 324,000 annually in New York City in 2013.

Significance of Wall Street

1. As an Economic Engine

Wall Street pay, in terms of salaries and bonuses and taxes, is an important part of the economy of New York City, the tri-state metropolitan area, and the United States. In 2008, after a downturn in the stock market, the decline meant $ 18 billion less in taxable income, with less money available for apartments, furniture, cars, clothing and services. A falloff in Wall Street's economy could have wrenching effects on the local and regional economies.

Estimates vary about the number and quality of financial jobs in the city. One estimate was that Wall Street firms employed close to 200,000 persons in 2008. Another estimate was that in 2007, the financial services industry which had a $ 70 billion profit became 22 percent of the city's revenue. Another estimate (in 2006) was that the financial services industry makes up 9% of the city's work force and 31% of the tax base. An additional estimate (2007) was that the securities industry accounts for 4.7 percent of the jobs in New York City but 20.7 percent of its wages. There were 175,000 securities-industries jobs in New York (both Wall Street area and midtown) paying an average of $ 350,000 annually. Between 1995 and 2005, the sector grew at an annual rate of about 6.6% annually, a respectable rate, but that other financial centers were growing faster. Another estimate (2008) was that Wall Street provided a fourth of all personal income earned in the city, and 10% of New York City's tax revenue. The city's securities industry, enumerating 163,400 jobs in August 2013, continues to form the largest segment of the city's financial sector and an important economic engine, accounting in 2012 for 5 percent of private sector jobs in New York City, 8.5 percent (US $ 3.8 billion) of the city's tax revenue, and 22 percent of the city's total wages, including an average salary of US $ 360,700.

The seven largest Wall Street firms in the 2000s were Bear Stearns, JPM organ Chase, Citigroup Incorporated, Goldman Sachs, Morgan Stanley, Merrill Lynch and Lehman Brothers. During the recession of 2008–2010, many of these firms, including Lehman, went out of business or were bought up at firesale prices by other financial firms. In 2008, Lehman filed for bankruptcy, Bear Stearns was bought by JP Morgan Chase forced by the U.S. government, and Merrill Lynch was bought by Bank of America in a similar shot-gun wedding. These failures marked a catastrophic downsizing of Wall Street as the financial industry goes through restructuring and change. Since New York's financial industry provides almost one-fourth of all income produced in the city, and accounts for 10% of the city's tax revenues and 20% of the state's, the downturn has had huge repercussions for government treasuries.

2. In the Public Imagination

Wall Street in a conceptual sense represents financial and economic power. To Americans, it can sometimes represent elitism and power politics, and its role has been a source of controversy throughout the nation's history, particularly beginning around the Gilded Age period in the late 19th century. Wall Street became the symbol of a country and economic system that many Americans see as having developed through trade, capitalism, and innovation.

Wall Street has become synonymous with financial interests, often used negatively. During the subprime mortgage crisis from 2007−2010, Wall Street financing was blamed as one of the causes, although most commentators blame an interplay of factors. The U.S. government with the Troubled Asset Relief Program bailed out the banks and financial backers with billions of taxpayer dollars, but the bailout was often criticized as politically motivated, and was criticized by journalists as well as the public. When the United States Treasury bailed out large financial firms, to ostensibly halt a downward spiral in the nation's economy, there was tremendous negative political fallout, particularly when reports came out that monies supposed to be used to ease credit restrictions were being used to pay bonuses to highly paid employees.

In addition, images of Wall Street and its figures have loomed large. The 1987 Oliver Stone film *Wall Street* created the iconic figure of Gordon Gekko who used the phrase 「greed is good」, which caught on in the cultural parlance. Stone commented in 2009 how the movie had had an unexpected cultural influence, not causing them to turn away from corporate greed, but causing many young people to choose Wall Street careers because of that movie.

Wall Street firms have however also contributed to projects such as Habitat for Humanity as well as done food programs in Haiti and trauma centers in Sudan and rescue boats during floods in Bangladesh.

3. As a Culture

According to the discipline of anthropology, the term culture represents the customs, values, morals, laws and rituals which a particular group or society shares. In the public imagination, Wall Street represents elitism, finance, economics and greed. However, although Wall Street employees may exhibit greedy and self-interested behaviours to the public, these behaviours are justified through their own value system and social practices. Various anthropologists have conducted research on Wall Street and it is their research which can confirm the negative views of Wall Street while providing the public with information that can contribute to a better understanding of how Wall Street workers perceive themselves. Through the perception of the public, financial investors take on a role that has already been established for them. It is both appropriate and fitting to call Wall Street a culture because of the system of values and practices it holds onto. Moreover, anthropological insight can help improve the general public's understanding of Wall Street and in turn allow the public to appreciate the culture of Wall

Street which is both logical and sensible to the workers themselves.

In situating global capitalisms: Wall Street Investment Bankers believe that working for Wall Street puts them at the top of the hierarchal ladder in society. The banker feels that everything goes through Wall Street, in terms of loans, investments, change or growth. From this point of view, Wall Street values are embedded in power. Actually, there is a 「dividing line between 「us on the inside」 and 「those on the outside」 」. These factors strengthen the power relations as well as establish a hierarchy between them as Wall Street employees, and the public.

Additionally, in disciplining investment Bankers, it disciplines the Economy: Wall Street's Institutional Culture of Crisis and the Downsizing of 「Corporate America」 states that as we continue to learn more about Wall Street, we learn about each independent banker. As the banker brings their life experiences into the business, we can see the reasons for their actions. Each investor has a unique identity which contributes to the culture of Wall Street. Ideally, they live in the moment. However, job insecurity and the volatile nature of the market creates a constant state of fear within the investor. Therefore, they must organize themselves and follow a pattern to ensure security, profit and prosperity for the long run. Wall Street should be viewed through the lens of the everyday investor and banker, as well as understanding the experiences and everyday situations that they must endure. The individuals within the public can counteract the stereotypes and negativity that both the media and society associates with Wall Street by learning more about the personal experiences of the investors and their everyday lives. Similarly to regular wage earners, Wall Street employees are just trying to earn a day's pay. Their work is sometimes undervalued, because the public does not see them in this manner. Thus, Wall Street cannot be understood in black and white terms. One needs to understand that they have a value system which is not only logical to them, but also reflective of North America's values of individual power, prestige, and social practices based on individualism. For example, throughout the 1940s and into the 1950s Manhattan was a 「white-only」 community. Within that time period, there was a lot of racial segregation. The values of America and the social practices were not like they are today, so African Americans were not within the Wall Street community.

Many people associated with Wall Street have become famous; although in most cases their reputations are limited to members of the stock brokerage and banking communities, others have gained national and international fame. For some, their fame is due to skillful investment strategies, financing, reporting, legal or regulatory activities, while others are remembered for their notable failures or scandal.

Part Ⅳ Financial Crisis and its Lessons

The financial crisis of 2007-2008, also known as the Global Financial Crisis and 2008 financial crisis, is considered by many economists to have been the worst financial crisis since the Great Depression of the 1930s. It threatened the collapse of large financial institutions, which was prevented by the bailout of banks by national governments, but stock markets still dropped worldwide. In many areas, the housing market also suffered, resulting in evictions, foreclosures and prolonged unemployment. The crisis played a significant role in the failure of key businesses, declines in consumer wealth estimated in trillions of U.S. dollars, and a downturn in economic activity leading to the 2008-2012 global recession and contributing to the European sovereign-debt crisis.

The bursting of the United States housing bubble, which peaked in 2004, caused the values of securities tied to U.S. real estate pricing to plummet, damaging financial institutions globally. The financial crisis was triggered by a complex interplay of policies that encouraged home ownership, providing easier access to loans for (lending) borrowers, overvaluation of bundled subprime mortgages based on the theory that housing prices would continue to escalate, questionable trading practices on behalf of both buyers and sellers, compensation structures that prioritize short-term deal flow over long-term value creation, and a lack of adequate capital holdings from banks and insurance companies to back the financial commitments they were making. Questions regarding bank solvency, declines in credit availability and damaged investor confidence had an impact on global stock markets, where securities suffered large losses during 2008 and early 2009. Economies worldwide slowed during this period, as credit tightened and international trade declined. Governments and central banks responded with unprecedented fiscal stimulus, monetary policy expansion and institutional bailouts. In the U.S., Congress passed the American Recovery and Reinvestment Act of 2009.

Many causes for the financial crisis have been suggested, with varying weight assigned by experts. The U.S. Senate's Levin-Coburn Report concluded that the crisis was the result of ⌈high risk, complex financial products; undisclosed conflicts of interest; the failure of regulators, the credit rating agencies, and the market itself to rein in the excesses of Wall Street.⌋ The Financial Crisis Inquiry Commission concluded that the financial crisis was avoidable and was caused by ⌈widespread failures in financial regulation and supervision,⌋ ⌈dramatic failures of corporate governance and risk management at many systemically important financial institutions,⌋ ⌈a combination of excessive borrowing, risky investments, and lack of transparency⌋ by financial institutions, ill preparation and inconsistent action by government that ⌈added to the uncertainty and panic,⌋ a ⌈systemic breakdown in accountability and ethics,⌋ ⌈collapsing mortgage-lending standards and the mortgage securitization pipeline,⌋ deregulation of over-the-counter derivatives, especially credit default swaps, and ⌈the failures of credit rating agencies⌋ to correctly price risk. Critics argued that credit rating agencies and investors failed to accurately price the risk involved with mortgage-related financial products, and that governments did not adjust their regulatory practices to address 21st-century financial markets. Research into the causes of the financial crisis has also focused on the role of interest rate spreads.

The immediate cause or trigger of the crisis was the bursting of the United States housing bubble which peaked in approximately 2005-2006. Already-rising default rates on ⌈subprime⌋ and adjustable-rate mortgages (ARM) began to increase quickly thereafter. As banks began to give out more loans to potential home owners, housing prices began to rise.

Easy availability of credit in the U.S., fueled by large inflows of foreign funds after the Russian debt crisis and Asian financial crisis of the 1997-1998 period, led to a housing construction boom and facilitated debt-financed consumer spending. Lax lending standards and rising real estate prices also contributed to the real estate bubble. Loans of various types (e.g., mortgage, credit card, and auto) were easy to obtain and consumers assumed an unprecedented debt load.

As part of the housing and credit booms, the number of financial agreements called mortgage-backed securities (MBS) and collateralized debt obligations (CDO), which derived their value from mortgage payments and housing prices, greatly increased. Such financial innovation enabled institutions and investors around the world to invest in the U.S. housing market. As housing prices declined, major global financial institutions that had borrowed and invested heavily in subprime MBS reported significant losses.

Falling prices also resulted in homes worth less than the mortgage loan, providing a financial incentive to enter foreclosure. The ongoing foreclosure epidemic that began in late 2006 in the U.S. continues to drain wealth from consumers and erodes the financial strength of banking institutions. Defaults and losses on other loan types also increased significantly as the crisis expanded from the housing market to other parts of the economy. Total losses are estimated in the trillions of U.S. dollars globally.

While the housing and credit bubbles were building, a series of factors caused the financial system to both expand and become increasingly fragile, a process called financialization. U.S. Government policy from the 1970s onward has emphasized deregulation to encourage business, which resulted in less oversight of activities and less disclosure of information about new activities undertaken by banks and other evolving financial institutions. Thus, policymakers did not immediately recognize the increasingly important role played by financial institutions such as investment banks and hedge funds, also known as the shadow banking system. Some experts believe these institutions had become as important as commercial (depository) banks in providing credit to the U.S. economy, but they were not subject to the same regulations.

These institutions, as well as certain regulated banks, had also assumed significant debt burdens while providing the loans described above and did not have a financial cushion sufficient to absorb large loan defaults. These losses impacted the ability of financial institutions to lend, slowing economic activity. Concerns regarding the stability of key financial institutions drove central banks to provide funds to encourage lending and restore faith in the commercial paper markets, which are integral to funding business operations. Governments also bailed out key financial institutions and implemented economic stimulus programs, assuming significant additional financial commitments.

The U.S. Financial Crisis Inquiry Commission reported its findings in January 2011. It concluded that「the crisis was avoidable and was caused by: widespread failures in financial regulation, including the Federal Reserve's failure to stem the tide of toxic mortgages; dramatic breakdowns in corporate governance including too many financial firms acting recklessly and taking on too much risk; an explosive mix of excessive borrowing and risk by households and Wall Street that put the financial system on a collision course with crisis; key policy makers ill prepared for the crisis, lacking a full understanding of the financial system they oversaw; and systemic breaches in accountability and ethics at all levels⌋.

Global Effects

The financial crisis is likely to yield the biggest banking shakeout since the savings-and-loan meltdown. Investment bank UBS stated on October 6 that 2008 would see a clear global recession, with recovery unlikely for at least two years. Three days later UBS economists announced that the ⌈beginning of the end⌋ of the crisis had begun, with the world starting to make the necessary actions to fix the crisis: capital injection by governments; injection made systemically; interest rate cuts to help borrowers. The United Kingdom had started systemic injection, and the world's central banks were now cutting interest rates. UBS emphasized the United States needed to implement systemic injection. UBS further emphasized that this fixes only the financial crisis, but that in economic terms ⌈the worst is still to come⌋. UBS quantified their expected recession durations on October 16: the Eurozone's would last two quarters, the United States' would last three quarters, and the United Kingdom's would last four quarters. The economic crisis in Iceland involved all three of the country's major banks. Relative to the size of its economy, Iceland's banking collapse is the largest suffered by any country in economic history.

At the end of October UBS revised its outlook downwards: the forthcoming recession would be the worst since the early 1980s recession with negative 2009 growth for the U.S., Eurozone, UK; very limited recovery in 2010; but not as bad as the Great Depression.

The Brookings Institution reported in June 2009 that U.S. consumption accounted for more than a third of the growth in global consumption between 2000 and 2007. ⌈The US economy has been spending too much and borrowing too much for years and the rest of the world depended on the U.S. consumer as a source of global demand.⌋ With a recession in the U.S. and the increased savings rate of U.S. consumers, declines in growth elsewhere have been dramatic. For the first quarter of 2009, the annualized rate of decline in GDP was 14.4% in Germany, 15.2% in Japan, 7.4% in the UK, 18% in Latvia, 9.8% in the Euro area and 21.5% for Mexico.

Some developing countries that had seen strong economic growth saw significant slowdowns. For example, growth forecasts in Cambodia show a fall from more than 10% in 2007 to close to zero in 2009, and Kenya may achieve only 3%–4% growth in 2009, down from 7% in 2007. According to the research by the Overseas Development Institute, reductions in growth can be attributed to falls in trade, commodity prices, investment and remittances sent from migrant workers (which reached a record $ 251 billion in 2007, but have fallen in many countries since). Especially states with a fragile political system have to fear that investors from Western states withdraw their money because of the crisis.

The World Bank reported in February 2009 that the Arab World was far less severely affected by the credit crunch. With generally good balance of payments positions coming into the crisis or with alternative sources of financing for their large current account deficits, such as remittances, Foreign Direct Investment (FDI) or foreign aid, Arab countries were able to avoid going to the market in the latter part of 2008. This group is in the best position to absorb the economic shocks. They entered the crisis in exceptionally strong positions. This gives them a significant cushion against the global downturn. The greatest impact of the global economic crisis will come in the form of lower oil prices, which remains the single most important determinant of economic performance. Steadily declining oil prices would force them to draw down reserves and cut down on investments. Significantly lower oil prices could cause a reversal of economic performance as has been the case in past oil shocks. Initial impact will be seen on public finances and employment for foreign workers.

The U.S. Federal Reserve and central banks around the world have taken steps to expand money supplies to avoid the risk of a deflationary spiral, in which lower wages and higher unemployment lead to a self-reinforcing decline in global consumption. In addition, governments have enacted large fiscal stimulus packages, by borrowing and spending to offset the reduction in private sector demand caused by the crisis. The U.S. executed two stimulus packages, totaling nearly $1 trillion during 2008 and 2009. The U.S. Federal Reserve's new and expanded liquidity facilities were intended to enable the central bank to fulfill its traditional lender-of-last-resort role during the crisis while mitigating stigma, broadening the set of institutions with access to liquidity, and increasing the flexibility with which institutions could tap such liquidity.

This credit freeze brought the global financial system to the brink of collapse. The response of the Federal Reserve, the European Central Bank, and other central banks was immediate and dramatic. During the last quarter of 2008, these central banks purchased US $2.5 trillion of government debt and troubled private assets from banks. This was the largest liquidity injection into the credit market, and the largest monetary policy action in world history. The governments of European nations and the USA also raised the capital of their national banking systems by $1.5 trillion, by purchasing newly issued preferred stock in their major banks.

Governments have also bailed out a variety of firms as discussed above, incurring large financial obligations. To date, various U.S. government agencies have committed or spent trillions of dollars in loans, asset purchases, guarantees, and direct spending.

United States President Barack Obama and key advisers introduced a series of regulatory proposals in June 2009. The proposals address consumer protection, executive pay, bank financial cushions or capital requirements, expanded regulation of the shadow banking system and derivatives, and enhanced authority for the Federal Reserve to safely wind-down systemically important institutions, among others.

European regulators introduced Basel III regulations for banks. It increased capital ratios, limits on leverage, narrow definition of capital (to exclude subordinated debt), limit counterparty risk, and new liquidity requirements.

The U.S. recession that began in December 2007 ended in June 2009. In April 2009 *TIME* magazine declared「More Quickly Than It Began, The Banking Crisis Is Over.」President Barack Obama declared on January 27, 2010,「the markets are now stabilized, and we've recovered most of the money we spent on the banks.」

Advanced economies led global economic growth prior to the financial crisis with「emerging」and「developing」economies lagging behind. The crisis completely overturned this relationship. The International Monetary Fund found that「advanced」economies accounted for only 31% of global GDP while emerging and developing economies accounted for 69% of global GDP from 2007 to 2014.

Glossary

Part I

bond   n. 債券
principal   n. 本金
maturity   n.（票據等的）到期
interval   n.（時間）間隔
underwriting   n. 包銷，承銷
Syndicate   n. 財團
bookrunner   n. 配售經辦人
tombstone   n. 發行公告
sovereign   adj.（國家）具有獨立主權的
entity   n. 實體
denominate   v. 命名
proceeds   n. 收入，收益
swap   n. 交換
hedge   n. 防範措施
creditworthiness   n. 商譽
nominal   adj. 票面上的
redeem   v. 償還；兌現
decimal   adj. 十進位的，小數的
decentralize   v. 權力分散（下放）
liquidity   n. 流動性；流動資金
hedge fund   避險基金，對沖基金
municipal   adj. 市政的
equities   n.（公司的）普通股
liquidate   v. 清算；清償
periodic   adj. 週期的；定期的
recapitalization   n. 資本結構的改變，資本額的調整
samurai   n.（日本封建時代的）武士

creditworthy　adj. 有信譽的
trillion　n. 萬億
yield curve　收益率曲線
futures　n. 期貨
glut　n. 供過於求
insulate　v. 使隔離, 使孤立
forward contract　期貨合同
derivative　n. 衍生性金融商品
open-outcry　n. 公開競價, 現場叫價
unveil　v. 推出; 出抬
novel　adj. 新穎的, 新奇的
mandate　n. 授權
statutory　adj. 法定的, 法令的
fare　v. 進展
level　v. 使對準
retrieval　n. 檢索
mandatory　adj. 強制的
securities　n. 有價證券
penalty　n. 懲罰

Part II

aggregation　n. 聚集
domicile　v. 定居, 以……為基地
institutionalized　adj. 制度化的
exorbitant　adj. 過度的, 過高的
oligopolistic　adj. 寡占的; 由少數壟斷的
counterparty　n. 對方, 另一方
default　v. 違約
disintermediation　n. 非居間化（銀行存款轉為直接證券投資）
rout　v. 大敗; 徹底打敗
accentuate　v. 使突出
abrupt　adj. 突然的; 意外的
grid　n.（輸送電力等的）系統網絡
misallocate　v. 錯配
dictate　v. 決定; 支配
speculative　adj. 投機的
halt　v. 使停止; 使中斷
confer　v. 授予, 賦予

facilitate   v. 促進；助長
simultaneously   adv. 同時地；一齊
hybrid   adj. 混合的
notable   adj. 顯著的；著名的
façade   n.（建築物的）正面，立面
precipitate   v. 突然降臨，加速
unveil   v. 使公之於眾；揭露
leverage   v. 舉債經營；為……融資
aftermath   n. 後果；餘波
executive   n.（公司或機構的）經理
remedy   v. 糾正，改進
trillion   n. 萬億
premises   n. 經營場所；辦公場所
sophisticated   adj. 複雜的；先進的
standalone   adj. 單獨的，獨立的

Part III

anchor   v. 與……有緊密聯繫；使固守
immense   adj. 極大的，巨大的
debris   n. 碎片，殘骸
dwarf   v. 使相形見絀
vehicular   adj. 車的，車輛的
bollard   n. 路樁
high-rise   n. 高層建築
spur   v. 加速，促進
residential   adj. 住宅的
sprout   v. 出現；（使）湧現出
exertions   n. 努力，運用
metropolitan   adj. 大都會的；大城市的
wrench   v. 使痛苦
respectable   adj. 可觀的
enumerate   v. 列舉，枚舉
shot-gun   adj. 強迫的
catastrophic adj. 災難的；慘重的
repercussion   n. 反響，影響
elitism   n. 精英主義
Gilded Age   繁榮昌盛時代（尤指美國內戰後的 28 年期間，約 1870—1898）；
ostensibly   adv. 表面上地

spiral   n. 急遽變化
fallout   n. 後果；餘波
bilk   v. 蒙騙
anthropology   n. 人類學
hierarchical   adj. 等級的；分層的
lens   n. 鏡頭
counteract   v. 抵消
segregation   n. 分離，隔離

Part IV

eviction   n. 逐出，趕出
foreclosure   n. 喪失抵押品贖回權
prolonged   adj. 持續很久的；時間長的
plummet   v. 驟然下跌，暴跌
escalate   v. 逐步上升
prioritize   v. 優先考慮；給……優先權
solvency   n. 償付能力
palliative   adj. 保守的
lax   adj. 寬鬆的
collateralize   v. 以……作抵押
epidemic   n. 盛行，泛濫
erode   v. 削弱，損害
proliferate   v. 激增
contrarian   adj. 採取相反態度的
spike   v. 迅速升值；急遽增值
contend   v. 聲稱，主張
concede   v. 承認
pronounced   adj. 明顯的，顯著的
trough   n. 低谷
remittance   n. 匯款金額
crunch   n. 危急情況
deflationary   adj. 通貨緊縮的
enact   v. 制定（法律），通過（法案）
stigma   n. 恥辱；羞恥
brink   n. 邊緣，初始狀態
proprietary   adj. 專有的，專利的
stabilization   n. 穩定性

Phrases

at par 與票面價值相等；按票面價格
at a premium 超出平常價；以高價
be subjected to 使……經受；使……遭受
back out 食言；退出
team up with 與……合作
track down 追查；查獲
adhere to 堅持，遵守，遵循
in excess of 多於，超出
spin off 剝離出，分立
file for 申請
fall through 落空；成為泡影
be synonymous with ……的同義詞；等同於
bail out （常指通過出資）幫助……脫離困境
rein in 控制，約束

Notes

M&A：Merger and Acquisition 的首字母合成，即合併；兼併，指的是兩家或者更多的獨立企業合併組成一家企業。通常由一家占優勢的公司收購一家或者多家公司。收購方承擔目標公司所有債權、負債的收購過程。

OTC：Over-The-Counter 場外交易，亦稱店頭交易、直接交易。在證券交易所之外所進行的證券交易。主要特點：①沒有一個集中的交易場所，買賣雙方分散於全國各地，買賣主要通過電話、計算機系統進行。②買賣對象以未上市證券為主，也有部分上市證券進行場外交易。③債券買賣較多，包括所有的政府公債和一些大公司債券，也有部分股票，特別是金融業和保險公司股票。④協商定價。

CME：Chicago Mercantile Exchange 首字母的縮寫，指芝加哥商業交易所，是美國最大的期貨交易所，也是世界上第二大買賣期貨和期貨期權合約的交易所。芝加哥商業交易所向投資者提供多項金融和農產品交易。

NYMEX：紐約商業交易所，地處紐約曼哈頓金融中心，與紐約證券交易所相鄰。它的交易主要涉及能源和稀有金屬兩大類產品，但能源產品交易大大超過其他產品的交易。交易所的交易方式主要是期貨和期權交易，到目前為止，期貨交易量遠遠超過期權交易量。紐約商業交易所於 2008 年被 CME 集團收購。

CBOT：芝加哥期貨交易所，成立於 1848 年，由 83 位穀物交易商發起組建。1865 年用標準的期貨合約取代了遠期合同，並實行了保證金制度。2006 年 10 月 17 日芝加哥商業交易所（CME）和芝加哥期貨交易所（CBOT）宣布已經就合併事宜達成最終協議，兩家交易所合併成全球最大的衍生品交易所——芝加哥交易所集團。

Euronext：歐洲交易所，是歐洲第一大證券交易所、世界第二大衍生產品交易所。2007 年 3 月底，歐洲證券交易所與紐約證券交易所合併組成紐約-泛歐交易所（NYSE Euronext），並於 2007 年 4 月 4 日在紐交所和歐交所同時掛牌上市。

JSE：約翰內斯堡證券交易所，成立於 1887 年 11 月。成立之初主要是為金礦開發籌資，此後融資方向開始多元化，目前礦業股仍占相當地位，但工業和金融股已成為交易所的主角。

SEC：美國證券交易委員會，成立於 1934 年，是直屬美國聯邦的獨立準司法機構，負責美國的證券監督和管理工作，是美國證券行業的最高機構。證券交易委員會的總部在華盛頓特區。美國證券交易委員會（SEC）具有準立法權、準司法權、獨立執法權。美國證券交易委員會的管理條例旨在加強信息的充分披露，保護市場上公眾投資利益不被玩忽職守和虛假信息所損害。

NASDAQ：納斯達克，指美國「全國證券交易商協會自動報價系統」，NASDAQ 是其英文縮寫。1971 年創立，是世界上第一個電子化證券市場，它通過計算機網絡將股票經紀人、做市商、投資者和監管機構聯繫起來，是世界上最成功和發展最快的證券市場。

Questions

1. When was the Chicago Board of Trade (CBOT) formed?
2. What mission does the U.S. Securities and Exchange Commission (SEC) have?
3. What is the importance of stock markets?
4. What securities are available for trading on the London Stock Exchange?
5. What caused Financial Crisis of 2007-2008 accarding to your opinion?
6. What global effects can financial crisis bring upon?

Chapter Ⅶ

Commercial Law and IPR Protection

Commercial law, also known as trade law, is the body of law that applies to the rights, relations, and conduct of persons and businesses engaged in commerce, merchandising, trade, and sales. It is often considered to be a branch of civil law and deals with issues of both private law and public law.

The need to regulate trade and commerce and resolve business disputes helped shape the creation of law and courts. Commercial law is a very detailed and well-established body of rules that evolved over a very long period of time applies to commercial transactions. The Code of Hammurabi dates back to about 1772 BC for example, and contains provisions that relate, among other matters, to shipping costs and dealings between merchants and brokers.

Commercial law includes within its compass such titles as principal and agent; carriage by land and sea; merchant shipping; guarantee; marine, fire, life, and accident insurance; bills of exchange, negotiable instruments, contracts and partnership. It can also be understood to regulate corporate contracts, hiring practices, and the manufacture and sales of consumer goods. Many countries have adopted civil codes that contain comprehensive statements of their commercial law.

Intellectual Property Rights (IPR) include patents, copyright, industrial design rights, trademarks, plant variety rights, trade dress, geographical indications, and in some jurisdictions trade secrets. There are also more specialized or derived varieties of exclusive rights, such as circuit design rights (called mask work rights in the US) and supplementary protection certificates for pharmaceutical products (after expiry of a patent protecting them) and database rights (in European law). The term 「industrial property」 is sometimes used to refer to a large subset of intellectual property rights including patents, trademarks, industrial designs, utility models, service marks, trade names, and geographical indications.

Part Ⅰ Commercial Law and Corporate Governance

In many countries it is difficult to compile all the laws that can affect a business into a single reference source. Laws can govern treatment of labour and employee relations, worker protection and safety, discrimination on the basis of age, gender, disability, race, and in some jurisdictions, sexual orientation, and the minimum wage, as well as unions, worker compensation, and working hours and leave.

So, Commercial law spans general corporate law, employment and labor law, health-care law, securities law, mergers and acquisitions, tax law, employee benefit plans, food and drug regulation, intellectual property law on copyrights, patents, trademarks and such, telecommunications law, etc..

Some specialized businesses may also require licenses, either due to laws governing entry into certain trades, occupations or professions, that require special education, or to raise revenue for local governments. Professions that require special licenses include law, medicine, piloting aircraft, selling liquor, radio broadcasting, selling investment securities, selling used cars, and roofing. Local jurisdictions may also require special licenses and taxes just to operate a business.

Some businesses are subject to ongoing special regulation, for example, public utilities, investment securities, banking, insurance, broadcasting, aviation, and health care providers. Environmental regulations are also very complex and can affect many businesses.

Businesses that have gone public are subject to regulations concerning their internal governance, such as how executive officers' compensation is determined, and when and how information is disclosed to shareholders and to the public. In the United States, these regulations are primarily implemented and enforced by the United States Securities and Exchange Commission (SEC). Other Western nations have comparable regulatory bodies. In China, the regulations are implemented and enforced by the China Securities Regulation Commission (CSRC). In Singapore, the regulation authority is the Monetary Authority of Singapore (MAS), and in Hong Kong, it is the Securities and Futures Commission (SFC).

Corporate Law

The proliferation and increasing complexity of the laws governing business have forced increasing specialization in corporate law. Corporate law (also 「company」 or 「corporations」 law) is the study of how shareholders, directors, employees, creditors, and other stakeholders such as consumers, the community and the environment interact with one another. Corporate law is a part of a broader companies law (or law of business associations). Under corporate law, corporations of all sizes have separate legal personality, with limited or unlimited liability for its shareholders. Shareholders control the company through a board of directors which, in turn, typically delegates control of the corporation's day-to-day operations to a full-time executive. Corporate law deals with firms that are incorporated or registered under the corporate or company law of a sovereign state or their sub-national states. The four defining characteristics of the modern corporation are:

· Separate legal personality of the corporation (access to tort and contract law in a manner similar to a person)

· Limited liability of the shareholders (a shareholder's personal liability is limited to the value of their shares in the corporation)

· Shares (if the corporation is a public company, the shares are traded on a stock exchange)

· Delegated management; the board of directors delegates day-to-day management of the company to executives

In many developed countries outside of the English speaking world, company boards are appointed as representatives of both shareholders and employees to 「co-determine」 company strategy. Corporate law is often divided into corporate governance (which concerns the various power relations within a corporation) and corporate finance (which concerns the rules on how capital is used).

Corporate Governance

Corporate governance broadly refers to the mechanisms, processes and relations by which corporations are controlled and directed. Governance structures identify the distribution of rights and responsibilities among a corporation's senior executives, its board of directors and those who elect them (shareholders in the 「general meeting」 and employees). It also concerns other stakeholders, such as creditors, consumers, the environment and the community at large. One of the main differences between different countries in the internal form of companies is between a two-tier and a one tier board. The United Kingdom, the United States, and most Commonwealth countries have single unified boards of directors. In Germany, companies have two tiers, so that shareholders (and employees) elect a 「supervisory board」, and then the supervisory board chooses the 「management board」. There is the option to use two tiers in France, and in the new European Companies.

The most important rules for corporate governance are those concerning the balance of power between the board of directors and the members of the company. Authority is given or 「delegated」 to the board to manage the company for the success of the investors. Certain specific decision rights are often reserved for shareholders, where their interests could be fundamentally affected. There are necessarily rules on when directors can be removed from office and replaced. To do that, meetings need to be called to vote on the issues.

Corporate governance includes the processes through which corporations' objectives are set and pursued in the context of the social, regulatory and market environment. Governance mechanisms include monitoring the actions, policies and decisions of corporations and their agents. Corporate governance practices are affected by attempts to align the interests of stakeholders. Interest in the corporate governance practices of modern corporations, particularly in relation to accountability, increased following the high-profile collapses of a number of large corporations during 2001–2002, most of which involved accounting fraud; and then again after the recent financial crisis in 2008. Corporate scandals of various forms have maintained public and political interest in the regulation of corporate governance.

In contemporary business corporations, the main external stakeholder groups are shareholders, debtholders, trade creditors and suppliers, customers, and communities affected by the corporation's activities. Internal stakeholders are the board of directors, executives, and other employees.

Much of the contemporary interest in corporate governance is concerned with mitigation of the conflicts of interests between stakeholders. In large firms where there is a separation of ownership and management and no controlling shareholder, the principal-agent issue arises between upper-management (the 「agent」) which may have very different interests, and by definition considerably more information, than shareholders (the 「principals」). The danger arises that, rather than overseeing management on behalf of shareholders, the board of directors may become insulated from shareholders and beholden to management. This aspect is particularly present in contemporary public debates and developments in regulatory policy.

Ways of mitigating or preventing these conflicts of interests include the processes, customs, policies, laws, and institutions which have an impact on the way a company is controlled. An important theme of governance is the nature and extent of corporate accountability. A related discussion at the macro level focuses on the impact of a corporate governance system on economic efficiency, with a strong emphasis on shareholders' welfare.

One of the key legal features of corporations are their separate legal personality, also known as 「personhood」 or being 「artificial persons」.

As artificial persons, companies can only act through human agents. The main agent who deals with the company's management and business is the board of directors, but in many jurisdictions other officers can be appointed too. The board of directors is normally elected by the members, and the other officers are normally appointed by the board. These agents enter into contracts on behalf of the company with third parties.

In most jurisdictions, directors owe strict duties of good faith, as well as duties of care and skill, to safeguard the interests of the company and the members.

The standard of skill and care that a director owes is usually described as acquiring and maintaining sufficient knowledge and understanding of the company's business to enable him to properly discharge his duties.

Directors are also strictly charged to exercise their powers only for a proper purpose. For instance, were a director to issue a large number of new shares, not for the purposes of raising capital but in order to defeat a potential takeover bid, that would be an improper purpose.

Directors have a duty to exercise reasonable skill care and diligence. This duty enables the company to seek compensation from its director if it can be proved that a director has not shown reasonable skill or care which in turn has caused the company to incur a loss.

Directors also owe strict duties not to permit any conflict of interest or conflict with their duty to act in the best interests of the company. This rule is so strictly enforced that, even where the conflict of interest or conflict of duty is purely hypothetical, the directors can be forced to disgorge all personal gains arising from it.

Members of a company generally have rights against each other and against the company, as framed under the company's constitution. However, members cannot generally claim against third parties who cause damage to the company which results in a diminution in the value of their shares or others membership interests because this is treated as 「reflective loss」 and the law normally regards the company as the proper claimant in such cases.

In relation to the exercise of their rights, minority shareholders usually have to accept that, because of the limits of their voting rights, they cannot direct the overall control of the company and must accept the will of the majority (often expressed as *majority rule*). However, majority rule can be iniquitous, particularly where there is one controlling shareholder. Accordingly, a number of exceptions have developed in law in relation to the general principle of majority rule.

· Where the majority shareholder (s) are exercising their votes to perpetrate a fraud on the minority, the courts may permit the minority to sue

· members always retain the right to sue if the majority acts to invade their personal rights, e.g. where the company's affairs are not conducted in accordance with the company's constitution (this position has been debated because the extent of a personal right is not set in law).

· in many jurisdictions it is possible for minority shareholders to take a representative or derivative action in the name of the company, where the company is controlled by the alleged wrongdoers.

Companies generally raise capital for their business ventures either by debt or equity. Capital raised by way of equity is usually raised by issued shares or warrants.

A share is an item of property, and can be sold or transferred. Holding a share makes the holder a member of the company, and entitles them to enforce the provisions of the company's constitution against the company and against other members. Shares also normally have a nominal or par value, which is the limit of the shareholder's liability to contribute to the debts of the company on an liquidation.

Many companies have different classes of shares, offering different rights to the shareholders. For example, a company might issue both ordinary shares and preference shares, with the two types having different voting and/or economic rights. For example, a company might provide that preference shareholders shall each receive a cumulative preferred dividend of a certain amount per annum, but the ordinary shareholders shall receive everything else.

The total number of issued shares in a company is said to represent its *capital*. Many jurisdictions regulate the minimum amount of capital which a company may have, although some countries only prescribe minimum amounts of capital for companies engaging in certain types of business (e.g. banking, insurance etc.).

Similarly, most jurisdictions regulate the maintenance of capital, and prevent companies returning funds to shareholders by way of distribution when this might leave the company financially exposed. In some jurisdictions this extends to prohibiting a company from providing financial assistance for the purchase of its own shares.

Liquidation is the normal means by which a company's existence is brought to an end. It is also referred to (either alternatively or concurrently) in some jurisdictions as winding up or dissolution. Liquidations generally come in two forms, either compulsory liquidations and voluntary liquidations. Where a company goes into liquidation, normally a liquidator is appointed to gather in all the company's assets and settle all claims against the company. If there is any surplus after paying off all the creditors of the company, this surplus is then distributed to the members.

As its names imply, applications for compulsory liquidation are normally made by creditors of the company when the company is unable to pay its debts. However, in some jurisdictions, regulators have the power to apply for the liquidation of the company on the grounds of public good, i.e. where the company is believed to have engaged in unlawful conduct, or conduct which is otherwise harmful to the public at large.

Voluntary liquidations occur when the company's members decide voluntarily to wind up the affairs of the company. This may be because they believe that the company will soon become insolvent, or it may be on economic grounds if they believe that the purpose for which the company was formed is now at an end, or that the company is not providing an adequate return on assets and should be broken up and sold off.

Insider trading is the trading of a corporation's stock or other securities (e.g. bonds or stock options) by individuals with potential access to non-public information about the company. In most countries, trading by corporate insiders such as officers, key employees, directors, and large shareholders may be legal, if this trading is done in a way that does not take advantage of non-public information. However, the term is frequently used to refer to a practice in which an insider or a related party trades based on material non-public information obtained during the performance of the insider's duties at the corporation, or otherwise in breach of a fiduciary or other relationship of trust and confidence or where the non-public information was misappropriated from the company. Illegal insider trading is believed to raise the cost of capital for securities issuers, thus decreasing overall economic growth.

In the United States and several other jurisdictions, trading conducted by corporate officers, key employees, directors, or significant shareholders (in the U.S., defined as beneficial owners of ten percent or more of the firm's equity securities) must be reported to the regulator or publicly disclosed, usually within a few business days of the trade. Many investors follow the summaries of these insider trades in the hope that mimicking these trades will be profitable. While 「legal」 insider trading cannot be based on material non-public information, some investors believe corporate insiders nonetheless may have better insights into the health of a corporation (broadly speaking) and that their trades otherwise convey important information (e.g., about the pending retirement of an important officer selling shares, greater commitment to the corporation by officers purchasing shares, etc.)

Part II   Intellectual Property Rights Protection

Businesses often have important 「intellectual property」 that needs protection from competitors for the company to stay profitable. This could require patents, copyrights, trademarks or preservation of trade secrets. Most businesses have names, logos and similar branding techniques that could benefit from trademarking. Patents and copyrights in the United States are largely governed by federal law, while trade secrets and trademarking are mostly a matter of state law. Because of the nature of intellectual property, a business needs protection in every jurisdiction in which they are concerned about competitors. Many countries are signatories to international treaties concerning intellectual property, and thus companies registered in these countries are subject to national laws bound by these treaties. In order to protect trade secrets, companies may require employees to sign non-compete clauses which will impose limitations on an employee's interactions with stakeholders, and competitors.

Trademark

A trademark, trade mark, or trade-mark is typically a name, word, phrase, logo, symbol, design, image, or a combination of these elements to identify products or services of a particular source from those of others. There is also a range of non-conventional trademarks comprising marks which do not fall into these standard categories, such as those based on color, smell, or sound (like jingles). The trademark owner can be an individual, business organization, or any legal entity. A trademark may be located on a package, a label, a voucher or on the product itself. For the sake of corporate identity trademarks are also being displayed on company buildings.

The term *trademark* is also used informally to refer to any distinguishing attribute by which an individual is readily identified, such as the well-known characteristics of celebrities. When a trademark is used in relation to services rather than products, it may sometimes be called a service mark, particularly in the United States.

A trademark may be designated by the following symbols:

- ™ (the ⌈trademark symbol⌋, which is the letters ⌈TM⌋, for an unregistered trademark, a mark used to promote or brand goods)
- ℠ (which is the letters ⌈SM⌋ in superscript, for an unregistered service mark, a mark used to promote or brand services)
- ® (the letter ⌈R⌋ surrounded by a circle, for a registered trademark)

The essential function of a trademark is to exclusively identify the commercial source or origin of products or services, so a trademark, properly called, *indicates source* or serves as a *badge of origin*. In other words, trademarks serve to identify a particular business as the source of goods or services. The use of a trademark in this way is known as *trademark use*. Certain exclusive rights attach to a registered mark.

It should be noted that trademark rights generally arise out of the use of, or to maintain exclusive rights over, that sign in relation to certain products or services, assuming there are no other trademark objections.

Different goods and services have been classified by the International (Nice) Classification of Goods and Services into 45 Trademark Classes (1 to 34 cover goods, and 35 to 45 services). The idea behind this system is to specify and limit the extension of the intellectual property right by determining which goods or services are covered by the mark, and to unify classification systems around the world.

The law considers a trademark to be a form of property. Proprietary rights in relation to a trademark may be established through actual use in the marketplace, or through registration of the mark with the trademarks office (or 「trademarks registry」) of a particular jurisdiction. In some jurisdictions, trademark rights can be established through either or both means. Certain jurisdictions generally do not recognize trademarks rights arising through use. If trademark owners do not hold registrations for their marks in such jurisdictions, the extent to which they will be able to enforce their rights through trademark infringement proceedings will therefore be limited. In cases of dispute, this disparity of rights is often referred to as 「first to file」 as opposed to 「first to use.」 Other countries such as Germany offer a limited amount of common law rights for unregistered marks where to gain protection, the goods or services must occupy a highly significant position in the marketplace—where this could be 40% or more market share for sales in the particular class of goods or services.

In the United States, the registration process includes several steps. First, the trademark owner files an application to register the trademark. About three months after it is filed, the application is reviewed by an examining attorney at the U.S. Patent and Trademark Office. The examining attorney checks for compliance with the rules of the Trademark Manual of Examination Procedure. This review includes procedural matters such as making sure the applicant's goods or services are identified properly. It also includes more substantive matters such as making sure the applicant's mark is not merely descriptive or likely to cause confusion with a pre-existing applied-for or registered mark. If the application runs afoul of any requirement, the examining attorney will issue an office action requiring the applicant to address certain issues or refusals prior to registration of the mark. If the examining attorney approves the application, it will be 「published for opposition.」 During this 30-day period third parties who may be affected by the registration of the trademark may step forward to file an Opposition Proceeding to stop the registration of the mark. If an Opposition proceeding is filed it institutes a case before the Trademark Trial and Appeal Board to determine both the validity of the grounds for the opposition as well as the ability of the applicant to register the mark at issue. Finally, provided that no third-party opposes the registration of the mark during the opposition period or the opposition is ultimately decided in the applicant's favor the mark will be registered in due course. Once an application is reviewed by an examiner and found to be entitled to registration a registration certificate is issued subject to the mark being open to opposition for a period of typically 6 months from the date of registration.

A registered trademark confers a bundle of exclusive rights upon the registered owner, including the right to exclusive use of the mark in relation to the products or services for which it is registered. The law in most jurisdictions also allows the owner of a registered trademark to prevent unauthorized use of the mark in relation to products or services which are identical or 「colourfully」 similar to the 「registered」 products or services, and in certain cases, prevent use in relation to entirely dissimilar products or services. The test is always whether a consumer of the goods or services will be confused as to the identity of the source or origin. An example may be a very large multinational brand such as 「Sony」 where a non-electronic product such as a pair of sunglasses might be assumed to have come from Sony Corporation of Japan despite not being a class of goods that Sony has rights in.

Once trademark rights are established in a particular jurisdiction, these rights are generally only enforceable in that jurisdiction. However, there is a range of international trademark laws and systems which facilitate the protection of trademarks in more than one jurisdiction.

In most systems, a trademark can be registered if it is able to distinguish the goods or services of a party, will not confuse consumers about the relationship between one party and another, and will not otherwise deceive consumers with respect to the qualities.

Trademarks rights must be maintained through actual lawful use of the trademark. These rights will cease if a mark is not actively used for a period of time, normally 5 years in most jurisdictions. In the case of a trademark registration, failure to actively use the mark in the lawful course of trade, or to enforce the registration in the event of infringement, may also expose the registration itself to become liable for an application for the removal from the register after a certain period of time on the grounds of 「non-use」. It is not necessary for a trademark owner to take enforcement action against all infringement if it can be shown that the owner perceived the infringement to be minor and inconsequential. This is designed to prevent owners from continually being tied up in litigation for fear of cancellation. An owner can at any time commence action for infringement against a third party as long as it had not previously notified the third party of its discontent following third party use and then failed to take action within a reasonable period of time (called acquiescence). The owner can always reserve the right to take legal action until a court decides that the third party had gained notoriety which the owner 「must」 have been aware of. It will be for the third party to prove their use of the mark is substantial as it is the onus of a company using a mark to check they are not infringing previously registered rights. In the US, owing to the overwhelming number of unregistered rights, trademark applicants are advised to perform searches not just of the trademark register but of local business directories and relevant trade press. Specialized search companies perform such tasks prior to application.

All jurisdictions with a mature trademark registration system provide a mechanism for removal in the event of such *non use*, which is usually a period of either three or five years.

In the U.S., failure to use a trademark for this period of time will result in *abandonment* of the mark, whereby any party may use the mark. An abandoned mark is not irrevocably in the public domain, but may instead be re-registered by any party which has re-established exclusive and active use, and must be associated or linked with the original mark owner. A mark is registered in conjunction with a description of a specific type of goods, and if the party uses the mark but in conjunction with a different type of goods, the mark may still be considered abandoned. If a court rules that a trademark has become 「generic」 through common use (such that the mark no longer performs the essential trademark function and the average consumer no longer considers that exclusive rights attach to it), the corresponding registration may also be ruled invalid.

Unlike other forms of intellectual property (e.g., patents and copyrights) a registered trademark can, theoretically, last forever. So long as a trademark's use is continuous a trademark holder may keep the mark registered with the U.S. Patent and Trademark Office as required.

While trademark law seeks to protect indications of the commercial source of products or services, patent law generally seeks to protect new and useful inventions, and registered designs law generally seeks to protect the look or appearance of a manufactured article. Trademarks, patents and designs collectively form a subset of intellectual property known as industrial property because they are often created and used in an industrial or commercial context.

By comparison, copyright law generally seeks to protect original literary, artistic and other creative works. Continued active use and re-registration can make a trademark perpetual, whereas copyright usually lasts for the duration of the author's lifespan plus 70 years for works by individuals.

Although intellectual property laws such as these are theoretically distinct, more than one type may afford protection to the same article. For example, the particular design of a bottle may qualify for copyright protection as a non-utilitarian [sculpture], or for trademark protection based on its shape, or the 「trade dress」 appearance of the bottle as a whole may be protectable. Titles and character names from books or movies may also be protectable as trademarks while the works from which they are drawn may qualify for copyright protection as a whole. Trademark protection does not apply to utilitarian features of a product such as the plastic interlocking studs on Lego bricks.

Drawing these distinctions is necessary, but often challenging for the courts and lawyers, especially in jurisdictions where patents and copyrights pass into the public domain, depending on the jurisdiction. Unlike patents and copyrights, which in theory are granted for one-off fixed terms, trademarks remain valid as long as the owner actively uses and defends them and maintains their registrations with the competent authorities. This often involves payment of a periodic renewal fee.

As a trademark must be used to maintain rights in relation to that mark, a trademark can be 「abandoned」 or its registration can be cancelled or revoked if the mark is not continuously used. By comparison, patents and copyrights cannot be 「abandoned」 and a patent holder or copyright owner can generally enforce their rights without taking any particular action to maintain the patent or copyright. Additionally, patent holders and copyright owners may not necessarily need to actively police their rights. However, a failure to bring a timely infringement suit or action against a known infringer may give the defendant a defense of implied consent or estoppel when suit is finally brought.

Like patents and copyrights, trademarks can be bought, sold, and transferred from one company or another. Unlike patents and copyrights, trademarks may not remain intact through this process. Where trademarks have been acquired for the purpose of marketing generic (non-distinctive) products, courts have refused to enforce them.

Part III   Limits and defenses to claims of infringement

Trademark Infringement

Trademark infringement is a violation of the exclusive rights attached to a trademark without the authorization of the trademark owner. Infringement may occur when one party, the 「infringer」, uses a trademark which is identical or confusingly similar to a trademark owned by another party, in relation to products or services which are identical or similar to the products or services which the registration covers. An owner of a trademark may commence civil legal proceedings against a party which infringes its registered trademark. In the United States, the Trademark Counterfeiting Act of 1984 criminalized the intentional trade in counterfeit goods and services.

The owner of a trademark may pursue legal action against trademark infringement. Most countries require formal registration of a trademark as a precondition for pursuing this type of action. The United States, Canada and other countries also recognize common law trademark rights, which means action can be taken to protect an unregistered trademark if it is in use. Still common law trademarks offer the holder in general less legal protection than registered trademarks.

An example is that although Maytag owns the trademark 「Whisper Quiet」, makers of other products may describe their goods as being 「whisper quiet」 so long as these products do not fall under the same category of goods the trademark is protected under.

Another example is that Audi can run advertisements saying that a trade publication has rated an Audi model higher than a BMW model, since they are only using 「BMW」 to identify the competitor. In a related sense, an auto mechanic can truthfully advertise that he services Volkswagens, and a former *Playboy* Playmate of the Year can identify herself as such on her website.

A trademark is *diluted* when the use of similar or identical trademarks in other non-competing markets. Dilution protection law aims to protect sufficiently strong trademarks from losing their singular association in the public mind with a particular product. Under trademark law, dilution occurs either when unauthorized use of a mark 「blurs」 the 「distinctive nature of the mark」 or 「tarnishes it.」 Likelihood of confusion is not required.

A trademark cannot be offensive. Yet, trademarks can be licensed to others; for example, Bullyland obtained a license to produce Smurf figurines; the Lego Group purchased a license from Lucasfilm in order to be allowed to launch Lego Star Wars. The unauthorized usage of trademarks by producing and trading counterfeit consumer goods is known as brand piracy.

In various jurisdictions a trademark may be sold with or without the underlying goodwill. However, this is not the case in the United States, where the courts have held that this would 「be a fraud upon the public」. In the U.S., trademark registration can therefore only be sold and assigned if accompanied by the sale of an underlying asset. Examples of assets whose sale would ordinarily support the assignment of a mark include the sale of the machinery used to produce the goods that bear the mark, or the sale of the corporation (or subsidiary) that produces the trademarked goods.

Licensing means the trademark owner (the licensor) grants a permit to a third party (the licensee) in order to commercially use the trademark legally. It is a contract between the two, containing the scope of content and policy. The essential provisions to a trademark license identify the trademark owner and the licensee, in addition to the policy and the goods or services agreed to be licensed.

Most jurisdictions provide for the use of trademarks to be licensed to third parties. The licensor must monitor the quality of the goods being produced by the licensee to avoid the risk of trademark being deemed abandoned by the courts. A trademark license should therefore include appropriate provisions dealing with quality control, whereby the licensee provides warranties as to quality and the licensor has rights to inspection and monitoring.

Well-known trade mark status is commonly granted to famous international trade marks in less-developed legal jurisdictions.

If the mark is deemed well known it is an infringement to apply the same or a similar mark to dissimilar goods/services where there is confusion, including where it takes unfair advantage of the well-known mark or causing detriment to it.

A well-known trademark does not have to be registered in the jurisdiction to bring a trade mark infringement action.

Many countries protect unregistered well-known marks in accordance with their international obligations under the Paris Convention for the Protection of Industrial Property and the Agreement on Trade-Related Aspects of Intellectual Property Rights (the TRIPS Agreement). Consequently, not only big companies but also SMEs may have a good chance of establishing enough goodwill with customers so that their marks may be recognized as well-known marks and acquire protection without registration. It is, nevertheless, advisable to seek registration, taking into account that many countries provide for an extended protection of registered well-known marks against dilution (Art. 16. 3 TRIPS), i.e., the reputation of the mark being weakened by the unauthorized use of that mark by others.

The Community Trade Mark (CTM) system is the trademark system which applies in the European Union, whereby registration of a trademark with the Office for Harmonization in the Internal Market (OHIM, the trademarks office of the European Union), leads to a registration which is effective throughout the EU as a whole.

One of the tasks of a CTM owner is the monitoring of the later applications whether any of those is similar to his/her earlier trademark. Monitoring is not easy and usually requires professional expertise. To conduct a monitoring there is the so-called Trademark Watching service where it can be checked if someone tries to get registered marks that are similar to the existing marks.

The major international system for facilitating the registration of trademarks in multiple jurisdictions is commonly known as the 「Madrid system」. Madrid provides a centrally administered system for securing trademark registrations in member jurisdictions by extending the protection of an 「international registration」obtained through the World Intellectual Property Organization. This international registration is in turn based upon an application or registration obtained by a trade mark applicant in its home jurisdiction.

The primary advantage of the Madrid system is that it allows a trademark owner to obtain trademark protection in many jurisdictions by filing one application in one jurisdiction with one set of fees, and make any changes (e.g. changes of name or address) and renew registration across all applicable jurisdictions through a single administrative process. Furthermore, the 「coverage」of the international registration may be extended to additional member jurisdictions at any time.

The advent of the domain name system has led to attempts by trademark holders to enforce their rights over domain names that are similar or identical to their existing trademarks. The domain name owner actually uses the domain to compete with the trademark owner. Cybersquatting, an unlicensed user registers a domain name identical to a trademark, and offers to sell the domain to the trademark owner. Typosquatters—those registering common misspellings of trademarks as domain names—have also been targeted successfully in trademark infringement suits. 「Gripe sites」, on the other hand, tend to be protected as free speech, and are therefore more difficult to attack as trademark infringement.

Enforcing trademark rights over domain name owners involves protecting a trademark outside the obvious context of its consumer market, because domain names are global and not limited by goods or service.

This clash of the new technology with preexisting trademark rights resulted in several high profile decisions as the courts of many countries tried to coherently address the issue (and not always successfully) within the framework of existing trademark law. As the website itself was not the product being purchased, there was no actual consumer confusion.

Most courts particularly frown on cybersquatting, and have since amended their trademark laws to address domain names specifically, and to provide explicit remedies against cybersquatters.

Comparison of Patent Infringement

Patent infringement is the commission of a prohibited act with respect to a patented invention without permission from the patent holder. Permission may typically be granted in the form of a license. The definition of patent infringement may vary by jurisdiction, but it typically includes using or selling the patented invention. In many countries, a use is required to be *commercial* (or to have a *commercial* purpose) to constitute patent infringement.

The scope of the patented invention or the extent of protection is defined in the claims of the granted patent. In other words, the terms of the claims inform the public of what is not allowed without the permission of the patent holder.

Patents are territorial, and infringement is only possible in a country where a patent is in force. For example, if a patent is granted in the United States, then anyone in the United States is prohibited from making, using, selling or importing the patented item, while people in other countries may be free to exploit the patented invention in their country. The scope of protection may vary from country to country, because the patent is examined-or in some countries not substantively examined-by the patent office in each country or region and may be subject to different patentability requirements.

Comparison of Copyright Infringement

Copyright infringement is the use of works protected by copyright law without permission, infringing certain exclusive rights granted to the copyright holder, such as the right to reproduce, distribute, display or perform the protected work, or to make derivative works. The copyright holder is typically the work's creator, or a publisher or other business to whom copyright has been assigned. Copyright holders routinely invoke legal and technological measures to prevent and penalize copyright infringement.

Copyright infringement disputes are usually resolved through direct negotiation, a notice and take down process, or litigation in civil court. Egregious or large-scale commercial infringement, especially when it involves counterfeiting, is sometimes prosecuted via the criminal justice system. Shifting public expectations, advances in digital technology, and the increasing reach of the Internet have led to such widespread, anonymous infringement that copyright-dependent industries now focus less on pursuing individuals who seek and share copyright-protected content online, and more on expanding copyright law to recognize and penalize—as 「indirect」 infringers—the service providers and software distributors which are said to facilitate and encourage individual acts of infringement by others.

Part Ⅳ   Franchising and Chain Stores

Franchising is the practice of the right to use a firm's business model and brand for a prescribed period of time. For the franchisor, the franchise is an alternative to building 「chain stores」 to distribute goods that avoids the investments and liability of a chain. The franchisor's success depends on the success of the franchisees. The franchisee is said to have a greater incentive than a direct employee because he or she has a direct stake in the business.

Essentially, and in terms of distribution, the franchisor is a supplier who allows an operator, or a franchisee, to use the supplier's trademark and distribute the supplier's goods. In return, the operator pays the supplier a fee.

Thirty three countries—including the United States and Australia—have laws that explicitly regulate franchising, with the majority of all other countries having laws which have a direct or indirect impact on franchising.

Three important payments are made to a franchisor: (a) aroyalty for the trademark, (b) reimbursement for the training and advisory services given to the franchisee, and (c) a percentage of the individual business unit's sales. These three fees may be combined in a single 「management」 fee. A fee for 「disclosure」 is separate and is always a 「front-end fee」.

A franchise usually lasts for a fixed time period (broken down into shorter periods, which each require renewal), and serves a specific territory or geographical area surrounding its location. One franchisee may manage several such locations. Agreements typically last from five to thirty years, with premature cancellations or terminations of most contracts bearing serious consequences for franchisees. A franchise is merely a temporary business investment involving renting or leasing an opportunity, not the purchase of a business for the purpose of ownership.

Franchise fees are on average 6.7% with an additional average marketing fee of 2%.

Although franchisor revenues and profit may be listed in a franchise disclosure document (FDD), no laws require an estimate of franchisee profitability, which depends on how intensively the franchisee 「works」 the franchise. Therefore, franchisor fees are typically based on 「gross revenue from sales」 and not on profits realized.

A Franchise Agreement is a legal, binding contract between a franchisor and franchisee. In the United States franchise agreements are enforced at the State level.

Prior to a franchisee signing acontract, the US Federal Trade Commission regulates information disclosures under the authority of The Franchise Rule. The Franchise Rule requires a franchisee be supplied a Franchise Disclosure Document (FDD) (originally called Uniform Franchise Offering Circular (UFOC)) prior to signing a franchise agreement, a minimum of ten days before signing a franchise agreement.

Once the Federal ten day waiting period has passed, the Franchise Agreement becomes a State level jurisdiction document. Each state has unique laws regarding franchise agreements.

A franchise agreement contents can vary significantly in content depending upon the franchise system, the state jurisdiction of the franchisor, franchisee, and arbitrator.

It overall provides the investor with a product, a branded name and recognition, and a support system.

Franchise brokers help franchisors find appropriate franchisees. There are also main 「master franchisors」 who obtain the rights to sub-franchise in a territory. According to the International Franchise Association approximately 44% of all businesses in the United States are franchisee-worked.

Franchisors provide national or international advertising, training and other support services.

A franchise can be exclusive, non-exclusive or 「sole and exclusive」.

The displacement of independent businesses by chains has sparked increased collaboration among independent businesses and communities to prevent chain proliferation. These efforts include community-based organizing through Independent Business Alliances (in the U.S. and Canada) and 「buy local」 campaigns.

A variety of small towns in the United States whose residents wish to retain their distinctive character — such as Provincetown, Massachusetts, Idaho, Washington, and California — closely regulate, even exclude, chain stores. They don't exclude the chain itself, only the standardized formula the chain uses. For example, there could often be a restaurant owned by McDonald's that sells hamburgers, but not the formula franchise operation with the golden arches and standardized menu, uniforms, and procedures. The reason these towns regulate chain stores is to protect independent businesses from competition.

Franchising is one of the only means available to access venture capital without the need to give up control of the operation of the chain and build a distribution system for servicing it. After the brand and formula are carefully designed and properly executed, franchisors are able to sell franchises and expand rapidly across countries and continents using the capital and resources of their franchisees while reducing their own risk.

There is also risk for the people that are buying the franchises; failure rates are actually higher for franchise businesses than independent business startups, and it's important for today's franchise-seekers to be aware of that fact.

Franchisor rules imposed by the franchising authority are becoming increasingly strict. Some franchisors are using minor rule violations to terminate contracts and seize the franchise without any reimbursement.

Each party to a franchise has several interests to protect. The franchisor is involved in securing protection for the trademark, controlling the business concept and securing know-how. The franchisee is obligated to carry out the services for which the trademark has been made prominent or famous. There is a great deal of standardization required. The place of service has to bear the franchisor's signs, logos and trademark in a prominent place. The uniforms worn by the staff of the franchisee have to be of a particular design and color. The service has to be in accordance with the pattern followed by the franchisor in the successful franchise operations. Thus, franchisees are not in full control of the business, as they would be in retailing.

A service can be successful if equipment and supplies are purchased at a fair price from the franchisor or sources recommended by the franchisor. A coffee brew, for example, can be readily identified by the trademark if its raw materials come from a particular supplier. If the franchisor requires purchase from his stores, it may come under anti-trust legislation or equivalent laws of other countries. So too the purchase things like uniforms of personnel and signs, as well as the franchise sites, if they are owned or controlled by the franchisor.

The franchisee must carefully negotiate the license and must develop a marketing or business plan with the franchisor. The fees must be fully disclosed and there should not be any hidden fees. The start-up costs and working capital must be known before the license is granted. There must be assurance that additional licensees will not crowd the 「territory」 if the franchise is worked according to plan. The franchisee must be seen as an independent merchant. It must be protected by the franchisor from any trademark infringement by third parties. A franchise attorney is required to assist the franchisee during negotiations.

Often the training period-the costs of which are in great part covered by the initial fee-is too short in cases where it is necessary to operate complicated equipment, and the franchisee has to learn on their own from instruction manuals. The training period must be adequate, but in low-cost franchises it may be considered expensive. Many franchisors have set up corporate universities to train staff online. This is in addition to providing literature, sales documents and email access.

Also, franchise agreements carry no guarantees or warranties and the franchisee has little or no recourse to legal intervention in the event of a dispute. Franchise contracts tend to be unilateral and favor of the franchisor, who is generally protected from lawsuits from their franchisees because of the non-negotiable contracts that franchisees are required to acknowledge, in effect, that they are buying the franchise knowing that there is risk, and that they have not been promised success or profits by the franchisor. Contracts are renewable at the sole option of the franchisor. Most franchisors require franchisees to sign agreements that mandate where and under what law any dispute would be litigated.

Chain Stores

Chain stores or *retail chain* are retail outlets that share a brand/trademark and central management, and usually have standardized business methods and practices. In retail, dining, and many service categories, chain businesses have come to dominate the market in many parts of the world. A franchise retail establishment is one form of chain store.

The first recorded chain store was British-owned W H Smith. Founded in London in 1792 by Henry Walton Smith and his wife, the store sells books, stationery, magazines, newspapers, and entertainment products.

In the U.S., chain stores began with the founding of The Great Atlantic & Pacific Tea Company (A&P) in 1859. By the early 1920s, the U.S. boasted three national chains: A&P, Woolworth's, and United Cigar Stores. By the 1930s, chain stores had come of age, and stopped increasing their total market share. Court decisions against the chains' price-cutting appeared as early as 1906, and laws against chain stores began in the 1920s, along with legal countermeasures by chain-store groups.

A restaurant chain is a set of related restaurants in many different locations that are either under shared corporate ownership (e.g., McDonald's in the U.S.) or franchising agreements. Typically, the restaurants within a chain are built to a standard format through architectural prototype development and offer a standard menu and/or services.

Chains most often share a single name but occasionally may adopt different names in separate regions of their operation. This may occur for a number of reasons including the controlling corporation finding that their business name has already been locally trademarked in a region they plan to expand into. This happened with Burger King who found the name was already trademarked in Australia leading them to utilize the name Hungry Jack's in that country. Another common reason for regional name differences is that two chains in separate regions may be merged and, while the architecture and services of the two chains may be conformed together to the point of being exactly the same, the name of the two businesses are kept within their respective regions so as not to confuse or alienate their existing customer base, as is the case with both Checkers/Rally's and Hardees/Carl's Jr. A simpler reason may simply be that the corporation finds that different names may be better marketed for each region such as in the case of Souplantation who market themselves by the name Sweet Tomatoes on the east coast of America. Also a number of locations within a chain may keep an earlier historical name for the business after the chain expands with a different name such as St. Louis Bread Company expanding to become Panera Bread but retaining the original name in its city of origin.

Restaurant chains are often found near highways, shopping malls and tourist areas.

The following U.S. listing tabulates the early 2010 ranking of major franchises along with the number of sub-franchisees (or partners) from data available for 2004. The United States is a leader in franchising, a position it has held since the 1930s when it used the approach for fast-food restaurants, food inns and, slightly later, motels at the time of the Great Depression. As of 2005, there were 909, 253 established franchised businesses, generating $ 880.9 billion of output and accounting for 8.1 percent of all private, non-farm jobs. This amounts to 11 million jobs, and 4.4 percent of all private sector output.

(1) Subway (sandwiches and salads) | *startup costs* $ 84,300 - $ 258,300 (22,000 partners worldwide in 2004).

(2) McDonald's | *startup costs* in 2010, $ 995,900 - $ 1,842,700 (37,300 partners in 2010)

(3) 7-Eleven Inc. (convenience stores) | *startup costs* in 2010 $ 40,500 - $ 775,300 (28, 200 partners in 2004)

(4) Hampton Inns & Suites (midprice hotels) | *startup costs* in 2010 $ 3,716,000 - $ 15,148,800

(5) Great Clips (hair salons) | *startup costs* in 2010 $ 109,000 - $ 203,000

(6) H&R Block (tax preparation and now e-filing) | *startup costs* $ 26,427 - $ 84,094 (11, 200 partners in 2004)

(7) Dunkin' Donuts | *startup costs* in 2010 $ 537,750 - $ 1,765,300

(8) Jani-King (commercial cleaning) | *startup costs* $ 11,400 - $ 35,050, (11,000 partners worldwide in 2004)

(9) Servpro (insurance and disaster restoration and cleaning) | *startup costs* in 2010 $ 102, 250 - $ 161, 150

(10) MiniMarkets (convenience store and gas station) | *startup costs* in 2010 $ 1,835,823 - $ 7,615,065

China has the most franchises in the world but the scale of their operations is relatively small. Each system in China has an average of 43 outlets, compared to more than 540 in the United States. Together, there are 2,600 brands in some 200,000 retail markets. KFC was the most significant foreign entry in 1987 and is widespread. Many franchises are in fact joint-ventures, as at their forming the franchise law was not explicit. For example, McDonald's is a joint venture. Pizza Hut, TGIF, Wal-mart, Starbucks followed a little later. But total franchising is only 3% of retail trade, which seeks foreign franchise growth.

The year 2005 saw the birth of an updated franchise law, 「Measures for the Administration of Commercial Franchise」. Previous legislation (1997) made no specific inclusion of foreign investors. Today the franchise law is much clearer by virtue of the 2007 law, a revision of the 2005 law.

In recent years, the idea of franchising has been picked up by the social enterprise sector, which hopes to simplify and expedite the process of setting up new businesses. Social franchising also refers to a technique used by governments and aid donors to provide essential clinical health services in the developing world.

Social Franchise Enterprises objective is to achieve development goals by creating self sustainable activities by providing services and goods in un-served areas. They use the Franchise Model characteristics to deliver Capacity Building, Access to Market and Access to Credit/Finance.

A number of business ideas, such as soap making, wholefood retailing, aquarium maintenance, and hotel operation have been identified as suitable for adoption by social firms employing disabled and disadvantaged people.

Glossary

Part I

proliferation   n. 激增；擴散
mechanism   n. 機制
tort   n. 民事侵權行為
two-tier   adj. 雙重的
align   v. 使一致
accountability   n. 會計責任
mitigation   n. 緩解
artificial person   法人；非自然人
hypothetical   adj. 假設的
disgorge   v. 退出
diminution   n. 減少
claimant   n. 原告
iniquitous   adj. 不公正的
perpetrate   v. 犯（罪）；干（壞事）
par   adj. 票面的
confer   v. 授予
preemption   n. 先買權；優先權
prescribe   v. 指定；規定
dissolution   n. 解散
fiduciary   n. 受託人
mimic   n. 模仿；模擬
pending   adj. 待定的；即將到的

Part II

signatory   n. 簽字人；簽約國

entity   n. 實體
voucher   n. 憑證；票券
attribute   n. 品質，特徵
designate   v. 標示；表明
superscript   n. 上標
badge   n. 象徵；標記
specify   v. 具體說明；明確規定
infringement   n. 侵權；違反；違背；
proceeding   n. 訴訟
attorney   n. 律師
inconsequential   adj. 不重要的；微不足道的
acquiescence   n. 默許；默認
onus   n. 義務；責任
irrevocably   adv. 不能取消地；不能撤回地
generic   adj. 一般的；非專利的
perpetual   adj. 永久的；無期限的
infringer   n. 侵權人
estoppel   n. 禁止；防止
intact   adj. 完整無缺的

Part III

counterfeit   v. 仿造；假冒
dilution   n. 削弱；淡化
blur   v.（使）變模糊；（使）難以區分
tarnish   v. 玷污；敗壞
replica   n. 複製品
piracy   n. 盜版行為
detriment   n. 損害；傷害
advent   n. 出現；到來
amend   v. 修改；修訂
territorial   adj. 區域的；地方的
substantively   adv. 真實地；實質上
invoke   v. 援用；援引
penalize   v. 懲罰；處罰
egregious   adj. 極壞的；極其惡劣的
prosecute   v. 控告；起訴

Part Ⅳ

franchise   n. 特許；特權   v. 給予……特許權
reimbursement   n. 償還；補償
master franchisor   二級特許經營者
spark   v. 觸發；引發
rationale   n. 根據
terminate   v. 結束；使終結
recourse   n. 求援；訴諸
unilateral   adj. 單邊的；一方的
mandate   v. 批准
boast   v. 以有……而自豪
tabulate   v. 將……制成表格；以表格形式排列
expedite   v. 加快進展；迅速完成
aquarium   n. 水族館；養魚缸

Phrases

at large   一般地；詳細地
per annum   每年
wind up   關停，關閉；以……告終
on the grounds of   以……為理由；根據
in breach of   違反
run afoul of   （與法律、規章等）相抵觸；有衝突
in due course   在適當的時候；到一定的時候
a bundle of   一束，一捆
frown on   不讚成；不許可
in effect   實際上；事實上
conform to   與……符合；遵照
by virtue of   憑藉，由於

Notes

　　MAS：新加坡金融監管局，於 1971 年成立，是新加坡的中央銀行，掌管著貨幣、銀行、保險、證券和金融部門的這項法規，具備發行貨幣的職能。
　　SFC：香港證券及期貨事務監察委員會。1989 年成立，是獨立於政府公務員架構外的法定組織，負責監管香港的證券期貨市場的運作。
　　USPTO：美國專利商標局。1802 年成立，是美國商務部下的一個機構，主要負責為發明家和他們的相關發明提供專利保護、商品商標註冊和知識產權證明。

Volkswagens：大眾汽車，是一家總部位於德國沃爾夫斯堡的汽車製造公司，也是世界四大汽車生產商之一的大眾集團的核心企業。

TRIPS：《與貿易有關的知識產權協議》的簡稱，於 1994 年 1 月 1 日簽定。其宗旨是：期望減少國際貿易中的扭曲和障礙，促進對知識產權充分、有效的保護，同時保證知識產權的執法措施與程序不至於變成合法的障礙。這個文件是知識產權保護的國際標準。

SME：英文 Small and Medium Enterprises 的縮寫，是中小型企業的意思，不同的國家對中小型企業的定義標準不同。比如，歐盟國家現在的標準是雇員少於 49 人的企業是小型企業，少於 249 人的是中型企業。在美國，雇員少於 99 人的企業是小型企業，少於 500 人的是中型企業。

CTM：歐盟商標制度，於 1996 年 4 月 1 日實施。主要涉及歐洲地區統一的商標申請的提交及審查的一個歐洲地區商標條約。由歐盟內部市場協調局審查核准的歐盟商標權，自動在歐盟聯盟的所有會員國直接獲得商標權保護。

OHIM：歐盟內部市場協調局，又稱歐盟商標局。

Madrid System：馬德里體系，是商標國際註冊體系，它受兩個條約約束：1891 年簽訂的《商標國際註冊馬德里協定》和 1989 年通過的《商標國際註冊馬德里協定》有關議定書。

Domain Name：簡稱域名、網域，是由一串用點分隔的名字組成的 Internet 上某一臺計算機或計算機組的名稱，用於在數據傳輸時標示計算機的電子方位（有時也指地理位置）；是因特網的一項核心服務，它作為可以將域名和 IP 地址相互映射的一個分佈式數據庫，能夠使人更方便地訪問互聯網。

Cybersquatting：域名搶註，是指搶先一步去登記含有著名企業或名人商標的互聯網域名後，再高價賣給該企業或名人以賺取暴利。

UFOC：統一特許經營要約公告。從 1971 年開始，在美國，為了監管本州特許經營權，有些州開始通過法律規定，特許人必須對潛在受許人進行信息披露，且向其所在州的州政府登記備案，備案登記程序包括對特許人提供的披露文件材料進行行政審核，重點審核特許人是否按照 UFOC 規定的格式填寫披露聞訊表，是否披露了全部信息。

Questions

1. What is the definition of「corporate law」according to the passage?

2. Do shares usually confer a number of rights on the holder? If yes, what rights are normally included?

3. When and where was the first recorded chain store founded? And what does the store sell?

4. Why must trademark rights be maintained through actual lawful use of the trademark?

5. What are the main differences and similarities among trademark law, patent law and copyright law?

6. What are you going to do for the intellectual property rights protection in your daily life?

Chapter VIII

IT Industry and Electro-technologies

The Internet is the global system of interconnected computer networks that use the Internet protocol suite (TCP/IP) to link devices worldwide. It is a network of networks that consists of private, public, academic, business, and government networks of local to global scope, linked by a broad array of electronic, wireless, and optical networking technologies. The Internet carries a vast range of information resources and services, such as the inter-linked hypertext documents and applications of the World Wide Web (WWW), electronic mail, telephony, and file sharing.

The origins of the Internet date back to research commissioned by the federal government of the United States in the 1960s to build robust, fault-tolerant communication with computer networks. The primary precursor network, the ARPANET, initially served as a backbone for interconnection of regional academic and military networks in the 1980s. The funding of the National Science Foundation Network as a new backbone in the 1980s, as well as private funding for other commercial extensions, led to worldwide participation in the development of new networking technologies, and the merger of many networks. The linking of commercial networks and enterprises by the early 1990s marked the beginning of the transition to the modern Internet, and generated a sustained exponential growth as generations of institutional, personal, and mobile computers were connected to the network. Although the Internet was widely used by academia since the 1980s, commercialization incorporated its services and technologies into virtually every aspect of modern life.

Part I International Standards and Internet Functions

Use of the standards ensures that products and services are safe, reliable and of good quality. The standards help businesses increase productivity while minimizing errors and waste. By enabling products from different markets to be directly compared, they facilitate companies in entering new markets and assist in the development of global trade on a fair basis. The standards also serve to safeguard consumers and the end-users of products and services, ensuring that certified products conform to the minimum standards set internationally.

ISO

Founded on 23 February 1947, The International Organization for Standardization (ISO) is an independent, non-governmental organization, the members of which are the standards organization of the 164 member countries. It is the world's largest developer of voluntary international standards and facilitates world trade by providing common standards between nations. Nearly twenty thousand standards have been set covering everything from manufactured products and technology to food safety, agriculture and healthcare.

The organization promotes worldwide proprietary, industrial and commercial standards. It is headquartered in Geneva, Switzerland. It was one of the first organizations granted general consultative status with the United Nations Economic and Social Council.

The three official languages of the ISO are English, French, and Russian.

Both the name 「ISO」 and the logo are registered trademarks, and their use is restricted.

ISO has formed joint committees with the International Electrotechnical Commission (IEC) to develop standards and terminology in the areas of electrical, electronic and related technologies.

IEC

The International Electro-technical Commission (IEC) is a non-profit, non-governmental international standards organization that prepares and publishes International Standards for all electrical, electronic and related technologies–collectively known as 「electro-technology」. IEC standards cover a vast range of technologies from power generation, transmission and distribution to home appliances and office equipment, semiconductors, fibre optics, batteries, solar energy, nanotechnology and marine energy as well as many others. The IEC also manages three global conformity assessment systems that certify whether equipment, system or components conform to its International Standards.

The IEC charter embraces all electro-technologies including energy production and distribution, electronics, magnetics and electromagnetics, electroacoustics, multimedia, telecommunication and medical technology, as well as associated general disciplines such as terminology and symbols, electromagnetic compatibility, measurement and performance, dependability, design and development, safety and the environment.

Today, the IEC is the world's leading international organization in its field, and its standards are adopted as national standards by its members. The work is done by some 10,000 electrical and electronics experts from industry, government, academia, test labs and others with an interest in the subject.

IEC standards have numbers in the range 60000 - 79999 and their titles take a form such as *IEC* 60417: *Graphical symbols for use* on equipment. The numbers of older IEC standards were converted in 1997 by adding 60000, for example IEC 27 became IEC 60027.

The 60000 series of standards are also found preceded by EN to indicate the IEC standards harmonized as European standards; for example IEC 60034 would be EN 60034.

IEC standards are also being adopted as harmonized standards by other certifying bodies such as BSI (United Kingdom), CSA (Canada), UL & ANSI/INCITS (United States), SABS (South Africa), SAI (Australia), SPC/GB (China) and DIN (Germany). IEC standards harmonized by other certifying bodies generally have some noted differences from the original IEC standard.

UPnP

Universal Plug and Play (UPnP) is a set of networking protocols that permits networked devices, such as personal computers, printers, Internet gateways, Wi-Fi access points and mobile devices to seamlessly discover each other's presence on the network and establish functional network services for data sharing, communications, and entertainment. UPnP is intended primarily for residential networks without enterprise-class devices.

The UPnP technology is promoted by the UPnP Forum, a computer industry initiative to enable simple and robust connectivity to stand-alone devices and personal computers from many different vendors. The Forum consists of over eight hundred vendors involved in everything from consumer electronics to network computing.

The UPnP architecture allows device-to-device networking of consumer electronics, mobile devices, personal computers, and networked home appliances. It is a distributed, open architecture protocol based on established standards such as the Internet Protocol Suite (TCP/IP), HTTP, XML, and SOAP.

UPnP AV architecture is an audio and video extension of the UPnP, supporting a variety of devices such as TVs, VCRs, CD/DVD players/jukeboxes, settop boxes, stereos systems, MP3 players, still image cameras, camcorders, electronic picture frames (EPFs), and personal computers. The UPnP AV architecture allows devices to support different types of formats for the entertainment content, including MPEG2, MPEG4, JPEG, MP3, Windows Media Audio (WMA), bitmaps (BMP), and NTSC, PAL or ATSC formats.

Internet

As of December 2014, 37.9 percent of the world's human population has used the services of the Internet within the past year-over 100 times more people than were using it in 1995. Internet use grew rapidly in the West from the mid-1990s to early 2000s and from the late 1990s to present in the developing world.

Most traditional communications media, including telephony and television, are being reshaped or redefined by the Internet, giving birth to new services such as voice over Internet Protocol (VoIP) and Internet Protocol television (IPTV). Newspaper, book, and other print publishing are adapting to website technology, or are reshaped into blogging and web feeds. The entertainment industry, including music, film, and gaming, was initially the fastest growing online segment. The Internet has enabled and accelerated new forms of human interactions through instant messaging, Internet forums, and social networking. Online shopping has grown exponentially both for major retailers and small artisans and traders. Business-to-business and financial services on the Internet affect supply chains across entire industries.

The Internet carries many network services, Email is an important communications service available on the Internet. The concept of sending electronic text messages between parties in a way analogous to mailing letters or memos predates the creation of the Internet. Pictures, documents and other files are sent as email attachments.

Internet telephony is another common communications service made possible by the creation of the Internet. The idea began in the early 1990s with walkie-talkie-like voice applications for personal computers. The benefit is that, as the Internet carries the voice traffic, VoIP (Voice-over-Internet Protocol) can be free or cost much less than a traditional telephone call, especially over long distances and especially for those with always-on Internet connections such as cable or ADSL. VoIP is maturing into a competitive alternative to traditional telephone service. Interoperability between different providers has improved and the ability to call or receive a call from a traditional telephone is available. Simple, inexpensive VoIP network adapters are available that eliminate the need for a personal computer.

File sharing is an example of transferring large amounts of data across the Internet. A computer file can be emailed to customers, colleagues and friends as an attachment. It can be uploaded to a website or FTP server for easy download by others. It can be put into a 「shared location」 or onto a file server for instant use by colleagues. The load of bulk downloads to many users can be eased by the use of 「mirror」 servers or peer-to-peer networks. In any of these cases, access to the file may be controlled by user authentication, the transit of the file over the Internet may be obscured by encryption, and money may change hands for access to the file. The price can be paid by the remote charging of funds from, for example, a credit card whose details are also passed-usually fully encrypted-across the Internet. The origin and authenticity of the file received may be checked by digital signatures or by MD5 or other message digests. These simple features of the Internet, over a worldwide basis, are changing the production, sale, and distribution of anything that can be reduced to a computer file for transmission. This includes all manner of print publications, software products, news, music, film, video, photography, graphics and the other arts. This in turn has caused seismic shifts in each of the existing industries that previously controlled the production and distribution of these products.

Streaming media is the real-time delivery of digital media for the immediate consumption or enjoyment by end users. Many radio and television broadcasters provide Internet feeds of their live audio and video productions. They may also allow time-shift viewing or listening such as Preview, Classic Clips and Listen Again features. These providers have been joined by a range of pure Internet 「broadcasters」 who never had on-air licenses. This means that an Internet-connected device, such as a computer or something more specific, can be used to access on-line media in much the same way as was previously possible only with a television or radio receiver. The range of available types of content is much wider, from specialized technical webcasts to on-demand popular multimedia services. Podcasting is a variation on this theme, where-usually audio-material is downloaded and played back on a computer or shifted to a portable media player to be listened to on the move. These techniques using simple equipment allow anybody, with little censorship or licensing control, to broadcast audio-visual material worldwide. Increasing amounts of data are transmitted at higher and higher speeds over fiber optic networks operating at 10-Gbit/s, 100-Gbit/s, or more.

World Wide Web browser software, such as Microsoft's Internet Explorer has also enabled individuals and organizations to publish ideas and information to a potentially large audience online at greatly reduced expense and time delay. Publishing a web page, a blog, or building a website involves little initial cost and many cost-free services are available. However, publishing and maintaining large, professional web sites with attractive, diverse and up-to-date information is still a difficult and expensive proposition. Many individuals and some companies and groups use *web logs* or blogs, which are largely used as easily updatable online diaries. Some commercial organizations encourage staff to communicate advice in their areas of specialization in the hope that visitors will be impressed by the expert knowledge and free information, and be attracted to the corporation as a result.

One example of this practice is Microsoft, whose product developers publish their personal blogs in order to pique the public's interest in their work. Collections of personal web pages published by large service providers remain popular, and have become increasingly sophisticated.

Advertising on popular web pages can be lucrative, and e-commerce or the sale of products and services directly via the Web continues to grow. During the late 1990s, it was estimated that traffic on the public Internet grew by 100 percent per year, while the mean annual growth in the number of Internet users was thought to be between 20% and 50%.

The prevalent language for communication on the Internet has been English. This may be a result of the origin of the Internet, as well as the language's role as a lingua franca. Early computer systems were limited to the characters in the American Standard Code for Information Interchange (ASCII), a subset of the Latin alphabet.

After English (27%), the most requested languages on the World Wide Web are Chinese (25%), Spanish (8%), Japanese (5%), Portuguese and German (4% each), Arabic, French and Russian (3% each), and Korean (2%). By region, 42% of the world's Internet users are based in Asia, 24% in Europe, 14% in North America, 10% in Latin America and the Caribbean taken together, 6% in Africa, 3% in the Middle East and 1% in Australia/Oceania. The Internet's technologies have developed enough in recent years, especially in the use of Unicode, that good facilities are available for development and communication in the world's widely used languages.

Internet provides a particularly good venue for crowdsourcing (outsourcing tasks to a distributed group of people) since individuals tend to be more open in web-based projects where they are not being physically judged or scrutinized and thus can feel more comfortable sharing.

Crowdsourcing systems are used to accomplish a variety of tasks. For example, the crowd may be invited to develop a new technology, carry out a design task, refine or carry out the steps of an algorithm, or help capture, systematize, or analyze large amounts of data.

Wikis have also been used in the academic community for sharing and dissemination of information across institutional and international boundaries. In those settings, they have been found useful for collaboration on grant writing, strategic planning, departmental documentation, and committee work. The United States Patent and Trademark Office uses a wiki to allow the public to collaborate on finding prior art relevant to examination of pending patent applications. Queens, New York has used a wiki to allow citizens to collaborate on the design and planning of a local park.

The English Wikipedia has the largest user base among wikis on the World Wide Web and ranks in the top 10 among all Web sites in terms of traffic.

The Internet has achieved new relevance as a political tool. The presidential campaign of Howard Dean in 2004 in the United States was notable for its success in soliciting donation via the Internet. Many political groups use the Internet to achieve a new method of organizing for carrying out their mission. The New York Times suggested that social media websites, such as Facebook and Twitter, helped people organize the political revolutions in Egypt, by helping activists organize protests, communicate grievances, and disseminate information.

The spread of low-cost Internet access in developing countries has opened up new possibilities for peer-to-peer charities, which allow individuals to contribute small amounts to charitable projects for other individuals. Websites, such as DonorsChoose and GlobalGiving, allow small-scale donors to direct funds to individual projects of their choice.

Many people use the World Wide Web to access news, weather and sports reports, to plan and book vacations and to pursue their personal interests. People use chat, messaging and email to make and stay in touch with friends worldwide, sometimes in the same way as some previously had pen pals.

Social networking websites such as Facebook, Twitter, and Myspace have created new ways to socialize and interact. Users of these sites are able to add a wide variety of information to pages, to pursue common interests, and to connect with others. It is also possible to find existing acquaintances, to allow communication among existing groups of people. Sites like LinkedIn foster commercial and business connections. YouTube and Flickr specialize in users' videos and photographs.

While social networking sites were initially for individuals only, today they are widely used by businesses and other organizations to promote their brands, to market to their customers and to encourage posts to「go viral」.「Black hat」social media techniques are also employed by some organizations, such as Spam accounts and Astroturfing.

A risk for both individuals and organizations writing posts (especially public posts) on social networking websites, is that especially foolish or controversial posts occasionally lead to an unexpected and possibly large-scale backlash on social media from other internet users. This is also a risk in relation to controversial *offline* behavior, if it is widely made known.

Some websites, such as Reddit, have rules forbidding the posting of personal information of individuals (also known as doxxing), due to concerns about such postings leading to mobs of large numbers of Internet users directing harassment at the specific individuals thereby identified.

Children also face dangers online such as cyber bullying and approaches by sexual predators, who sometimes pose as children themselves. Children may also encounter material which they may find upsetting, or material which their parents consider to be not age-appropriate. Due to naivety, they may also post personal information about themselves online, which could put them or their families at risk, unless warned not to do so. Many parents choose to enable internet filtering, and/or supervise their children's online activities, in an attempt to protect their children from inappropriate material on the internet. The most popular social networking websites, such as Facebook and Twitter, commonly forbid users under the age of 13. However, these policies are typically trivial to circumvent by registering an account with a false birth date, and a significant number of children aged under 13 join such sites anyway.

While much has been written of the economic advantages of Internet-enabled commerce, there is also evidence that some aspects of the Internet such as maps and location-aware services may serve to reinforce economic inequality and the digital divide. Electronic commerce may be responsible for consolidation and the decline of mom-and-pop, brick and mortar businesses resulting in increases in income inequality.

Internet resources, hardware and software components, are the target of malicious attempts to gain unauthorized control to cause interruptions, or access private information. Such attempts include computer viruses which copy with the help of humans, computer worms which copy themselves automatically, denial of service attacks, ransomware, botnets, and spyware that reports on the activity and typing of users. Usually these activities constitute cybercrime. Defense theorists have also speculated about the possibilities of cyber warfare using similar methods on a large scale.

The vast majority of computer surveillance involves the monitoring of data and traffic on the Internet. In the United States for example, under the Communications Assistance For Law Enforcement Act, all phone calls and broadband Internet traffic (emails, web traffic, instant messaging, etc.) are required to be available for unimpeded real-time monitoring by Federal law enforcement agencies.

Some governments, such as those of Burma, Iran, North Korea, Saudi Arabia and the United Arab Emirates restrict access to content on the Internet within their territories, especially to political and religious content, with domain name and keyword filters.

In Norway, Denmark, Finland, and Sweden, major Internet service providers have voluntarily agreed to restrict access to sites listed by authorities. While this list of forbidden resources is supposed to contain only known child pornography sites, the content of the list is secret. Many countries, including the United States, have enacted laws against the possession or distribution of certain material, such as child pornography, via the Internet, but do not mandate filter software. Many free or commercially available software programs, called content-control software are available to users to block offensive websites on individual computers or networks, in order to limit access by children to pornographic material or depiction of violence.

Part II   Silicon Valley and American IT Corporations

Silicon Valley is a nickname for the southern portion of the San Francisco Bay Area in California, United States. It is home to many of the world's largest high-tech corporations, as well as thousands of tech startup companies. The region occupies roughly the same area as the Santa Clara Valley where it is centered, including San Jose and surrounding cities and towns. The term originally referred to the large number of silicon chip innovators and manufacturers in the region, but eventually came to refer to all high tech businesses in the area, and is now generally used as a metonym for the American high-technology economic sector.

Silicon Valley is a leading hub and startup ecosystem for high-tech innovation and development, accounting for one-third of all of the venture capital investment in the United States. Geographically, Silicon Valley is generally thought to encompass all of the Santa Clara Valley, San Francisco, the San Francisco peninsula, and southern portions of the East Bay.

The term *Silicon Valley* gained widespread use in the early 1980s, at the time of the introduction of the IBM PC and numerous related hardware and software products to the consumer market.

Perhaps the strongest thread that runs through the Valley's past and present is the drive to 『play』 with novel technology, which, when bolstered by an advanced engineering degree and channeled by astute management, has done much to create the industrial powerhouse we see in the Valley today.

Stanford University, its affiliates, and graduates have played a major role in the development of this area.

After World War II, universities were experiencing enormous demand due to returning students. To address the financial demands of Stanford's growth requirements, and to provide local employment opportunities for graduating students, Frederick Terman proposed the leasing of Stanford's lands for use as an office park, named the Stanford Industrial Park (later Stanford Research Park). Leases were limited to high technology companies. Its first tenant was Varian Associates, founded by Stanford alumni in the 1930s to build military radar components. However, Terman also found venture capital for civilian technology start-ups. One of the major success stories was Hewlett-Packard. Founded in Packard's garage by Stanford graduates William Hewlett and David Packard, Hewlett-Packard moved its offices into the Stanford Research Park shortly after 1953. In 1954, Stanford created the Honors Cooperative Program to allow full-time employees of the companies to pursue graduate degrees from the University on a part-time basis. The initial companies signed five-year agreements in which they would pay double the tuition for each student in order to cover the costs. Hewlett-Packard has become the largest personal computer manufacturer in the world, and transformed the home printing market when it released the first thermal drop-on-demand ink jet printer in 1984. Other early tenants included

Eastman Kodak, General Electric, and Lockheed.

Silicon Valley was born when several contributing factors intersected, including a skilled STEM research base housed in area universities, plentiful venture capital, and steady U.S. Department of Defense spending. Stanford University leadership was especially important in the valley's early development. Together these elements formed the basis of its growth and success. It was in Silicon Valley that the silicon-based integrated circuit, the microprocessor, and the microcomputer, among other key technologies, were developed. As of 2013 the region employed about a quarter of a million information technology workers.

The rise of Silicon Valley was also bolstered by the development of appropriate legal infrastructure to support the rapid formation, funding, and expansion of high-tech companies, as well as the development of a critical mass of litigators and judges experienced in resolving disputes between such firms. From the early 1980s onward, many national (and later international) law firms opened offices in San Francisco and Palo Alto in order to provide Silicon Valley startups with legal services.

By the early 1970s, there were many semiconductor companies in the area, computer firms using their devices, and programming and service companies serving both. Industrial space was plentiful and housing was still inexpensive. The growth was fueled by the emergence of the venture capital industry on Sand Hill Road, beginning with Kleiner Perkins in 1972; the availability of venture capital exploded after the successful $ 1.3 billion IPO of Apple Computer in December 1980.

In 1980 *Intelligent Machines Journal*, a hobbyist journal, changed its name to *Info World*, and, with offices in Palo Alto, began covering the explosive emergence of the microcomputer industry in the valley.

Although semiconductors are still a major component of the area's economy, Silicon Valley has been most famous in recent years for innovations in software and Internet services. Silicon Valley has significantly influenced computer operating systems, software, and user interfaces.

In 1995 the internet was opened to commercial use and the initial wave of internet startups, Amazon. com, eBay, and the predecessor to Craigs list began operations.

Silicon Valley is generally considered to have been the center of the dot-com bubble, which started in the mid-1990s and collapsed after the NASDAQ stock market began to decline dramatically in April 2000. During the bubble era, real estate prices reached unprecedented levels. For a brief time, Sand Hill Road was home to the most expensive commercial real estate in the world, and the booming economy resulted in severe traffic congestion.

After the dot-com crash, Silicon Valley continues to maintain its status as one of the top research and development centers in the world. *The Wall Street Journal* story found in 2015 that 12 of the 20 most inventive towns in America were in California, and 10 of those were in Silicon Valley.

Silicon Valley has a social and business ethos that supports innovation and entrepreneurship. Attempts to create 「Silicon Valleys」 in environments, such as Europe, where disruptive innovation does not go over well have a poor track record.

Apple Inc.

Apple Inc. is an American multinational technology company headquartered in Cupertino, California, that designs, develops, and sells consumer electronics, computer software, online services, and personal computers. Its best-known hardware products are the Mac line of computers, the iPod media player, the iPhone smartphone, the iPad tablet computer, and the Apple Watch smartwatch. Its online services include iCloud, the iTunes Store, and the App Store. Apple's consumer software includes the OS X and iOS operating systems, the iTunes media browser, the Safariweb browser, and the iLife and iWork creativity and productivity suites.

Apple was founded by Steve Jobs, Steve Wozniak, and Ronald Wayne on April 1, 1976, to develop and sell personal computers. It was incorporated as **Apple Computer, Inc.** on January 3, 1977.

In 1985, a power struggle developed between Jobs and CEO John Sculley. Jobs resigned from Apple and founded NeXT Inc. the same year.

In 1994, Apple allied with IBM and Motorola in the AIM alliance with the goal of creating a new computing platform, which would use IBM and Motorola hardware coupled with Apple software.

In 1996, Gil Amelio as CEO made numerous changes at Apple. He purchased NeXT and its NeXTSTEP operating system and brought Steve Jobs back to Apple.

On July 9, 1997, Jobs acted as the interim CEO and began restructuring the company's product line; it was during this period that he identified the design talent of Jonathan Ive, and the pair worked collaboratively to rebuild Apple's status.

At the 1997 Macworld Expo, Jobs announced that Apple would join Microsoft to release new versions of Microsoft Office for the Macintosh, and on November 10, 1997, Apple introduced the Apple Online Store, which was tied to a new build-to-order manufacturing strategy.

On August 15, 1998, Apple introduced a new all-in-one computer reminiscent of the Macintosh 128K: the iMac. The iMac design team was led by Ive, who would later design the iPod and the iPhone.

During this period, Apple completed numerous acquisitions to create a portfolio of digital production software for both professionals and consumers.

During his keynote speech at the Macworld Expo on January 9, 2007, Jobs announced that Apple Computer, Inc. would from that point on be known as 「Apple Inc.」, because the company had shifted its emphasis from computers to mobile electronic devices. This event also saw the announcement of the iPhone and the Apple TV. The following day, Apple shares hit $97.80, an all-time high at that point. Apple achieved widespread success with its iPhone, iPod Touch and iPad products, which introduced innovations in mobile phones, portable music players and personal computers respectively.

In July 2008, Apple launched the App Store to sell third-party applications for the iPhone and iPod Touch. Within a month, the store sold 60 million applications and registered an average daily revenue of $ 1 million. By October 2008, Apple was the third-largest mobile handset supplier in the world due to the popularity of the iPhone.

After years of speculation and multiple rumored 「leaks」, Apple announced a large screen, tablet-like media device known as the iPad on January 27, 2010. The iPad ran the same touch-based operating system as the iPhone, and many iPhone apps were compatible with the iPad. This gave the iPad a large app catalog on launch, despite very little development time before the release. Later that year on April 3, 2010, the iPad was launched in the US. It sold more than 300,000 units on its first day, and 500,000 by the end of the first week. In May of the same year, Apple's market cap exceeded that of competitor Microsoft for the first time since 1989. Apple became the most valuable consumer-facing brand in the world.

On August 24, 2011, Jobs resigned his position as CEO of Apple.

On October 5, 2011, Apple announced that Jobs had died, marking the end of an era for Apple.

Corporate Identity

According to Steve Jobs, the company's name was inspired by his visit to an apple farm while on a fruitarian diet. Jobs thought the name 「Apple」 was 「fun, spirited and not intimidating」.

The logo was designed with a bite so that it would not be confused with a cherry. This logo is often wrongly referred to as a tribute to Alan Turing, with the bite mark a reference to his method of suicide. Both Janoff and Apple deny any homage to Turing in the design of the logo.

From 1997 to 2002, the slogan 「Think Different」 was used in advertising campaigns, and is still closely associated with Apple. Apple also has slogans for specific product lines — for example, 「iThink, therefore iMac」 was used in 1998 to promote the iMac, and 「Say hello to iPhone」 has been used in iPhone advertisements.

Apple's high level of brand loyalty is considered unusual for any product. People have an incredibly personal relationship with Apple's products. Apple Store openings can draw crowds of thousands, with some waiting in line as much as a day before the opening or flying in from other countries for the event. The opening of New York City's Fifth Avenue 「Cube」 store had a line half a mile long; a few Mac fans used the setting to propose marriage. The line for the Ginza opening in Tokyo was estimated to include thousands of people and exceeded eight city blocks.

Fortune magazine named Apple the most admired company in the United States in 2008, and in the world from 2008 to 2012. On September 30, 2013, Apple surpassed Coca-Cola to become the world's most valuable brand.

Apple has 453 retail stores (as of March 2015) in 16 countries and anonline store available in 39 countries. Each store is designed to suit the needs of the location and regulatory authorities. Apple has received numerous architectural awards for its store designs, particularly its midtown Manhattan location on Fifth Avenue.

Corporate culture

Apple was one of several highly successful companies founded in the 1970s that bucked the traditional notions of corporate culture. Jobs often walked around the office barefoot even after Apple became a Fortune 500 company. By the time of the 「1984」television commercial, Apple's informal culture had become a key trait that differentiated it from its competitors. According to a 2011 report in *Fortune*, this has resulted in a corporate culture more akin to a startup rather than a multinational corporation.

As the company has grown and been led by a series of differently opinionated chief executives, it has arguably lost some of its original character. Nonetheless, it has maintained a reputation for fostering individuality and excellence that reliably attracts talented workers, particularly after Jobs returned to the company.

Microsoft

Microsoft Corporation (commonly known as Microsoft) is an American multinational technology company headquartered in Redmond, Washington, that develops, manufactures, licenses, supports and sells computer software, consumer electronics and personal computers and services. Its best known software products are the Microsoft Windows line of operating systems, Microsoft Office office suite, and Internet Explorer web browser. It is the world's largest software maker measured by revenues. It is also one of the world's most valuable companies.

Microsoft is a portmanteau of the words micro computer and soft ware., founded by Bill Gates and Paul Allen, childhood friends with a passion for computer programming, sought to make a successful business utilizing their shared skills. In 1972 they founded their first company, which offered a rudimentary computer that tracked and analyzed automobile traffic data. Allen went on to pursue a degree in computer science at the University of Washington, later dropping out of school to work at Honeywell. Gates began studies at Harvard. They officially established Microsoft on April 4, 1975, with Gates as the CEO.

While jointly developing a new OS with IBM in 1984, Microsoft released Microsoft Windows, a graphical extension for MS-DOS. On March 13, 1986, the company went public; the ensuing rise in the stock would make an estimated four billionaires and 12,000 millionaires from Microsoft employees. Due to the partnership with IBM, in 1990 the Federal Trade Commission set its eye on Microsoft for possible collusion; it marked the beginning of over a decade of legal clashes with the U.S. Government.

In 1990, Microsoft introduced its office suite, Microsoft Office. The software bundled separate office productivity applications, such as Microsoft Word and Microsoft Excel. Both Office and Windows became dominant in their respective areas.

Following Bill Gates's internal 「Internet Tidal Wave memo」on May 26, 1995, Microsoft began to redefine its offerings and expand its product line into computer networking and the World Wide Web. The company released Windows 95 on August 24, 1995.

Bill Gates handed over the CEO position on January 13, 2000, to Steve Ballmer, an old college friend of Gates and employee of the company since 1980, creating a new position for himself as Chief Software Architect.

Released in January 2007, Microsoft Office 2007, was a significant departure from its predecessors. Relatively strong sales of both titles helped to produce a record profit in 2007.

As the smartphone industry boomed beginning in 2007, Microsoft struggled to keep up with its rivals Apple and Google in providing a modern smartphone operating system. As a result, in 2010, Microsoft revamped their aging flagship mobile operating system, Windows Mobile, replacing it with the new Windows Phone OS; along with a new strategy in the smartphone industry that has Microsoft working more closely with smartphone manufacturers, such as Nokia, and to provide a consistent user experience across all smartphones using Microsoft's Windows Phone OS. It used a new user interface design language, codenamed 「Metro」, which prominently used simple shapes, typography and iconography, and the concept of minimalism.

Following the release of Windows Phone, Microsoft underwent a gradual rebranding of its product range throughout 2011 and 2012—the corporation's logos, products, services, and websites adopted the principles and concepts of the Metro design language.

In June 2012, Microsoft entered the personal computer production market for the first time, with the launch of the Microsoft Surface, a line of tablet computers.

On October 26, 2012, Microsoft launched Windows 8 and the Microsoft Surface. Three days later, Windows Phone 8 was launched.

On September 3, 2013, Microsoft agreed to buy Nokia's mobile unit for $ 7 billion.

In line with the maturing PC business, in July 2013 Microsoft announced that it would reorganize the business into 4 new business divisions by function: Operating System, Apps, Cloud and Devices. All previous divisions will be diluted into new divisions without any workforce cut.

As of 2013, Microsoft is market dominant in both the IBM PC-compatible operating system and office software suitemarkets (the latter with Microsoft Office). The company also produces a wide range of other software for desktops and servers, and is active in areas including Internet search (with Bing), the video game industry (with the Xbox, Xbox 360 and Xbox One consoles), the digital services market (through MSN), and mobile phones (via the Windows Phone OS).

The company is run by a board of directors made up of mostly company outsiders, as is customary for publicly traded companies. Board members are elected every year at the annual shareholders' meeting using a majority vote system. There are five committees within the board which oversee more specific matters. These committees include the Audit Committee, which handles accounting issues with the company including auditing and reporting; the Compensation Committee, which approves compensation for the CEO and other employees of the company; the Finance Committee, which handles financial matters such as proposing mergers and acquisitions; the Governance and Nominating Committee, which handles various corporate matters including nomination of the board; and the Antitrust Compliance Committee, which attempts to prevent company practices from violating antitrust laws.

When Microsoft went public and launched its initial public offering (IPO) in 1986, the opening stock price was $ 21; after the trading day, the price closed at $ 27.75. The stock price peaked in 1999 at around $ 119. The company began to offer a dividend on January 16, 2003. Though the company had subsequent increases in dividend payouts, the price of Microsoft's stock remained steady for years.

One of Microsoft's business tactics, described by an executive as 「embrace, extend and extinguish,」 initially embraces a competing standard or product, then extends it to produce their own version which is then incompatible with the standard, which in time extinguishes competition that does not or cannot use Microsoft's new version. Various companies and governments sue Microsoft over this set of tactics, resulting in billions of dollars in rulings against the company. Microsoft claims that the original strategy is not anti-competitive, but rather an exercise of its discretion to implement features it believes customers want.

Standard and Poor's and Moody's have both given a AAA rating to Microsoft.

As of January 2014, Microsoft's market capitalization stood at $ 314B, making it the 8th largest company in the world by market capitalization.

On November 14, 2014, Microsoft overtook Exxon Mobil to become the 2nd most valuable company by market capitalization, behind only Apple Inc. Its total market value was over $ 410B — with the stock price hitting $ 50.04 a share, the highest since early 2000.

On August 23, 2012, Microsoft unveiled a new corporate logo. The new logo also includes four squares with the colors of the then-current Windows logo which have been used to represent Microsoft's four major products: Windows (blue), Office (red), Xbox (green), and Bing (yellow).

Microsoft

2012 - **present**

IBM

The International Business Machines Corporation (commonly referred to as **IBM**) is an American multinational technology and consulting corporation, with headquarters in Armonk, New York. IBM manufactures and markets computer hardware and software, and offers infrastructure, hosting and consulting services in areas ranging from mainframe computers to nanotechnology.

The company originated in 1911 as the Computing-Tabulating-Recording Company (CTR) through a merger of the Tabulating Machine Company, the International Time Recording Company, and the Computing Scale Company. CTR was changed to 「International Business Machines」 in 1924. The initialism **IBM** followed. The nickname **Big Blue** is adopted for its size and common use of the color in products, packaging, and logo.

In 1937, IBM's tabulating equipment enabled organizations to process unprecedented amounts of data, its clients including the U.S. Government. In 1947, IBM opened its first office in Bahrain, as well as an office in Saudi Arabia to service the needs of the Arabian-American Oil Company that would grow to become Saudi Business Machines (SBM).

In 1956, the company demonstrated the first practical example of artificial intelligence.

In 1963, IBM employees and computers helped NASA track the orbital flight of the Mercury astronauts. The latter half of the 1960s saw IBM continue its support of space exploration, participating in the 1965 Gemini flights, 1966 Saturn flights, and 1969 lunar mission.

On April 7, 1964, IBM announced the first computer system family, the revolutionary IBM System/360. Sold between 1964 and 1978, it spanned the complete range of commercial and scientific applications from large to small, allowing companies for the first time to upgrade to models with greater computing capability.

In 1974, IBM engineer developed the Universal Product Code. On October 11, 1973, IBM introduced the IBM 3666, a laser-scanning point-of-sale barcode reader which would become the backbone of retail checkouts.

In 2003, three slogans were emerged, expressed to implement company values in practice, as: 「Dedication to every client's success」, 「Innovation that matters—for our company and for the world」, and 「Trust and personal responsibility in all relationships」.

In 2005, the company sold its personal computer business to Lenovo. Later in 2009, IBM's Blue Gene supercomputing program was awarded the National Medal of Technology and Innovation by U.S. President Barack Obama. In 2011, IBM gained worldwide attention for its artificial intelligence program Watson, which won against game-show champions Ken Jennings and Brad Rutter.

IBM's closing value of $ 214 billion on September 29, 2011 surpassed Microsoft's $ 213.2 billion valuation. It was the first time since 1996 that IBM's closing price exceeded that of its software rival.

IBM has 12 research laboratories worldwide, bundled into IBM Research. As of 2015, IBM had been the top annual recipient of U.S. patents for 22 consecutive years.

In 2012, *Fortune* ranked IBM the No. 2 largest U.S. firm in terms of number of employees (435,000 worldwide), the No. 4 largest in terms of market capitalization, the No. 9 most profitable and the No. 19 largest firm in terms of revenue. Globally, the company was ranked the No. 31 largest in terms of revenue by *Forbes* for 2011.

In November 2014, IBM and Twitter announced a global landmark partnership which they claim will change how institutions and businesses understand their customers, markets and trends. With Twitter's data on people and IBM's cloud-based analytics and customer-engagement platforms they plan to help enterprises make better, more informed decisions. The partnership will give enterprises and institutions a way to make sense of Twitter's mountain of data using IBM's Watson supercomputer.

Part Ⅲ Zhongguancun and Chinese IT Corporations

Zhongguancun (中關村), or Zhong Guan Cun, is a technology hub in Haidian District, Beijing, China. It is geographically situated in the northwestern part of Beijing city, in a band between the northwestern Third Ring Road and the northwestern Fourth Ring Road. Zhongguancun is very well known in China, and is often referred to as 「China's Silicon Valley」.

Zhongguancun has long existed since 1950s and only became a household name in the early 1980s. The first person who envisioned the future for Zhongguancun was Chen Chunxian, a member of the Chinese Academy of Sciences (CAS), who came up with the idea for a Silicon Valley in China after he visited the U.S. as part of a government-sponsored trip. The location of the Chinese Academy of Sciences within Zhongguancun reinforced, and perhaps was in part responsible for the technological growth in this area.

Throughout the 1980s and still today, Zhongguancun was known as 「electronics avenue,」 because of its connections to information technology and the preponderance of stores along a central, crowded street.

Zhongguancun was officially recognized by the central government of China in 1988. It was given the wordy name 「Beijing High-Technology Industry Development Experimental Zone.」

However, officially (as of 1999) Zhongguancun has become the 「Zhongguancun Science & Technology Zone.」 It is a zone with seven parks, including Haidian Park, Fengtai Park, Changping Park, Electronics City (in Chaoyang), Yizhuang Park, Desheng Park, and Jianxiang Park.

The original Zhongguancun is now known as the Haidian Park of the Zhongguancun Zone.

Due to the proximity and participation of China's two most prestigious universities, Peking University and Tsinghua University, along with the Chinese Academy of Sciences, many analysts elsewhere are optimistic about Zhongguancun's future prospects.

The most famous companies that grew up in Zhongguancun are Stone Group, Founder Group, and Lenovo Group. They were all founded in 1984-1985. Stone was the first successful technology company to be operated by private individuals outside the government of China. Founder is a technology company that spun off Peking University. Lenovo Group spun off from Chinese Academy of Sciences with Liu Chuanzhi, a hero of Zhongguancun and current Chairman, eventually taking the helm. Lenovo purchased IBM's PC division with $1.75 billion in 2005, making it the world's third-largest PC maker. Both Founder and Lenovo Group maintain strong connections to their academic backers, who are significant shareholders.

According to the 2004 Beijing Statistical Yearbook, there are over 12,000 high-tech enterprises throughout Zhongguancun's seven parks, with 489,000 technicians employed. Many world renowned technology companies built their Chinese headquarters and research centers in Zhongguancun Technology Park, such as Google, Intel, AMD, Oracle Corporation, Motorola, Sony, and Ericsson. Microsoft has built its Chinese research headquarters in the park that costs $280 million and can accommodate 5000 employees, which is completed in April, 2011. Microsoft Research Asia is in that building.

In addition, many conferences are held in this location, including the annual ChinICT conference-which is the largest Information technology Development and Entrepreneurship event in China.

Huawei

Huawei Technologies Co. Ltd. is a Chinese multinational networking and telecommunications equipment and services company headquartered in Shenzhen, Guangdong. It is the largest telecommunications equipment maker in the world, having overtaken Ericsson in 2012.

Huawei was founded in 1987 by Ren Zhengfei, a former engineer in the People's Liberation Army. At the time of its establishment Huawei was focused on manufacturing phone switches, but has since expanded its business to include building telecommunications networks; providing operational and consulting services and equipment to enterprises inside and outside of China; and manufacturing communications devices for the consumer market. Huawei has over 140,000 employees, around 46% of whom are engaged in research and development (R&D). It has 21 R&D institutes in countries including China, the United States, Canada, UK, Pakistan, France, Belgium, Germany, Colombia, Sweden, Ireland, India, Russia, and Turkey, and in 2013 invested US $5 billion in R&D.

In 2010, Huawei recorded profit of 23.8 billion CNY (3.7 billion USD). Its products and services have been deployed in more than 140 countries and it currently serves 45 of the world's 50 largest telecoms operators.

Huawei is the official English transliteration of the firm's Chinese name (華為). The character 「華」 means 「flower」, it can also mean 「splendid」 or 「magnificent」, but nowadays mostly prefer to 「China/Chinese」. The character 「為」 means 「action」 or 「achievement」, thus Huawei literally means 「China's achievement」.

Ren Zhengfei, a former deputy director of the People's Liberation Army engineering corp, founded Huawei in 1987 in Shenzhen. Rather than relying on joint ventures to secure technology transfers from foreign companies, Ren focused on indigenous research and development to produce the switches. At a time when 100% of China's telecommunications technology was imported from abroad, Ren hoped to build a domestic Chinese telecommunication company that could take on foreign competitors.

The company's first major breakthrough came in 1993, when it launched its C&C08 program controlled telephone switch. It was by far the most powerful switch available in China at the time. By initially deploying in small cities and rural areas and placing emphasis on service and customizability, the company gained market share and made its way into the mainstream market.

In 1997, Huawei won its first overseas contract, providing fixed-line network products to Hong Kong company Hutchison Whampoa. Later that year, Huawei launched its wireless GSM-based products and eventually expanded to offer CDMA and UMTS. In 1999, the company opened a research and development (R&D) center in Bangalore, India to develop a wide range of telecom software. From 1998 to 2003, Huawei contracted with IBM for management consulting, and underwent significant transformation of its management and product development structure. After 2000, Huawei increased its speed of expansion into overseas markets, having achieved international sales of more than US $ 100 million by 2000 and establishing an R&D center in Stockholm, Sweden. In 2001, Huawei established four R&D centers in the United States.

In July 2010, Huawei was included in the Global Fortune 500, 2010 list published by the U.S. magazine *Fortune* for the first time, on the strength of annual sales of US $ 21.8 billion and net profit of US $ 2.67 billion.

Huawei has focused on expanding its mobile technology and networking solutions through a number of partnerships. In March 2003, Huawei and 3Com Corporation formed a joint venture company, 3Com-Huawei (H3C), which focused on the R&D, production and sales of data networking products. In 2005, Huawei began a joint venture with Siemens, called TD Tech, for developing 3G/ TD-SCDMA mobile communication technology products. In 2006, Huawei established a Shanghai-based joint R&D center with Motorola to develop UMTS technologies. Later that year, Huawei also established a joint venture with Telecom Venezuela. Telecom Venezuela holds a 65% stake while Huawei holds the remaining 35% stake.

Huawei and American security firm Symantec announced in May 2007 the formation of a joint-venture company to develop security and storage solutions to market to telecommunications carriers. Huawei Technologies was one of six telecom industry companies included in the World's Most Respected 200 Companies list compiled by Forbes magazine in May 2007. In December 2008, *Business Week* magazine included Huawei in their inaugural list of 「The World's Most Influential Companies」.

In 2008, Huawei launched a joint venture with UK-based marine engineering company, Global Marine Systems, to deliver undersea network equipment and related services. In 2009,

Huawei won the Green Mobile Award at the GSMA Mobile Awards 2009.

As of the beginning of 2010, approximately 80% of the world's top 50 telecoms companies had worked with Huawei. Prominent partners include BT, Vodafone, Motorola, etc..

In May 2011 Huawei won a contract with Everything Everywhere, the UK's biggest communication company, to enhance its 2G network. The four-year deal represents Huawei's first mobile network deal in the UK.

Huawei Technologies Co Ltd, is the world's largest telecom equipment maker and China's largest telephone-network equipment maker. As of 2008, Huawei ranked first in terms of global market share in the mobile softswitches market, tied with Sony Ericsson for lead market share in mobile broadband cards by revenue, ranked second in the optical hardware market, stayed first in the IP DSLAM market, and ranked third in mobile network equipment. In 2009, Huawei was ranked No. 2 in global market share for radio access equipment.

According to theWorld Intellectual Property Organization (WIPO) on 27 January 2009, Huawei was ranked as the largest applicant under WIPO's Patent Cooperation Treaty (PCT). In 2014, Huawei became the world's No. 1 applicant for international patents in 2014, with 3,442 patents.

As part of its international support for technology and telecommunications education and training, Huawei has contributed funding and equipment to a number of universities and training centers in countries such as Kenya, India, Indonesia, Bangladesh, and Nigeria. In the U.S.

Lenovo

Lenovo Group Ltd. is a Chinese multinational computer technology company with headquarters in Beijing, China, and Morrisville, North Carolina, United States. It designs, develops, manufactures and sells personal computers, tablet computers, smartphones, workstations, servers, electronic storage devices, IT management software and smart televisions.

Lenovo was founded in Beijing in 1984 as **Legend** and was incorporated in Hong Kong in 1988. For the first 20 years of its existence, the company's English name was 「Legend」 (in Chinese 「聯想」). In 2002, Yang Yuanqing decided to abandon use of the Legend brand name in order to expand outside of China. The 「Legend」 name was already in use by many other businesses worldwide, making it impossible to register in most jurisdictions. In April 2003, the company publicly announced its new name, 「Lenovo.」

Liu chuanzhi founded Lenovo in 1984 with a group of ten engineers in Beijing with 200,000 yuan.

Their first significant effort, an attempt to import televisions, failed. The group rebuilt itself within a year by conducting quality checks on computers for new buyers. Lenovo soon started developing a circuit board that would allow IBM-compatible personal computers to process Chinese characters. This product was Lenovo's first major success. Lenovo also tried and failed to market a digital watch. Liu said,「Our management team often differed on which commercial road to travel. This led to big discussions, especially between the engineering chief and myself. He felt that if the quality of the product was good, then it would sell itself. But I knew this was not true, that marketing and other factors were part of the eventual success of a product.」Lenovo's early difficulties were compounded by the fact that its staff had little business experience.「We were mainly scientists and didn't understand the market,」Liu said.「We just learned by trial-and-error, which was very interesting—but also very dangerous,」said Liu. In 1990, Lenovo started to manufacture and market computers using its own brand name.

In May 1988, Lenovo placed its first advertisement seeking employees. The ad was placed on the front page of the *China Youth News*, and it was quite rare in China at that time. Out of the 500 respondents, 280 were selected to take a written employment exam. 120 of these candidates were interviewed in person. Although interviewers initially only had authority to hire 16 people, 58 were given offers. The new staff included 18 people with graduate degrees, 37 with undergraduate degrees, and three students with no university-level education. Their average age was 26. Yang Yuanqing, the current CEO of Lenovo, was among that group.

Liu Chuanzhi, received government permission to open a subsidiary in Hong Kong and was allowed to move there along with five other employees. Liu's father, already in Hong Kong, furthered his son's ambitions through mentoring and facilitating loans. Liu moved to Hong Kong in 1988. In order to save money during this period, Liu and his co-workers walked instead of taking public transportation. In order to keep up appearances, they rented hotel rooms for meetings.

Lenovo became publicly traded after a 1994 Hong Kong listing that raised nearly US $ 30 million. Prior to its IPO, many analysts were optimistic about Lenovo. The company was praised for its good management, strong brand recognition, and growth potential. When Lenovo was first listed, its managers thought the only purpose of going public was to raise capital. They had little understanding of the rules and responsibilities that went along with running a public company. The first time Liu traveled to Europe to discuss his company's stock, he was shocked by the skeptical questions he was subjected to and felt offended. Liu later came to understand that he was accountable to shareholders. Legend began to think about issues of credibility, and learn how to become a truly international company.」

From 1990 to 2007, Lenovo successfully integrated Western-style accountability into its corporate culture. Lenovo's emphasis on transparency earned it a reputation for the best corporate governance among mainland Chinese firms. All major issues regarding its board, management, major share transfers, and mergers and acquisitions were fairly and accurately reported. While Hong Kong listed firms were only required to issue financial reports twice per year, Lenovo followed the international norm of issuing quarterly reports. Lenovo created an audit committee and a compensation committee with non-management directors.

Lenovo works to integrate the management of each newly acquired company into its larger culture. Lenovo has a dedicated mergers and acquisitions team that tracks the progress of these integrations. Lenovo has an annual meeting where the management of newly acquired companies meet with its top 100 executives. In these meetings, held in English, Lenovo explains its global strategy and how new executives fit in.

In regards to the purchase of IBM's personal computer division, Liu Chuanzhi said,「We benefited in three ways from the IBM acquisition. We got the ThinkPad brand, IBM's more advanced PC manufacturing technology and the company's international resources, such as its global sales channels and operation teams. These three elements have shored up our sales revenue in the past several years.」

On January 27, 2011, Lenovo formed a joint venture to produce personal computers with Japanese electronics firm NEC. This joint venture was intended to boost Lenovo's worldwide sales by expanding its presence in Japan, a key market for personal computers. NEC spun off its personal computer business into the joint venture. As of 2010, NEC controlled about 20% of Japan's market for personal computers while Lenovo had a 5% share. Lenovo and NEC also agreed to explore cooperating in other areas such as servers and tablet computers.

In June 2011, Lenovo announced acquiring control of Medion, a German electronics manufacturing company. The deal, which closed in the third quarter of the same year, was the first in which a Chinese company acquired a well-known German company. This acquisition gave Lenovo 14% of the German computer market.

Lenovo entered the smartphone market in 2012 and quickly became the largest vendor of smartphones in Mainland China. Entry into the smartphone market was paired with a change of strategy from「the one-size-fits-all」to a diverse portfolio of devices. These changes were driven by the popularity of Apple's iPhone and Lenovo's desire to increase its market share in mainland China. Lenovo passed Apple to become the No. 2 provider of smartphones to the Chinese market in 2012. However, due to there being about 100 smartphone brands sold in China, this second only equated to a 10.4% market share.

In September 2012, Lenovo acquired the Brazil-based electronics company Digibras, which sells products under the brand-name CCE. Lenovo cited their desire to take advantage of increased sales due to the 2014 World Cup that was hosted by Brazil and the 2016 Summer Olympics and CCE's reputation for quality.

In September 2012, Lenovo acquired the United States-based software company Stoneware in order to gain access to new technology and efforts to improve and expand its cloud-computing services.

In April 2014, Lenovo purchased a portfolio of patents from NEC related to mobile technology. These included over 3,800 patent families in countries around the world. The purchase included standards-essential patents for 3G and LTE cellular technologies and other patents related to smartphones and tablets.

On 29 January 2014, Google announced selling Motorola Mobility to Lenovo for US $ 2.91 billion in a cash-and-stock deal. As of February 2014, Google owns about 5.94% of Lenovo's stock. Lenovo got the future Motorola Mobility product roadmap. Google retained the Advanced Technologies & Projects unit and Lenovo received royalty free licenses to all the patents retained by Google.

In 2015, Lenovo revealed a new logo at Lenovo Tech World in Beijing, with the slogan 「Innovation Never Stands Still」(Chinese: 創新無止境).

Lenovo's corporate culture differs significantly from most large Chinese companies. While Lenovo was founded using seed capital from the state-owned Chinese Academy of Sciences, Lenovo is run as a private enterprise with little or no interference by the state. Lenovo's senior executives, including many non-Chinese, rotate between two head offices, one in Beijing and the other in Morrisville, North Carolina, and Lenovo's research and development center in Japan. Two Westerners have served as Lenovo's CEO.

English is Lenovo's official language. Lenovo's CEO, Yang Yuanqing, initially did not understand English well, but relocated his family to Morrisville in order to improve his language skills and soak up American culture. One American Lenovo executive interviewed by *The Economist* praised Yang for his efforts to make Lenovo a friendly place for foreigners to work. He said that Yang had created a 「performance culture」in place of the traditional Chinese work style of 「waiting to see what the emperor wants.」

When Yang took over Lenovo's personal computer division, he strongly discouraged the use of formal titles and required staff to address each other by their given names. Yang even required managers to stand outside their offices each morning to greet their employees while carrying signs with their first names. Yang wanted his people to think and act like high-tech workers in developed markets.

In 2012, Yang received a $3 million bonus as a reward for record profits, which he inturn redistributed among staff working in positions such as production and reception who received an average of 2,000 yuan or about US $314. This was almost equivalent to a monthly salary of an average worker in China. Yang made a similar gift of $3.25 million again in 2013.

Liu Chuanzhi is the founder and chairman of Lenovo. Liu was trained as an engineer at a military college and later went on to work at the Chinese Academy of Sciences. Like many young people during the Cultural Revolution, Liu was denounced and sent to the countryside where he worked as a laborer on a rice farm.

Liu claims Hewlett-Packard as a key source of inspiration. In an interview with *The Economist* he stated that 「Our earliest and best teacher was Hewlett-Packard.」For more than ten years, Lenovo was Hewlett-Packard's distributor in China. In reference to Lenovo's later acquisition of IBM's personal computer unit Liu said, 「I remember the first time I took part in a meeting of IBM agents. I was wearing an old business suit of my father's and I sat in the back row. Even in my dreams, I never imagined that one day we could buy the IBM PC business. It was unthinkable. Impossible.」

Founder Group

Founder Group (Chinese: 方正集團) is a major Chinese technology conglomerate that deals with information technology, pharmaceuticals, real estate, finance, and commodities trading. It is divided into five major industry groups, each covering a separate industry: PKU Founder IT Group (IT), PKU Healthcare Group (healthcare and pharmaceuticals), PKU Resource Group (real estate), Founder Financial (finance), and Founder Commodities (commodities trading).

Founder Group was established in 1986 by Peking University. Professor Wang Xuan of Peking University became Founder's first key person, as the Chinese-character laser phototypesetting system that he invented provided the foundation on which Founder was developed. Wang brought Founder into the television and radio industries, positioned the company to expand overseas, and supported the diversification of the group. By 1989, total orders for the phototypesetting system exceeded 100 million yuan.

Between 1990 and 1994, under the guidance of Wang Xuan, Founder released multiple technologies, including a long-distance newspaper transfer technology, a color desktop publishing system, a computer management system for gathering and editing news, and the new generation of software and hardware systems. Founder's publishing system became the most popular product of its kind, capturing 80% of the Chinese newspaper market in Hong Kong, Southeast Asia, and North America.

Throughout the late 1990s, publishing systems developed by Founder's researchers dominated the domestic market. Additionally, they entered the international market, with products being exported to dozens of countries all over the world. In the meantime, Founder Group sold its core technologies with independent intellectual rights to global manufacturers, who then applied these technologies in their products around the world.

Founder Group currently has six public companies listed in stock exchanges of Shanghai, Shenzhen, and Hong Kong, and more than 80 independently funded enterprises and joint ventures. Founder's motto is 「世界在變 創新不變」, which roughly translates to 「The world is changing; innovation is not」. The company is moving to establish itself as a computer chip designer.

Part Ⅳ E-commerce and Its Industries

E-commerce, short for **electronic commerce**, is trading in products or services using computer networks, such as the Internet. Electronic commerce draws on technologies such as mobile commerce, electronic funds transfer, supply chain management, Internet marketing, online transaction processing, electronic data interchange (EDI), inventory management systems, and automated data collection systems. E-commerce seeks to add revenue streams using the Internet to build and enhance relationships with clients and partners. Modern electronic commerce typically uses the World Wide Web for at least one part of the transaction's life cycle, although it may also use other technologies such as e-mail.

E-commerce may employ some or all of the following:

· Online shopping web sites for retail sales direct to consumers

· Providing or participating in online marketplaces, which process third-party business-to-consumer or consumer-to-consumer sales

· Business-to-business buying and selling

· Gathering and using demographic data through web contacts and social media

· Business-to-business electronic data interchange

· Marketing to prospective and established customers by e-mail or fax (for example, with newsletters)

Alibaba Group

Alibaba Group Holding Limited (NYSE: BABA) is a Chinese e-commerce company that provides consumer-to-consumer, business-to-consumer and business-to-business sales services via web portals. It also provides electronic payment services, a shopping search engine and data-centric cloud computing services. The group began in 1999 when Jack Ma founded the website Alibaba. com, a business-to-business portal to connect Chinese manufacturers with overseas buyers. In 2012, two of Alibaba's portals handled 1.1 trillion yuan ($ 170 billion) in sales. The company primarily operates in the People's Republic of China (PRC), In September 2013, the company sought an IPO in the United States after a deal could not be reached with Hong Kong regulators. On 19 September 2014, the date of its initial public offering (IPO), Alibaba's market value was measured as US $ 231 billion.

Alibaba's consumer-to-consumer portal Taobao, similar to eBay. com, features nearly a billion products and is one of the 20 most-visited websites globally. The Group's websites accounted for over 60% of the parcels delivered in China by March 2013, and 80% of the nation's online sales by September 2014. Alipay, an online payment service, accounts for roughly half of all online payment transactions within China.

Alibaba reported sale of more than $ 9 billion on China's Singles' Day in 2014.

The company was founded in Hangzhou in eastern China, as Ma explained: One day I was in San Francisco in a coffee shop, and I was thinking Alibaba is a good name. And then a waitress came, and I said,「Do you know about Alibaba?」And she said yes. I said,「What do you know about Alibaba?」, and she said,「Open Sesame」. And I said,「Yes, this is the name!」Then I went onto the street and found 30 people and asked them,「Do you know Alibaba?」People from India, people from Germany, people from Tokyo and China… they all knew about Alibaba. Alibaba — open sesame. Alibaba is a kind, smart business person, and he helped the village. So… easy to spell, and globally known. Alibaba opens sesame for small-to medium-sized companies. We also registered the name 「Alimama」, in case someone wants to marry us!」

Alibaba. com, the primary company of Alibaba, is the world's largest online business-to-business trading platform for small businesses.

Alibaba. com has three main services. The company's English language portal Alibaba. com handles sales between importers and exporters from more than 240 countries and regions. The Chinese portal 1688. com was developed for domestic business-to-business trade in China. In addition, Alibaba. com offers a transaction-based retail website, AliExpress. com, which allows smaller buyers to buy small quantities of goods at wholesale prices.

Taobao, is China's largest consumer-to-consumer online shopping platform. Founded in 2003, it offers a variety of products for retail sale. In January 2015 it was the second most visited web site in China, according to Alexa. com. Taobao's growth was attributed to offering free registration and commission-free transactions using a free third-party payment platform.

Advertising makes up 85 percent of the company's total revenue. The number of stores on Taobao with annual sales under 100 thousand yuan increased by 60% between 2011 and 2013. Over the same period, the number of stores with sales between 10 thousand and 1 million yuan increased by 30%, and the number of stores with sales over 1 million yuan increased by 33%. Taobao's total sales (including Tmall) exceeded 1 trillion yuan (USD 160 billion) in 2012. And on 11 November 2012, the biggest online shopping promotion activity, Taobao accomplished 19. 1 billion yuan (USD 3. 07 billion) sales in one day.

Tmall. com was introduced in April 2008 as an online retail platform to complement the Taobao consumer-to-consumer portal and became a separate business in June 2011. As of October 2013 it was the eighth most visited web site in China, offering global brands to an increasingly affluent Chinese consumer base.

Launched in 2004, Alipay is a third-party online payment platform with no transaction fees. It also provides an escrow service, in which buyers can verify whether they are happy with goods they have bought before releasing money to the seller. Alipay has the biggest market share in China with 300 million users and control of just under half of China's online payment market in February 2014. In 2013, Alipay launched a financial product platform called Yu'ebao (餘額寶).

Alibaba Cloud Computing (www. aliyun. com) aims to build a cloud computing service platform, including e-commerce data mining e-commerce data processing, and data customization. It was established in September 2009 in conjunction with the 10th anniversary of Alibaba Group. It has R&D centers and operators in Hangzhou, Beijing and Silicon Valley. In July 2014, Aliyun entered into a partnership deal with Inspur, the largest high-end cloud computing company in China.

Launched in 2010, AliExpress. com is an online retail service made up of mostly small Chinese businesses offering products to international online buyers. It is the most visited e-commerce website in Russia.

Baidu

Baidu 百度, Inc. incorporated on January 18, 2000, is a Chinese web services company headquartered at the Baidu Campus in Beijing's Haidian District.

Baidu offers many services, including a Chinese language-search engine for websites, audio files and images. Baidu offers 57 search and community services including Baidu Baike (an online, collaboratively-built encyclopedia) and a searchable, keyword-based discussion forum. Baidu was established in 2000 by Robin Li and Eric Xu. Both of the co-founders are Chinese nationals who studied and worked overseas before returning to China. In March 2015, Baidu ranked 4th overall in the Alexa Internet rankings. In December 2007, Baidu became the first Chinese company to be included in the NASDAQ-100 index.

The name *Baidu* is a quote from the last line of Xin Qiji's classical poem「Green Jade Table in The Lantern Festival」saying:「Having searched thousands of times in the crowd, suddenly turning back, She is there in the dimmest candlelight.」

As of 2006, Baidu provided an index of over 740 million web pages, 80 million images, and 10 million multimedia files. Baidu offers multimedia content including MP3 music, and movies, and is the first in China to offer Wireless Application Protocol (WAP) and personal digital assistant (PDA) -based mobile search.

Baidu offers several services to locate information, products and services using Chinese-language search terms, such as, search by Chinese phonetics, advanced search, snapshots, spell checker, stock quotes, news, knows, postbar, images, video and space information, and weather, train and flight schedules and other local information.

• *Baidu Map*-a desktop and mobile mapping solution similar to Google Maps, but covering only the Greater China region.

• *Baidu Yun* or *Baidu Cloud*（百度雲）is a cloud storage service that offers 2 TB of free data storage.

• *Baidu News* provides links to a selection of local, national and international news, and presents news stories in a searchable format, within minutes of their publication on the Web. Baidu News uses an automated process to display links to related headlines, which enables people to see many different viewpoints on the same story.

• *Baidu Knows*（百度知道）provides users with a query-based searchable community to share knowledge and experience. Through Baidu Knows, registered members of Baidu Knows can post specific questions for other members to respond and also answer questions of other members.

• *Baidu MP3 Search* provides algorithm-generated links to songs and other multimedia files provided by Internet content providers. Baidu started with a popular music search feature called「MP3 Search」and its comprehensive lists of popular Chinese music, *Baidu* 500, based on download numbers. Baidu locates file formats such as MP3, WMA and SWF. The multimedia search feature is mainly used in searches for Chinese pop music. While such works are copyrighted under Chinese law, Baidu claims on its legal disclaimer that linking to these files does not break Chinese law. This has led other local search engines to follow the practice, including Google China (Hong Kong), which uses an intermediate company called Top100 to offer a similar MP3 Search service.

• *Baidu Image Search* enables users to search millions of images on the Internet. Baidu Image Search offers features such as search by image size and by image file type. Image listings are organized by various categories, which are updated automatically through algorithms.

• *Baidu Video Search* enables users to search for and access through hyperlinks of online video clips that are hosted on third parties' Websites.

• Baidu Space the social networking service of Baidu, allows registered users to create personalized homepages in a query-based searchable community. Registered users can post their Web logs, or blogs, photo album and certain personal information on their homepages and establish their own communities of friends who are also registered users. By July 2009, it had reached 100 million registered users

• Baidu Baike is similar to Wikipedia as an encyclopedia; however, unlike Wikipedia, only registered users can edit the articles due to Chinese laws.

• *China Digital Village Encyclopedia*, in June 2009, Baidu announced it would compile the largest digital rural encyclopedia in China, according to China Securities Journal. It is expected to include 500,000 administrative villages in China, covering 80% of the total 600,000 villages in China. Baidu is creating the content of this encyclopedia largely from participants of its「rural information competition」, on which it has spent roughly five million yuan on incentives. Baidu sees China's rural areas as great potential for electronic business (e-business), evidenced by the fact that revenue grew the fastest from agriculture, forestry, animals, and fishery in the company's keyword promotion project, a crucial source of Baidu's total revenue.

• *Baidu Search Ranking* provides listings of search terms based on daily search queries entered on Baidu.com. The listings are organized by categories and allow users to locate search terms on topics of interest.

• *Baidu Web Directory* enables users to browse and search through websites that have been organized into categories.

• *Baidu Government Information Search* allows users to search various regulations, rules, notices, and other information announced by People's Republic of China government entities.

• *Baidu Postal Code Search* enables users to search postal codes in hundreds of cities in China.

• *Educational Website Search* allows users to search the Websites of educational institutions. Baidu University Search allows users to search information on or browse through the Websites of specific universities in China.

• *Baidu Legal Search* enables users to search a database that contains national and local laws and regulations, cases, legal decisions, and law dictionaries.

· *Baidu Love* is a query-based searchable community where registered users can write and post messages to loved ones.

· *Baidu Patent Search* enables users to search for specific Chinese patents and provides basic patent information in the search results, including the patent's name, application number, filing date, issue date, inventor information and brief description of the patent.

· *Baidu Games* is an online channel that allows users to search or browse through game-related news and content.

· *Baidu Statistics Search* enables users to search statistics that have been published by the Government of the People's Republic of China.

· *Baidu Entertainment* is an online channel for entertainment-related news and content. Users can search or browse through news and other information relating to specific stars, movies, television series and music.

· *Baidu Dictionary* provides users with lookup and text translation services between Chinese and English.

· *Baidu Desktop Search*, a free, downloadable software, which enables users to search all files saved on their computer without launching a Web browser.

· *Baidu Sobar*, a free, downloadable software, displayed on a browser's tool bar and makes the search function available on every Web page that a user browses.

· *Baidu Wireless* provides various services for mobile phones, including a Chinese-input front end processor (FEP) for various popular operating systems including Android, Symbian S60v5, and Windows Mobile.

· *Baidu Anti-Virus* offers anti-virus software products and computer virus-related news.

· *Baidu Safety Center*, launched in 2008, provides users with free virus scanning, system repair and online security evaluations.

· *Baidu Internet TV* (known as *Baidu Movies*) allows users to search, watch and download free movies, television series, cartoons, and other programs hosted on its servers.

· *Baidu Library* is an open online platform for users to share documents. All the documents in Baidu Library are uploaded by the users and Baidu does not edit or change the documents. Users can read and download lecture notes, exercises, sample exams, presentation slides, materials of various subjects, variety of documents templates, etc. However, it is not completely free. In order to download some documents, users should have enough Baidu points to cover the points asked by the uploaders. Users could gain Baidu points by making contribution to Baidu Library and other users, such as uploading documents, categorizing documents, evaluating documents, etc.

· *Baidu Experience* is a product of Baidu primarily focusing on supporting the users with practical problems. In other words, it helps the users to solve the 「how to do」problem. It was launched in October 2010. In architecture, Baidu Experience has integrated and reformatted Baidu Encyclopedia and Baike Knows. The first difference between Baidu Experience and Baidu Knows is that the former concentrates on specific 「how to do」problems while the later contains a wider range of problems. The second difference is that users could share their experience without being asked on Baidu Experience.

Baidu focuses on generating revenues primarily from online marketing services. Baidu's pay for placement (P4P) platform enables its customers to reach users who search for information related to their products or services. Customers use automated online tools to create text-based descriptions of their web pages and bid on keywords that trigger the display of their webpage information and link. Baidu's P4P platform features an automated online sign-up process that customers use to activate their accounts at any time. The P4P platform is an online marketplace that introduces Internet search users to customers who bid for priority placement in the search results. Baidu also uses third-party distributors to sell some of its online marketing services to end customers and offers discounts to these distributors in consideration of their services.

Baidu offers certain consultative services, such as keyword suggestions, account management and performance reporting. Baidu suggests synonyms and associated phrases to use as keywords or text in search listings. These suggestions can improve click through rates of the customer's listing and increase the likelihood that a user will enter into a transaction with the customer. Baidu also provides online daily reports of the number of click throughs, clicked keywords and the total costs incurred, as well as statistical reports organized by geographic region.

Baidu competes with 360 Search (www.haosou.com), Sogou Search (www.sogou.com), Sina, Wikipedia, Tencent's Soso.com and Alibaba's Taobao, etc.. Baidu is the No. 1 search engine in China, controlling 63 percent of China's market share as of January 2010. The number of Internet users in China had reached 513 million by the end of December 2011. On January 9, 2013, Baidu was still number one in the market, with 64.5% of the users.

Tencent

Tencent Holdings Limited is a Chinese investment holding company whose subsidiaries provide media, entertainment, internet and mobile phone value-added services, and operate online advertising services in China. Its headquarters are in Nanshan District, Shenzhen. Tencent offers a diverse mix of services and counts both consumers and businesses as customers.

Tencent's many services include social network, web portals, e-commerce, and multiplayer online games. Its offerings include the well-known (in China) instant messenger Tencent QQ and one of the largest web portals in China, QQ.com.. QQ is one of the most popular instant messaging platforms in its home market. As of December 31, 2010, there were 647.6 million active Tencent QQ IM user accounts, making Tencent QQ the world's largest online community at the time. The number of QQ accounts simultaneously online has sometimes exceeded 100 million.

Mobile chat service WeChat has helped bolster Tencent's continued expansion into smartphone services.

WeChat, literally micro message, is a mobile text and voice messaging communication service developed by Tencent in China, first released in January 2011. The app is available on Android, iPhone, BlackBerry, Windows Phone. As of August 2014, WeChat has 438 million active users; with 70 million outside of China.

WeChat provides text messaging, hold-to-talk voice messaging, broadcast (one-to-many) messaging, sharing of photographs and videos, and location sharing. It can exchange contacts with people nearby via Bluetooth, as well as providing various features for contacting people at random if desired (if these are open to it) and integration with social networking services such as those run by Facebook and Tencent QQ. Photographs may also be embellished with filters and captions, and a machine translation service is available.

Tencent sells virtual goods for use in their MMOs, IM client, social networking sites, and for mobile phones. Income from the sale of virtual goods was a large proportion of Tencent's revenue in 2009.

Tencent's online currency, Q Coins, can be used to purchase virtual goods. These range from the offbeat, such as virtual pets and the virtual clothing, jewelry, and cosmetics, etc..

Tencent used to offer a number of online, multiplayer games through its game portal QQ Games.

Tencent established in 2014 exclusive in-China distribution agreements with several large music producers, including Sony, Warner Music Group and YG Entertainment.

Dididache (滴滴打車) is a smartphone application which matches passengers and willing taxi drivers who are situated in close proximity. For passengers, a list of nearby taxicabs is created via GPS, and a signal is sent out indicating an expression of interest. Conversely, for taxi drivers with the app installed on their phones, the GPS system quickly lists and localizes nearby potential clients; and once a match is created, the taxi can efficiently pick up awaiting passengers.

Dididache is a dominant player in China's taxi-hailing arena, with a market share exceeding 60% and service extending to 32 cities including the Tier-1 Beijing, Shanghai, Guangzhou, and Shenzhen. Dididache in 2014 has 40 million registered users, a doubling from 2013's user base; and every month, more than 21 million cab rides are booked through the service, or 700,000 bookings per day. Additionally, from the taxicab perspective, Dididache already has an extensive user base of taxi drivers of more than 350,000 vehicles across China.

TenPay is an online payment system similar to PayPal. It supports B2B, B2C, and C2C payments. In some Chinese cities individuals can use TenPay for utility payments and to refill their public transport cards. Co-branded credit cards are available, and credit card bills can also be paid using the service. offline recharging of your TenPay account is possible, as the company sends employees to collect customer money in person.

On April 13, 2015, the market value of Tencent exceeded US $ 200 billion for the first time, hitting US $ 206 billion. It is one of the largest Internet companies in the world and competes with Google, Facebook, Twitter, Amazon, Ebay, and Alibaba.

Google Search

Google Search, is a web search engine owned by Google Inc. It is the most-used search engine on the World Wide Web, handling more than three billion searches each day. As of February 2015 it is the most used search engine in the US with 64.5% market share.

The main purpose of Google Search is to hunt for text in publicly accessible documents offered by web servers.

Universal search was launched by Google on May 16, 2007. It was an idea which merged the results from different searches into one. Prior to Universal search, a standard Google search would consist of links to different websites. Universal search incorporates a wide variety of information such as websites, news, pictures, maps, blogs, videos, and more to display as search results. With Universal search, Google attempted to break down the walls that traditionally separated various search properties and integrate the vast amounts of information available into one simple set of search results. Google wants to help people find the very best answer, even if there don't know where to look.

A Google Search mobile app is available for Android and iOS devices. In addition to allowing users to perform web searches, the app implements Google Now, Google's voice recognition and intelligent personal assistant software. Google Now uses a natural language user interface to answer questions, make recommendations, and perform actions by delegating requests to a set of web services. Along with answering user-initiated queries, Google Now passively delivers information to the user that it predicts they will want, based on their search habits.

Searches made by search engines, including Google, leave traces. This raises concerns about privacy. In principle, if details of a user's searches are found, those with access to the information—principally state agencies responsible for law enforcement and similar matters—can make deductions about the user's activities. This has been used for the detection and prosecution of lawbreakers; for example a murderer was found and convicted after searching for terms such as 「tips with killing with a baseball bat」.

Google is available in many languages and has been localized completely or partly for many countries. At the same time, Google has to compete world-wide with many websites, which include Baidu and Soso. com in China; Naver. com and Daum Communications in South Korea; Yandex in Russia; Seznam. cz in the Czech Republic; Yahoo! in Japan, Taiwan and the US, as well as Bing and DuckDuckGo.

Facebook

Facebook is an online social networking service headquartered in Menlo Park, California. Its website was launched on February 4, 2004, by Mark Zuckerberg with his college roommates and fellow Harvard University students Eduardo Saverin, Andrew McCollum, Dustin Moskovitz and Chris Hughes. The founders had initially limited the website's membership to Harvard students, but later expanded it to colleges in the Boston area, the Ivy League, and Stanford University. It gradually added support for students at various other universities and later to high-school students. Since 2006, anyone who is at least 13 years old is allowed to become a registered user of the website, though the age requirement may be higher depending on applicable local laws.

After registering to use the site, users can create a user profile, add other users as 「friends」, exchange messages, post status updates and photos, share videos and receive notifications when others update their profiles. Additionally, users may join common-interest user groups, organized by workplace, school or college, or other characteristics, and categorize their friends into lists such as 「People From Work」 or 「Close Friends」. By January 2014, Facebook's market capitalization had risen to over $ 134 billion. At the end of January 2014, 1.23 billion users were active on the website every month.

The company celebrated its 10th anniversary during the week of February 3, 2014. In each of the first three months of 2014, over one billion users logged into their Facebook account on a mobile device.

Facebook had over 1.44 billion monthly active users as of March 2015. Because of the large volume of data users submit to the service, Facebook has come under scrutiny for their privacy policies. Facebook, Inc. held its initial public offering in February 2012 and began selling stock to the public three months later, reaching an original peak market capitalization of $ 104 billion. As of February 2015 Facebook reached a market capitalization of $ 212 Billion.

Twitter

Twitter is an online social networking service that enables users to send and read short 140-character messages called 「tweets」.

Registered users can read and post tweets, but unregistered users can only read them. Users access Twitter through the website interface, SMS, or mobile device app. Twitter Inc. is based in San Francisco and has more than 25 offices around the world.

Twitter was created in March 2006 by Jack Dorsey, Evan Williams, Biz Stone and Noah Glass and launched by July 2006. The service rapidly gained worldwide popularity, with more than 100 million users who in 2012 posted 340 million tweets per day. The service also handled 1.6 billion search queries per day. In 2013 Twitter was one of the ten most-visited websites. As of May 2015, Twitter has more than 500 million users, out of which more than 302 million are active users.

Twitter has been adopted as a communication and learning tool in educational settings mostly in colleges and universities. It has been used as a back channel to promote student interactions, especially in large-lecture courses. Research has found that using Twitter in college courses helps students communicate with each other and faculty, promotes informal learning, allows shy students a forum for increased participation, increases student engagement, and improves overall course grades.

In May 2008, *The Wall Street Journal* wrote that social networking services such as Twitter 「elicit mixed feelings in the technology-savvy people who have been their early adopters. Fans say they are a good way to keep in touch with busy friends. But some users are starting to feel 「too」 connected, as they grapple with check-in messages at odd hours, higher cellphone bills and the need to tell acquaintances to stop announcing what they're having for dinner.」

World leaders and their diplomats have taken note of Twitter's rapid expansion and have been increasingly utilizing Twitter diplomacy, the use of Twitter to engage with foreign publics and their own citizens. US Ambassador to Russia, Michael A. McFaul has been attributed as a pioneer of international Twitter diplomacy. He used Twitter after becoming ambassador in 2011, posting in English and Russian. On October 24, 2014, Queen Elizabeth II sent her first tweet to mark the opening of the London Science Museum's Information Age exhibition. A 2013 study by website Twiplomacy found that 153 of the 193 countries represented at the United Nations had established government Twitter accounts. The same study also found that those accounts amounted to 505 Twitter handles used by world leaders and their foreign ministers, with their tweets able to reach a combined audience of over 106 million followers.

According to an analysis of accounts, the heads of state of 125 countries and 139 other leading politicians have Twitter accounts that have between them sent more than 350,000 tweets and have almost 52 million followers.

Twitter's usage spikes during prominent events. For example, a record was set during the 2010 FIFA World Cup when fans wrote 2,940 tweets per second in the thirty-second period after Japan scored against Cameroon on June 14. The record was broken again when 3,085 tweets per second were posted after the Los Angeles Lakers' victory in the 2010 NBA Finals on

June 17, and then again at the close of Japan's victory over Denmark in the World Cup when users published 3,283 tweets per second. The record was set again during the 2011 FIFA Women's World Cup Final between Japan and the United States, when 7,196 tweets per second were published. When American singer Michael Jackson died on June 25, 2009, Twitter servers crashed after users were updating their status to include the words「Michael Jackson」at a rate of 100,000 tweets per hour.

Amazon.com

amazon.com

Amazon.com, Inc. is an American electronic commerce company with headquarters in Seattle, Washington. It is the largest Internet-based retailer in the United States. Amazon.com started as an online bookstore, but soon diversified, selling DVDs, Blu-rays, CDs, video downloads, MP3 downloads, software, video games, electronics, apparel, furniture, food, toys and jewelry. The company also produces consumer electronics—notably, Amazon Kindle e-book readers, Fire tablets, Fire TV and Fire Phone — and is a major provider of cloud computing services.

Jeff Bezos, the founder, selected the name Amazon by looking through the dictionary, and settled on「Amazon」because it was a place that was「exotic and different」just as he planned for his store to be; the Amazon river, he noted was by far the「biggest」river in the world, and he planned to make his store the biggest in the world. Bezos placed a premium on his head start in building a brand, telling a reporter,「There's nothing about our model that can't be copied over time. But you know, McDonald's got copied. And it still built a huge, multibillion-dollar company. A lot of it comes down to the brand name. Brand names are more important online than they are in the physical world.」

After reading a report about the future of the Internet which projected annual Web commerce growth at 2,300%, Bezos created a list of 20 products which could be marketed online. He narrowed the list to what he felt were the five most promising products which included: compact discs, computer hardware, computer software, videos, and books. Bezos finally decided that his new business would sell books online, due to the large world-wide demand for literature, the low price points for books, along with the huge number of titles available in print.

Amazon has separate retail websites for United States, United Kingdom & Ireland, France, Canada, Germany, Italy, Spain, the Netherlands, Australia, Brazil, Japan, China, India and Mexico. Amazon also offers international shipping to certain other countries for some of its products. In 2011, it had professed an intention to launch its websites in Poland and Sweden.

eBay

eBay Inc. is an American multinational corporation and e-commerce company, providing consumer to consumer & business to consumer sales services via Internet. It is headquartered in San Jose, California, United States. eBay was founded by Pierre Omidyar in 1995, and became a notable success story of the dot-com bubble. Today, it is a multi-billion dollar business with operations localized in over thirty countries.

eBay generates revenue by a complex system of fees for services, listing product features, and a *Final Value Fee* for sales proceeds by sellers. The company manages eBay. com, an online auction and shopping website in which people and businesses buy and sell a broad variety of goods and services worldwide. In addition to its auction-style sales, the website has since expanded to include「Buy It Now」shopping; shopping by UPC, ISBN, or other kind of SKU (via Half. com); online classified advertisements (via Kijiji or eBay Classifieds); online event ticket trading (via StubHub); online money transfers (via PayPal) and other services.

On October 3, 2002, PayPal became a wholly owned subsidiary of eBay. Its corporate headquarters are in San Jose, California, United States at eBay's North First Street satellite office campus. The company also has significant operations in Omaha, Scottsdale, Charlotte, Austin, and Boston in the United States; Chennai in India; Dublin in Ireland; Kleinmachnow in Germany; and Tel Aviv in Israel. From July 2007, PayPal has operated across the European Union as a Luxembourg-based bank. The company's business strategy includes increasing international trade. eBay has already expanded to over two dozen countries including China and India.

Glossary

Part I

facilitate   v. 使……便利；促進，推進
certified   adj. 有保證的；通過相關證明的
proprietary   adj. 專有的；專賣的
Geneva   n. 日內瓦
Switzerland   n. 瑞士
consultative   adj. 商議的
restrict   v. 限制
terminology   n. 術語
appliance   n. 用具；器具

nanotechnology   n. 納米技術
magnetics   n. 磁學
harmonize   v. 使……協調，使……一致
protocols   n. 協議
precursor   n. 初期形式
exponential   adj. 越來越快的；指數的，冪數的
encryption   n. 加密；編密碼
seismic   adj. 很有撼動力的；震撼世界的
podcast   v. 發布播客視頻
pique   v. 激起；挑起
sophisticated   adj. 複雜的
lucrative   adj. 獲利多的，賺錢的
scrutinize   v. 仔細檢查
algorithm   n. 運算法則；計算程序
dissemination   n. 散播，宣傳；浸染
solicit   v. 徵求；懇求
philanthropy   n. 慈善活動；慈善事業
backlash   v. 激烈反應；反擊
harassment   n. 騷擾，擾亂
encounter   v. 遇見；碰到
naivety   n. 天真；幼稚
circumvent   v. （用欺騙手段）避開
vulnerable   adj. 易受攻擊的；易受傷的
malicious   adj. 蓄意的；預謀的；存心不良的
surveillance   n. 監督；［法］管制；監視
censorship   n. 審查制度；審查機構
pornography   n. 色情；色情描寫
depiction   n. 描寫；敘述
cyber bullying   網絡詐欺
lingua franca   通用語
mom-and-pop   （店鋪等）夫妻經營的
brick and mortar   實際存在的；實體的；（公司等）有廠房和店鋪的
domain name   域名、網域
keyword filters   關鍵字過濾器

Part II

metonym   n. 代名詞
peninsula   n. 半島

bolster   v. 支持；支撐
astute   adj. 機敏的；精明的
affiliate   n. 分支機構；附屬企業
litigator   n. 訴訟律師
interim   adj. 過渡期間的
collaboratively   adv. 合作地
reminiscent   adj. 使人聯想的
fruitarian   n. 常食水果的人
intimidating   adj. 令人生畏的
trait   n. 特點，特性
portmanteau   n. 混成詞
rudimentary   adj. 基本的；初步的
architect   n. 設計師；建築師
revamp   v. 將（某物）更新；翻新
flagship   n. 最重要的一個；佼佼者
prominently   adv. 顯著地；重要地
typography   n. 印刷
iconography   n. 圖
minimalism   n. 簡約；至簡主義
compensation   n. 補償，賠償
extinguish   v. 使……不復存在
sue   v. 起訴；控告；控訴
discretion   n. 慎重；考慮周到
tabulate   v. 製表
recipient   n. 接受者
analytics   n. 分析學，解析學，分析論
garner   v. 獲得
high-technology economic sector   高科技經濟區
integrated circuits   集成電路
a valuation of   估價
floppy disk   軟盤

Part Ⅲ

envision   v. 想像；展望
reinforce   v. 加固；強化
preponderance   n. 數量上的優勢
proximity   n. 接近；鄰近
prestigious   adj. 有聲望的

eminent　adj. 傑出的；卓越的
indigenous　adj. 固有的；本地的
marine　adj. 海的；海軍的
billboard　n. 廣告牌；告示牌
transcendence　n. 超越；卓越
respondent　n. 回應者
profitability　n. 收益性；利益率
skeptical　adj. 懷疑性的；好懷疑的
coupon　n. 優惠券；息票；通票
commentator　n. 評論員
iconic　adj. 突出的；傑出的
rotate　v. 圍繞……運行
denounce　v. 告發；公開指責
pharmaceutical　n. 藥物
Chinese character　漢字
real estate　房地產

Part Ⅳ

prospective　adj. 未來的；預期的
affluent　adj. 富裕的；富足的
escrow　n. 由第三者保存附帶條件委付蓋印的契約
privacy　n. 隱私；秘密
encyclopedia　n. 百科全書
incentive　n. 鼓勵；刺激
template　n. 模板；樣板
trigger　v. 引發；觸發
detection　n. 偵查；檢查
prosecution　n. 控告；起訴
synonym　n. 同義詞
simultaneously　adv. 同時地
literally　adv. 逐字地；照字面地
embellish　v. 修飾；裝飾
filter　n. 濾波器；過濾器
caption　n. 標題；說明文字
conversely　adv. 反過來；反之
notification　n. 通知；公布
scrutiny　n. 關注；監督
apparel　n.（商店出售的）衣服

notably   adv. 尤其；顯著地
exotic   adj. 奇異的；吸引人的
oracle   n. 聖賢；哲人
officious   adj. 過分殷勤的，愛管閒事的，
uncouth   adj. 粗野的；不文明的
skyrocket   v. 突升；猛漲

Phrases

on a fair basis   在公平的基礎上
be preceded by   在……之前
be intended primarily for   主要是為了……
under the name of   名叫……；以……名字出現
in venture with   和……合夥投資
be analogous to   與……相似
be obscured by   被……掩蓋
speculate about   推斷；猜測
on a large scale   大規模地
be diluted into   被細分成……
be bundled into   捆綁成……
spin off from   從……分拆出來
take the helm   掌管；把舵
take on（foreign competitors）   與（外國競爭者）較量
be on track to   走在……的軌道上；將……
shore up   支撐住
in a combination of   結合在一起
soak up   吸收；大量而迅速地吸取

Notes

IEC：the International Electrotechnical Commission，國際電工委員會，成立於 1906 年，是世界上成立最早的國際性電工標準化機構，負責有關電氣工程和電子工程領域中的國際標準化工作。國際電工委員會的總部最初位於倫敦，1948 年搬到了位於日內瓦的現總部處。1947 年作為一個電工部門並入國際標準化組織（ISO），1976 年又從 ISO 中分立出來。宗旨是促進電工、電子和相關技術領域有關電工標準化等所有問題上（如標準的合格評定）的國際合作。該委員會的目標是：有效滿足全球市場的需求；保證在全球範圍內優先並最大程度地使用其標準和合格評定計劃；評定並提高其標準所涉及的產品質量和服務質量；為共同使用複雜系統創造條件；提高工業化進程的有效性；提高人類健康和安全；保護環境。

UPnP：Universal Plug and Play，計算機外設的即插即用，UPnP 協議即通用即插即用，英文是 Universal Plug and Play，縮寫為 UPnP。UPnP 規範基於 TCP/IP 協議和針對

設備彼此間通訊而制訂的新的 Internet 協議。UPnP 是各種各樣的智能設備、無線設備和個人電腦等實現遍布全球的對等網絡連接（P2P）的結構。UPnP 是一種分佈式的、開放的網絡架構，是獨立的媒介。在任何操作系統中，利用任何編程語言都可以使用 UPnP 設備。

Nazi Party：民族社會主義德國工人黨，簡稱「納粹黨」（Nazi，「民族的」和「社會主義的」兩個詞的德文縮寫），是 20 世紀前半葉的一個德國政黨。納粹黨前身為魏瑪共和國時期於 1919 年創立的德國工人黨，於 1920 年 4 月 1 日更名。1921 年 6 月 29 日，阿道夫·希特勒任黨首，開始宣揚納粹主義、反共產主義、反猶主義，在大蕭條時期贏得了很多狂熱分子的支持。1933 年希特勒被任命為德國總理後，通過「國會縱火案」而成為納粹德國唯一執政黨，實行一黨專政。1945 年 5 月，德國在第二次世界大戰中戰敗及由盟國占領後，盟國管制理事會第 2 號法令將納粹黨解散並宣布其為非法組織，其領導者被逮捕並在紐倫堡審判上被宣判犯有危害人類罪。

Fukushima Disaster：福島核電站事故，福島核電站地處日本福島工業區。它是當時世界上最大的在役核電站，由福島第一核電站、福島第二核電站組成，共 10 臺機組（一站 6 臺，二站 4 臺），均為沸水堆。2011 年 3 月 11 日日本東北太平洋地區發生里氏 9.0 級地震，繼發生海嘯，該地震導致福島第一核電站、福島第二核電站受到嚴重的影響。2011 年 3 月 12 日，日本經濟產業省原子能安全和保安院宣布，受地震影響，福島第一核電廠的放射性物質泄漏到外部。2011 年 4 月 12 日，日本原子力安全保安院（Nuclear and Industrial Safety Agency，NISA）將福島核事故等級定為核事故最高分級 7 級（特大事故），與切爾諾貝利核事故同級。福島縣在核事故後以縣內所有兒童約 38 萬人為對象實施了甲狀腺檢查。截至 2018 年 2 月，已診斷 159 人患癌，34 人疑似患癌。其中被診斷為甲狀腺癌並接受手術的 84 名福島縣內患者中，約一成的 8 人癌症復發，再次接受了手術。

VoIP：Voice-over-Internet Protocol，網絡語言電話服務，是傳輸語音的一種方式，它把語音分解成構成數據的字節通過互聯網傳輸到目的地。在目的地，這些被傳輸過來的字節再被還原成語音。你的語音就像網頁及音頻文件等其他互聯網數據一樣在網絡上傳輸。普通電話要求用戶使用一個專用電路，而 VoIP 是利用所有用戶共享的互聯網空間。因此，VoIP 技術的效率要高於普通電話技術。

IPTV：Internet Protocol Television，互聯網協議電視，是一種利用寬帶有線電視網，集互聯網、多媒體、通訊等多種技術於一體，向家庭用戶提供包括數字電視在內的交互式網絡電視。它利用計算機或機頂盒+電視完成接收視頻點播節目、視頻廣播及網上衝浪等功能，採用高效的視頻壓縮技術，使視頻流傳輸帶寬在 800Kb/s 時可以有接近 DVD 的收視效果，可以開展視頻類業務如因特網上視頻直播、遠距離真視頻點播、節目源製作等。

Silicon Valley：即「硅谷」，位於美國加利福尼亞州的舊金山，是美國重要的電子工業基地，也是世界最為知名的電子工業集中地。它是隨著 20 世紀 60 年代中期以來，微電子技術高速發展而逐步形成的，其特點是以附近一些具有雄厚科研力量的美國一流大學斯坦福、伯克利和加州理工等世界知名大學為依託，以高技術的中小公司群為基礎，並擁有思科、英特爾、惠普、朗訊、蘋果等大公司，融科學、技術、生產為一體。

Alan Turing：艾倫·麥席森·圖靈（Alan Mathison Turing，1912 年 6 月 23 日－1954

年6月7日），英國數學家、邏輯學家，被稱為計算機科學之父，人工智能之父。1931年圖靈進入劍橋大學國王學院，畢業後到美國普林斯頓大學攻讀博士學位，第二次世界大戰爆發後回到劍橋，後曾協助軍方破解德國的著名密碼系統 Enigma，幫助盟軍取得了二戰的勝利。圖靈對於人工智能的發展有諸多貢獻，提出了一種用於判定機器是否具有智能的試驗方法，即圖靈試驗，至今，每年都有試驗的比賽。此外，圖靈提出的著名的圖靈機模型為現代計算機的邏輯工作方式奠定了基礎。

World Intellectual Property Organization（WIPO）：世界知識產權組織，是聯合國保護知識產權的一個專門機構。根據《成立世界知識產權組織公約》而設立。該公約於1967年7月14日在斯德哥爾摩簽訂，於1970年4月26日生效。中國於1980年6月3日加入了該組織。該組織總部設在日內瓦。該組織的宗旨是：通過國家之間的合作，並在適當的情況下，與其他國際組織進行合作，以促進全世界範圍內保護知識產權；並保證知識產權組織各聯盟之間的行政合作。

Patent Cooperation Treaty（PCT）：專利合作協定，是專利領域的一項國際合作條約，被認為是該領域進行國際合作最具有意義的進步標誌。但是，它主要涉及專利申請的提交，檢索及審查以及其中包括的技術信息的傳播的合作性和合理性的一個條約。PCT 不具有「國際專利授權」，授予專利的任務和責任仍然只能由尋求專利保護的各個國家的專利局或行使其職權的機構掌握。PCT 並非與《巴黎公約》競爭，事實上是其補充。的確，它是在《巴黎公約》下只對《巴黎公約》成員國開放的一個特殊協議。

Questions

1. How many standards have been set and what do the standards cover? Why is it necessary to set standards for products and services?

2. With the smartphone industry booming, how did Microsoft struggle to keep up with its rivals Apple and Google?

3. In which ways did Lenovo benefit in regards to the purchase of IBM's personal computer division?

4. Searches made by search engines leave traces and this raises concerns about privacy. What's your understanding of the fact?

5. What is Dididache? And why is it that Dididache is a dominant player in China's taxi-hailing arena?

6. Give examples to show that world leaders and diplomats have been increasingly utilizing Twitter diplomacy, the use of Twitter to engage with foreign public and their own citizens.

Chapter IX

Social Responsibility and Corporate Practice

Social responsibility is the idea that businesses should balance profit-making activities with activities that benefit society. It involves developing businesses with a positive relationship to the society in which they operate. The International Organization for Standardization (ISO) emphasizes that a business's relationship to its society and environment is a critical factor in operating efficiently and effectively.

Social responsibility means that individuals and companies have a duty to act in the best interests of their environments and society as a whole. Social responsibility, as it applies to business, is known as corporate social responsibility (CSR). Many companies, such as those with 「green」 policies, have made social responsibility an integral part of their business models.

Additionally, some investors use a company's social responsibility, or lack thereof, as investment criteria. As such, a dedication to social responsibility can actually turn into profits, as the idea inspires investors to invest, and consumers to purchase goods and services from the company. Put simply, social responsibility helps companies develop good reputations.

Social responsibility takes on different meanings within industries and companies. For example, Starbucks Corp. and Ben & Jerry's Homemade Holdings Inc. have blended social responsibility into the core of their operations. Both companies purchase Fair Trade Certified ingredients to manufacture their products and actively support sustainable farming in the regions where they source ingredients. Big-box retailer Target Corp., also well known for its social responsibility programs, has donated money to communities in which the stores operate, including education grants.

In general, social responsibility is more effective when a company takes it on voluntarily, as opposed to being required by the government to do so through regulations. Social responsibility can boost company morale, and this is especially true when a company can engage employees with its social cause.

Part I   Corporations and Incorporations

Corporations

A corporation is a company, a firm or a group of people authorized to act as a single entity (legally a person) and recognized as such in law. Corporations come in many flavors but are usually divided by the law of the jurisdiction where they are chartered into two kinds: by whether or not they can issue stock, or by whether or not they are for profit.

Where local law distinguishes corporations by ability to issue stock, corporations allowed to do so are referred to as 「stock corporations」, ownership of the corporation is through stock, and owners of stock are referred to as 「stockholders.」 Corporations not allowed to issue stock are referred to as 「non-stock」 corporations, those who are considered the owners of the corporation are those who have obtained membership in the corporation, and are referred to as a 「member」 of the corporation.

Corporations chartered in regions where they are distinguished by whether they are allowed to be for profit or not are referred to as 「for profit」 and 「not-for-profit」 corporations, respectively.

There is some overlap between stock/non-stock and for profit/not-for-profit in that not-for-profit corporations are always non-stock as well. A for profit corporation is almost always a stock corporation, but some for profit corporations may choose to be non-stock.

Most jurisdictions now allow the creation of new corporations through registration. Registered corporations have legal personality and are owned by shareholders, whose liability is limited to their investment. Shareholders do not typically actively manage a corporation; shareholders instead elect or appoint a board of directors to control the corporation.

In American English the word *corporation* is most often used to describe large business corporations. In British English and in the Commonwealth countries, the term *company* is more widely used to describe the same sort of entity while the word *corporation* encompasses all incorporated entities.

Despite not being human beings, corporations, as far as the law is concerned, are legal persons, and have many of the same rights and responsibilities as natural persons do. Corporations can exercise human rights against real individuals and the state, and they can themselves be responsible for human rights violations. Corporations can be 「dissolved」 either by statutory operation, order of court, or voluntary action on the part of shareholders. Insolvency may result in a form of corporate failure, when creditors force the liquidation and dissolution of the corporation under court order, but it most often results in a restructuring of corporate holdings. Corporations can even be convicted of criminal offenses, such as fraud and manslaughter. However corporations are not considered living entities in the way that humans are.

Chartered corporations

Early incorporated entities were established by charter (i.e. by an act granted by a monarch or passed by a parliament or legislature). A chartered company is an association formed by investors or shareholders for the purpose of trade, exploration, and colonization.

Many European nations chartered corporations to lead colonial ventures, such as the Dutch East India Company or the Hudson's Bay Company. These chartered companies became the progenitors of the modern corporation.

In England, the government created corporations under a Royal Charter or an Act of Parliament with the grant of a monopoly over a specified territory. The best known example was the East India Company of London.

The East India Company (EIC), was an English joint-stock company. Originally, chartered as the 「Governor and Company of Merchants of London trading into the East Indies」, the company rose to account for half of the world's trade, particularly trade in basic commodities that included cotton, silk, indigo dye, salt, saltpetre, tea and opium. The company also ruled the beginnings of the British Empire in India.

The company received a Royal Charter from Queen Elizabeth I on 31 December 1600, making it the oldest among several similarly formed European East India Companies. Wealthy merchants and aristocrats owned the Company's shares. The government owned no shares and had only indirect control.

Queen Elizabeth I granted The East India Company the exclusive right to trade with all countries to the east of the Cape of Good Hope, but which ended up trading mainly with the Indian subcontinent and Qing China. Some corporations at this time would act on the government's behalf, bringing in revenue from its exploits abroad. Subsequently the Company became increasingly integrated with English and later British military and colonial policy, just as most corporations were essentially dependent on the Royal Navy's ability to control trade routes.

Labeled by both contemporaries and historians as 「the grandest society of merchants in the universe」, the English East India Company would come to symbolize the dazzlingly rich potential of the corporation, as well as new methods of business that could be both brutal and exploitative. By 1611, shareholders in the East India Company were earning a return on their investment of almost 150 per cent. Subsequent stock offerings demonstrated just how lucrative the Company had become.

Acting under a charter sanctioned by the Dutch government, the Dutch East India Company defeated Portuguese forces and established itself in the Moluccan Islands in order to profit from the European demand for spices. Investors in the chartered company were issued paper certificates as proof of share ownership, and were able to trade their shares on the original Amsterdam stock exchange. Shareholders are also explicitly granted limited liability in the company's royal charter.

The Dutch East India Company is often considered to have been the first multinational corporation in the world and it was the first company to issue stock. It was a powerful company, possessing quasi-governmental powers, including the ability to wage war, imprison and execute convicts, negotiate treaties, strike its own coins, and establish colonies.

Having been set up in 1602, to profit from the Malukan spice trade, in 1619 the Dutch India Company established a capital in the port city of Jayakarta and changed the city name into Batavia (now Jakarta). Over the next two centuries the Company acquired additional ports as trading bases and safeguarded their interests by taking over surrounding territory. It remained an important trading concern and paid an 18% annual dividend for almost 200 years.

Weighed down by corruption in the late 18th century, the Company went bankrupt and was formally dissolved in 1800, its possessions and the debt being taken over by the government of the Dutch Batavian Republic. The Company's territories became the Dutch East Indies and were expanded over the course of the 19th century to include the whole of the Indonesian archipelago, and in the 20th century formed the Republic of Indonesia.

Chartered companies in many cases benefited from the trade monopolies, which in many cases included functions-such as security and defence-usually reserved for a sovereign state, some companies achieved relative autonomy, in effect making them a state within a state.

More chartered companies were formed during the late nineteenth century's 「Scramble for Africa」 with the purpose of seizing, colonizing and administering the last 「virgin」 African territories, but these proved generally less profitable than earlier trading companies. In time, most of their colonies were either lost (often to other European powers) or transformed into crown colonies.

Multinational corporations

A multinational corporation or multinational enterprise is an organization that owns or controls production of goods or services in one or more countries other than their home country. It can also be referred as an international corporation, a 「transnational corporation」, or a stateless corporation.

A multinational corporation is usually a large corporation which produces or sells goods or services in various countries. It may be described as a multinational corporation when it is registered in more than one country or has operations in more than one country.

Multinational corporations take many different forms and engage in many different activities:
- Importing and exporting goods and services
- Making significant investments in a foreign country
- Buying and selling licenses in foreign markets
- Engaging in contract manufacturing—permitting a local manufacturer in a foreign country to produce their products
- Opening manufacturing facilities or assembly operations in foreign countries

One of the first multinational business organizations, the East India Company, arose in 1600. After East India Company, came the Dutch East India Company, founded March 20, 1602, which would become the largest company in the world for nearly 200 years.

The history of multinational corporations is closely intertwined with the history of colonialism. Examples of such corporations include the British East India Company, the Swedish Africa Company, and the Hudson's Bay Company. These early corporations facilitated colonialism by engaging in international trade and exploration, and creating colonial trading posts. Many of these corporations, such as the South Australia Company and the Virginia Company, played a direct role in formal colonization by creating and maintaining settler colonies. Without exception these early corporations created differential economic outcomes between their home country and their colonies via a process of exploiting colonial resources and labour, and investing the resultant profits and net gain in the home country. The end result of this process was the enrichment of the colonizer and the impoverishment of the colonized. Some multinational corporations, such as the Royal African Company, were also responsible for the logistical component of the Atlantic Slave Trade, maintaining the ships and ports required for this vast enterprise. During the 19th century formal corporate rule over colonial holdings largely gave way to state-controlled colonies, however corporate control over colonial economic affairs persisted in a majority of colonies.

During the process of decolonization the European colonial charter companies were disbanded. However the economic impact of corporate colonial exploitation has proved to be lasting and far reaching, with some commentators asserting that this impact is among the chief causes of contemporary global income inequality.

In the world economy facilitated by multinational corporations, capital will increasingly be able to play workers, communities, and nations off against one another as they demand tax, regulation and wage concessions while threatening to move. Besides, the aggressive use of tax avoidance schemes allows multinational corporations to gain competitive advantages over small and medium-sized enterprises. Some negative outcomes generated by multinational corporations include increased inequality, unemployment, and wage stagnation.

Incorporations

Incorporation is the forming of a new corporation. Due to the abandonment of mercantilist economic theory in late 18th century and the rise of classical liberalism and laissez-faire economic theory, corporations transitioned from being government or guild affiliated entities to being public and private economic entities free of government direction.

In the U.K., the process of incorporation is generally called company formation. The United Kingdom is one of the quickest locations to incorporate, with a fully electronic process and a very fast turnaround by the national registrar of companies, the Companies House. The current Companies House record is five minutes to vet and issue a certificate of incorporation for an electronic application. There are many different types of UK companies:

- Public limited company (PLC)
- Private company limited by shares (Ltd.)
- Company limited by guarantee
- Unlimited company (Unltd.)
- Limited liability partnership (LLP)
- Community interest company
- Industrial and provident society (IPS)
- Royal charter (RC)

In the United States, The Certificate of Incorporation (Requirements) differs in different states. However, there are some common information that are asked by almost all the states and so, must be included in the Certificate of Incorporation, accordingly. They are as follows:

• **Business purpose** —It would describe the incorporated tasks a company has to do or provide. At present, only two types of business purpose clauses are used. They are:

1. General — General purpose clauses are accepted by some and not all states. It indicates that the budding company has been formed to carry out 「all lawful business」 in the region.

2. Specific — Alternatively, some states have made it mandatory for the business owners to furnish a more detailed explanation of the products and/or services to be offered by their companies.

• **Corporate name** —A chosen name must be added to the Certificate of Incorporation. This should be followed with the corporate identifier like 「Corporation」, 「Incorporated」, 「Company」, or one of the abbreviations like 「Inc」. In case of online incorporation, the state will have final say with regards to the name chosen for the company and that the name shouldn't deceive or mislead the consumers.

• **Registered agent** —Almost all the states require every corporation to have a registered agent of their own in the state of incorporation. Registered agents will receive all the important legal as well as tax documents on behalf of the corporation. A typical registered agent will need a physical address (P. O box nos.) in the state of incorporation and should be accessible during normal business hours.

• **Incorporator** —An incorporator is the person who prepares and files the Certificate of Incorporation with the concerned state.

• **Share par value** — It refers to the stated minimum value, and generally doesn't correspond to the actual value. Usually, $ 0.01, $ 1.00 or no par are some of the common par values. In reality, the value of a share is based on its fair market value, or whatever amount a buyer is willing to pay for the same.

• **Number of authorized shares of stock** —An incorporation needs to stipulate the exact number of shares they as a company are willing to authorize. Moreover, it is mandatory for every corporation, be it small or large, to have stock. A stock represents ownership in the corporation.

• **Protection of personal assets** . One of the most important legal benefits is the safeguarding of personal assets against the claims of creditors and lawsuits. Sole proprietors and general partners in a partnership are personally and jointly responsible for all the liabilities of a business such as loans, accounts payable, and legal judgments. In a corporation, however, stockholders, directors and officers typically are not liable for the company's debts and obligations. They are limited in liability to the amount they have invested in the corporation. For example, if a shareholder purchased $ 100 in stock, no more than $ 100 can be lost. Corporations and limited liability companies (LLCs) may hold assets such as real estate, cars or boats. If a shareholder of a corporation is personally involved in a lawsuit or bankruptcy, these assets may be protected. A creditor of a shareholder of a corporation or LLC cannot seize the assets of the company. However, the creditor can seize ownership shares in the corporation, as they are considered a personal asset.

- **Transferable ownership**. Ownership in a corporation or LLC is easily transferable to others, either in whole or in part. Some state laws are particularly corporate-friendly. For example, the transfer of ownership in a corporation incorporated in Delaware is not required to be filed or recorded.
- **Taxation**. In the United States, corporations are taxed at a lower rate than individuals are. Also, they can own shares in other corporations and receive corporate dividends 80% tax-free. There are no limits on the amount of losses a corporation may carry forward to subsequent tax years. A sole proprietorship, on the other hand, cannot claim a capital loss greater than $3,000 unless the owner has offsetting capital gains.
- **Raising funds through sale of stock**. A corporation can easily raise capital from investors through the sale of stock.
- **Durability**. A corporation is capable of continuing indefinitely. Its existence is not affected by the death of shareholders, directors, or officers of the corporation.
- **Credit rating**. Regardless of an owner's personal credit scores, a corporation can acquire its own credit rating, and build a separate credit history by applying for and using corporate credit.

Part II Entrepreneurship and Intrapreneurship

A business opportunity consists of four integrated elements all of which are to be present within the same timeframe and most often within the same domain or geographical location, before it can be claimed as a business opportunity. These four elements are:
- A need
- The means to fulfill the need
- A method to apply the means to fulfill the need and;
- A method to benefit

With any one of the elements missing, a business opportunity may be developed, by finding the missing element. The more unique the combination of the elements, the more unique the business opportunity. The more control an institution (or individual) has over the elements, the better they are positioned to exploit the opportunity and become a niche market leader.

While entrepreneurship is the process of starting a business, a startup company or other organization, intrapreneurship is the act of behaving like an entrepreneur while working within a large organization. The entrepreneur develops a business plan, acquires the human and other required resources, and is fully responsible for its success or failure. Intrapreneurship is known as the practice of a corporate management style that integrates risk-taking and innovation approaches, as well as the reward and motivational techniques.

Intrapreneurship refers to employee initiatives in organizations to undertake something new, without being asked to do so. Hence, the *intrapreneur* focuses on innovation and creativity, and transforms an idea into a profitable venture, while operating within the organizational environment. Thus, intrapreneurs are *Inside entrepreneurs* who follow the goal of the organization. Intrapreneurship is an example of motivation through job design, either formally or informally. Employees, such as marketing executives or perhaps those engaged in a special project within a larger firm, are encouraged to behave as entrepreneurs, even though they have the resources, capabilities and security of the larger firm to draw upon.

Another characteristic of intrapreneurs is their courage and flexibility to think outside of the box, which allows them to work on ideas that may change strategic direction. Even though many managers are afraid of radical changes, they are often the only way to help companies grow.

Intrapreneurs are able to search for opportunities and shape them into high-potential innovations through teamwork and with access to corporate resources. This assumes the right conditions of good leadership, communication and the appropriate environment to support creativity, these are essential for entrepreneurial outcomes to take place.

One of the most well-known examples of intrapreneurship is the「Skunk Works」group at Lockheed Martin. The group was originally named after a reference in a cartoon, and was first brought together in 1943 to build the P-80 fighter jet. Because the project was to eventually become a part of the war effort, the project was internally protected and secretive. Kelly Johnson, later famous for Kelly's 14 rules of intrapreneurship, was the director of this group.

Another example could be 3M, who encourage many projects within the company. They give certain freedom to employees to create their own projects, and they even give them funds to use for these projects. (In the days of its founders, HP *used to* have similar policies and just such an innovation-friendly atmosphere and intrapreneurial reputation) Besides 3M, Intel also has a tradition of implementing intrapreneurship. Google is also known to be intrapreneur friendly, allowing their employees to spend up to 20% of their time to pursue projects of their choice.

Other companies such as Xerox, Virgin, Siemens and Microsoft are also looking for unique solutions to promote CE (corporate entrepreneurship) in their own businesses, e.g. by developing separate research and development departments. Siemens-Nixdorf took a different approach, designing a 2-year corporate program to turn 300 managers into intrapreneurs, skilled in spotting new business opportunities with notable potential.

Part Ⅲ   Business Ethics and Corporate Social Responsibility

Business Ethics

Business ethics (also corporate ethics) is a form of professional ethics that examines ethical principles and moral or ethical problems that arise in a business environment. It applies to all aspects of business conduct and is relevant to the conduct of individuals and entire organizations.

The range and quantity of business ethical issues reflects the interaction of profit-maximizing behavior with non-economic concerns. Interest in business ethics accelerated dramatically during the 1980s and 1990s, both within major corporations and within academia. For example, most major corporations today promote their commitment to non-economic values under headings such as ethics codes and social responsibility charters. Governments use laws and regulations to point business behavior in what they perceive to be beneficial directions. Ethics implicitly regulates areas and details of behavior that lie beyond governmental control.

Corporate Social Responsibility (CSR)

Corporate social responsibility (corporate conscience, corporate citizenship) is a form of corporate self-regulation integrated into a business model. CSR policy functions as a self-regulatory mechanism whereby a business monitors and ensures its active compliance with the spirit of the law, ethical standards and international norms. With some models, a firm's implementation of CSR goes beyond compliance and engages in 「actions that appear to further some social good, beyond the interests of the firm and that which is required by law.」 CSR aims to embrace responsibility for corporate actions and to encourage a positive impact on the environment and stakeholders including consumers, employees, investors, communities, and others.

Business dictionary defines CSR as 「A company's sense of responsibility towards the community and environment (both ecological and social) in which it operates. Companies express this citizenship (1) through their waste and pollution reduction processes, (2) by contributing educational and social programs and (3) by earning adequate returns on the employed resources.」 A broader definition expands from a focus on stakeholders to include philanthropy and volunteering.

The term 「corporate social responsibility」 became popular in the 1960s and has remained a term used indiscriminately by many to cover legal and moral responsibility more narrowly construed.

CSR is titled to aid an organization's mission as well as a guide to what the company stands for to its consumers. ISO 26000 is the recognized international standard for CSR. Public sector organizations (the United Nations for example) adhere to 「the Triple Bottom Line」 (TBL): 「People, planet and profit」. 「People」 refers to fair labour practices, the community and region where the business operates. 「Planet」 refers to sustainable environmental practices. Profit is the economic value created by the organization after deducting the cost of all inputs, including the cost of the capital. TBL is widely accepted that CSR adheres to similar principles, but with no formal act of legislation.

Most consumers agree that while achieving business targets, companies should do CSR at the same time. Most consumers believe companies doing charity will receive a positive response. Consumers are usually loyal and willing to spend more on retailers that support charity. They also believe that retailers selling local products will gain loyalty.

CSR may be based within the human resources, business development or public relations departments of an organization, or may be a separate unit reporting to the CEO or the board of directors. Common CSR actions include:

· Environmental sustainability: recycling, waste management, water management, renewable energy, reusable materials, 「greener」 supply chains, reducing paper use and adopting Leadership in Energy and Environmental Design (LEED) building standards.

· Community involvement: This can include raising money for local charities, providing volunteers, sponsoring local events, employing local workers, supporting local economic growth, engaging in fair trade practices, etc.

· Ethical marketing: Companies that ethically market to consumers are placing a higher value on their customers and respecting them as people who are ends in themselves. They do not try to manipulate or falsely advertise to potential consumers. This is important for companies that want to be viewed as ethical.

A CSR program can be an aid to recruitment and retention, particularly within the competitive graduate student market. Potential recruits often consider a firm's CSR policy. CSR can also help improve the perception of a company among its staff, particularly when staff can become involved through payroll giving, fundraising activities or community volunteering. CSR has been credited with encouraging customer orientation among customer-facing employees.

Managing risk is an important executive responsibility. Reputations that take decades to build up can be ruined in hours through corruption scandals or environmental accidents. These draw unwanted attention from regulators, courts, governments and media. CSR can limit these risks.

CSR can help build customer loyalty based on distinctive ethical values. Some companies use their commitment to CSR as their primary positioning tool, e.g. the Co-operative Group, The Body Shop and American Appare.

Some companies use CSR methodologies as a strategic tactic to gain public support for their presence in global markets, helping them sustain a competitive advantage by using their social contributions as another form of advertising.

Corporations are keen to avoid interference in their business through taxation and/or regulations. A CSR program can persuade governments and the public that a company takes health and safety, diversity and the environment seriously, reducing the likelihood that company practices will be closely monitored.

Appropriate CSR programs can increase the attractiveness of supplier firms to potential customer corporations. e.g., a fashion merchandiser may find value in an overseas manufacturer that uses CSR to establish a positive image—and to reduce the risks of bad publicity from uncovered misbehavior.

Walmart Foundation and TESCO's Commitment

Wal-Mart Stores, Inc. is an American multinational retail corporation that operates a chain of discount department stores and warehouse stores. The company was founded by Sam Walton in 1962 and incorporated on October 31, 1969. It has over 11,000 stores in 28 countries, under a total 65 banners. The company operates under the Walmart name in the United States and Canada. It operates as Walmart de México y Centroamérica in Mexico, as Asda in the United Kingdom, as Seiyu in Japan, and as Best Price in India. It also owns and operates the Sam's Club retail warehouses.

Walmart is the world's largest company by revenue, according to the Fortune Global 500 list in 2014, as well as the biggest private employer in the world with 2.2 million employees. Walmart is a family-owned business, as the company is controlled by the Walton family. Sam Walton's heirs own over 50 percent of Walmart through their holding company, It is also one of the world's most valuable companies by market value.

Walmart Foundation dramatically increased charitable giving. For example, in 2005, Walmart donated $20 million in cash and merchandise for Hurricane Katrina relief. Today, Walmart's charitable donations approach $1 billion each year. Sam Walton believed that the company's contribution to society was the fact that it operated efficiently, thereby lowering the cost of living for customers, and therefore in that sense was a 「powerful force for good」, despite his refusal to contribute cash to philanthropic causes. He explained that while he believed his family had been fortunate and wished to use his wealth to aid worthy causes like education, they could not be expected to 「solve every personal problem that comes to [their] attention」.

Tesco PLC is a British multinational grocery and general merchandise retailer. It is the third largest retailer in the world measured by profits and second-largest retailer in the world measured by revenues. It has stores in 12 countries across Asia and Europe and is the grocery market leader in the UK, Ireland, Hungary, Malaysia, and Thailand.

Tesco was founded in 1919 by Jack Cohen as a group of market stalls. Originally a UK-focused grocery retailer, since the early 1990s Tesco has increasingly diversified geographically and into areas such as the retailing of books, clothing, electronics, furniture, toys, petrol and software; financial services; telecoms and internet services.

Tesco has made a commitment to corporate social responsibility in the form of contributions of 1.87% in 2006 of its pre-tax profits to charities/local community organizations. This compares favourably with Marks & Spencer's 1.51% but not well with Sainsbury's 7.02%.

In 1992, Tesco started a 「computers for schools scheme」, offering computers in return for schools and hospitals getting vouchers from people who shopped at Tesco. The scheme has been also implemented in Poland.

Starting during the 2005–2006 football season, the company now sponsors the Tesco Cup, a football competition for young players throughout the UK.

In 2009 Tesco used the phrase, 「Change for Good」 as advertising, which is trade marked by Unicef for charity usage but not for commercial or retail use, which prompted the agency to say, 「It is the first time in Unicef's history that a commercial entity has set out to capitalize on one of our campaigns which several of our programmes for children are dependent on.」 They went on to call on the public 「... who have children's welfare at heart, to consider carefully who they support when making consumer choices.」

Tesco's own labels for personal care and household products are cruelty-free—this means they are not tested on animals.

Apple's Dedication and Huawei's Social Responsibility

Apple is the world's second-largest information technology company by revenue after Samsung Electronics. On November 25, 2014, in addition to being the largest publicly traded corporation in the world by market capitalization, Apple became the first U.S. company to be valued at over $ 700 billion. As of March 2015, Apple employs 98, 000 permanent full-time employees, maintains 453 retail stores in sixteen countries.

Apple enjoys a high level of brand loyalty and, according to the 2014 edition of the Interbrand Best Global Brands report, is the world's most valuable brand with a valuation of $ 118. 9 billion.

Following a Greenpeace protest, Apple released a statement on April 17, 2012 committing to ending its use of coal and shifting to 100% clean energy. By 2013 Apple was using 100% renewable energy to power their data centers. Overall, 75% of the company's power came from renewable sources.

In 2010, Climate Counts, a nonprofit organization dedicated to directing consumers toward the greenest companies, gave Apple a score of 52 points out of a possible 100, which puts Apple in their top category. This was an increase from May 2008, when Climate Counts only gave Apple 11 points out of 100, which placed the company last among electronics companies.

As of 2014, Apple is listed as a partner of the Product RED campaign. The campaign's mission is to prevent the transmission of HIV from mother to child by 2015. In November 2012, Apple donated $ 2. 5 million to the American Red Cross to aid relief efforts after Hurricane Sandy.

Huawei Technologies Co. Ltd. is a Chinese multinational networking and telecommunications equipment and services company headquartered in Shenzhen, Guangdong. It is the largest telecommunications equipment maker in the world, having overtaken Ericsson in 2012. Its products and services have been deployed in more than 140 countries and it currently serves 45 of the world's 50 largest telecoms operators.

As part of its international support for technology and telecommunications education and training, Huawei has contributed funding and equipment to a number of universities and training centers in countries such as Kenya, India, Indonesia, Bangladesh, and Nigeria. In the U.S., since 2008, Huawei has sponsored MIT's Communications Futures Program, a research collaboration that studies the future of the telecommunications industry.

In 2010, Huawei joined the Broadband Commission for Digital Development, formed by the ITU and UNESCO to support broadband deployment to developing nations. In the same year, Huawei joined the Green Touch consortium, an industry group that aims to make communications networks 1000 times more energy efficient than they are today.

In June 2011, Huawei signed a five-year agreement to contribute donated services, equipment and technical expertise worth over US $ 1.4 million to Carleton University, in Ottawa, Canada, to establish a research lab dedicated to cloud computing technology and services. The same month, Huawei published its 2010 Corporate Social Responsibility (CSR) Report.

Samsung's Environmental Records and ebay's Solarcity

Samsung Electronics Co., Ltd. is a South Korean multinational electronics company. It is the flagship subsidiary of the Samsung Group, accounting for 70% of the group's revenue in 2012, and has been the world's largest information technology company by revenue since 2009. Samsung Electronics has assembly plants and sales networks in 80 countries and employs around 370,000 people.

Samsung has long been a major manufacturer of electronic components such as lithium-ion batteries, semi-conductors, chips, flash memory and hard drive devices for clients such as Apple, Sony, HTC and Nokia.

In recent years, the company has diversified into consumer electronics. It is the world's largest manufacturer of mobile phones and smartphones fueled by the popularity of its Samsung Galaxy line of devices. The company is also a major vendor of tablet computers, particularly its Android-powered Samsung Galaxy Tab collection, and is generally regarded as pioneering the phablet market through the Samsung Galaxy Note family of devices.

Samsung has been the world's largest manufacturer of LCD panels since 2002, the world's largest television manufacturer since 2006, and world's largest manufacturer of mobile phones since 2011. Samsung Electronics displaced Apple Inc. as the world's largest technology company in 2011 and is a major part of the South Korean economy.

The company is listed in Greenpeace's Guide to Greener Electronics, which rates electronics companies on policies and practices to reduce their impact on the climate, produce greener products, and make their operations more sustainable. In November 2011 Samsung was ranked 7th out of 15 leading electronics makers with a score of 4.1/10. In the newly re-launched guide Samsung moved down two places (occupying 5th position in October 2010) but scored maximum points for providing verified data and its greenhouse gas emissions and also scored well for its Sustainable Operations with the guide praising its relatively good e-waste take-back programme and information.

In June 2004, Samsung was the first major electronics company to publicly commit to eliminate PVC and BFRs from new models of all its products.

The company has been taking the lead in industry efforts to reduce greenhouse gas emissions, the company has been awarded as one of global top-ten companies in the Carbon Disclosure Leadership Index (CDLI). It was the only Asian company among top ten companies. In addition, the company is listed in Dow Jones Sustainability Index (DJSI).

The company's achievement ratio of products approaching the Global Ecolabel level (「Good Eco-Products」 within the company) is 11 percentage points above the 2010 goal (80 percent). As of the first half of 2010, Samsung earned the Global Ecolabel for its 2,134 models, thereby becoming the world's number-one company in terms of the number of products meeting Global Ecolabel standards.

The company is also accelerating its effort to recover and recycle electronic wastes. The amount of wastes salvaged throughout 60 countries during 2009 was as much as 240,000 tons. The 「Samsung Recycling Direct」 program, the company's voluntary recycling program under way in the United States, was expanded to Canada.

In 2008, the company was praised for its recycling effort by the U.S. advocacy group Electronics Take Back Coalition as the 「best eco-friendly recycling program」.

eBay was founded by Pierre Omidyar in 1995, and became a notable success story of the dot-com bubble. Today, it is a multi-billion dollar business with operations localized in over thirty countries.

On May 8, 2008, eBay announced the opening of its newest building on the company's North Campus in San Jose, which is the first structure in the city to be built from the ground up to LEED Gold standards. The building, the first the company had built in its 13-year existence, uses an array of 3,248 solar panels, spanning 60,000 square feet (5,600 m^2), and providing 650 kilowatts of power to eBay's campus. The array can supply 15% – 18% of the company's total energy requirements, reducing the amount of greenhouse gases that would be produced to create that energy by other means. SolarCity, the company responsible for designing the array, estimates that the solar panels installed on eBay's campus will prevent 37 million pounds of carbon dioxide from being released into the environment as a result of replaced power production over the next three decades. Creating an equivalent impact to remove the same amount of carbon dioxide from the atmosphere would require planting 322 acres (1.30 km^2) of trees. The design of the building also incorporates other elements to reduce its impact on the environment. The building is equipped with a lighting system that detects natural ambient light sources and automatically dims artificial lighting to save 39% of the power usually required to light an office building. eBay's newest building also reduces demand on local water supplies by incorporating an eco-friendly irrigation system, and low-flow shower heads and faucets. Even during construction, more than 75% of the waste from construction was recycled.

eBay also runs buses between San Francisco and the San Jose campus to reduce the number of commuting vehicles. In 2014, eBay and several other Oregon businesses signed the Oregon Business Climate Declaration to promote local job growth and slow carbon pollution.

Part Ⅳ   Illegal Economy and Mal-practice of Incorporations

Illegal economies, or underground economies are omnipresent, existing in market oriented as well as in centrally planned nations, be they developed or developing. Those engaged in underground activities circumvent, escape or are excluded from the institutional system of rules, rights, regulations and enforcement penalties that govern formal agents engaged in production and exchange. Different types of underground activities are distinguished according to the particular institutional rules that they violate. Four specific underground economies can be identified:

(1) the illegal economy.

(2) the unreported economy.

(3) the unrecorded economy.

(4) the informal economy.

The 「illegal economy」 consists of the income produced by those economic activities pursued in violation of legal statutes defining the scope of legitimate forms of commerce. Illegal economy participants engage in the production and distribution of prohibited goods and services, such as drug trafficking, arms trafficking.

The 「unreported economy」 consists of those economic activities that circumvent or evade the institutionally established fiscal rules as codified in the tax code. A summary measure of the unreported economy is the amount of income that should be reported to the tax authority but is not so reported. A complementary measure of the unreported economy is the 「tax gap」, namely the difference between the amount of tax revenues due the fiscal authority and the amount of tax revenue actually collected.

The 「unrecorded economy」 consists of those economic activities that circumvent the institutional rules that define the reporting requirements of government statistical agencies. A summary measure of the unrecorded economy is the amount of unrecorded income, namely the amount of income that should (under existing rules and conventions) be recorded in national accounting systems (e.g. National Income and Product Accounts) but is not. Unrecorded income is a particular problem in transition countries that switched from a socialist accounting system to UN standard national accounting. New methods have been proposed for estimating the size of the unrecorded (non-observed) economy. But there is still little consensus concerning the size of the unreported economies of transition countries.

The 「informal economy」 comprises those economic activities that circumvent the costs and are excluded from the benefits and rights incorporated in the laws and administrative rules covering property relationships, commercial licensing, labor contracts, torts, financial credit and social security systems. A summary measure of the informal economy is the income generated by economic agents that operate informally. The informal sector is defined as the part of an economy that is not taxed, monitored by any form of government, or included in any gross national product (GNP), unlike the formal economy. In developed countries the informal sector is characterized by unreported employment. This is hidden from the state for tax, social security or labour law purposes but is legal in all other aspects.

A black market is a market in which goods or services are traded illegally. The key distinction of a black market trade is that the transaction itself is illegal. The goods or services may or may not themselves be illegal to own, or to trade through other legal channels. Because the transactions are illegal, the market itself is forced to operate outside the formal economy that is supported by the established state power. Common motives for operating in black markets are to trade contraband, avoid taxes, or skirt price controls (Table 1).

Table 1　Size of the global black markets

Largest black markets	Estimated annual market value (Billion USD)
Total	1,144
Counterfeit pharmaceutical drugs	200
Prostitution	187
Counterfeit electronics	169
Marijuana	142
Cocaine	85
Prescription drugs	73
Opium and heroin	68
Software piracy	59
Movie piracy	58
Gas and oil smuggling	53
Cigarette smuggling	50

A grey market is the trade of a commodity through distribution channels which are legal but are unofficial, unauthorized, or unintended by the original manufacturer. The most common type of grey market is the sale, by individuals or small companies not authorized by the manufacturer, of imported goods which would otherwise be either more expensive in the country to which they are being imported, or unavailable altogether. An example of this would be the import and subsequent re-sale of Apple products by unlicensed intermediaries in countries such as South Korea where Apple does not currently operate retail outlets and licensed reseller markups are high.

Grey market goods refer to legal, non-counterfeit goods sold outside normal distribution channels by entities which may have no relationship with the producer of the goods. This commonly takes place with electronic equipment such as cameras. Entrepreneurs buy the product where it is available cheaply, often at retail but sometimes at wholesale, and import it legally to the target market. They then sell it at a price high enough to provide a profit but under the normal market price. Because of the nature of grey markets, it is difficult or impossible to track the precise numbers of grey market sales. Grey market goods are often new, but some grey market goods are used goods. A market in used goods is sometimes nicknamed a green market

Smuggling is the illegal transportation of objects or people, such as out of a house or buildings, into a prison, or across an international border, in violation of applicable laws or other regulations.

There are various motivations to smuggle. These include the participation in illegal trade, such as in the drug trade, in illegal immigration or illegal emigration, tax evasion, providing contraband to a prison inmate, or the theft of the items being smuggled. Examples of non-financial motivations include bringing banned items past a security checkpoint (such as airline security) or the removal of classified documents from a government or corporate office.

Money laundering is the process of transforming the proceeds of crime into ostensibly legitimate money or other assets.

Money obtained from certain crimes, such as extortion, insider trading, drug trafficking and illegal gambling is 「dirty」. It needs to be cleaned to appear to have been derived from legal activities. So, placing 「dirty or filthy」 money in a service company, such as banks or other financial institutions, where it is layered with legitimate income and then integrated into the flow of money, is a common form of money laundering.

Money laundering is commonly defined as happening in three steps: the first step involves introducing cash into the financial system by some means (「placement」); the second involves carrying out complex financial transactions to camouflage the illegal source (「layering」); and the final step entails acquiring wealth generated from the transactions of the illicit funds (「integration」). Some of these steps may be omitted, depending on the circumstances. For example, non-cash proceeds that are already in the financial system would have no need for placement.

The term money laundering has become conflated with other forms of financial crime, and sometimes used more generally to include misuse of the financial system (involving things such as securities, digital currencies, credit cards, and traditional currency), including terrorism financing and evasion of international sanctions. Most anti-money laundering laws openly conflate money laundering with terrorism financing when regulating the financial system.

Formed in 1989 by the G7 countries, the FATF (Financial Action Task Force) is an intergovernmental body whose purpose is to develop and promote an international response to combat money laundering. The FATF Secretariat is housed at the headquarters of the OECD in Paris. In October 2001, FATF expanded its mission to include combating the financing of terrorism. FATF is a policy-making body that brings together legal, financial, and law enforcement experts to achieve national legislation and regulatory AML (Anti-Money Laundering) reforms. As of 2014 its membership consists of 36 countries and territories and two regional organizations. FATF works in collaboration with a number of international bodies and organization. These entities have observer status with FATF, which does not entitle them to vote, but permits them full participation in plenary sessions and working groups.

Securities fraud, also known as stock fraud and investment fraud, is a deceptive practice in the stock or commodities markets that induces investors to make purchase or sale decisions on the basis of false information, frequently resulting in losses, in violation of securities laws offers of risky investment opportunities to unsophisticated investors who are unable to evaluate risk adequately.

Securities fraud can also include outright theft from investors (embezzlement by stockbrokers), stock manipulation, misstatements on a public company's financial reports, and lying to corporate auditors. The term encompasses a wide range of other actions, including corporate misconduct, dummy corporations, internet fraud, insider trading, accountant fraud and other illegal acts on the trading floor of a stock or commodity exchange.

Fraud by high level corporate officials became a subject of wide national attention during the early 2000s, as exemplified by corporate officer misconduct at Madoff Investment Securities LLC.

The Madoff investment scandal broke in December 2008, when former NASDAQ Chairman Bernard Madoff admitted that the wealth management arm of his business was an elaborate Ponzi scheme. Madoff's business, in the process of liquidation, was one of the top market makers on Wall Street and in 2008, the sixth-largest. Madoff's personal and business asset freeze created a chain reaction throughout the world's business and philanthropic community, forcing many organizations to at least temporarily close, including the Robert I. Lappin Charitable Foundation, the Picower Foundation, and the JEHT Foundation.

It became a problem of such scope that the Bush Administration announced what it described as an 「aggressive agenda」against corporate fraud.

Dummy corporations may be created by fraudsters to create the illusion of being an existing corporation with a similar name. Fraudsters then sell securities in the dummy corporation by misleading the investor into thinking that they are buying shares in the real corporation.

According to enforcement officials of the Securities and Exchange Commission, criminals engage in pump-and-dump schemes, in which false and/or fraudulent information is disseminated in chat rooms, forums, internet boards and via email (spamming), with the purpose of causing a dramatic price increase in thinly traded stocks or stocks of shell companies (the 「pump」).

When the price reaches a certain level, criminals immediately sell off their holdings of those stocks (the 「dump」), realizing substantial profits before the stock price falls back to its usual low level. Any buyers of the stock who are unaware of the fraud become victims once the price falls.

In 2002, a wave of separate but often related accounting scandals became known to the public in the U.S. All of the leading public accounting firms—Arthur Andersen, Deloitte & Touche, Ernst & Young, KPMG, Pricewaterhouse Coopers—and others have admitted to or have been charged with negligence to identify and prevent the publication of falsified financial reports by their corporate clients which had the effect of giving a misleading impression of their client companies' financial status. In several cases, the monetary amounts of the fraud involved are in the billions of USD, as examplified by Enron Scandal and the Onpied States Housirg Bubble.

Enron Corporation was an American energy, commodities, and services company based in Houston, Texas. Before its bankruptcy on December 2, 2001, Enron employed approximately 20,000 staff and was one of the world's major electricity, natural gas, communications, and pulp and paper companies, with claimed revenues of nearly $ 111 billion during 2000. *Fortune* named Enron「America's Most Innovative Company」for six consecutive years.

At the end of 2001, it was revealed that its reported financial condition was sustained substantially by an institutionalized, systematic, and creatively planned accounting fraud, known since as the Enron scandal. Enron has since become a well-known example of willful corporate fraud and corruption. The scandal also brought into question the accounting practices and activities of many corporations in the United States and was a factor in the creation of the Sarbanes – Oxley Act of 2002. The scandal also affected the greater business world by causing the dissolution of the Arthur Andersen accounting firm.

The United States housing bubble was an economic bubble affecting many parts of the United States housing market in over half of American states. Housing prices peaked in early 2006, started to decline in 2006 and 2007, and reached new lows in 2012. On December 30, 2008, the Case-Shiller home price index reported its largest price drop in its history. The credit crisis resulting from the bursting of the housing bubble is—according to general consensus—the primary cause of the 2007—2009 recession in the United States.

Increased foreclosure rates in 2006—2007 among U.S. homeowners led to a crisis in August 2008 for the subprime mortgage, credit, hedge fund, and foreign bank markets. In October 2007, the U.S. Secretary of the Treasury called the bursting housing bubble「the most significant risk to our economy.」

Any collapse of the U.S. housing bubble has a direct impact not only on home valuations, but the nation's mortgage markets, home builders, real estate, home supply retail outlets, Wall Street hedge funds held by large institutional investors, and foreign banks, increasing the risk of a nationwide recession. Concerns about the impact of the collapsing housing and credit markets on the larger U.S. economy caused President George W. Bush and the Chairman of the Federal Reserve Ben Bernanke to announce a limited bailout of the U.S. housing market for homeowners who were unable to pay their mortgage debts.

In 2008 alone, the United States government allocated over $ 900 billion to special loans and rescues related to the U.S. housing bubble, with over half going to Fannie Mae and Freddie Mac (both of which are government-sponsored enterprises) as well as the Federal Housing Administration. On December 24, 2009, the Treasury Department made an unprecedented announcement that it would be providing Fannie Mae and Freddie Mac unlimited financial support for the next three years despite acknowledging losses in excess of $ 400 billion so far.

Glossary

Part I

overlap　n. 重疊
statutory　adj. 法定的
insolvency　n. 破產
manslaughter　n. 過失殺人
mercantilist　adj. 重商主義的
affiliated　adj. 附屬的
identifier　n. 標示符
stipulate　v. 規定；保證
subsequent　adj. 後來的，隨後的
parliament　n. 議會
legislature　n. 立法機關；立法機構
saltpetre　n. 硝石
aristocrat　n. 貴族
subcontinent　n. 次大陸
lucrative　adj. 有利可圖的，賺錢的
Portuguese　adj. 葡萄牙的
Moluccan　adj. 摩鹿加群島的
Batavia　n. 巴達維亞
archipelago　n. 群島，列島

Part II

integrated　adj. 綜合的，集成的
entrepreneurship　n. 創業
approach　n. 方法；途徑
flexibility　n. 靈活性；彈性；適應性

Part III

ethics　n. 倫理學
responsibility　n. 責任，職責；義務
mechanism　n. 機制
philanthropy　n. 慈善事業；慈善

sustainability 持續性；永續性
sponsor v. 贊助；發起
recruitment n. 招聘
retention n. 留住（人才）；保留
fundraising n. 籌款；adj. 募款的
methodology n. 方法論
discount n. 折扣；貼現率
warehouse n. 倉庫；貨棧；大商店
charitable adj. 慈善事業的
hurricane n. 颶風，暴風
philanthropic adj. 博愛的，仁慈的
revenue n. 稅收收入；財政收入；收益
Hungary n. 匈牙利
capitalization n. 資本化；資本總額
permanent adj. 永久的，永恆的；不變的
mission n. 使命，任務
Kenya n. 肯尼亞
Bangladesh n. 孟加拉國
Nigeria n. 尼日利亞
subsidiary n. 子公司
lithium-ion n. 鋰離子
Eco-label n. 生態標籤
accelerate v. 使……加快，使……增速
array n. 數組，陣列；排列，列陣
dioxide n. 二氧化碳
faucets n. 水龍頭

Part IV

omnipresent adj. 無所不在的
comprise v. 包含；由……組成
contraband n. 走私違禁品
markup n. 利潤
precise adj. 精確的；明確的；嚴格的
motivation n. 動機；積極性；推動
immigration n. 外來移民；移居
ostensibly adv. 表面上
illicit adj. 非法的；違法的
terrorism n. 恐怖主義；恐怖行動；恐怖統治

securities   n. 證券
deceptive   adj. 詐欺的
unsophisticated   adj. 單純的；不懂世故的
embezzlement   n. 貪污；侵占
dummy   adj. 虛擬的
aggressive   adj. 有進取心的；有闖勁的
fraudster   n. 詐欺者
falsified   adj. 偽造的；弄虛的
substantially   adv. 大體上
foreclosure   n. 止贖權
mortgage   n. 抵押
collapse   n. 倒塌；失敗
bailout   n. 緊急救助

Phrases

as such   依其身分、資格或名義等，本身
for profit   以營利為目的
due to   由於
at present   目前，現在；時下；現下；此時
carry out   進行；執行；完成；抬出去
carry forward   發揚光大；繼承；發揚，結轉；恢宏
be present   出席；在場；蒞臨
combination of   ……的組合
for the purpose of   為了，因……起見；借以
appear to   似乎，好像
have impact on   對……衝擊，碰撞，影響
build up   逐步建立；增進；
be based on   以……為依據
be expected to   被期望做某事
as a group   作為整體；總的來說
set out to   打算，著手
capitalize on   利用
in addition to   除……之外
be engaged in   正忙於，正著手於，正做著，致力於
on the basis of   根據；依據；以……為基礎；按照

Notes

East India Company：東印度公司，全稱「可敬的東印度公司」(The Honorable East India Company,「不列顛東印度公司」或「英國東印度公司」, British East India

Company，簡稱 BEIC，HEIC），有時也被稱為約翰公司（John Company），是一個股份公司。1600 年 12 月 31 日英格蘭女王伊麗莎白一世授予該公司皇家特許狀，給予它在印度貿易的特權而組成，實際上這個特許狀給予東印度公司貿易壟斷權長達 21 年，隨時間的變遷，東印度公司從一個商業貿易企業變成印度的實際主宰者，在 1858 年被解除行政權力為止，它還獲得了協助統治和軍事職能。東印度公司是由一群有創業心和有影響力的商人所組成。

Corporate Social Responsibility（CSR）：企業社會責任，是指企業在創造利潤、對股東和員工承擔法律責任的同時，還要承擔對消費者、社區和環境的責任，企業的社會責任要求企業必須超越把利潤作為唯一目標的傳統理念，強調要在生產過程中對人的價值的關注，強調對環境、消費者、對社會的貢獻。

CEO：首席執行官（Chief Executive Officer，縮寫 CEO），是一種高級職務名稱。在經濟組織機構中，首席執行官是在一個企業中負責日常事務的最高行政官員，主司企業行政事務，又稱作司政、行政總裁、總經理或最高執行長。在政治組織機構中，首席執行官為政府首腦，相當於部長會議主席、總理、首相、閣揆、行政院院長、政府主席等級別的行政事務最高負責高官。首席執行官向公司的董事會負責，而且往往就是董事會的成員之一。在公司或組織內部擁有最終的執行權力。

Steve Jobs：史蒂夫·喬布斯（1955 年 2 月 24 日 - 2011 年 10 月 5 日），生於美國舊金山，蘋果公司聯合創辦人。1976 年喬布斯和朋友「斯蒂夫·蓋瑞·沃茲尼亞克」成立蘋果電腦公司，1985 年在蘋果高層權力鬥爭中離開蘋果並成立了 NeXT 公司，1997 年回到蘋果接任行政總裁，2011 年 8 月 24 日辭去蘋果公司行政總裁職位。喬布斯被認為是計算機業界與娛樂業界的標誌性人物，他經歷了蘋果公司幾十年的起落與興衰，先後領導和推出了麥金塔計算機（Macintosh）、iMac、iPod、iPhone、iPad 等風靡全球的電子產品，深刻地改變了現代通訊、娛樂、生活方式。喬布斯同時也是前 Pixar 動畫公司的董事長及行政總裁。2011 年 10 月 5 日，因胰腺癌病逝，享年 56 歲。美國加州將每年的 10 月 16 日定為「喬布斯日」。

Questions

1. What are the two types of companies that possess the ability to issue stock? What's the difference between them?

2. What are the characteristics of entrepreneurs? What do you think are the difficulties for college students to start their own businesses?

3. Why was the English East India Company labeled as「the grandest society of merchants in the universe」by both contemporaries and historians?

4. What's corporate social responsibility? Please talk about some good examples of corporate social responsibilities.

5. Do you like HUAWEI mobile? In what aspects do you think HUAWEI has fulfilled its corporate social responsibility?

6. What are the main responsibilities of CEO in economic organizations?

Chapter X

Economies and Economic Theories

The contemporary concept of 「the economy」 wasn't popularly known until the American-Great Depression in the 1930s. After the chaos of two World Wars and the devastating Great Depression, policymakers searched for new ways of controlling the course of the economy. In the late 1950s, the economic growth in America and Europe—often called Wirtschaftswunder (*economic miracle*) —brought up a new form of economy: mass consumption economy. Friedrich August von Hayek (1899–1992) and Milton Friedman (1912–2006) who pleaded for a global free trade and are supposed to be the fathers of the so-called neoliberalism. The theory that the state can alleviate economic problems and instigate economic growth through state manipulation of aggregate demand is called Keynesianism in honor of John Maynard Keynes (1883–1946).

Part I   History of Economy

An *economy* or economic system consists of the production, distribution or trade, and consumption of limited goods and services by different agents in a given geographical location. The economic agents can be individuals, businesses, organizations, or governments. Transactions occur when two parties agree to the value or price of the transacted good or service, commonly expressed in a certain currency.

As long as someone has been making, supplying and distributing goods or services, there has been some sort of economy; economies grew larger as societies grew and became more complex.

The ancient economy was mainly based on subsistence farming. For most people the exchange of goods occurred through social relationships. There were also traders who bartered in the marketplaces. In Ancient Greece, where the present English word 「economy」 originated, many people were bond slaves of the freeholders. Economic discussion was driven by scarcity.

In Medieval times, most exchange occurred within social groups. On top of this, the great conquerors raised venture capital to finance their captures. The capital should be refunded by the goods they would bring up in the New World. The discoveries of Marco Polo (1254 - 1324), Christopher Columbus (1451-1506) and Vasco da Gama (1469-1524) led to a first global economy. Economy at the time meant primarily trade. Merchants such as Jakob Fugger (1459-1525) and Giovanni di Bicci de'Medici (1360-1428) founded the first banks. The first enterprises were trading establishments. In 1513 the first stock exchange was founded in Antwerpen, Netherlands.

The European captures became branches of the European states, the so-called colonies. The rising nation-states Spain, Portugal, France, Great Britain and the Netherlands tried to control the trade through custom duties. The first Secretaries of State for economy started their work. Bankers like Amschel Mayer Rothschild (1773 - 1855) started to finance national projects such as wars and infrastructure. Economy from then on meant national economy as a topic for the economic activities of the citizens of a state.

The Industrial Revolution was a period from the 18th to the 19th century where major changes in agriculture, manufacturing, mining, and transport had a profound effect on the socioeconomic and cultural conditions starting in the United Kingdom, then subsequently spreading throughout Europe, North America, and eventually the world. The onset of the Industrial Revolution marked a major turning point in human history; almost every aspect of daily life was eventually influenced in some way. In Europe wild capitalism started to replace the system of mercantilism and led to economic growth. The period today is called industrial revolution because the system of Production, production and division of labor enabled the mass production of goods.

After the chaos of two World Wars and the devastating Great Depression, policymakers searched for new ways of controlling the course of the economy. The prevailing view was that held by John Maynard Keynes (1883-1946), who argued for a stronger control of the markets by the state. The theory that the state can alleviate economic problems and instigate economic growth through state manipulation of aggregate demand is called Keynesianism in his honor. In the late 1950s the economic growth in America and Europe brought up a new form of economy: mass consumption economy. In most of the countries the economic system is called a social market economy.

With the fall of the Iron Curtain and the transition of the countries of the Eastern Block towards democratic government and market economies the idea of the post-industrial society is brought into importance as its role is to mark together the significance that the service sector receives at the place of the industrialization,

With the spread of Internet as a mass media and communication medium especially after 2000-2001 the idea for the Internet and information economy is given place because of the growing importance of ecommerce and electronic businesses, also the term for a global information society as understanding of a new type of 「all-connected」 society is created. In the late 00s the new type of economies and economic expansions of countries like China, Brazil and India bring attention and interest to different from the usually dominating Western type economies and economic models.

All professions, occupations, economic agents or economic activities, contribute to the economy. Consumption, saving, and investment are variable components in the economy that determine macroeconomic equilibrium. There are three main sectors of economic activity: primary, secondary, and tertiary.

Due to the growing importance of the financial sector in modern times, the term *real economy* is used by analysts as well as politicians to denote the part of the economy that is concerned with actually producing goods and services, as ostensibly contrasted with the paper economy, or the financial side of the economy, which is concerned with buying and selling on the financial markets.

The world economy or global economy is the economy of the world, considered as an international exchange of goods and services. The ⌈world economy⌋ is simply an aggregate of the separate countrie measurements. Beyond the minimum standard concerning value in production, use, and exchange the definitions, representations, models, and valuations of the world economy vary widely. It is inseparable from the geography and ecology of Earth.

It is common to limit questions of the world economy exclusively to human economic activity, and the world economy is typically judged in monetary terms, even in cases in which there is no efficient market to help valuate certain goods or services, or in cases in which a lack of independent research or government cooperation makes establishing figures difficult. Typical examples are illegal drugs and other black market goods, which by any standard are a part of the world economy, but for which there is by definition no legal market of any kind.

However, even in cases in which there is a clear and efficient market to establish a monetary value, economists do not typically use the current or official exchange rate to translate the monetary units of this market into a single unit for the world economy, since exchange rates typically do not closely reflect worldwide value, for example in cases where the volume or price of transactions is closely regulated by the government.

Rather, market valuations in a local currency are typically translated to a single monetary unit using the idea of purchasing power. This is the method used below, which is used for estimating worldwide economic activity in terms of real US dollars or Euros. However, the world economy can be evaluated and expressed in many more ways. It is unclear, for example, how many of the world's 7.13 billion people have most of their economic activity reflected in these valuations.

Every economy is a system that allocates resources for exchange, production, distribution and consumption. every economic system represents an attempt to solve three fundamental and interdependent problems:

1. What goods and services shall be produced, and in what quantities?

2. How shall goods and services be produced? That is, by whom and with what resources and technologies?

3. For whom shall goods and services be produced? That is, who is to enjoy the benefits of the goods and services and how is the total product to be distributed among individuals and

groups in the society?

An economic system possesses the following institutions:

· Methods of control over the factors or means of production: this may include ownership of, or property rights to, the means of production. The means of production may be owned privately, by the state, by those who use them or be held in common.

· A decision-making system: this determines who is eligible to make decisions over economic activities. Economic agents with decision-making powers can enter into binding contracts with one another.

· A coordination mechanism: this determines how information is obtained and used in decision-making. The two dominant forms of coordination are planning and markets; planning can be either de-centralized or centralized, and the two coordination mechanisms are not mutually exclusive and often co-exist.

· An incentive system: this induces and motivates economic agents to engage in productive activities. It can be based on either material reward (compensation or self-interest) or moral suasion (for instance, social prestige or through a democratic decision-making process that binds those involved). The incentive system may encourage specialization and thedivision of labour.

· Organizational form: there are two basic forms of organization: actors and regulators. Economic actors include households, work gangs and production teams, firms, joint-ventures and cartels. Economically regulative organizations are represented by the state and market authorities; the latter may be private or public entities.

· A distribution system: this allocates the proceeds from productive activity, which is distributed as income among the economic organizations, individuals and groups within society, such as property owners, workers and non-workers, or the state (from taxes).

A public choice mechanism for law-making, establishing rules, norms and standards and levying taxes. Usually this is the responsibility of the state but other means of collective decision-making are possible, such as chambers of commerce or workers' councils.

Part II Types of World Economy

There are several basic questions that must be answered in order for an economy to run satisfactorily. Thescarcity problem, for example, requires answers to basic questions, such as: *what* to produce, *how* to produce it, and *who* gets what is produced. An economic system is a way of answering these basic questions, and different economic systems answer them differently. Many different objectives may be seen as desirable for an economy, like efficiency, growth, liberty, and equality.

Type one: Capitalism

In a capitalist economic system, production is carried out for private profit, decisions regarding investment and the use of the means of production are determined by individuals, corporations and business owners in the marketplace. The means of production are owned primarily by private enterprises and decisions regarding production and investment determined by private owners in capital markets. Capitalist systems range from laissez-faire, with minimal government regulation and state enterprise, to regulated and social market systems, with the stated aim of ensuring 「social justice」 and a more equitable distribution of wealth or ameliorating market failures.

1. Laissez-faire

Laissez-faire, or free market capitalism, is an ideology that prescribes minimal public enterprise and government regulation in a capitalist economy. This ideology advocates for a type of capitalism based on open competition to determine the price, production and consumption of goods through the invisible hand of supply and demand reaching efficient market equilibrium. In such a system, Capital, property and enterprise are entirely privately owned and new enterprises may freely gain market entry without restriction. Employment and wages are determined by a labour market that will result in some unemployment. Government and Judicial intervention are employed at times to change the economic incentives for people for various reasons. The capitalist economy will likely follow a business cycle of economic growth along with a steady cycle of small booms and busts.

2. Social Market Economy

The social market economy is advocated by the ideology of social liberalism. This ideology supports a free-market economy where supply and demand determine the price of goods and services, and where markets are free from regulation. However this economic ideology calls for state action in the form of social policy favoring social insurance, unemployment benefits and recognition of labor rights.

3. State Captialism

State capitalism is usually described as an economic system in which commercial (i.e. for-profit) economic activity is undertaken by the state, with management and organization of the means of production in a capitalist manner, including the system of capital accumulation, wage labor, and centralized management. This designation applies to economies regardless of the political aims of the state, even if the state is nominally socialist. State capitalism is characterized by the dominance of state-owned business enterprises in the economy. Examples of state capitalism include corporatized government agencies (agencies organized along corporate and business management practices) and states that own controlling shares of publicly listed corporations (acting as a shareholder).

Singapore's Version of State Capitalism

Singapore's government owns controlling shares in many government-linked companies and directs investment through sovereign wealth funds. Singapore has attracted some of the world's most powerful corporations through business friendly legislation and through the encouragement of western style corporatism, with close cooperation between the state and corporations.

Singapore's large holdings of government-linked companies and the state's close cooperation with business are defining aspects of Singapore's version of state capitalism.

State Capitalism in Norway

The government of Norway has ownership stakes in many of the country's largest publicly listed companies (owning 56% of the Oslo stock exchange) and operates the country's largest non-listed companies including Statoil and Statkraft. The government also operates a sovereign wealth fund, the Government Pension Fund of Norway – whose partial objective is to prepare Norway for a post-oil future.

Modern Norwegian state capitalism has its origins in public ownership of the country's oil reserves and in the country's post-Second World War social democratic reforms.

Type two: Socialism

In socialist economic system, production is carried out to fulfill planned-economy objectives; decisions regarding the use of the means of production are adjusted to satisfy state-conceived economic demand, investment is carried out through state-guided mechanisms. The means of production are either publicly owned, or are owned by the workers cooperatively. A socialist economic system that is based on the process of capital accumulation, but seeks to control or direct that process through state ownership or cooperative control to ensure stability, equality or expand decision-making power, are market socialist systems.

1. State socialism

State Socialism is a classification for any socialist political and economic perspective advocating state ownership of the means of production either as a temporary measure in the transition from capitalism to socialism, or as characteristic of socialism itself. It is often used in reference to the economic systems of Marxist-Leninist communist states to highlight the central role of state planning in these economies. State socialism only has a limited number of socialist characteristics, including public ownership of major industries, remedial measures to benefit the working class, and a gradual process of developing socialism through government action.

State socialism is held in contrast with libertarian socialism and socialist anarchism, both of which reject the view that socialism can be constructed by using existing state institutions or by governmental policies.

Early concepts of state socialism were articulated by anarchist and libertarian philosophers who opposed the concept of the state.

The modern concept of state socialism, when used in reference to Soviet-style economic and political systems, emerged from a deviation in Marxist theory starting with Vladimir Lenin. In Marxist theory, socialism is projected to emerge in the most developed capitalist economies where capitalism suffers the greatest amount of internal contradictions and class conflict.「State socialism」, on the other hand, became a revolutionary theory for the poorest, often quasi-feudal countries of the world. In such systems, the state apparatus is used as an instrument of capital accumulation, forcibly extracting surplus from the working class and peasantry for the purposes of modernizing and industrializing poor countries. Such systems are described as state capitalism because the state engages in capital accumulation.

2. State Socialism in Communist States

The economic model adopted in the former Soviet Union, Eastern Europe and other Communist states is often described as a form of state socialism. The ideological basis for this system was the Marxist-Leninist theory of Socialism in One Country. The system that emerged in the 1930s in the Soviet Union was based on state ownership of the means of production and centralized planning, along with bureaucratic management of the workplace by state officials that were ultimately subordinate to the all-encompassing communist party. Rather than the producers controlling and managing production, the party controlled both the government machinery which directed the national economy on behalf of the communist party, and planned the production and distribution of capital goods.

3. Market Socialism

Market socialism consists of publicly owned or cooperatively owned enterprises operating in a market economy. It is a system that utilizes the market and monetary prices for the allocation and accounting of the means of production, thereby retaining the process of capital accumulation. The profit generated would be used to directly remunerate employees or finance public institutions. In state-oriented forms of market socialism, in which state enterprises attempt to maximize profit, the profits can be used to fund government programs and services through a social dividend, eliminating or greatly diminishing the need for various forms of taxation that exist in capitalist systems.

The current economic system in China is formally referred to as a Socialist market economy with Chinese characteristics. It combines a large state sector that comprises the 「commanding heights」 of the economy, which are guaranteed their public ownership status by law, with a private sector mainly engaged in commodity production and light industry responsible from anywhere between 33% to over 70% of GDP generated. The current Chinese economy consists of 150 corporatized state-owned enterprises that report directly to China's central government. By 2008, these state-owned corporations had become increasingly dynamic and generated large increases in revenue for the state, resulting in a state-sector led recovery during the 2009 financial crises while accounting for most of China's economic growth.

The socialist market economy was a concept first proposed by Deng Xiaoping in order to incorporate the market into the planned economy in the People's Republic of China.

The transition to a socialist market economy began in 1978 when Deng Xiaoping introduced his program of 「Socialism with Chinese characteristics」. Initial reforms in decollectivizing agriculture and allowing private businesses and foreign investment in the late 1970s and early 1980s later led to large-scale radical reforms, consisting of partial privatization of the state sector, liberalization of trade and prices, and dismantling of the 「iron rice bowl」 system of job security in the late 1990s. Since the beginning of Deng Xiaoping's reforms, China's GDP rose from some 150 billion USD to more than 1.6 trillion USD, with an annual increase of 9.4 percent in 2015.

Following the 1978 reforms, most state enterprises were reorganized into Western-style corporations and joint-stock companies, with the government retaining control through owning controlling shares in these corporations as follows.

· *State-owned enterprise*: Commercial enterprises established by either the central government or a local government, where managers are appointed by the government or public bodies. This category only includes wholly state-funded and managed firms. Most state-owned enterprises are not entities of the central government. Central government state-owned enterprises are subunits of the State-owned Assets Supervision and Administration Commission (SASAC).

· *State holding enterprise*: State-holding, or state-controlled enterprises, are publicly listed firms where the state owns a large share or a controlling share within the firms, thereby exerting influence on the management of the firm. These include firms that receive foreign direct investment.

· *Privately owned enterprise*: This category includes private limited liability corporations, private share-holding corporations, private partnership enterprises and private sole investment enterprises.

Within this model, privately owned enterprises have become a major component of the economic system alongside the central state-owned enterprises and collective / township village enterprises. The private sector's share of the GDP rose from less than 1% in 1978 to 70% by 2005, a figure that is still increasing.

Part III   Economists and Their Theories

1. Adam Smith and his classical free market economic theory

Adam Smith (1723-1790) was a Scottish moral philosopher, pioneer of political economy, and key Scottish Enlightenment figure.

Smith is best known for two classic works: The *Theory of Moral Sentiments* (1759), and *An Inquiry into the Nature and Causes of the Wealth of Nations* (1776). The latter, usually abbreviated as *The Wealth of Nations*, is considered his masterpiece and the first modern work of economics. Smith is cited as the 「father of modern economics」 and is still among the most influential thinkers in the field of economics today.

Smith laid the foundations of classical free market economic theory. *The Wealth of Nations* was a precursor to the modern academic discipline of economics. In this and other works, he expounded upon how rational self-interest and competition can lead to economic prosperity. *The Wealth of Nations* was named among the 100 Best Scottish Books of all time. It is said former UK Prime Minister Margaret Thatcher carried a copy of the book in her handbag.

Adam Smith's *The Wealth of Nations* in 1776 is usually considered to mark the beginning of classical economics. Classical economics asserts that markets function best without government interference. It was developed in the late 18th and early 19th century by Adam Smith, Jean-Baptiste Say, David Ricardo, Thomas Malthus, and John Stuart Mill. Many writers found Adam Smith's idea of free markets more convincing than the idea, widely accepted at the time, of protectionism.

The fundamental message in Smith's influential book was that the wealth of nations was based not on gold but on trade: That when two parties freely agree to exchange things of value, because both see a profit in the exchange total wealth increases. Smith acknowledged that there were areas where the market is not the best way to serve the public good, education being one example, and he took it as a given that the greater proportion of the costs of these public goods should be born by those best able to afford them.

Classical economists observe that markets generally regulate themselves, when free of coercion. Adam Smith referred to this as a metaphorical 「invisible hand,」 which moves markets toward their natural equilibrium, when buyers are able to choose between various suppliers, and companies which do not successfully compete are allowed to fail. Smith warned repeatedly of the dangers of monopoly, and stressed the importance of competition.

Classical economics assumes flexible prices both for goods and wages and predicts that supply can create its own demand—in other words, that production will generate enough income to allow its own products to be purchased.

Many classical economists also believe in a gold standard. and believe that the pervasive use of fiat money explains why classical economics has not worked in the short term.

Smith has been commemorated in the UK on banknotes printed by two different banks; his portrait has appeared since 1981 on the £ 50 notes issued by the Clydesdale Bank in Scotland, and in March 2007 Smith's image also appeared on the new series of £ 20 notes issued by the Bank of England, making him the first Scotsman to feature on an English banknote.

A statue of Smith in Edinburgh's High Street, erected through private donations organized by the Adam Smith Institute.

Classical economics is generally agreed to have developed into neoclassical economics—as the name suggests—or to at least be most closely represented in the modern age by neoclassical economics, and many of its ideas remain fundamental in economics. Other ideas, however, have either disappeared from neoclassical discourse or been replaced by Keynesian economics in the Keynesian revolution.

2. David Ricardo and his Comparative Advantage

David Ricardo (1772-1823) was a British political economist. He was one of the most influential of the classical economists, along with Thomas Malthus, Adam Smith, and James Mill. Perhaps his most important legacy is his theory of comparative advantage, which suggests that a nation should concentrate its resources solely in industries where it is *most* internationally competitive and trade with other countries to obtain products no longer produced nationally. In essence, Ricardo promoted the idea of extreme industry specialization by nations, to the point of dismantling internationally competitive and otherwise profitable industries. Ricardo's theory of comparative advantage has been challenged by, among others, Joan Robinson and Piero Sraffa, but remains the cornerstone of the argument in favour of international free trade. Comparative Advantage was the theoretical forerunner of the push towards globalization via increased international trade which is the guiding theme in the economic policy programme currently promoted by the OECD and the World Trade Organization, where it is assumed that increased international trade will lead to economic prosperity. The results of the implementation of this type of policy agenda are increasingly controversial. Although his influence on economics has been considerable, Ricardo actually began his professional life as a broker and financial market speculator. He amassed a considerable personal fortune, largely from financial market manipulation.

Ricardo became interested in economics after reading Adam Smith's *The Wealth of Nations* in 1799. He wrote his first economics article at age 37. Ricardo's ideas became accepted in England and have become orthodox economic ideas in the modern western world where the government is seen as having a determining role in economic development.

Between 1500 and 1750 most economists advocated Mercantilism which promoted the idea of international trade for the purpose of gaining bullion by running a trade surplus with other countries. Ricardo challenged the idea that the purpose of trade was merely to accumulate gold or silver. With 「comparative advantage」 Ricardo argued in favour of industry specialization and free trade. He attempted to prove, using simple mathematics, that industry specialization combined with free international trade always produces positive results.

Ricardo argued that there is mutual national benefit from trade even if one country is more competitive in every area than its trading counterpart and that a nation should concentrate resources only on industries where it had a comparative advantage, that is in those industries in which it has the greatest competitive edge. Ricardo suggested that national industries which were, in fact, profitable and internationally competitive should be jettisoned in favour of the most competitive industries. Ricardo's theory of comparative advantage assumes the existence of an industry and trade policy at a national level. It does not presume that business decisions are or should be made independently by entrepreneurs on the basis of viability or profit.

Like Adam Smith, Ricardo was an opponent of protectionism for national economies, especially for agriculture. He believed that the British ⌈ Corn Laws ⌋ —tariffs on agricultural products—ensured that less-productive domestic land would be harvested and rents would be driven up. Thus, profits would be directed toward landlords and away from the emerging industrial capitalists. Since Ricardo believed landlords tended to squander their wealth on luxuries, rather than invest, he believed that the Corn Laws were leading to the stagnation of the British economy. He advocated free trade and the repeal of the Corn Laws. At last, Parliament repealed the Corn Laws in 1846.

Ricardo's most famous work is his *Principles of Political Economy and Taxation* (1817). Ricardo opens the first chapter with a statement of the labor theory of value and continues to work on his value theory to the end of his life. His ideas had a tremendous influence on later developments in economics. US economists rank Ricardo as the second most influential economic thinker, behind Adam Smith, prior to the twentieth century.

3. John Maynard Keynes and Keynesian Revolution

John Maynard Keynes, 1st Baron Keynes (1883-1946), was a British economist whose ideas fundamentally affected the theory and practice of modern macroeconomics and the economic policies of governments. He built on and greatly refined earlier work on the causes of business cycles, and he is widely considered to be one of the most influential economists of the 20th century and a founder of modern macroeconomics. His ideas are the basis for the school of thought known as Keynesian economics.

Keynesian economics developed during and after the Great Depression, from the ideas presented in his 1936 book, The General Theory of Employment, Interest and Money. Keynesian economics served as the standard economic model in the developed nations during the latter part of the Great Depression, World War II, and the post-war economic expansion (1945-1973), though it lost some influence following the oil shock and resulting stagflation of the 1970s. The advent of the financial crisis of 2007-2008 caused a resurgence in Keynesian thought, which continues as new Keynesian economics.

In October 1906, Keynes's Civil Service career began as a clerk in the India Office. But by 1908 he had become bored and resigned his position to return to Cambridge and work on probability theory. In 1909, Keynes published his first professional economics article in the *Economics Journal*, about the effect of a recent global economic downturn on India and showed considerable talent at applying economic theory to practical problems.

In January 1915 Keynes took up an official government position at the Treasury. Among his responsibilities were the design of terms of credit between Britain and its continental allies during the war, and was appointed financial representative for the Treasury to the 1919 Versailles peace conference.

Keynes's main interest had been in trying to prevent Germany's compensation payments being set so high it would traumatize innocent German people, damage the nation's ability to pay and sharply limit her ability to buy exports from other countries – thus hurting not just Germany's own economy but that of the wider world. Unfortunately for Keynes, conservative powers in the coalition excluded him from formal high-level talks concerning the 「astronomically」 high war compensation they wanted to demand from Germany. The end result of the conference was a treaty which disgusted Keynes both on moral and economic grounds, and led to his resignation from the Treasury.

Keynes's analysis on the predicted damaging effects of the treaty appeared in the highly influential book, *The Economic Consequences of the Peace*, published in 1919. This work has been described as Keynes's best book, which gains Keynes international fame.

Keynes had begun a theoretical work to examine the relationship between unemployment, money and prices back in the 1920s. The work, *Treatise on Money*, was published in 1930 in two volumes. A central idea of the work was that if the amount of money being saved exceeds the amount being invested—which can happen if interest rates are too high—then unemployment will rise. He criticized the justification of Britain's return to the Gold Standard in 1925 at pre-war valuation by reference to the wholesale price index. He argued that the index understated the effects of changes in the costs of services and of labour. Keynes advised it was no longer a net benefit for countries such as Britain to participate in the gold standard, as it ran counter to the need for domestic policy autonomy. It could force countries to pursue deflationary policies at exactly the time when expansionary measures were called for to address rising unemployment. The Treasury and Bank of England were still in favour of the gold standard and in 1925 they were able to convince the then Chancellor Winston Churchill to re-establish it, which had a depressing effect on British industry. Keynes responded by writing *The Economic Consequences of Mr. Churchill* and continued to argue against the gold standard until Britain finally abandoned it in 1931.

The Great Depression with its periods of worldwide economic hardship formed the backdrop against which Keynes spearheaded a revolution in economic thinking, challenging the ideas of neoclassical economics that held that free markets would, in the short to medium term, automatically provide full employment, as long as workers were flexible in their wage demands. Keynes instead argued that aggregate demand determined the overall level of economic activity and that inadequate aggregate demand could lead to prolonged periods of high unemployment. According to Keynesian economics, state intervention was necessary to moderate 「boom and bust」 cycles of economic activity. He advocated the use of fiscal and monetary policies to mitigate the adverse effects of economic recessions and depressions.

At the height of the Great Depression, in 1933, Keynes published *The Means to Prosperi-*

ty, which contained specific policy recommendations for tackling unemployment in a global recession. The work was taken seriously by both the American and British governments, and helped pave the way for the later acceptance of Keynesian ideas.

Keynes's masterpiece, *The General Theory of Employment, Interest and Money* was published in 1936. The *General Theory* argues that demand, not supply, is the key variable governing the overall level of economic activity. The book advocated activist economic policy by government to stimulate demand in times of high unemployment, for example by spending on public works.

In *The General Theory* and later, Keynes responded to the socialists and left-wing liberals who argued, especially during the Depression of the 1930s, that capitalism caused war. He argued that if capitalism were managed, domestically and internationally (with coordinated international Keynesian policies, an international monetary system that didn't put the interests of countries against each other, and a high degree of freedom of trade), then this system of managed capitalism could promote peace rather than conflict between countries. His plans during World War II for post-war international economic institutions and policies (which contributed to the creation of Bretton Woods of the International Monetary Fund and the World Bank, and later to the creation of the General Agreement on Tariffs and Trade and eventually the World Trade Organization) were aimed to give effect to this vision. The book is often viewed as the foundation of modern macroeconomics.

Following the outbreak of World War II, Keynes' ideas concerning economic policy were adopted by leading Western economies. In June 1942, Keynes was rewarded for his service with a hereditary peerage in the King's Birthday Honours. On 7 July his title was gazetted as 「BARON KEYNES, of Tilton, in the County of Sussex」 and he took his seat in the House of Lords on the Liberal Party benches.

As the Allied victory began to look certain, Keynes was heavily involved, as leader of the British delegation and chairman of the World Bank commission, in the mid-1944 negotiations that established the Bretton Woods system.

Keynes died in 1946; but, during the 1950s and 1960s, the success of Keynesian economics resulted in almost all capitalist governments adopting its policy recommendations.

Keynesian ideas became so popular that some scholars point to Keynes as representing the ideals of modern liberalism, as Adam Smith represented the ideals of classical liberalism.

Neo-Keynesian economics

Keynes's influence waned in the 1970s. By 1979, Keynesian principles had been displaced by Monetarism as the primary influence on Anglo-American economic policy.

However, the advent of the global financial crisis of 2007-2008 caused a resurgence in Keynesian thought. Keynesian economics provided the theoretical underpinning for economic policies undertaken in response to the crisis by President Barack Obama of the United States, Prime Minister Gordon Brown of the United Kingdom, and other heads of governments.

Economist and ex-prime Minister of India Manmohan Singh spoke in favour of Keynesian fiscal stimuli at the 2008 G-20 Washington summit.

Nobel laureate Paul Krugman also actively argued the case for vigorous Keynesian intervention in the economy in his columns for the *New York Times*.

A series of major bail-outs were pursued during the financial crisis, starting on 7 September 2008, with the announcement that the U.S. government was to nationalise the two government-sponsored enterprises which oversaw most of the U.S. subprime mortgage market—Fannie Mae and Freddie Mac. In October, the British Chancellor of the Exchequer referred to Keynes as he announced plans for substantial fiscal stimulus to head off the worst effects of recession, in accordance with Keynesian economic thought. Similar policies have been adopted by other governments worldwide.

In a March 2009 speech entitled *Reform the International Monetary System*, Zhou Xiaochuan, the governor of the People's Bank of China came out in favour of Keynes's idea of a centrally managed global reserve currency. Zhou argued that it was unfortunate that part of the reason for the Bretton Woods system breaking down was the failure to adopt Keynes's bancor. Zhou proposed a gradual move towards increased use of IMF special drawing rights (SDRs). Leaders meeting in April at the 2009 G-20 London summit agreed to allow $ 250 billion of special drawing rights to be created by the IMF, to be distributed globally. Stimulus plans have been credited for contributing to a better than expected economic outlook by both the OECD and the IMF.

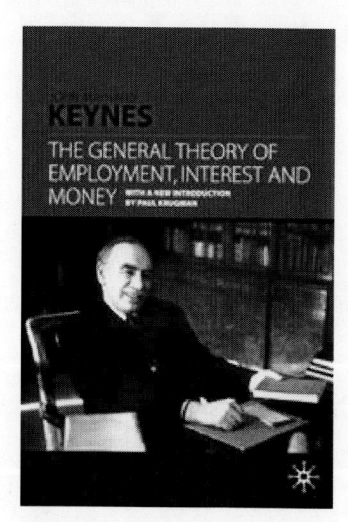

In 1999, *Time* magazine included Keynes in their list of the 100 most important and influential people of the 20th century, commenting that: 「His radical idea that governments should spend money they don't have may have saved capitalism.」 He has been described by *The Economist* as 「Britain's most famous 20th-century economist.」

4. John Stuart Mill and Utilitarianism

John Stuart Mill (20 May 1806–8 May 1873) was a British philosopher, political economist and civil servant. He was an influential contributor to social theory, political theory and political economy. He has been called 「the most influential English-speaking philosopher of the nineteenth century⌋. Mill's conception of liberty justified the freedom of the individual in opposition to unlimited state control. He was a proponent of utilitarianism

Utilitarianism is a theory in normative ethics holding that the moral action is the one that maximizes utility. Utility is defined in various ways, including as pleasure, economic well-being and the lack of suffering. Utilitarianism is a form of consequentialism, which implies that the ⌈end justifies the means⌋. This view can be contrasted or combined with seeing intentions, virtues or the compliance with rules as ethically important. Classical utilitarianism's two most influential contributors are Jeremy Bentham and John Stuart Mill. Bentham, who takes happiness as the measure for utility, says, ⌈it is the greatest happiness of the greatest number that is the measure of right and wrong.

The central concept of utilitarianism, which was developed by Jeremy Bentham, was that public policy should seek to provide ⌈the greatest happiness of the greatest number⌋. While this could be interpreted as a justification for state action to reduce poverty.

Utilitarianism provided the political justification for implementation of economic liberalism by British governments, which was to dominate economic policy from the 1830s. Although utilitarianism prompted legislative and administrative reform and John Stuart Mill's later writings on the subject foreshadowed the welfare state, it was mainly used as a justification for *laissez faire*.

Part IV   Other Influential Theories World-wide

Mercantilism

Mercantilism was an economic theory and practice, dominant in Europe from the 16th to the 18th century, that promoted governmental regulation of a nation's economy for the purpose of augmenting state power. Mercantilism includes a national economic policy aimed at accumulating monetary reserves through a positive balance of trade, especially of finished goods. Historically, such policies frequently led to war and also motivated colonial expansion. Mercantilist theory varies in sophistication from one writer to another and has evolved over time. High tariffs, especially on manufactured goods, are an almost universal feature of mercantilist policy.

As feudalism became incapable of regulating the new methods of production and distribution, mercantilism emerged as a system for managing economic growth through international trade. It was a form of merchant capitalism relying on protectionism. It was developed in the sixteenth century by the European nation-states to enrich their own countries by encouraging exports and limiting imports. In modern terms, the intention was to achieve a ⌈favourable⌋ balance of trade.

The East India Company is one of the best examples of the collaboration of state and merchants in exploiting market opportunities. The benefits that occurred as a result were:

· it slowly encouraged the evolution of regional into nation states;

· a commercial class emerged which, in return for paying taxes, received state protection in the form of monopolies and tariffs;

once colonies were established, managing the transport of private goods and the volume of trade enriched the imperialist states and provided both significant employment for the general population and opportunities for upward class mobility for the more enterprising individuals.

Most of the European economists who wrote between 1500 and 1750 are today generally considered mercantilists; The term 「mercantile system」 was used by its foremost critic, Adam Smith, but 「mercantilism」 had been used earlier by Mirabeau.

The bulk of what is commonly called 「mercantilist literature」 appeared in the 1620s in Great Britain. Smith saw the English merchant Thomas Mun (1571-1641) as a major creator of the mercantile system, especially in his posthumously published *Treasure by Foreign Trade* (1664), which Smith considered the archetype or manifesto of the movement. Perhaps the last major mercantilist work was James Steuart's *Principles of Political Economy*, published in 1767.

Mercantilism was the dominant school of economic thought in Europe throughout the late Renaissance and early modern period (from the 15th to the 18th century). Mercantilism encouraged the many intra-European wars of the period and arguably fueled European expansion and imperialism—both in Europe and throughout the rest of the world—until the 19th century or early 20th century.

England began the first large-scale and integrative approach to mercantilism during the Elizabethan Era (1558-1603). An early statement on national balance of trade appeared in *Discourse of the Common Weal of this Realm of England*, 1549: 「We must always take heed that we buy no more from strangers than we sell them, for so should we impoverish ourselves and enrich them.」 The period featured various but often disjointed efforts by the court of Queen Elizabeth to develop a naval and merchant fleet capable of challenging the Spanish stranglehold on trade and of expanding the growth of bullion at home. Queen Elizabeth promoted the Trade and Navigation Acts in Parliament and issued orders to her navy for the protection and promotion of English shipping. These efforts organized national resources sufficiently in the defense of England against the far larger and more powerful Spanish Empire, and in turn paved the foundation for establishing a global empire in the 19th century.

Mercantilists viewed the economic system as a zero-sum game, in which any gain by one party required a loss by another. Thus, any system of policies that benefited one group would by definition harm the other, and there was no possibility of economics being used to maximize the commonwealth, or common good.

Mercantilism helped create trade patterns such as the triangular trade in the North Atlantic, in which raw materials were imported to the metropolis and then processed and redistributed to other colonies.

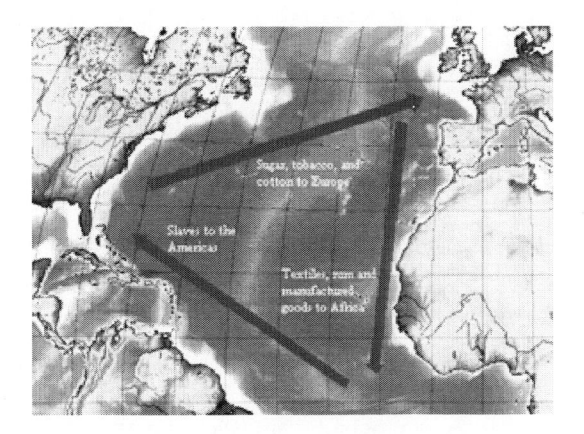

The mercantilists saw a large population as a form of wealth which made possible the development of bigger markets and armies. The idea of mercantilism was to protect the markets, but it also helped to maintain the agriculture and those who were dependent upon it.

The Austrian lawyer and scholar Philipp Wilhelm von Hornick, detailed a nine-point program of what he deemed effective national economy, which sums up the tenets of mercantilism comprehensively:

· That every little bit of a country's soil be utilized for agriculture, mining or manufacturing.

· That all raw materials found in a country be used in domestic manufacture, since finished goods have a higher value than raw materials.

· That a large, working population be encouraged.

· That all export of gold and silver be prohibited and all domestic money be kept in circulation.

· That all imports of foreign goods be discouraged as much as possible.

· That where certain imports are indispensable they be obtained at first hand, in exchange for other domestic goods instead of gold and silver.

· That as much as possible, imports be confined to raw materials that can be finished [in the home country].

· That opportunities be constantly sought for selling a country's surplus manufactures to foreigners, so far as necessary, for gold and silver.

· That no importation be allowed if such goods are sufficiently and suitably supplied at home.

Adam Smith and David Hume were the founding fathers of anti-mercantilist thought. Much of Adam Smith's *The Wealth of Nations* is an attack on mercantilism. A number of scholars found important flaws with mercantilism long before Adam Smith developed an ideology that could fully replace it. Critics like Hume, Dudley North, and John Locke undermined much of mercantilism, and it steadily lost favor during the 18th century.

In Europe, especially in Britain, in light of the arguments of Adam Smith and the classical economists, the repeal of the Corn Laws symbolized the emergence of free trade as an alternative system.

Neomercantilism is a 20th-century economic policy that uses the ideas and methods of neoclassical economics. The new mercantilism has different goals and focuses on more rapid economic growth based on advanced technology.

Neo-mercantilism is a policy regime that encourages exports, discourages imports, controls capital movement, and centralizes currency decisions in the hands of a central government. The objective of neo-mercantilist policies is to increase the level of foreign reserves held by the government, allowing more effective monetary policy and fiscal policy.

This is generally believed to come at the cost of lower standards of living than an open economy would bring at the same time, but offers the advantages to the government in question of having greater autonomy and control. China, Japan and Singapore are described as neo-mercantilist. It is called 「neo-」 because of the change in emphasis from classical mercantilism on military development, to economic development.

Its policy recommendations sometimes echo the mercantilism of the early modern period. These are generally protectionist measures in the form of high tariffs and other import restrictions to protect domestic industries combined with government intervention to promote industrial growth, especially manufacturing. At its simplest level, it proposes that economic independence and self-sufficiency are legitimate objectives for a nation to pursue, and systems of protection are justified to allow the nation to develop its industrial and commercial infrastructure to the point where it can compete on equal terms in international trade. In macro-economic terms, it emphasizes a fixed currency and autonomy over monetary policy over capital mobility.

Laissez-faire

Laissez-faire is an economic system in which transactions between private parties are free from government interference such as regulations, privileges, tariffs, and subsidies. The phrase *laissez-faire* usually means 「let it be」, or 「let it go」.

Being a system of thought, *laissez-faire* rests on the following axioms:

1. The individual is the basic unit in society.
2. The individual has a natural right to freedom.
3. The physical order of nature is a harmonious and self-regulating system.
4. Corporations are creatures of the State and therefore must be watched closely by the citizenry due to their propensity to disrupt the Smithian spontaneous order.

Laissez-faire was proclaimed by the Physiocrats in the eighteenth-century France, thus being the very core of the economic principles, and was more developed by famous economists, beginning with Adam Smith. 「It is with the physiocrats and the classical political economy that the term 」 laissez faire 「 is ordinarily associated.」 The book *Laissez Faire and the General-Welfare State* mentions that, 「The physiocrats, reacting against the excessive mercantilist regulations of the France of their day, expressed a belief in a 「natural order」 or liberty under which individuals in following their selfish interests contributed to the general good. Since, in their view, this natural order functioned successfully without the aid of government, they advised the state to restrict itself to upholding the rights of private property and individual liberty, to removing all artificial barriers to trade, and to abolishing all useless laws.」

Laissez-faire, a product of the Enlightenment, was「conceived as the way to unleash human potential through the restoration of a natural system, a system unhindered by the restrictions of government.」In a similar vein, Adam Smith viewed the economy as a natural system and the market as an organic part of that system. Smith saw *laissez-faire* as a moral program, and the market its instrument to ensure men the rights of natural law. By extension, free markets become a reflection of the natural system of liberty.「For Smith, *laissez-faire* was a program for the abolition of laws constraining the market, a program for the restoration of order and for the activation of potential growth.」

However, Adam Smith, and the notable classical economists, such as Thomas Malthus, and David Ricardo, did not use the phrase. Jeremy Bentham used the term. Though Smith never actually used the term himself. he first used the metaphor of an「invisible hand」, to which the idea and the doctrine of *laissez-faire* have always been closely related.

Classical liberalism and Neo-liberalism

Classical liberalism is a political ideology, a branch of liberalism which advocates civil liberties and political freedom with representative democracy under the rule of law and emphasizes economic freedom.

Classical liberalism developed in the 19th century in Europe and the United States. Although classical liberalism built on ideas that had already developed by the end of the 18th century, it advocated a specific kind of society, government and public policy as a response to the Industrial Revolution and urbanization. Notable individuals whose ideas have contributed to classical liberalism include John Locke, Thomas Malthus, and David Ricardo. It drew on the economics of Adam Smith and on a belief in natural law, utilitarianism, and progress.

In the late 19th century, classical liberalism developed into neo-classical liberalism, which argued for government to be as small as possible to allow the exercise of individual freedom. In its most extreme form, it advocated Social Darwinism.

Neo-liberalism was originally an economic philosophy that emerged among European liberal scholars in the 1930s in an attempt to trace a so-called「Third」or「Middle Way」between the conflicting philosophies of classical liberalism and collectivist central planning. The impetus for this development arose from a desire to avoid repeating the economic failures of the early 1930s, which were mostly blamed on the economic policy of classical liberalism. In the decades that followed, the use of the term neoliberal tended to refer to theories at variance with the more *laissez-faire* doctrine of classical liberalism, and promoted instead a market economy under the guidance and rules of a strong state, a model which came to be known as the social market economy.

Neo-liberalism is famously associated with the economic policies introduced by Margaret Thatcher in the United Kingdom and Ronald Reagan in the United States.

Neo-liberalism is a term whose usage and definition have changed over time. Since the 1980s, the term has been used primarily by scholars and critics in reference to the resurgence of 19th century ideas associated with *laissez-faire* economic liberalism beginning in the 1970s and 1980s, whose advocates support extensive economic liberalization policies such as privatization, fiscal austerity, deregulation, free trade, and reductions in government spending in order to enhance the role of the private sector in the economy.

Glossary

Part I

geographical   adj. 地理的
transacted   adj. 交易的
subsistence farming   自給農業
barter   v. 交易
freeholder   n. 世襲地產保有人
scarcity   n. 短缺
colony   n. 殖民地
mercantilism   n. 重商主義
chaos   n. 混亂
instigate   v. 刺激
manipulation   n. 操縱，操作
ostensibly   adv. 表面上
volume   n. 量
eligible   adj. 有資格的
decentralized   adj. 分散管理的
incentive   adj. 激勵的，刺激的
suasion   n. 勸告
prestige   n. 榮譽，聲望
gang   n. 幫派
cartel   n. 聯合企業
allocate   v. 分配，指定
levy   v. 徵收
chamber   n. 會所

Part II

desirable   adj. 令人滿意的，滿足需要的
laissez-faire   n. 自由放任主義
equitable   adj. 公平的，公正的
ameliorate   v. 改善

capital accumulation　資本累積
designation　n. 指定，選派
nominally　adv. 名義上地
marxist-leninist　n. 馬克思列寧主義者
remedial　adj. 補救的
articulate　v. 表達，表明
anarchist　n. 無政府主義者
libertarian　n. 自由主義者
quasi-feudal　adj. 類似封建制度的
forcibly　adv. 強制地
bureaucratic　adj. 官僚的
all-encompassing　adj. 包羅萬象的
remunerate　v. 給予酬勞
dividend　n. 紅利，股息
initial　adj. 初始的
radical　adj. 根本的，基礎的
dismantling　n. 廢除
joint-stock　adj. 合資的
exert　v. 施以影響
alongside　prep. 在……旁邊

Part Ⅲ

abbreviate　v. 縮寫
precursor　n. 先驅
expound　v. 詳細說明
interference　n. 干預
coercion　n. 強制
pervasive　adj. 普遍的
commemorate　v. 紀念
neoclassical　adj. 新古典主義的
dismantle　v. 廢除
cornerstone　n. 基礎
speculator　n. 投機者
orthodox　adj. 正統的
jettison　v. 捨棄，放棄
squander　v. 揮霍
stagnation　n. 停滯
allies　n. 同盟國

traumatize   v. 使……精神受損
innocent   adj. 無辜的
coalition   n. 聯盟
astronomically   adv. 天文學般
compassion   n. 憐憫，同情
servitude   n. 勞役，奴役
abhorrent   adj. 令人厭惡的
detestable   adj. 可恨的
prolonged   adj. 持續很久的
destitute   adj. 窮困的
hereditary   adj. 世襲的
Peerage   n. 貴族
gazette   v. 在報上刊載
resurgence   n. 復興
underpinning   n. 基礎
nationalize   v. 把……收歸國有
Bancor   n. 國際貨幣單位班柯爾
utilitarianism   n. 功利主義
consequentialism   n. 結果論
justification   n. 理由
foreshadow   v. 預示

Part Ⅳ

sophistication   n. 複雜性
feudalism   n. 封建主義，封建制度
collaboration   n. 合作，協作
imperialist   adj. 帝國主義的
posthumously   adv. 去世後
archetype   n. 原型
manifesto   n. 宣言
arguably   adv. 可爭論地
impoverish   v. 使貧窮
disjoint   v. 使脫節
metropolis   n. 大都市
tenet   n. 原則
indispensable   adj. 不可缺少的
Neo-mercantilism   n. 新重商主義
regime   n. 政權，政體

legitimate　adj. 合法的
infrastructure　n. 基礎設施
dominance　n. 優勢
isolationism　n. 孤立主義
interventionism　n. 干涉主義
axiom　n. 原理
proclaim　v. 宣布
physiocrats　n. 重農學派
impetus　n. 動力

Phrases

on top of　在……之上，另外
the onset of　開啓，來臨
Bring... into　使……開始，使……進入某種狀態
act as　擔當，充當
in reference to　關於
in contrast with　與……形成對比
subordinate to　服從，從屬於
free of　擺脫……，無……
develop into　發展成為
in essence　本質上，大體上
in favor of　有利於，支持
bear out　證實，支持
give effect to　實行，生效
head off　轉移方向，出發
in accordance with　依照，與……一致
in return for　作為對……報答
in light of　根據，鑒於
by extension　相關地，引申開來
at variance with　與……不和

Notes

Great Depression：大蕭條（The Great Depression），是指 1929—1933 年發源於美國，後來波及整個資本主義世界的經濟危機，其中包括美國、英國、法國、德國和日本等資本主義國家。大蕭條的普遍影響導致了：①提高了政府對經濟的政策參與性，即凱恩斯主義；②以關稅的形式強化了經濟的民族主義；③激起了作為共產主義替代物的浪漫—極權主義政治運動（如德國納粹）。大蕭條相對於其他單一原因來說是最能夠解釋為什麼在 1932—1938 年歐洲大陸和拉丁美洲各國政治逐漸右翼化。④使德國、義大利、日本為了擺脫大蕭條開始走上了對外侵略擴張的道路與法西斯主義道路；⑤阿道

夫·希特勒、貝尼托·墨索里尼、東條英機等獨裁者的崛起，間接造成第二次世界大戰爆發；⑥為蘇聯的工業發展提供了有利時期。

　　Keynesianism：凱恩斯主義指出，通過利率把儲蓄轉化為投資和借助於工資的變化來調節勞動供求的自發市場機制，並不能自動地創造出充分就業所需要的那種有效需求水準；在競爭性私人體制中，三大規律（邊際消費傾向遞減、資本邊際效率遞減和流動偏好）使有效需求往往低於社會的總供給水準，從而導致就業水準總是處於非充分就業的均衡狀態。因此，要實現充分就業，就必須拋棄自由放任的傳統政策，政府必須運用積極的財政與貨幣政策，以確保足夠水準的有效需求。凱恩斯最根本的理論創新就在於從經濟學理論上證明了國家干預經濟的合理性，這是凱恩斯主義出現以前任何經濟學都根本做不到的。

Questions

1. Where and when was the first stock exchange founded? What can be regarded as a major turning point in human history?
2. For an economic system, how many institutions does it possess?
3. According to the text, who was thought of as the「father of modern economics」and what was his theory?
4. Which book is viewed as the foundation of modern macroeconomics?
5. Who was the founding father of anti-mercantilist thought?
6. How many axioms does laissez-faire have and what are they?

國家圖書館出版品預行編目（CIP）資料

新時代：商務英語職場應用 / 何文賢 編著. -- 第一版.
-- 臺北市：財經錢線文化, 2020.05
　　面；　公分
POD版

ISBN 978-957-680-437-3(平裝)

1.商業英文 2.讀本

805.18 109006943

書　　名：新時代：商務英語職場應用
作　　者：何文賢 編著
發 行 人：黃振庭
出 版 者：財經錢線文化事業有限公司
發 行 者：財經錢線文化事業有限公司
E-mail：sonbookservice@gmail.com
粉 絲 頁：　　　　　　網　址：
地　　址：台北市中正區重慶南路一段六十一號八樓 815 室
8F.-815, No.61, Sec. 1, Chongqing S. Rd., Zhongzheng
Dist., Taipei City 100, Taiwan (R.O.C.)
電　　話：(02)2370-3310 傳　真：(02) 2388-1990
總 經 銷：紅螞蟻圖書有限公司
地　　址：台北市內湖區舊宗路二段 121 巷 19 號
電　　話：02-2795-3656 傳真:02-2795-4100　　網址：
印　　刷：京峯彩色印刷有限公司（京峰數位）

　本書版權為西南財經大學出版社所有授權崧博出版事業股份有限公司獨家發行電子書及繁體書繁體字版。若有其他相關權利及授權需求請與本公司聯繫。

定　價：399元
發行日期：2020 年 05 月第一版
◎ 本書以 POD 印製發行